STRANGE SCREAMS
OF DEATH

Also by Nigel McCrery in Pocket Books

SILENT WITNESS

STRANGE SCREAMS OF DEATH

Nigel McCrery

POCKET
BOOKS

LONDON · SYDNEY · NEW YORK · TOKYO · SINGAPORE · TORONTO

First published in Great Britain by Pocket Books, 1997
An imprint of Simon & Schuster Ltd
A Viacom Company

Simon & Schuster Ltd
West Garden Place
Kendal Street
London W2 2AQ

Simon & Schuster of Australia Pty Ltd
Sydney

A CIP catalogue record for this book is available
from the British Library

ISBN 0-671-00529-4

Typeset in Sabon 10.5/12.5pt by
Palimpsest Book Production Limited,
Polmont, Stirlingshire FK2 0NZ
Printed and bound in Great Britain by
Caledonian International Book Manufacturing Ltd,
Glasgow

For
Wyn Copson
in memory of
Richard Copson
1921–1987

Acknowledgements

With grateful thanks to the following: Dr Helen Witwell, Forensic Pathologist; Professor Bernard Knight, Forensic Pathologist; FBI Academy, Quantico; Atlanta Police Department; Atlanta Sheriff's Department; Dr John Conway, GP and Art Historian; Peter Qu Rose, Botanist; Sue Andrews, Botanist, Kew Gardens; Oliver Crimmond, Fish Department, Natural History Museum; Security Police and Press Office USAF Mildenhall, Cambridge-shire. With thanks, also, to all others who have helped with the technical advice on the book.

The night has been unruly: where we lay . . .
Lamentings heard i'th'air, strange screams of death
Macbeth, Act II, Scene 3

PROLOGUE

St Mary's Hospital for the Criminally Insane, Washington, DC

They'd been lucky this time. He'd been seen at the last moment, climbing over one of the walls using a rope ladder made from sections of sheets and curtains. He'd seriously injured the first guard to arrive on the scene, and only by weight of numbers were they finally able to subdue him. Many of the inmates seemed to possess an unnatural strength born of their mental condition. Christopher Amery had been a nurse at the institute for almost five years now, and had seen many forms of insanity, and not only inside the hospital – Christ, he thought, you only had to walk through the Bronx to see most of them – but he'd never come across anything quite like this.

This was terrifying: an anger so great that it felt evil. Nobody entered the cell unless they had to, and even then never alone. Never.

Amery was normally good at dealing with the disturbed of society, but he hated dealing with this man in any capacity. It wasn't that he was always violent.

Much of the time he was calm and rational – but that, as they had learnt to their cost over the years, was when he was at his most dangerous. His particular demons glowered and festered within him and some part of his brain was always occupied with plans and fantasies. He didn't have a name that they were aware of, only a number, 2452, and that was what everyone had to call him. No one ever visited him and he never sent or received any letters. Occasionally, a group of unknown officials would arrive and spend the day monitoring him but then they would depart in silence and wouldn't be seen again for months.

Amery was no coward but this one frightened him. Even going to the cell made him go cold and he found he could never look for long into those red-tinged eyes before turning away, fighting against nausea. Still more alarming was the fact that there were others like him in other institutions around the country. Amery shuddered to think of the consequences if one of them should ever escape.

Still screaming and kicking, 2452 was wrestled back into his cell and the steel door slammed shut behind him.

CHAPTER ONE

Fulton County, Georgia, USA

FBI Agent Edward Doyle watched closely as a school of tiny, brilliantly blue sunfish darted through the clear waters of the lake and took cover in a nearby reedbank. He strained to follow their progress but they disappeared. He dipped his once-white handkerchief into the water and wiped it across his broad face and fleshy neck before pushing the damp rag back into his trouser pocket. It was one of the hottest summers on record and he was decidedly uncomfortable. It wasn't that he didn't like the heat – after all he'd been brought up in California, where the sun shone for most of the year – but the air on his part of the West Coast was dry, almost welcoming, whereas here it was humid and oppressive, clinging tightly to the skin like a fever waiting to break.

Doyle was a large, lumbering man in his late forties who was at least fifty pounds overweight and didn't carry it well. He'd ceased caring what he looked like some years before. He'd never been an attractive man, and since his wife had left him he'd given up completely, persuading himself that it was achievements, not appearances, that counted in life. He'd been true to this philosophy ever since.

He raised his hand to shield his eyes from the midday sun. The movement exposed an unsightly damp stain; sweat had oozed from beneath his arm and run down the sleeve of his ill-fitting cotton shirt. The ageing launch was close to the bank now, sitting so low in the water that Doyle could see the end of the black plastic body-bag. It had been laid unceremoniously along the floorboards and bounced rhythmically in tune with the boat's movement, as if its grisly contents had come back to life and were struggling to get out.

The boat wasn't an official police launch but had been borrowed from the man who discovered the body. It was in such a poor state of repair that Doyle wondered how it stayed afloat. Green and red paint flaked from every part of its decaying wooden frame, exposing several large holes in a hull that was slowly rotting away. It was clearly more used to carrying the odd fisherman and his dog than half the county's Sheriff's Department. The underpowered diesel engine strained with the unaccustomed weight of a rather rotund medical examiner and the four burly deputies who were acting as crew. Doyle always felt better when he met or saw someone larger than himself: it allowed him to justify his own lamentable lack of fitness.

He also wondered why none of the boat's occupants seemed to have considered the fact that, as the body had been discovered on a small island at the centre of the lake and there were no other boats nearby, the killer had almost certainly used this boat to transport his victim to the island in the first place. Any forensic evidence there might have been on board would now have been well and truly adulterated or ground into the decaying wood and lost for ever. Still, he thought, what could you expect from backwoodsmen?

He looked across at his partner, Catherine Solheim, who was interviewing the local hick who had discovered the body. He was sitting on a log smoking a hand-rolled cigarette with a pretence of nonchalance, but was clearly enjoying his newfound importance. His role had not been a particularly dramatic one, but would undoubtedly be enhanced as he recounted the tale in full graphic and gory detail in his favourite bar that evening. Most people lead relatively humdrum lives, and finding a body, especially that of a murder victim, would be a major event for the average citizen. The guy would probably dine out on the story for years.

The arrival of a dark-blue saloon car drew Doyle's attention away from the scene. The car stopped at the top of the bank and from it emerged the two men who had been tracking his every move for the past year. They were equipped with standard-issue blue suits and dark glasses and somehow managed to look cool, even under these conditions. They made no attempt to approach, but remained leaning against the side of the car, watching.

The first time they'd arrived at the scene of one of the murders Doyle had confronted them and demanded to know who they were and, more importantly, who they represented. They told him if he had a problem with their presence he should complain to his boss, Mark Bartoc, at the Bureau. Doyle saw Bartoc at his first opportunity, but had been given the runaround. Bartoc had been ambiguous and even defensive, and he'd got nowhere. The two men turned up at the next and all subsequent murder scenes and they slowly began to accept one another's presence, though without becoming friendly. They'd never interfered with the enquiry, but Doyle couldn't help speculating on what might be happening behind the scenes.

Ignoring his two unwanted guests, he turned back to the lake as the launch swung in to the bank. Solheim had concluded her interview and came over to join her partner. Doyle adopted an air of studied indifference, pretending to ignore her while actually being acutely aware of her every action. She was tall and attractive, one of the new intake of highly intelligent and motivated agents who were destined to reach the top of their profession. He couldn't help but admire – and even desire – her but he accepted his limitations and tried to remain cool and detached when they were together. She'd caught him looking at her 'unprofessionally' on a number of occasions, forcing him to look away quickly, feeling awkward and embarrassed at the power her youth and appearance had over him. Still, he was senior to her and, for the time being anyway, she had to obey his orders. He enjoyed that, enjoyed the control. It was one of the small pleasures his authority afforded him.

The body-bag was pulled from the boat by the sheriff and several of his deputies, who dropped it casually on the hard-baked earth by the side of the lake, one end of the bag dipping into the water.

Doyle looked across at the medical examiner and asked, 'What can you tell us?'

The examiner shrugged his huge, rounded shoulders. 'She's dead. Unnatural causes. I'll see you at the post mortem.'

He lumbered off towards the two suits, who were now standing away from the car and waiting to speak to him. It was as much information as Doyle had expected and he knew he wouldn't learn any more until after the PM. He shook his head, registering his irritation. He looked across at one of the deputies and nodded towards the body-bag. He had a certain status in situations like this and he wasn't about to demean himself by kneeling in the dirt and exposing the contents himself. The deputy squatted down and unzipped the bag, slowly revealing the badly decomposed remains of a young woman.

This one had been dead for some time. The pathologist would be able to give them no more than an approximate time of death. Doyle knew they wouldn't know for sure how long she'd been there until she was identified. Then would come the long and laborious task of collecting witness statements in order to establish her movements during the final few days or, with luck, hours of her life. In a world which was becoming increasingly uninterested and anonymous, he knew that was going to take time, and time, as always, was in short supply. The one thing he was already sure of, however, from viewing the pitiful remains, was that the post mortem, booked for later that day at the Fulton County mortuary, would confirm that she was victim number twelve.

As if reading his thoughts, Solheim glanced across at

him and nodded. He had to give her her due: she'd got guts. As the bag was opened, even some of Georgia's finest had stood back or looked away, gulping in mouthfuls of air to control their nausea. Solheim, however, had stood impassively, watchful and professional. Doyle liked that.

Crouching down, he examined one of the girl's wrists. Although the body had been out in the open for some time, there was still enough flesh stretched across the bones to try and make some rudimentary judgements. There were no signs of abrasion or of any rope or handcuff burns. Like the last two victims, she had been subdued in some other way.

There had been a clear change in the killer's MO over the past few months. The first few victims had been tied and gagged before being butchered. The last three, however, showed no signs of this: they had been subdued in some way which, frustratingly, had still to be discovered. Apart from the single knife wound to the stomach there had been no signs of violence, and toxicology tests had drawn a complete blank. If the modus operandi of the killings hadn't been so alike, they might almost have been committed by different people. In the light of this, the killer's profile, which Doyle had spent so many months piecing together, was now being completely redrawn to take in his new style.

As he considered this, several flies seized their chance to escape from the bag and buzz their way to freedom. Doyle was unsure whether they had been locked in there when the bag was zipped shut or were newly born and just emerging from some warm dark cavity within the festering body. He pulled the zip up, trapping any further would-be escapees in the darkness.

He looked up at the least green-faced deputy. 'Did you find her clothes?'

The deputy nodded. 'They were folded neatly, like you said they would be.'

'Her shoes?'

He shook his head. 'No sign.'

Doyle looked back across the lake towards the tree-covered island.

The headlines surrounding the series of murders had been dramatic and lurid as the media battled to attach the most graphic and disturbing pseudonym to the killer: 'The Stalker', 'The Slasher', 'Cannibal Killer'. Doyle reckoned such nicknames would glorify the killer in his own eyes, and refused to use them, referring to the killer only as 'he' or 'him'. Too much information had already been released to the press, both officially and unofficially, for Doyle's liking. Some should have been held back, otherwise every nut and his dog would be turning up wanting to confess to the murders, knowing just enough detail to waste his time.

Doyle had dreamt about 'him' since they'd discovered the third body in Arizona two years before. The dreams were dark and menacing, their disturbing quality coming not from the technicolour images of horror and mayhem his mind conjured up, but from a gut-wrenching awareness of evil. Ephemeral, shapeless and unidentifiable, the malevolence intensified as he cast around blindly through the grey mists of his mind, trying to locate and identify the source of the horror. Even after he woke, the odour of death and decay did not leave him, but lingered momentarily in his nasal cavities and across the surface of his lips.

Doyle was aware that 'he' was just waiting for the tensions within him to reach breaking point again before fulfilling another fantasy and finding another victim. As with most serial killers, the periods between murders when he was still able to control his desires were becoming shorter, and the body count was rising with increasing rapidity.

The roar of a B17 jet streaking low overhead shattered his thoughts and caused the smooth waters of the lake to ripple in its wake. Doyle looked up to see the silver-bodied fighter twist the full three hundred and sixty degrees of a victory roll before climbing almost vertically and disappearing into a clear turquoise sky.

Suddenly a voice broke through the roar. 'Over here! Over here!'

One of the sheriff's deputies had just emerged from a small clump of trees that overhung the lake. He was almost dancing with excitement, and kept pointing back towards the trees. Doyle didn't react. He didn't need to see what the deputy had discovered. He already knew what it was.

Leeminghall US Air Force Base, Cambridgeshire

The rhythmic sound of Glen Miller's 'In The Mood' beat out around the giant aircraft hangar, sending young American airmen and their excited partners spinning out on to the dance floor to fight for their piece of the rapidly decreasing space. A shout of enjoyment escaped from Sam as she felt herself being spun effortlessly round, first one way and then the other, before being pulled back towards her partner and lifted bodily over his back. She had no control over what was happening to her, and she didn't care. She just followed where her partner led and hoped she wasn't going to be sent sprawling across the dance floor. She needn't have worried. She was in expert hands.

Eventually, the music stopped and Sam turned, breathless, and clapped her appreciation of the band's playing. She was so exhilarated by the evening and the dancing that she found herself jumping up and down and whistling with the rest of the revellers. She looked across at her partner, Major Robert Hammond, who was waving a fist in the air and grunting his own approval. Sam was pleased with herself, pleased that she had decided to come. She felt relaxed and refreshed and appreciated the break from her routine.

She'd been surprised to receive an invitation to the dance and, having given the invitation card only a cursory glance, ignored it for some days, assuming it to be a semi-formal function of the type held occasionally to forge links between the US Air Force base and sections of the local community which were probably connected to her work. It was Trevor Stuart, her professional partner and the only other forensic pathologist in the county, who had revived her interest. He'd been invited to several of these occasions, and said they had been 'wild' and a great excuse to let his hair down a little. But then, Sam thought, Trevor's ongoing mid-life crisis, and the succession of young women who moved in and out of his life, probably meant that he saw the parties mainly as an ideal opportunity to meet more girls, possibly in uniform.

Leeminghall air-base was about ten miles outside Cambridge, a small oasis of American life and culture in the middle of the English countryside. It contained a baseball pitch, football ground and even its own shops and restaurants. The base had been there for over fifty years and had been one of the US Air Force's main bomber command stations during the Second World War. As she gazed around the dance floor at the eager and excited faces of the airmen, Sam wondered how many other young men had come to functions like this during the war, only to die somewhere over Germany as their aircraft were blown up beneath them. She was glad that the young men enjoying this dance would live to enjoy another, and felt a surge of gratitude towards those who had gone before.

Sam had met Bob Hammond at one of the many crime seminars that seemed increasingly to litter her diary. The seminars covered everything from serial killers and psychological profiling to scenes of crime and handwriting analysis. Being one of only five female Home Office forensic pathologists in England and Wales, she was expected to attended most of these functions and be shown off as an example of sexual liberation within the world of forensic pathology. It was all nonsense, of course, but she attended willingly and followed the party line.

Sam had given a talk on establishing the time of death

and afterwards Hammond came up to her during the coffee-break and introduced himself. He was the officer in command of the security police at Leeminghall and, as with most policemen, military or otherwise, the detection of crime was clearly much more than a job to him. He'd begun by asking her a question about something she'd said during her talk, and they'd gone on to chat about various interesting or unusual cases. Normally Sam would soon have tired of the conversation, as these exchanges were generally predictable and boring, but there was a passion in Hammond that showed itself in the way he spoke about his work. It was a passion she shared.

Hammond was in his early forties, tall and attractive with an athletic figure and a strong face. He also possessed a keen sense of humour, which Sam always found attractive. He was in the last year of a three-year posting to England and, although he'd moved about a lot, was hoping to see his tour out at Leeminghall.

Sam thought she detected a distinct Boston twang to his accent and felt sure he must come from New England or somewhere nearby. She was surprised when she discovered he had been born and bred in Atlanta, Georgia, and wondered how he'd come to lose that distinctive Southern drawl. She knew her own Belfast accent was still evident, despite all the years she'd spent in England.

The invitation to the dance had been for two, but Tom was on duty and Marcia, her friend and colleague at the Scrivingdon forensic labs, was in Durham on a course. With the two obvious choices of companion unavailable,

Sam thought about going alone. At first she didn't much like the idea, then she thought, why not? After all, she was an adult woman and quite capable of looking after herself if an airman the worse for drink tried anything on. She wasn't sure whether it was the lure of an unusual evening out – she smiled, remembering Trevor's description of the parties as 'wild' – or the desire to meet Bob Hammond again on a social level. Whatever the reason, in the end she accepted the invitation and stopped trying to analyse her motives too closely.

On arrival Sam had been directed towards the car park where she soon found a parking space. The place was buzzing with young people making their way towards the music blasting out of a giant aircraft hangar on the opposite side of a large playing field. Sam sat in the car for a few minutes, watching the crowd stream towards the hangar like moths attracted to a light. They were all very young, very alive.

She pulled down the sun visor and gazed into the mirror. She was, as they say, 'good for her age'. She worked at it. She jogged, weight-trained and watched her diet but inevitably, no matter what she did, time marched on and she was realistic enough to accept that, although it was possible to delay the ageing process a bit, there was no way of stopping it.

The thought made her feel out of place, an interloper in a youthful world. The idea of relaxing in front of a roaring fire with a good book and a glass of wine seemed better than trying to compete with a bunch of twenty-year-olds. This was an unusual frame of mind for Sam, who was normally happy and comfortable with both her appearance and her lively outlook on life. She flicked the sun visor back into place and, replacing the key in the ignition, prepared to flee.

A knock on the driver's window stopped her with her hand still on the key. Looking up, she saw Bob Hammond smiling in at her from under his smart uniform cap. Pushing her unwelcome thoughts to the back of her mind, Sam smiled back, slipped her car keys into her handbag, opened the car door and climbed out.

Hammond was clearly pleased to see her. 'Just arrived?'

Sam nodded awkwardly, like a naughty schoolgirl caught in mid-mischief.

Hammond glanced quickly around. 'On your own? No Tom?'

'No, he's on an evening shift.'

'I'm sorry. I'd have liked to meet him.'

There was no hint of disappointment in Hammond's voice or posture, however. He was lying and it was transparent, but flattering. Sam wasn't sure how he knew about Tom; she'd thought their relationship was a well-kept secret. But then, considering what his job was, perhaps it wasn't so surprising he knew.

'Well,' he went on, 'in the absence of others I'd be delighted to be your escort for the evening.'

He held out his arm and Sam slipped her own arm through his. As she did so, he looked down at her and said, 'By the way, just in case I forget to tell you later, you look great.'

Sam smiled. She thought she might enjoy herself after all.

*　　*　　*

The mood of the music changed as the final dance was announced. Sam recognised the tune: 'Moonlight Serenade'. It had been one of her father's favourites. Bob Hammond drew her closer and smiled down at her. Whether because of the emotions aroused by the music or simply because of her unusual mood and the occasion, Sam wasn't sure, but she found herself resting her head on Hammond's shoulder as he guided her slowly round the dance floor. She wondered idly how many other local girls had fallen in love at dances like this over the past fifty years, and envied them.

The music came to an end and was abruptly replaced by the shrill sound of an air-raid siren, closely followed by the crash of explosions as fluorescent green and red fireworks exploded around the hangar in an imitation of German bombs. People ran from the dance floor and the hangar, laughing and screaming with delight.

'Works every time,' said Hammond, grinning. 'Best way I know to clear a place.' He took her hand and led her off towards one of the exits.

Still full of the evening's events, Mary West was half pulled and half carried from the hangar by Airman Ray Strachan, her boyfriend of the past few weeks. Mary was a local girl from Little Bonnington, a village on the fringes of the base. A little over eighteen years old, she was small and pretty with a crop of natural blond hair. She had never been short of admirers but had seen little of life outside her own village or county. She had met Strachan in the local pub some weeks before and had fallen for him at once. He reminded her of an American film star, the type who hung around with what the papers called the 'brat pack'. There was a confidence and a daring about him that excited her. She had never been happier.

Although she had lived close to the base all her life, she had never been on it before, so when Strachan asked her to go to the hangar dance she had accepted at once. She didn't tell her parents where she was going because she knew they would disapprove and try to stop her, and it would only lead to a row. Why her parents hated the base and the young American airmen so much she wasn't sure. In every other way they seemed perfectly rational people. Her mother had once even had an American boyfriend who'd been stationed at Leeminghall, and it must have been love because she'd almost gone to the States with him. But that was over eighteen years ago and perhaps Mum had forgotten how much fun Americans could be. So as far as her parents were concerned she was staying with a friend in St Ives.

Strachan led her into one of the large hangars. As soon as they reached the far end, he caught her to him, ran his hands through her hair and kissed her passionately on the lips before pushing her back against the hangar wall.

His face was very close to hers and he held her gaze as he said softly, 'I love you, Mary. I've loved you right from the beginning.'

She could hear the sincerity in his voice and believed he was telling the truth. She, in her turn, felt her feeling for him growing stronger. She took his handsome head in her hands and kissed him deeply. She'd never kissed any of the local boys like this and her entire body tingled with the passion of it.

As Strachan's hands moved slowly up her thighs, her passion began to turn to concern. She didn't stop kissing him, but she wasn't sure she wanted what he clearly wanted. Although she would never admit it, she was still a virgin. It wasn't that she was a prude – she'd been involved with a number of village boys and had always enjoyed the experience – but she had never gone 'all the way' and wasn't sure she wanted to now. Her dilemma was how to stop him without ruining the relationship. She wanted him, but not the sex, well, not right now, pushed up against a dirty hangar wall in the middle of the night. This wasn't how she'd imagined it in her dreams.

She grabbed his hand, stopping him as he pulled at her panties. 'No, not now, not here,' she pleaded. 'It's wrong, it's all wrong. Wait!'

Strachan glanced at her and hesitated for a moment. But he had no intention of stopping. He pulled her hands above her head, kissing her passionately to silence her protests, while he forced his knee between her legs and prised them apart. A few moments later, Mary felt her underclothes being torn from her body.

Sam waited by the entrance as the dozens of party-goers filed out of the hangar, shouting and laughing at each other as they headed for their homes and billets, their faces glowing with enjoyment. Before long, Bob Hammond returned with her coat and slipped it round her shoulders, then put his cap on and adjusted it to the correct military angle.

'I'll take you to your car.' Bob's voice was deep and slow. She thought it was just about the sexiest voice she'd ever heard.

As they made their way out of the hangar they were approached by a large, elderly man in his late fifties or early sixties. From the braid on his hat to the two inches of multi-coloured medal ribbons on his tunic, he was clearly a man of importance, and he knew it. He strode across to Bob Hammond, his hand outstretched. Bob straightened and saluted him before shaking hands.

'Bob, another excellent evening. I can see I was right to keep you with my command. Best retirement party I've ever had.'

Hammond was properly respectful. 'Thank you, sir, and thanks for the note. We're all going to miss you.'

The general smiled sarcastically. 'In a pig's eye you are.' He turned to Sam. 'And who might you be, young lady?'

'This is Doctor Samantha Ryan, sir. She's the forensic pathologist for the area, sir. Sam, this is General Arthur Wilmot Brown. The general is in charge of our Eastern Command and retires this week after—'

'Many years with the Air Force,' the general cut in. He shook hands with Sam. 'Should have gone years ago but they decided they couldn't do without me.'

Sam said merely, 'General.'

'Very unusual job for a woman,' Brown went on. He drew his hand away from Sam's and inspected it. 'I hope you've washed your hands.'

He turned to the officer behind him, chuckling. 'Good

to see that our boys are still getting the pretty ones, eh, Colonel?'

Colonel Richard Cully had been the base commander at Leeminghall for almost a year. He was a career officer who had developed the ability to make all the right moves and get to know all the right people into a fine art. Sam knew little of him; she didn't much like him either. 'All show and little substance' seemed to be most people's opinion and Sam felt sure they were right.

Cully nodded and smiled deferentially.

'It was the same in the last war,' said the general. 'All the nice girls.' He looked at Sam and put his hand to the side of his mouth as if about to reveal some great secret. 'I dare say there are a few around who could claim dual nationality.' He laughed loudly at his own joke, looking back at Cully, who laughed encouragingly in support of his superior.

Sam looked at him impassively without a hint of a smile. Seeing that his joke had not amused her, the general stopped laughing and moved on awkwardly, quickly followed by Cully, who glared across at Bob Hammond as if it was Hammond's fault that the general had been made to feel uncomfortable. Hammond raised his eyebrows apologetically at Sam. She smiled understandingly and took his arm.

Hammond felt it might be diplomatic to explain the top brass's conduct. 'General Arthur Wilmot Brown—'

'As in nose?' Sam interrupted.

Hammond gave a quick, soft laugh and continued, 'Played ball for the Air Force. Winner of the Congressional Medal of Honor, Silver Stars, Purple Heart three times, ace of aces in Vietnam and all-round American hero.'

Sam looked pointedly at the left-hand side of Hammond's tunic which bore almost as many medal ribbons as Brown's. 'Looks like you're a bit of a hero yourself.'

Hammond looked down at his chest. 'Oh, those. Most of them are for sitting in a deep bunker giving orders to men braver than I am.'

'I'm sure that's not true.'

'I'm no Brown. Do you know, he crashed in 'Nam and the old bastard cut his way through fifty miles of jungle, most of it held by the Vietcong, and managed to get back to base. It was in all the papers at the time.'

Sam looked up at him. 'Sounds like quite a man.'

'He's an institution back home. Still flies his own jet from base to base. The kids love him. They think he's John fucking Wayne.' Realising what he had just said, he coughed and said awkwardly, 'Sorry. Just slipped out.'

Sam smiled reassuringly. 'Rough soldiers' talk. My dad was a policeman. It was much the same.'

Relieved, Hammond continued, 'The truth is, he's a complete arsehole and the biggest bullshitter since MacArthur. Lives off his Vietnam days.'

'But you still call him "sir".'

'Yes, ma'am, I still call him "sir", and if push came to shove I'd kiss his butt and thank him for the privilege. But I want you to know that we don't all approve of his attitudes.'

Sam laughed quietly. She could think of a few con-
sultants whose 'butts' she'd been prepared to kiss in the
past, although she'd never admit it.

The evening had cooled considerably since she had
arrived and, though it wasn't far from the hangar to the
car park, Sam was glad of her coat. The car park was
crowded with young people keen to make their evening
last as long as possible. Hammond smiled wrily at one
couple who were oblivious of everything but each other.

As Sam followed his gaze, he voiced his thoughts:
''Twas ever thus.'

'It's still true then?'

Hammond looked puzzled.

'Over-sexed, over-paid and over here?'

Hammond's smile broadened. 'The pay ain't so good
these days.' He stared at her until Sam found herself
looking away, slightly flustered.

They reached her car and Sam put her hand out.
'Thanks for a wonderful evening.'

Hammond nodded and took her hand but instead of
shaking it, he pulled her to him, cupping her face gently
in his other hand and bending his head towards hers. At
the last moment Sam moved her head slightly to one side,
and Hammond found himself kissing her cheek instead
of her lips.

She stepped backwards and saw the disappointment
in his face. She liked Hammond and didn't want to
hurt him.

'Sorry. It wouldn't be fair to Tom. I don't think I
could cope with more than one relationship at a time.'

Hammond nodded, still keeping a tight hold on her

hand. 'I suppose at this point I should say he's a lucky guy. But I won't. If you ever get bored with the limey stiff, bear me in mind.'

Sam smiled and this time kissed him on the cheek, whispering in his ear, 'You're top of my list.'

Hammond smiled, his pride intact, as Sam jumped into her car and pulled away towards the main gate. She glanced into her rear-view mirror and saw him disappear into the darkness of the base.

It took Sam a little over an hour to travel from the base back to her cottage. Once she pulled off the straight, well-lit motorway the roads were dark and narrow, and her progress slowed. In the thin, hazy light of the quarter-moon, the trees, so proud and erect in daylight, looked crippled and grotesque, crouching low over her car and blocking out what little light the moon provided, their branches dipping into the beam of her headlights like long twisted fingers reaching out to pluck her from the comfortable interior of her car. Much as she loved the countryside, its monochrome appearance at night always reminded her of faded Victorian photographs of people and places that no longer existed. The imagination she normally kept firmly under control broke free under these circumstances, and childhood fears and superstitions rose through the veneer of logic and maturity like bubbles of gas from rotting vegetation at the bottom of a stagnant pool, bursting foully as they sent ripples over the calm surface.

After what seemed like an age, Sam turned off the road and climbed steadily along the farm track towards her cottage, swerving this way and that as she tried to avoid the pot-holes that seemed to increase daily. She had talked to the farmer about them more than once. He'd smiled sweetly at her, nodding his head and assuring her that it would be seen to at once, but nothing ever happened – in fact it continued to get worse.

Swinging the car through the cottage gates, she pulled up by the front door as the security light flicked on and illuminated the drive. As she got out of the car, Shaw, her ever-faithful tabby, appeared at her feet and began to rub himself around her ankles. Sam smiled and bent down to pick him up.

'What are you doing out?'

She stroked him quickly before slipping her key into the lock and opening the door.

Airmen First Class Carl Simons and William Johnson had missed the dance. The duty sergeant did his best to ensure that the base's security police rotated their shifts so they didn't miss too many events but on this occasion the two hapless policemen had been unlucky. But that's the way it went and they had both become philosophical about it. They'd been waiting outside when the dance had finished and watched as drunk and happy airmen flaunted their girl friends at them, their intentions for later that evening more than clear.

They had to admit that the dance seemed to have attracted more than its normal quota of young and good-looking women. Apparently the organisers had encouraged some of the female students from Cambridge to come along and had even laid on special transport to bring them into the base. It had certainly worked. The two security officers just hoped that at least a few of them had sisters or friends and that phone numbers and addresses had been left behind.

When the hangar had been cleared and the laughing, shouting revellers were finally on their way home, the two men breathed a deep sigh of relief and frustration. Relief that it had all passed off peacefully, with few problems and no arrests, and frustration at their inability to make the acquaintance of so many attractive girls.

Johnson looked across at his partner. 'So many women, so little time.'

Simons laughed. 'Hangar two?'

Johnson smiled wickedly. 'Hangar two.'

Hangar two was notorious as the place to which many airmen took their girl friends for a bit of 'privacy'. It was off limits, of course, which was why everybody went there. The two men had already decided that if they weren't going to have any fun that night, then neither was anyone else. Full of righteous intent, they strode towards the hangar.

Sam undressed quickly and slipped into bed. Tom Adams was already there, lying on his back with his head slightly to one side, breathing deeply. She snuggled close, entwining her arms and legs around his and absorbing the warmth from his body. Although nothing had happened with Bob Hammond, she felt a twinge of guilt that secretly she'd wanted it to and it was only her practical side that had stopped her. Now all she wanted to do was apologise to Tom for something that had never happened, except in her mind. Stupid, she knew, but she couldn't help herself. She needed to be reassured about their relationship and to convince herself that everything was all right. As she let her head fall on to his chest, she could hear the slow, rhythmic beating of his heart. It made her feel safe.

They had been together for almost a year now. She had steadfastly refused to allow him to move in with her, but he stayed most weekends and she enjoyed his company. However, she wasn't entirely happy with the way their relationship was developing. They seemed to spend endless hours arguing about their 'future together'. He wanted more, including marriage and children, but she wasn't sure she had any more to give and was beginning to resent the pressure.

With the exception of her father and now her nephew, Ricky, she'd never really been close to anyone. Even her love for her mother wasn't deep. It felt almost like a duty, something that was expected of her as a daughter, especially now her mother was ill. She wasn't very close to her sister either, a situation which she acknowledged with some regret. They were so different that Sam occasionally found it difficult to believe they came from the same parents. 'Too much like your father' was the accusation usually thrown at her when things weren't going quite right at home. If that was true – and it probably was – then Wyn was far too much like her mother.

Tom stirred and, leaning towards Sam, gently pushed her on to her back. He held her tightly and looked down into her face, his body lean and strong above hers.

'And what time of the night do you call this?'

'Sid. What do you call it?'

His faced was stern, like that of a father scolding his errant daughter. 'Have a good time?'

Sam realised it was a loaded question and wasn't about to admit she'd enjoyed herself without him. 'It would have been better if you'd been there.'

He knew the trick but was flattered anyway. 'Miss me, then?'

Sam decided she'd flattered him enough for one night, and said with a half-smile, 'Not for long. Far too many eligible young men about.'

His face relaxed and he smiled down at her, the wrinkles round his eyes deepening as he did so. His head moved slowly down towards hers, his lips brushing hers before he moved down her naked body, gently kissing her breasts and caressing her erect nipples, catching them between his teeth and tongue. He was a good lover, strong but gentle, and always enjoying her pleasure as much as his own. He was, in his own words, a bit of a 'flask and sandwiches man' who liked to take his time, savouring every moment as he came to it. He felt good, and Sam could feel herself slowly responding to him. Her breathing became more laboured, her heart beat faster. Her back arched as she wrapped her legs tightly around his body and she heard herself cry out as her lover reached his final destination.

It was late and both Johnson and Simons were ready for a break. Despite searching the usual places, the back of the hangar, the seating around the baseball stadium and football pitch, they hadn't managed to find a single couple. It was unusual for a hangar dance. They were usually at it like rabbits. Either the girls had suddenly become more puritanical or they had managed to find somewhere a little more comfortable. It spoilt their fun, though. They enjoyed watching for a while, giving the unsuspecting couple marks out of ten for performance, and then, just as they reached the point of no return, stepping out from their hiding-place and asking loudly and authoritatively, 'Can I ask what you're doing here?'

The results were usually hilarious and helped break the evenings up a bit. They had decided they were going to write a book on the various excuses they'd heard, not to mention the false names and addresses they'd been given, even by people they knew. Tonight, however, was different, just one long, cold drag. The one ray of hope in their otherwise dismal evening was a small black evening bag they recovered from the back of hangar two. A few feet from the bag, they also found a pair of red cotton ladies' panties which had been ripped apart and lay in tatters on the floor.

Johnson picked them up with his night-stick. 'Someone was in a hurry.'

Simons laughed. 'Only just missed them, then.'

'Looks like it.'

As he brandished the panties on the end of his stick he noticed a dark stain covering one side. He looked at them more closely and rubbed the thin cotton between his fingers. His suspicions were confirmed: it was blood.

He called out to Simons, 'There's blood on these panties.'

Simons had begun to examine the bag and was uninterested in his partner's discovery. 'Some girls just don't care when they do it.'

Johnson nodded his agreement, but the find had unsettled him. He flashed his torch around. A dark stain on the close-cut grass caught his attention. Although it didn't cover a large area, it seemed odd. It just didn't sit right in his mind. He walked over to it and, crouching down, ran his hand across it. It felt sticky. Turning his wrist he shone his torch on the flat of his hand. It was blood.

He said, 'There's more blood over here.'

'Scene of the crime,' said his partner. 'Probably where they did it.'

Johnson wasn't satisfied. 'Or someone's been hurt. Wouldn't be the first time.'

Simons shook his head and joined him, flashing his torch around the grass. He came to an immediate conclusion. 'The blood's only in one place. If something bad happened, why isn't there a trail of it? Besides, if there'd been that kind of trouble we'd have heard about it by now.'

Johnson took another look round and saw that the rest of the area was clean. Deciding his partner was probably right, he stood up. Simons was again searching through the handbag. Inside it, among the usual paraphernalia, he found a ticket to that night's dance, a purse containing about three pounds and a bus pass made out to a Mary West and with a nearby address printed on the front. The two men pored over her photograph.

'Cute,' said Simons. 'I could do her a big favour.'

Johnson agreed. 'Me too. Perhaps she'd like a three-way split, twice the fun and twice the taste.'

Simons laughed. They'd make up for an otherwise wasted evening by paying her a visit and asking some very awkward questions. They walked on, contemplating the future with a smile.

They were crossing the baseball ground *en route* to the main gate and the warmth of the control room, when Johnson noticed a faint light in one of the storage sheds at the far side of the field. The light moved around inside of the shed, flickering from place to place before coming to a standstill. The two men knew the shed contained only an assortment of well-worn equipment for the base's various sporting activities. They were pleased with themselves. It looked as though they had located at least one of the 'more comfortable' places that the couples had obviously discovered.

As they made their way quickly towards the shed, a shadowy figure emerged from its doorway, apparently carrying something. It could have been a bag but they were too far away to be sure. Johnson flashed his torch towards the figure but couldn't make out any details. He quickened his pace and shouted, 'Stop right there, mister. We know who you are!'

It was an old lie, which sometimes worked. The figure seemed to hesitate for a moment as if unsure what to do, then darted off into the darkness of the base.

Tucking his torch into his belt, Johnson gave chase, calling back to his colleague, 'Check the shed.'

Simons ran across to the door before anyone else had a chance to escape. He said loudly, 'Come on out. We know you're in there. There's not a problem, just come on out.'

There was no reply,

'Look, come on. I've really got better things to do. Don't make me come in there and get you. If I do, you won't like it.'

The shed remained silent. Simons pulled his night-stick from his belt and banged it twice against the shed door, hard. 'Last chance.'

Still there was silence.

'OK, if you want to be stupid about it it's up to you.'

He pushed the door wide and, flashing his torch before him, stepped slowly inside.

At the other side of the field, the figure Johnson was chasing had disappeared among the store sheds and supply wagons at the far side of the base. Realising his task was hopeless, and expecting to get the man's name from whoever was in the shed with him anyway, Johnson stuck his night-stick back in his belt and gave up the chase.

'I'll see you later, bud, whoever you are!'

With that final warning he turned and made his way back towards the shed. It took him only a few moments to get back to where they'd first seen the figure. He was looking forward to seeing who Simons had caught inside. He half hoped it was the girl whose photo they'd seen on the bus pass. Perhaps, he thought, she could be persuaded to 'co-operate' with their enquiries in return for their not taking the matter any further. Smiling in anticipation, he quickened his step, fearful of losing out to his partner.

He was almost at the shed when he saw Simons stagger backwards through the door, as if he'd been punched or beaten with some unseen object, before twisting downwards, falling to his knees and being violently sick, retching, the contents of his stomach gushing over the grass in front of him. Startled, Johnson drew his pistol. Every shadow suddenly seemed sinister, and he looked around more than a little nervously for his partner's hidden attacker. But he saw no one, nothing. He crouched down and put a comforting hand on his friend's shoulder, while still peering through the darkness to locate the enemy.

'For Christ's sake, Carl, what the fuck is the matter?'

Simons, still retching and holding his stomach, was unable to speak and instead pointed shakily towards the shed door. Johnson went slowly inside, holding his pistol at arm's length ready to shoot anyone or anything that might suddenly emerge from the gloomy interior. He had gone only a few steps when he felt the soles of his boots begin to stick to the floor and make a strange sucking sound as he lifted his feet. He shone his torch down at the floor. It seemed to be moving, oozing around his feet, filling the gap his foot left as he lifted it from the floor. Gripping his gun more firmly, he aimed the torchlight down at the floor and along the liquid trail towards the rear of the shed until it finally reached a mass of matted blond hair. The hair surrounded the white, marbled face of a young woman, emphasising it like a macabre frame. Her head was angled unnaturally backwards and twisted

STRANGE SCREAMS OF DEATH

slightly to one side. Her eyes, half open, stared blankly towards him and her mouth hung wide open in a silent scream of agonised death.

Sam lay back across Tom's chest, stroking his face and running her fingers through his hair. He returned the caress by stroking the back of her head. As they lay there in the semi-darkness, she could almost hear his brain ticking over as he decided on the right moment and right tactic to bring up the subject they seemed to talk about constantly, especially after making love, when he thought her guard might be down and she was at her weakest. She half wished he smoked and then perhaps he would have something else to concentrate on. Eventually he stirred and the inevitable assault began.

'How long have we been together now?'

Christ, he's predictable, Sam thought. Aloud, she said, 'It's our anniversary next month.'

'A year next month.' He smiled down at her. 'Goes quickly when you're enjoying yourself, doesn't it?'

She nodded into his chest. 'Longest year of my life.'

He gave her hair a gentle tweak. 'Thanks a lot.'

Sam lifted her head and smiled up at him. 'And are you enjoying yourself?'

'Yes, but I'd like to enjoy myself a bit more.'

She knew what he meant. 'Not yet. I'm not ready.' She laid her head back on his chest and waited for his endless list of good reasons why they should marry.

'Why not? We get on, don't we? We seem compatible in most departments, and to be frank I miss you. That bloody flat of mine's even emptier than it used to be.'

'You'll have to be patient.'

'It's been a year, and I think that is being patient. How patient do I have to be?'

'I don't know. It's a big decision. Soon.' She looked up at him again. 'When I decide to share my life with someone, I want it to be for ever. So I want to be sure.'

Tom produced his hurt look. She knew it of old and it usually had the desired effect. She really didn't want to hurt him but this was becoming stale ground and she was mildly irritated at his persistence.

'It's not you, it's me. Perhaps I've been on my own too long, got too set in my ways. Just give me a bit of space and a bit more time.'

'More space, Sam? I only see you at weekends now, and that's only when one of us isn't on call.'

'We're both on call this weekend and we're still together.'

'So far so good, but it's one hell of a way to carry on a relationship. It's like going out with a microwave: when you hear the bleep, turn it off.'

She sighed. She knew she'd have to make her mind up soon or risk losing him, and it was a dilemma she could have done without. Before she had time to continue, Tom's bleeper brought the conversation to an end.

He looked down at her. 'It's that microwave again.'

Saved by the bell, Sam thought with relief. She rolled over, giving him room to read his bleeper and move across the bed to the phone. He began to punch the numbers in quickly. Before he'd had time to reach the final digit, Sam leant across and slammed her hand down hard on the receiver. Tom looked up in surprise.

'One four one first, if you please,' she said crisply. 'I don't want every copper in the force knowing who you spend your nights with.'

Tom nodded his understanding and pressed the 141 key before completing the number.

Sam whispered in his ear, 'I'm going to have a shower.'

A night of strenuous activity, from dancing at the base to making love with Tom, had left her feeling hot and sticky, and although it was late the thought of cool, fresh water was bliss. She slipped out of the bed and began to walk, naked, towards the bathroom. Tom watched her go as he waited for his call to be answered. She might not be twenty any more, he thought, but my God she looked good. He sighed appreciatively as his call was finally answered.

'Detective Inspector Adams. You want me?'

The voice at the other end of the phone was cool and matter-of-fact, typical of a control-room operator, he thought.

'They've found the body of a girl at the Yanks' air-base at Leeminghall. Superintendent Farmer's on her way and would like you to join her as soon as possible.'

He scribbled down the details in the notebook Sam kept beside the bed. 'Do we know who she is yet?'

There was a pause at the other end of the phone while the controller examined his computer screen.

'Haven't got that information yet. I'll try and get an update as soon as I can.'

'OK, I'll be right there.'

The operator didn't seem entirely satisfied. 'Sorry, sir, would you mind letting me know what number you're calling from? There seems to be a problem with my computer. Your number hasn't registered for some reason.'

Tom Adams knew there was no problem. 'Yes, I would mind, you nosy git.'

He slammed the phone down, annoyed at the controller's inquisitiveness, and forced himself out of bed. He ripped the page out of the notebook and tucked it into his trouser pocket, then hurried to the bathroom. Sam was just stepping out of the shower. He picked up her towel and stood for a second, admiring her.

Sam asked, 'Are you going to pass me the towel or are you just going to stand there looking at me.'

'I'm just going to stand here looking at you.'

Sam reached out and grabbed the towel from his hands, wrapping it round her as she walked back into the bedroom.

He followed and began to pull on his clothes. 'I've got to go. They've found a girl's body.'

Sam began to dry herself. 'Where?'

'Leeminghall air-base.'

'What? I was there only a few hours ago.'

'Interesting twist. That makes you a suspect.'

'Who is she? Someone from the base?'

Tom shrugged. 'They don't know yet.'

'Was she at the hangar dance?'

'I told you, I don't know. Nor do I know how she was killed, why she was killed, or if they have a

36

suspect yet. I'll give you a call later and bring you up to date.'

As he spoke the phone rang.

'I don't think you'll have to,' Sam said. 'I think they're playing my tune.'

Tom frowned.

'I'm on call, remember?'

He nodded. 'I'll wait till you're ready, then.'

Sam shook her head. 'You won't. It wouldn't take a genius to work out what was going on if we turned up together.'

'And that would never do, would it?' he said acidly.

Sam ignored him and picked up the phone. 'Dr Ryan speaking.'

Hammond had followed procedure to the letter. After viewing the girl's body briefly, he had taped off the area and immediately contacted the local civilian authorities. Simons and Johnson had been stripped of their clothing, which was bagged and labelled, and initial statements had been taken from both of them. Colonel Cully arrived about half an hour after the body was found. He was in a foul and slightly hysterical mood. He marched across to Hammond and snapped, 'What the fuck's going on, Bob?'

Hammond stood up straight and saluted formally before answering, 'Dead girl, sir. Looks like murder.'

'Shit, this is all I need, specially with the general still here. Are you sure it's a murder?'

Hammond nodded.

'Who is she?'

'We can't be entirely sure just yet, we think—'

'Don't think, Bob, find out,' Cully cut in. 'With my luck she's probably related to the fucking Churchills or something.'

Hammond said calmly, 'We think it might be a local girl called Mary West. She was at the dance tonight. The two men who found the body discovered these at the back of hangar two a little while before.'

He handed Cully the bus pass and torn panties. Cully examined the bus pass. 'Cute,' he said.

'Not any more, she isn't.'

Cully handed the pass back. 'No, I don't suppose she is. How long before you know for sure?'

'We're doing our best, sir. The local police have been informed. A Superintendent Farmer is on her way here, and I understand they're sending one of their uniformed officers round to the address on the pass.'

Cully began to pace agitatedly around. Unmoved, Hammond waited in silence. He knew Cully's moods of old and knew it would be better to let him get on with it.

'This is all I fucking need. This'll be in every paper in the country. Fuck, it'll be in every paper in the US. Shit, Bob, how the fuck could you let this happen? Well, I can kick my promotion up the arse. Limey bitch! Why'd she have to get herself killed on my base?'

Hammond said, 'I'm sure her parents will apologise, sir.'

Cully swung round, flushed with anger. The two men eyed each other for a moment, then Cully backed off. He'd known Hammond for years and appreciated his worth. If anyone could clean this mess up, and do it quickly, Hammond could. He seemed to make it his business to know all the civilian authorities within weeks of moving on to a base and had the knack of getting them to do what he wanted. To alienate him just now would be damn foolishness.

Cully stepped towards the shed, ducking beneath the marker tape. 'Well, let's have a look at the mess.'

Hammond tried to stop him. 'I'm not sure that . . .'

Before he had finished his sentence, Cully was by the shed door and peering in. Hammond moved forwards quickly in an attempt to limit the damage his senior officer might do to the crime scene.

'It's perhaps best that you don't go in, sir. I mean, it's pretty unpleasant.'

Cully wasn't put off. 'When you've served in a real war, like 'Nam, then lecture to me on unpleasant sights, Major.' Hammond had seen military service in both Grenada and the Gulf but Cully often intimated that he didn't consider them real wars.

Under his breath, Hammond said sardonically, 'I love the smell of napalm in the morning.' It was the colonel's favourite line from *Apocalypse Now*.

Arc-lights had already been assembled around the shed, their lights piercing the gloom of the interior. Cully nearly slipped on coagulating blood as he made his way across to the girl's body, while Hammond considered the excuses he was going to have to make to the British police when they arrived.

In truth, Cully had been a pen-pusher attached to the staff in Saigon and had seen little real action. What he had seen wouldn't have prepared him for this. Hammond knew that war created an atmosphere all of its own. It was a shared experience, and the knowledge that you were all in it together, and not alone, helped prepare you for what might happen, what you might see and, ultimately, how you might deal with death.

Here, however, on a peacetime base in the middle of the English countryside, Cully was not ready for what he found. The sight of a dead teenage girl, her life's blood sticking to the soles of his highly polished shoes, set his head spinning. He grabbed the side of the door as the world began to revolve. Hammond saw Cully's legs begin to buckle and grabbed his commanding officer firmly under the arms, dragging him out of the shed before his body had a chance to hit the ground. It was done not out of kindness or respect for Cully but out of need to preserve the scene and stop it being damaged further. Cully had already had his size tens all over it, which Hammond knew would reflect on *his* professionalism not Cully's.

Hammond looked at his commanding officer lying face down on the floor in the recovery position, groaning and twitching like a drunk on a downtown sidewalk. 'So, napalm sticks to kids, eh?' Hammond quoted inwardly. Still, he preferred Cully this way: at least he couldn't do any more damage.

CHAPTER TWO

Sam arrived at the scene early for once. She passed through the base's main checkpoint with its high security towers and automatic gates. It was guarded by both a civilian and a military policeman and the contrast between the two was striking. The American trooper cut a dashing figure in his sharp, dark-green uniform, his beret pulled down to one side of his head at a rakish angle, while across his shoulder he balanced a semi-automatic rifle. The British policeman, on the other hand, was dressed in an ill-fitting dark-blue uniform and jacket with a traditional but out-of-place pointed helmet perched precariously on his head, and was probably carrying nothing more than a long wooden stick with which to guard democracy against all comers. Sam flashed her pass at him and announced herself: 'Doctor Ryan, Home Office pathologist.'

The policeman nodded. 'They're expecting you, ma'am.'

He quickly jotted down her name, profession and time of arrival before directing her towards the car park at the centre of the base. Sam already knew the way, of course, but she listened politely before driving off. It seemed odd that only hours before she had been at the same place, enjoying herself and looking forward to her next meeting with Hammond. She hadn't realised it was going to be so soon or in such inauspicious circumstances.

As she pulled into her parking space she saw Hammond was there, waiting to meet her. She picked up her medical bag from the passenger seat and stepped out of her car before locking the door and checking it. Even in situations like this, Sam was always careful about her personal security. During the ten years she had been a Home Office pathologist her car had been broken into twice and damaged four times – and that when there had been dozens of policemen around. She began to make her way towards the bright lights that indicated the location of the murder.

Hammond joined her as she walked. 'I was kind of hoping to see you in more favourable surroundings.'

Sam smiled at him. 'I was just thinking that myself.' She switched to professional mode. 'Where was the body found?'

'Storage shed back of one of the hangars. It's pretty isolated, used for storing old sports equipment, that sort of thing.'

'Who is she? One of yours?'

'No, not at all. We're pretty sure she's a local kid, Mary West. Comes from Little Bonnington a few miles down the road. According to her parents, she should have been staying with a friend tonight in St Ives.'

'But she was playing hooky?'

Hammond nodded. 'Something like that. Two of our security policemen found an evening bag at the back of one of the hangars. It contained a ticket for tonight's dance and a bus pass with her photograph on. Looks like her – well, what she might have looked like when she was alive.'

'You've been in, then?'

Hammond realised the question was loaded. He raised a hand defensively. 'No, ma'am. We are taught a *little* about the preservation of murder scenes, even in the United States Air Force.'

Sam nodded. 'Good.'

'I just peeked in through the door. That was enough.'

Sam considered that he should not have even done that, but let it pass.

'Your guys in the white suits, Scene of Crime Officers? They're in there now. Seem to know what they're doing.'

Sam bristled slightly. 'They do. Any suspects?'

'One of ours, I'm afraid. Young airman called Ray Strachan, medical orderly. According to the guys who bunk with him, he's been seeing her for some weeks but she wanted it kept secret – her parents don't approve of Americans for some reason. He left the dance with her when it finished and no one's seen him since.'

'Does he live on the base?'

'Yep. We've searched his room, but no sign. Left all his kit behind, though, so it looks like he left in one big hurry. We've got men out looking for him now.'

'What about the British police?'

'We're searching inside the camp. They're doing the rest.'

As they reached the scene Sam noticed that the tape marking off the area was made up of long thin strips of bunting with stars and stripes and the words 'Happy New Year' printed on it at regular intervals. 'Unusual tape,' she commented.

Hammond looked slightly embarrassed. 'It's all we had. It was left over from the New Year's Eve party. This kind of thing doesn't happen on the base too often. Your Crime Scene Manager wasn't too impressed.'

'No, he wouldn't have been.'

'He's arranging for something more formal. Should be here soon.'

Sam smiled as she visualised the look on Colin Flannery's face when he saw the American version of marker tape. He was such a stickler for procedure.

The murder scene was as chaotic as usual, only this time there seemed to be twice as many people as usual attempting to get involved. They were like ants moving purposefully to and fro, each with a particular task. Dragon lights and exhibit bags stuck to their cold hands. Apart from the white-suited SOCOs there was the usual array of pale-faced CID officers called out of bed unexpectedly and feeling the worse for it. Especially if they'd been on one of their usual drinking binges the night before, which was very likely. Walking and kneeling around the scene were the Special Operations Units, huge, tough-looking men, their dark woolly hats pulled tightly around their ears as they conducted fingertip and general search patterns through the base, their long sticks probing nearby bushes and undergrowth, hoping to find a vital clue. To complicate matters, the American security police were also in evidence, advising, watching and directing. This was the biggest thing to happen on the base for years and although the investigation was a matter for the British police they were determined not to miss out completely.

Sam stopped on the edge of the marked-off area. Flannery approached her and handed over a protective white suit. She pulled it over her clothes quickly, then slipped into a pair of protective overshoes.

'How far have you got, Colin?'

'All the temperatures have been taken, except the body's, of course. Thought we'd leave that one for you. We've had the oblique lighting in there and photographed the body, floors and wall, and we've dropped in the stepping-plates to protect the floor.' Stepping-plates were essential in a murder of this type. They were small raised platforms, normally made of plastic, which sat over a murder scene and prevented any direct contact with the floor, thus preserving any vital forensic evidence which might be located beneath.

'There were a few bootprints, but we understand they came from the two American policemen who found her.'

'Have you managed to get hold of them?'

Flannery nodded. 'All bagged and tagged.'

'What about the body?'

'Her hands and feet have been bagged and the visible skin surface taped for debris. It was quite difficult: she's a bit of a mess.'

'Right.'

Sam was keen to get on. She ducked under the tape and headed for the shed, but Flannery hadn't quite finished.

'Arthur Knight's still in there. He shouldn't be long. He's just scanning the body for any prints.'

Sam waved back at him to show she had heard and Flannery moved on. DI Tom Adams and Superintendent Harriet Farmer approached, and Sam braced herself. To her surprise, however, the first string of instructions and questions were fired not at her but at Hammond, who had followed her through the tape.

'Major Hammond?' said Farmer.

Hammond was instantly alert.

'I want the names of all the base personnel, with their addresses. I also want to know who has visited the base over the past twenty-four hours, and that includes everyone from generals to dustmen and cleaners.'

Hammond nodded, pulling a notebook from his top jacket pocket.

'I also want to know who has clearance to enter the base, whether they were here recently or not.'

Hammond was scribbling at speed as Farmer continued, 'Also whether there have been any breaches in security over the past three months and the names of any personnel who visited the murder scene prior to our arrival.'

Hammond wasn't happy with Farmer's requests. 'Is all this really necessary, Superintendent? I think we can assume who our killer is. Wouldn't it be better to wait until we've got him?'

Farmer glared at him. 'Assumption is the mother of disaster, Major. You've got my instructions and I'd appreciate your co-operation.'

She turned away from him and said to Adams, 'Tom,

46

go and see the search parties are all out. Get some more men in if you need them. Have the airports and ports been done?'

Adams nodded.

'Good. Then let's start the door-to-door enquiries in the nearest villages. Strachan might be hiding in one of them.'

'Right.'

Farmer called out to Hammond, who was disappearing rapidly towards his office to deal with her first set of instructions, 'Oh and Major, I also want to know everyone Strachan associated with, friends, family, people he worked with, girls he slept with!'

He raised a hand in acknowledgement and disappeared into the darkness of the base. Farmer glanced down at her watch and then at Sam. 'I'm impressed. Got here only half an hour after Inspector Adams.'

Farmer had an uncanny knack of always knowing what was going on, especially within her own squad. What irritated Sam was the snide way she chose to let you know she knew. Sam supposed it made her feel powerful, in charge.

The superintendent continued, 'Hope you didn't break any speed limits,' and smiled at her. For some reason Sam didn't feel Farmer's smile and comments had the usual hard sarcastic edge, but perhaps it was just that she was becoming inured to Farmer's style.

This, though, was not the time to analyse the situation. She went quickly into the shed. Moving carefully across the stepping-plates, she made her way towards

Knight. He was crouched beside the body, a torch in one hand and his magnifying glass in the other. The shed resembled a slaughterhouse and the smell was already overpowering. The blood which had spurted and oozed from the body had washed across the floor like a red carpet, before finally congealing against the edge of the door. The walls, ceiling and most of the equipment were streaked and splattered with blood. Macabre but strangely compelling patterns were splashed against every surface like a modern painting of an image of hell.

Knight looked up. 'Morning, Sam. Fancy seeing you here.'

She hunkered down beside him. 'Anything?'

'Shed's covered in prints – a lot of eliminations to do – but not much on the body. Bit of a half-print here.' He indicated the area just below Mary West's left arm. 'But even that's smudged, so we'll probably have trouble getting a match.'

'Even with a suspect?'

'Depends on how many points of comparison there are. Courts are still a bit funny about things like that. On the other hand, it might not even belong to our killer.' His tone changed to one of sarcasm. 'You know how people like to help.'

'They've got a log of who's been in and out of the shed, so it shouldn't be too difficult to match.'

'They've got a log all right, but I wonder how many people dropped in for a quick look before they started to keep it.'

Sam nodded ruefully. In a perfect world there would

be no problems, but murder scenes were always far from perfect, which every defence counsel worth their salt realised.

'Seen her clothes?' she asked.

He pointed to a twisted grey plastic chair by the side of the body. On it, carefully folded, were Mary West's skirt, blouse and jacket, on top of which, again neatly folded, were her bra, suspenders and stockings. 'Her pants and shoes are missing.'

'Probably outside.'

'Possibly. Why do you think the clothes are folded?'

Sam mused for a moment. 'She might have done it keep them clean and tidy while they were romping around the shed.'

Knight wasn't convinced. 'Maybe, but I think it's a little odd. In my day it was all passion, and to hell with where your clothes landed.'

'And there was me thinking you were still a virgin.'

He looked up and laughed. 'Right, I've finished. It's all yours. I'll have a quick word with Flannery about the handling of the body when it's moved. Try and make sure the print we've got isn't wiped away.'

'Has it been photographed?'

He nodded. 'Still nothing quite like the real thing, though. See you later.'

As Knight made for the door, he hesitated for a moment. Nodding towards the wall behind Mary West's head, he said, 'You might like to take a look at that as well when you've got a moment. Very odd, very odd.'

She followed his glance. Painted in what, at this stage, she assumed was West's blood, was the last letter in

49

the Greek alphabet, omega: Ω. Its significance was immediately obvious to Sam, who knew it was the symbol for 'the end' and the destruction of the world. Its presence, under these circumstances, was heavy with portent. She hadn't noticed it when she entered the shed, because she had been concentrating on Knight and West's body. She stepped closer to the symbol, which surrounded an old, rusted nail. What arrested her attention, however, wasn't so much the nail as the strip of white paper caught on it.

On its own it didn't seem particularly unusual but there were blood splashes surrounding it. Up to the area close to the nail they followed a familiar and expected pattern. Forming a shallow arc across the wall, the droplets were thick at the bottom and thinned as they moved upwards, indicating the direction of the instrument from which they had flown. These patterns were normally created by the slashing motion of a knife or blunt instrument which flicked blood from its edges as it was swung around. In this case, however, a large part of the pattern seemed to be missing. The droplets started thickly enough at the base of the arc and gradually diminished as the line was traced upwards, indicating the direction of the movement. However, there was a gap in the pattern, after which a few thin, dispersed streaks and splashes completed the sequence. Sam could only surmise that some object, probably a sheet of paper, had been attached to the nail and had, some time after the murder, been removed. She looked around the floor but could see nothing which might have been the object. She wondered if Flannery or one of his

SOCOs had removed it before she arrived. If they had, then it was very remiss of them to leave a small fragment behind. No, she concluded, the paper had been ripped down after the murder and without the care that one of Flannery's team would have taken.

Ideally, the fragment should have been photographed *in situ*, but because of its precarious position Sam decided to move it for safe keeping. She retrieved a pair of tweezers from her bag and used them to remove the paper from the nail, dropping it into a small plastic exhibit bag, which she stored carefully in her bag. Once she'd finished, she turned back to the girl's body: she was now alone with it. She stood over it for a moment, scanning every inch and making her preliminary judgements.

Did she recognise the girl from the dance? It was possible, but she might well be wrong. Dozens of similar girls had been there last night, and she'd been too occupied to remember any of them in particular. It was chilling to remember the laughter and revelry they had all been enjoying while this poor young scrap had been losing her battle for life.

Mary West's body lay towards the back of the shed. She was naked. Her head lay towards the far wall. Her stomach had been ripped open and its contents exposed. Judging by the amount of blood inside the shed, Sam concluded that the girl had still been alive when it had been done. Her entire body was covered in congealing blood. The wall by the side of the body and the remains of an old table-tennis table above her head were splattered with blood. The spurts had spread across both surfaces in long, reducing patterns away from the body.

Examination of the blood splashes on the wall suggested to Sam that the body had been opened with a very violent and forceful cut which began at the top of the pubic bone and ran up to the base of her sternum, at which point the force of the cutting action had caused the knife to deflect off the bone and swing upwards and to the right as it was freed from the restriction of flesh and sinew. She opened her bag, snapped on her surgical gloves and picked up her tape-recorder.

Kneeling down by the body she began to dictate her observations. 'Storage shed, Leeminghall US Air Force base, 4.45 a.m., Sunday the 22nd of May 1996. Also present at the scene are Major Bob Hammond of the US Air Force Security Police, Detective Superintendent Farmer, Detective Inspector Adams, Mr Colin Flannery, the Crime Scene Manager, and Mr Arthur Knight, the fingerprint officer. The body is that of a well-developed white female in her late teens or early twenties.'

Sam ran her hands round the head, face and neck. 'The body is still warm to the touch.' She took the thermometer from her pack and pushed it into Mary's left armpit. Taking the right arm, she moved it up and down in a slight circular movement before putting it back in place.

'There is no evidence of rigor mortis. There is a deep wound made by a sharp instrument of some sort that stretches from her sternum to the tip of her pubic region. The body has been crudely opened, exposing its contents. Most of the abdominal contents – stomach, intestine and bowel – all lie across the body, with some extending to the floor.'

Sam hadn't seen injuries like this for some time and then they had usually been the result of a serious car smash or bombing, when victim and murderer were normally miles apart from each other. These injuries had clearly been committed not just close to but face-to-face, with all the horror and fascination that must have held for her killer.

'There is too much damage to make any further judgements at this point, but it appears that some organs may have been removed.' That was a bit of a snap judgement, but on the basis of what she had observed she was sure she was right.

She stood up and packed her bag away before looking down at West's body once more. There were already many, many questions she wanted to ask. She could almost guess what the police were thinking. Strachan brought her here for sex, she objected, there was a quarrel and he probably raped and killed her in a fit of sexual frustration. But, if Strachan had done it, he had made sure that everyone knew it was him. He was certainly the last person to be seen with her. And why were the clothes folded so neatly? If he'd raped her, why had he taken so much trouble over her clothes? What was her bag doing on the other side of the camp? And why did Strachan kill her with such savagery?

No. This murder had been contrived, arranged, thought about. Perhaps Mary had been picked out, stalked, and finally savagely murdered. Sam felt a sudden sense of great evil, as if something of the killer's presence had remained in the shed. It was so strong that it made her look quickly round the shed, searching for a presence she knew wasn't there. She felt herself shudder. This wasn't the work of an over-amorous airman. This was something far more sinister.

All at once the atmosphere inside the shed was claustrophobic and menacing. She could feel herself becoming hot. Grabbing her bag, she hurried outside, almost falling off one of the stepping-plates in her rush.

Outside, Sam was glad to feel the rush of fresh air against her face and to fill her lungs. She leant against the shed for a moment, recovering herself and taking in great gulps of air.

'Are you OK?' She felt Farmer take her arm, which was something she'd never done before.

Sam nodded and gently disengaged her arm. 'Yes, I'm fine. Just a bit warm in there.'

Farmer nodded. 'Anything?' she asked.

Sam came abruptly back to reality. 'Not yet. We'll need to get her back to the mortuary.'

'Cause of death?'

Sam felt she had to say something. 'Without wishing to state the glaringly obvious, she's certainly been stabbed and disembowelled, but that's about as much as I can tell you at the moment. Any sign of the murder weapon?'

Farmer shook her head.

'You said the men found her bag at the back of one of the hangars. Did they find anything else?'

'Pair of ladies' knickers. We're assuming they're West's but they'll have to be identified.'

'Knickers? What kind of state were they in?'

'They'd been ripped. Looks like someone tugged them off. Oh, and there was blood on them.'

The more Sam learnt, the more questions she wanted to ask. She turned to Flannery, who had just joined them. 'Any blood near the pants?'

He nodded. 'Some. We've got samples from the scene and the pants have been bagged.'

Sam wasn't satisfied. 'What's the distance between the hangar and the shed?'

Flannery thought for a moment. 'Two or three hundred yards.'

Her mind began to race. So West could have been murdered by the hangar and then her body carried to the shed. But she was alive when she was stabbed – of that Sam was sure – and it still didn't explain the clothes. If the killer had ripped off her pants at the hangar, why not the rest of her clothes? Perhaps he raped her there, and then dragged her to the shed to murder her? It was all too implausible. The more Sam knew, the more puzzled she became.

She asked, 'Have her shoes been found yet?'

Flannery shook his head. 'We're still looking. They'll turn up.'

Sam could think of nothing else to say for the moment and knew she, like the rest of them, would have to wait until after the PM to know more. She looked down at her watch. 'PM at 10 a.m., if that suits everyone?' There were nods of approval.

She stepped out of her protective suit and overshoes, and handed them back to Flannery. 'Colin, I think you might have to tape the stomach closed to stop anything dropping out when you move her.'

'Not a problem.' He called across to one of the SOCOs and together they walked towards the shed.

In the early hours of that morning, a man trudged along the track leading to Sam's cottage. The taxi driver had been reluctant to take him along the uneven lane in the middle of the night, so the passenger was forced to leave the taxi at the main road and walk the rest of the way. When he finally reached Sam's cottage, it was in darkness, but he had expected that. As he turned in to the drive, the security light flickered into life, then into a blaze, blinding him for a moment and casting his shadow long and thin behind him.

'That won't last long,' he thought. He walked across to the front door, shielding his eyes while they adjusted to the brightness. He knocked loudly and waited. When, after a few moments, there was no response, he tried again. This time he pressed the bell, holding his finger on it long and hard. He could hear its loud shrill echoing around the inside of the house. After holding the button down long enough to wake the devil himself, he released it and waited. Still nothing. No lights, no sound of footsteps coming hurriedly down the stairs.

Suddenly the security light flickered again and went out, leaving him and the drive in total darkness. He moved determinedly round the house, using the moon as a lantern to see by. He searched for an open window, a catch that might not have been fastened properly, a broken pane that hadn't yet been repaired. For a moment he contemplated smashing a window, but he realised that the place probably had an alarm system. He looked over the garden and spotted the shed. It wouldn't be the first time he'd slept in a shed, and they could be made quite comfortable. He walked across to it and tried the door. It wasn't locked. He stepped into the gloom, closing the door behind him, threw his suitcase on the floor and settled down to await Sam's return.

Dawn was spilling over the dark-edged Cambridge landscape when Sam got home. As her Range Rover pulled off the farm track on to the drive, she heard, with some pleasure, the familiar sound of gravel crunching beneath the wheels of her car. The security light, perched high on the front wall, came on uncertainly, hesitated for a moment, and then went out with a sharp ping, plunging the driveway into darkness as the bulb failed. She'd been meaning to replace it for weeks, aware that it must be approaching the end of its natural life, but had never managed to find the time. There was no point in asking Tom: he was about as practical around the house as she was. What she needed, she decided, was a handyman. Someone to come to the cottage occasionally to deal with all the annoying little things which needed replacement or renovation.

She dug around inside her handbag, searching for the cottage keys. Knowing her weakness when it came to keys, she always kept her cottage and car keys separate. It wasn't that she didn't lose her keys any less often, just that when she did, she didn't lose the whole lot. She'd kept a set under one of the stones in the garden for a while, but when she forgot which stone it was she had to admit that her plan was flawed. She still hadn't rediscovered it, six months later.

She unearthed her door keys, which were hidden beneath a collection of chewing-gum papers and old car-park tickets, in one of the several side pockets of her capacious handbag. Opening the front door, she switched on the hall light, bathing the low ceiling and uneven walls in welcome illumination, before slamming shut the solid oak door and leaning heavily against it.

She was exhausted. It wasn't only the physical strain of the work, although as the years passed she found it increasingly difficult to drag herself out of bed in the early hours of the morning, to work in some freezing field or other equally uninviting spot. Unless the death was due to a domestic murder, which most still were, the bodies tended to turn up in the most inhospitable locations, disposed of unceremoniously by the killer or killers, anxious to hide the incriminating evidence for as long as possible.

One thing Sam had learnt over the years was that getting rid of a body was far more difficult than people realised. She'd dealt with cases in which everything from dismemberment and burial to vats of acid had been used to try and hide or destroy the body. In almost every case, however, something had been left behind. Admittedly, on occasions this didn't amount to much, but it was frequently enough to give the police a starting-point for their investigation.

Wearily, she dragged herself away from the door, hung up her coat and made her way along the corridor to the kitchen. Through the kitchen window, she stared out into the garden. (There was so much to do; there always was.) She wanted to shake the last few hours off, push the experience away. She wasn't religious, didn't believe in any great Being who was responsible for every individual life and who guided every move, but for the first time in her life she had sensed genuine evil. It had been almost tangible, like an unseen force waiting to envelop and possess her. Although she hadn't admitted it to herself at the time, she had been very frightened, especially after Knight had left her alone at the scene. No wonder she was exhausted: fear was more tiring than even the most strenuous physical exercise.

Glancing at the clock on the wall she decided that there was very little point in returning to bed so, as there was now enough light to work by, she would do some gardening by way of therapy. She changed her shoes for wellington boots, and went down to the far end of the garden to complete the work she had started the previous afternoon. Her spade was still sticking out of the heavy clay soil, next to the hole she had been preparing for the violas which sat forlornly, still in their pots, where she'd abandoned them the previous afternoon.

She hated leaving her tools out, and was normally meticulous about cleaning and oiling them. However, Tom had arrived at the cottage in one of his silly moods and had rushed into the garden, picked her up and carried her up to bedroom, bellowing like Tarzan, pausing only to allow her to kick off her mud-covered boots. She had tried to protest but he wouldn't listen. He didn't like gardening and certainly didn't understand plants.

She crouched down and examined the violas. Although they had been left out in the afternoon sun and were a little dehydrated, no lasting damage seemed to have been done. She brought her nose down to one of the flowers and breathed in deeply. The scent was so sweet: if only she could bottle it, she'd make a fortune. Pulling her spade out of the ground she began to finish off the hole she had begun before her amorous partner had interrupted her.

The noise from the shed wasn't loud but it was distinct. Something had fallen or been toppled. Sam was surprised because she was very careful about the way she kept things in the shed. She stood looking at the rickety wooden construction for a moment, wondering what to do. Normally a noise like that wouldn't have bothered her, but, still on edge after the morning's events, she feared things that went bump in the night. Eventually, she made her way slowly down the slate path and across to the shed, holding her spade up in the air like a spear or club, ready for anything that might coming rushing through the twisted and broken door. She'd already had one unpleasant experience in a shed tonight, and that was quite enough.

When she reached the shed, she turned her head to bring her ear close to the gap between the door and the jamb. She listened intently, trying to decide what might be lurking inside. She suspected that it was probably an animal of some sort. Living in the country, she had become accustomed to the miscellany of sounds which emanated from the local wildlife, from foxes, which sounded like crying babies, to mating hedgehogs, whose passionate grunting sounded like something from another world. She decided to swing the shed door open and stand to one side, in the hope that whatever was lurking inside would see its chance to escape and make a run for it.

Holding the spade up in one hand while the other grabbed hold of the shed lock, she prepared to pull the door open.

Invisible hands seized her from behind, lifted her off her feet and sent her soaring high into the air. Dropping her spade, Sam screamed and lashed out, hoping to strike her attacker or push him away. After what seemed an age, she was dropped back to the ground but still held tightly around the middle and pressed firmly against a man's body.

'It's all right, it's all right. Steady on there, it's me, it's me!'

Tom's voice was calm and reassuring but Sam rounded on him in fury.

'When will you stop acting like an overgrown school boy and start acting your age?' she shouted.

He was unrepentant. 'Calm down. It was just a bit of fun.'

'It's always "just a bit of fun" with you. Grow up! I'm not a toy. You creep up behind me in the middle of the bloody night—'

'Morning,' he corrected her annoyingly.

She overrode him '—grab me from behind, giving me the fright of my life, and expect me to fall about laughing. Well, I'm sorry, but I just lost my sense of humour!'

The sound from the shed came again, more loudly this time. Whoever, or whatever, was inside had clearly been disturbed by the argument. Tom looked enquiringly at Sam.

She pointed at the shed and whispered, 'There's something, or someone, in the shed.'

He nodded his understanding. With one hand, he gestured to Sam to stand back. He yanked the shed door open with the other and stepped inside. There were immediate, alarming sounds of a struggle.

'Come here, you bastard!'

Sam picked up the spade and held it above her head, ready to strike down whoever came out, if it wasn't Tom.

The struggle continued.

'Will you bloody get off me!' The voice was clearly Irish and, for a moment, Sam thought she recognised it.

'Hold still, you bloody Mick.'

The door, which had swung shut because of the angle at which the shed leant, burst open again and two figures, locked together, lurched out on to the path.

'Sam,' panted one of them, 'will you tell your big ape of a friend here to get off me?'

Sam's eyes widened as she realised who it was. 'Liam?' she demanded.

Tom relaxed his hold and looked across at her. 'You know this prat?'

Sam nodded. 'Unfortunately.'

Tom released Liam's arm, which until then had been forced half-way up his back, and pushed him forward.

Liam stepped quickly away from him on to the flower bed, wincing and rubbing his arm.

Tom eyed him suspiciously. 'What were you doing in the shed?'

'Minding my own business, that's what I was doing in the shed.'

Tom took a step forward and Liam took another step away from him.

Sam moved hastily between them and asked, 'Why didn't you say you were coming?'

'I did,' said Liam indignantly. 'I sent you a card. It had a picture of the Blarney Stone on it.'

'Very appropriate, but that was months ago. And couldn't you have arrived at a more respectable hour?'

'Plane was delayed from Dublin, which meant I missed the train and so on. Besides, you know me, I like to take my time about things.'

Sam shook her head and smiled indulgently. 'Well, get off the garden before you cause any more damage.'

As Liam stepped back on to the path, Sam kissed him on the cheek, much to Tom's disgust. 'Well,' she said, 'it's good to see you. What *were* you doing in the shed?'

'There was no one in, so I thought it was as good a place as any to lay me head. Not that I got much sleep, mind you, not with all the bloody noise you two were making.'

Sam glanced across at Tom and then back at Liam. The two men were still eyeing each other warily.

'Tom, this is Liam, a friend from my childhood. Liam, this is Tom.'

Sam looked at Tom expectantly and he took the hint and held out his hand. 'Sorry about the misunderstanding. It's been a bad night.'

Liam, still rubbing his right arm, nodded. 'I accept your hand, but as you can see I can't take it.'

As Tom nodded in his turn, Sam seized the moment. 'Anyone fancy a cup of tea?'

Both men smiled. Liam said to Tom, 'I was wondering, now you've damaged my arm, whether you would be good enough to bring in my bag.' He rubbed his arm more vigorously. Sam struggled not to laugh at the look on Tom's face. She and Liam set off down the path towards the cottage, and Tom went grudgingly back into the shed to collect the suitcase.

Although Sam arrived at the mortuary early for once, Fred was already there. She knew, almost from the moment she entered the bright, sterile room, that he was about. He had a passion for strong Turkish cigarettes, and smoked them whenever he got the opportunity. The mortuary was a strict no-smoking area, and Fred normally satisfied his needs by standing just outside the front door.

Sam crept quietly up to his room and popped her head round the door. 'Morning, Fred. Any more tea in the pot?'

Fred was sitting back in his old armchair, a large mug of steaming tea in one hand, a long black cigarette in the other, and a copy of a crumpled tabloid on his lap. He jumped up, stubbing his cigarette out in an ashtray which was already full of stubs and bore witness to his guilt. He glanced at his watch. 'You're early, Doctor Ryan.'

Sam knew she'd got him. 'So it would seem.' She walked across to the table and picked up the ashtray. 'While the cat's away . . . ?'

Fred was speechless, which was unusual for him. Finally, he summoned up the right words. 'On call. Had to come in to accept the body. Time I'd finished there seemed little point in going home, and there was no one about.'

'So you thought you'd smoke yourself to death while you waited?'

'Something like that. Sorry.'

Sam tipped the nubs into the bin and put the ashtray back. Fred's help over the next few hours would be important, so she decided not to make an issue of it. Besides, now he'd been caught she doubted that he'd do it again. Her lenience would also make him far more co-operative for the next few weeks.

'What about that tea?' she said.

Fred wasn't sure what to expect. He liked Sam but had also been at the wrong end of her anger on more than one occasion and didn't like it much.

'It's a bit stewed. I'll make a fresh pot.'

He walked across to the small hob he'd somehow managed to get installed inside his little room and switched it on.

'We're not alone.'

Sam didn't understand. Beckoning her to follow, Fred went to the door. When she reached it, he pointed to the far end of the mortuary. Beside a stainless-steel fridge, a very youthful uniformed police officer sat perched on the edge of a grey plastic chair. He looked very uncomfortable.

'Been there since they brought the body in. Won't move. I asked him in for a chat and a warm but he didn't want to know. Something about continuity?'

'Continuity of evidence. He's obviously taking his job very seriously.'

Fred laughed sarcastically. 'Good to know one of them is. They'll corrupt him, give 'em time.'

Fred went back into his room to finish making the tea while Sam watched the young officer. He was nineteen or twenty years old, fresh-faced and eager. A lot of responsibility for one so young, she thought. He sat there on guard like a little tin soldier, sitting with a straight back, his helmet standing neatly on the floor beside his shiny boots. Sam guessed that he must be a probationer. If there were any long and boring jobs to do, it was always probationers who got them. A sort of 'rite of passage'. Fred returned and called across to him, 'Fancy a tea?'

He nodded and half stood, shy and awkward, before sitting down again. 'Thank you. No sugar.'

Fred looked at Sam. 'Sweet enough, I suppose.'

She dug her elbow into his ribs. 'I'll try and find a regulation cup. I'll be in my office.'

Sam took advantage of these few spare moments to try and catch up with some work. She began quickly to write up the notes she'd made at the murder scene. After a few minutes Fred came in and put a large mug of tea by her side.

'Thanks, Fred.'

'You've got a visitor.' As he spoke there was a tap on the internal office window, and Sam looked up to see Colin Flannery, the Crime Scene Manager, standing by the door.

She beckoned him inside. 'Colin. Fancy some tea?'

He shook his head. 'No thanks. Thought I'd have a quick word with you about the plan of action before you start the PM.'

The plan-of-action meeting before the full PM was a fairly recent development. Although initially hostile to what seemed another time-wasting intrusion into her work, Sam had begun to see its usefulness. During these meetings every aspect of the PM was covered, from the role each person present would play to a stage-by-stage analysis of the PM itself. Flannery was a meticulous man, both in his professional and in his private life – 'a bit of a trainspotter', as Fred put it – so meetings with him tended to be longer than most. Still, she thought, she had been glad of his professionalism on more than one occasion. He didn't miss much, so she tolerated his pernickety methodology.

By the time the meeting was over, all the interested parties had already arrived. Sam had hoped to slip up to her office before the PM started and bring herself up to date with her diary and mail, a privilege she hadn't enjoyed for several days. She knew Jean, her secretary, was becoming increasingly concerned at the backlog that was building up. The impatient looks and expectant air which greeted her the moment she suggested leaving the mortuary, however, quickly put paid to that idea.

Slipping into her gown and boots, she pushed her way into the dissecting room, where everything was ready.

As well as Fred, Colin Flannery was there with his team. Sam moved across to the mortuary table, where the remains of Mary West lay concealed beneath a black plastic body-bag. Before beginning her commentary, Sam glanced up at the gallery. Inside, keeping a well-experienced distance and protected behind a glass screen, were John Dale, the coroner's officer, Superintendent Farmer and Bob Hammond.

Sam was slightly surprised that Tom wasn't there. He'd left the cottage in a huff after she'd said Liam could stay while he was in Cambridge. She'd tried to find out what his plans were but he seemed reluctant to say anything while Tom was there. The only thing she had managed to glean was that he was in town for only a few days. While Liam was there, Sam didn't want Tom there too. She had tried, until her patience snapped, to explain that it was only for a couple of days, that Liam was an old family friend and that she was not ready to advertise their relationship just yet. But all attempts to placate Tom with promises to make it up to him later had failed improve his mood, and in the end she gave up trying. He'd stormed out of the cottage, annoyed with both her and the situation and making a scene which embarrassed her. She'd never seen that side of Tom's character before, and she didn't like it much.

Liam had been very tactful and pretended to be unaware of any tensions, but it didn't make her feel any better. When she'd left he was unpacking his things in the spare room, and he'd promised her a surprise when she got home. She prayed it was nothing stupid: she'd had more than enough of male pranks for one day. She hadn't time to concern herself with that now, but she knew it would have to be sorted out later, and the nagging thought irritated her and took the edge off her concentration.

Holding her hands up, she nodded across to Fred. He leant over and slowly began to undo the large metal zip on the body-bag. As the contents of the bag were exposed, the Scene of Crime photographer stepped forward. He took photographs at each stage of the revealing. Finally, the bag was carefully pulled from beneath the body and dropped into an exhibit bag, which in turn had an exhibit label tied round it, and was taken away for examination.

The second layer of protective wrapping was now removed. This consisted of a large, clear plastic bag which was wrapped tightly around the body in order to collect any previously unseen debris that might have fallen from the body when it was being transported. The fogged plastic gave the remains a surreal, even disturbing, appearance. Once again all the appropriate photographs were taken and the plastic sheet dropped into an exhibit bag, leaving Mary West's body naked and still on top of the cold stainless-steel table.

Sam looked expectantly across at Flannery. He was ready. He nodded to the SOCOs who moved across to the body and, with effortless efficiency, began to tape every part of Mary West's body.

Taping was done quite simply by wrapping commercial sticky tape around their hands several times and then pressing it lightly across every inch of the skin's surface to pick up any foreign bodies that might be lingering there. With Fred's assistance, this process was carried out all over the body. As each length of tape became spent it was dropped into an exhibit bag and a fresh piece was wound round the SOCO's hand. A third SOCO brushed vigorously through Mary West's hair, trapping any scraps and fibres in a small glass bowl, then moved down to her pubic hair and repeated the process.

Next, a minute examination of the body was conducted, first with the use of a magnifying glass and then with hand-held ultraviolet lights. As the cold, blue-tinted light searched along the body, any fibres missed by the tape stood out like flashing beacons against the goose-white flesh and were carefully recovered with either tape or tweezers.

Sam watched intently as the last few fibres were lifted from the body. Finally the men finished and, one by one, turned off their lights. Just before the last beam was extinguished, a tiny flash caught Sam's eye. She saw it for only a moment and felt sure that the SOCO working on that area must have noticed it. Only when he turned off his lamp, and it became apparent that he'd missed it, did she intervene.

'Excuse me.'

The SOCO looked up. Sam walked across to the body. 'There.' She pointed to the area where she'd seen the spark of light. 'Shine your light back on there.'

The SOCO seemed uncertain about Sam's intervention and glanced across at Flannery as if awaiting an instruction. Flannery was slow to react, and in the end

Sam impatiently pulled the torch from the man's grasp and switched it on. Bending close over the body, she scanned the area where she'd seen that fleeting glint.

Flannery came across to her. 'Have we got a problem here, Doctor Ryan?'

Sam held up her hand, silencing him, while she played the light around the underside of Mary West's arm. For a moment there was no sign of it and Sam began to think she'd been imagining things. Then, suddenly, there it was, by the side of her arm, flashing as brightly as before. She waved her free hand and, taking the hint, Colin dropped a magnifying glass into it. At last she could see it properly. It was small and transparent like an insect's wing, its colours changing and glittering as she moved the glass. She glanced up at Fred quickly, reluctant to take her eyes off the object for even for a moment.

'Scalpel.'

It was an order and Fred responded quickly, taking the torch from her outstretched hand and replacing it with a scalpel. Watching closely through the magnifying glass, she gently manoeuvred the scalpel under the object and slowly lifted it from the surface of the flesh. Flannery passed her a glass slide on to which she dropped it. Instinctively, Sam knew that this small translucent particle was important and needed to be handled with care. Flannery sealed the specimen and handed it to the exhibits officer, who bagged it and sealed the bag.

Sam stood up. She asked Flannery. 'Has your team finished?'

He looked around at his team, and they nodded in unison. He said, 'It's all yours, Doctor Ryan.'

She looked down at the body and began her PM commentary. 'Ten thirty-eight a.m., Sunday the 22nd of May 1996, Park Hospital, Cambridge. Post mortem on Mary West, an eighteen-year-old female whose body was discovered earlier this morning in a storage shed at the Leeminghall US Air Force base. Also present are Detective Superintendent Harriet Farmer of the Cambridgeshire Constabulary, Major Robert Hammond, representing the United States Air Force, Mr Colin Flannery, the Crime Scene Manager and Mr John Dale, representing the coroner.

'The body is that of a well-nourished white female. She weights a hundred and twelve pounds and is five feet eight inches tall.' Although the system had officially switched to metric some years before, Sam always found it difficult to convert the measurements in her head and still worked in pounds and ounces, feet and inches. Jean would convert it all to 'official' units when she typed up the reports later.

Starting at the head, Sam moved slowly down the body. 'She has long fair hair. The head is clear of any form of injury.' As she got to the neck she leant down to look more closely. 'There is a blister, about three inches long, on the left anterior of the neck. Looks like a scald or burn of some description.'

Sam didn't know what had caused it but for some reason it bothered her. 'Can I have several photographs of this, please?'

The SOCO photographer stepped forward and photographed the injury from several different angles before resuming his position. Sam then took several quick measurements. It was as if something hot had come into contact with the girl's neck. Judging by the blistering, the injury had clearly been sustained before death, but whether it was connected with her death was another matter.

She moved down to the chest and stomach area. 'There is a long, deep cut running from the centre of the chest to the top of the pubic region. From the look of the uneven edges to the cut, the knife used almost certainly had some sort of serrated edge.' Fred passed her a measure. 'It is twenty-two inches long. The cut has been forced open to reveal the intestines. Some of the stomach contents are hanging loosely and are spread across her abdomen. They have been deliberately pulled and cut from the body. There are no other visible injuries at this moment.'

Fred held out a small stainless-steel bowl containing several long swabs. Sam picked one up and began the examination of all the orifices. Her work had begun in earnest.

By the time the PM was finished, Sam just wanted to kick off her gown, go home and stand under a hot shower. She wanted the water to wash over her naked body, cleansing her and rinsing away the evil she'd just had to deal with.

Over the years pathologists became hardened to the baggage that death left behind. Bodies became just objects, with points of interest to be examined and explained. Sam had dealt with death in all its shapes and forms, from the old to the very young. Some died with dignity, while others raged against the darkness.

Sam often thought that the way people died was etched into the lines on their faces: lines of calmness, anger, even surprise. Occasionally, though, like Mary West's, the faces expressed horror, pain and disbelief. Such cases still chilled her and set her nerves jangling, unsettling her natural rhythms and requiring an act of will to banish them from her mind in order to restore her equilibrium.

People were murdered in a variety of different ways and for very different reasons. Often Sam could understand the motive, see the reason, no matter how nauseating that reason might be, but this ... This defied definition, this was pure evil. She wondered how much the papers already knew or were likely to find out. They seemed to have contacts everywhere, even within the hospital and police force. For the girl's family, the inquest would be traumatic enough, but to see the grisly details splashed over the front page of every national and local paper would, she felt, be almost unbearable.

The PM had taken longer than usual. It had been a difficult one, but Sam had been determined not to miss a thing. Something about the death of this young woman both frightened and fascinated her. She slipped out of her gown and threw it into the laundry basket, pulled her boots off and stepped into her shoes.

Leaving Fred and the team of SOCOs to tidy up, she left the mortuary and made her way quickly to her hospital office. Normally any post mortem meetings between herself and the police were held inside the small mortuary office, but today she urgently wanted to get away from its white-tiled and impersonal interior, away from all the horrors of Mary West's hideous death.

CHAPTER THREE

By the time Sam got back to her office, Farmer and Hammond had already arrived and made themselves comfortable. They were sipping tea that Jean had brought them, and looked very relaxed. For them, what had just occurred was, despite its horror, routine. Sam knew she should have felt the same, and that it was fanciful and unprofessional to allow herself to become emotionally involved in a case, but this time she couldn't help herself.

This case seemed to epitomise her reasons for entering the field of pathology in the first place. In her work she was a bit of a voyeur, peering into other people's lives and deaths. She wanted to know not just how a person had died but why, especially if their death was premature. What really inspired and fascinated her, however, was murder. Murder seemed to stretch her mind and challenge her abilities. It took her beyond the clinical certainties of the mortuary and satisfied the darker aspects of her soul which only its demands could fulfil.

She looked across at Farmer. 'Where's Inspector Adams?'

'He couldn't make it. Busy with other enquiries, apparently.'

Despite her efforts at self-control, Sam found herself frowning – she hoped Farmer wouldn't notice. Tom really was being childish, she thought.

Jean finished setting out the refreshments for the visitors and made to leave. 'There's a cup of camomile tea on the table.' She said it soothingly, as if she fully understood Sam's mood.

Sam walked across to her desk and sat down. Picking up her cup, she began sipping from it, grateful for the respite the action gave her.

Farmer put her cup down and looked across expectantly at Sam. 'Well, what can you tell us?'

Hammond said nothing, but his expression showed that he wanted to ask the same question but was too polite, or too politically aware, to make the first move in Farmer's presence.

Sam decided to get it over quickly. 'Death was caused by the obvious injuries to her abdomen and the subsequent massive internal damage. The knife was almost certainly large, over six inches long, possibly had a serrated edge. A hunting knife, perhaps? The abdominal contents were cut and pulled out of the cavity and both kidneys removed, probably using the same knife—'

'Someone who knew what they were doing then?' interrupted Farmer.

'Perhaps, but you'd need only a basic knowledge of anatomy and you could find that in any half-way decent book in the local library. There was no expertise. It was all rather crudely done. We're not talking transplant surgery here.'

Farmer turned to Hammond. 'Your man Strachan's an orderly, isn't he?' Hammond nodded and she continued, 'So he'd have a basic knowledge of anatomy?'

Hammond said, 'I reckon so, yes.'

Farmer nodded contentedly.

Sam went on, 'There's an injury to Mary West's neck about here.' She touched a finger to the side of her neck. 'It looks like a burn of some sort. I was wondering if you could find out whether she'd been involved in an accident of any kind over the last couple of days?'

'Is it relevant?'

'I don't know. It may be. That's why I'm asking. I'd like to know what happened for the record. It's an unusual injury but I haven't been able to link it to the murder at this stage.'

Farmer said, 'I'll see what I can find out.'

Sam nodded her thanks and continued. 'As neither kidney was found at the scene, presumably our killer took them away with him.'

Hammond broke in. 'Why would he do that?'

Sam shrugged, then glanced across at Farmer and said, with more than a hint of irony in her voice, 'I'm a pathologist, not a detective. Superintendent Farmer, that's more your domain, isn't it?'

Hammond turned to Farmer, and she said, 'One of your military policemen, in his statement, said that he thought he saw the figure which ran from the shed carrying a bag of some sort. They were probably in that.'

Hammond shook his head in disbelief.

Farmer returned her attention to Sam. 'Isn't there supposed to be some sort of transplant market? Organs for cash, that sort of thing?'

Sam said disgustedly, 'Well if there is, whoever gets Mary West's kidney's is going to be short-changed. It's not just the putting back that matters, it's also the removal, and this was very much a hack-and-grab procedure.'

Farmer changed tack. 'Was she raped?'

'Yes, I think so. The vaginal walls are certainly bruised and cut, suggesting that sex was forced, not consensual.'

'Any semen specimens?'

'Some.'

'Enough for a match?'

'Not my field, but I should think so.'

Farmer looked pleased. 'Well, that should help settle it.'

Hammond broke in again. 'If you can't find Strachan, how are you going to get a match?'

'He's alone in a foreign land with nowhere to go. We'll find him all right, but even if that takes time I'm sure we can get a cross-match from his parents, if they're still around and give their consent. And if they're not, I'm sure we can find another family member willing to help. It's been done before.'

Hammond doubted if the family would be willing to co-operate once they knew that what they were doing could be crucial evidence against Strachan, but held his peace.

Farmer picked up her cup again, and smiled at him over the rim. 'I'm sure we can count on the co-operation of our American cousins, can't we?'

Sam was rather enjoying the sparring match between Hammond and Farmer, but realised that it mustn't be allowed to get out of hand. She intervened quickly, before things got too edgy. 'Do you know Strachan?'

'No. It's a big base and I tend to know the bad boys and girls. He seems to have kept his nose clean. Most of the people who do know him seem to think he's all right. Certainly not the kind of boy to get involved in something like this.'

Farmer put in, 'Nor was Christie.'

Hammond didn't understand the allusion, so Sam helped him out. 'Famous British murderer.'

Hammond nodded. Sam continued, 'Is he a big man?'

'No, not really. Small and quite wiry, I understand. Why?'

'The bloodstains on her pants and behind hangar two probably mean she was attacked there and then carried or dragged to the shed.'

'She wasn't very big or heavy.'

'Still a dead weight, though, so difficult to move.'

'If that were so,' objected Farmer, 'and in view of the way she was murdered, wouldn't we have found a trail of blood from the hangar to the shed – especially considering how much there was at the scene?'

'That depends on how badly injured she was. I'm positive she was murdered in the shed.'

'Her clothes weren't damaged and there was no heavy bloodstaining, which you'd have expected.'

'They were having sex, remember,' said Sam. 'Could have been naked.'

'It's hardly likely that he'd carry a naked girl to the shed and then come back for her clothes, fold them neatly beside her and then murder her.'

Hammond took the point and, having run out of ideas, changed the subject. 'Superintendent, you will let me know when Strachan's picked up, won't you? He's still an American citizen and will probably need all the help and advice he can get.'

'I'm sure Mary West's parents feel just the same.'

Hammond was unamused by Farmer's sarcasm but tried hard not to show it.

Farmer continued, 'Don't worry, your people have already been in touch with my people, as I believe you say over there.' She turned back to Sam. 'Anything else?'

'Apart from the obvious fact that you're looking for a very dangerous man, the rest will be in my report.'

'Right, well, in that case, I'd better get on.'

Farmer and Hammond stood up, but Sam hadn't quite finished. 'How much are you going to tell the press?' It was, of course, nothing to do with her, nor the kind of question she had any right to ask, but she asked it all the same.

'Just what they need to know to give us some help,' said Farmer. 'If Strachan isn't picked up soon, we might have to issue a public appeal to try and catch him.'

Hammond frowned. 'Won't that jeopardise his chance of a fair trial? Almost like saying he's already been found guilty?'

Farmer looked coldly at him. 'Let's hope we catch him quickly, then. I'd hate to offend your keen sense of fair play. In the meantime, let's pray that a few more bodies don't turn up dotted around the countryside while we're being so terribly reasonable about it all.'

Hammond decided that he had pushed Farmer about as far as he dared and that, in the interests of peace and a continuing working relationship, he had better not say any more.

Farmer turned to Sam. 'Thanks for your time, Doctor Ryan. It's been illuminating, as always.'

Sam smiled coolly at her. 'Any time, Superintendent, you know that.'

Farmer turned back to Hammond. 'Nice to have met you, Major.' She held out her hand and he shook it. 'I'm sure we'll be seeing quite a bit of each other over the next few weeks.'

'I look forward to it, Superintendent.'

As soon as she was out of sight Hammond sat down again. He clearly still had something on his mind.

'Was there something I forgot to tell you?' she asked.

'No, not at all. It all seemed first-class to me. I was wondering whether it would be in order for me to have a copy of the PM report.'

Sam was interested. 'Why?'

'English girl killed on American soil. There's bound to be a lot of questions. I'd just like to have the right answers.'

'I'm not supposed to. Well, not without permission.'

'I realise that and I don't wish to take advantage of our friendship . . .'

'But you're going to.'

Hammond gave a rueful half-smile. 'Yep.'

Sam surprised herself by relenting. It seemed the common-sense thing to do, and going through official channels would take for ever. 'You didn't get it from me, OK?'

'It'll be our secret. Thanks a lot.'

'I'll get Jean to stick one in the post to you tomorrow.'

'Would it be easier and quicker if I sent a car?'

Sam nodded. 'As you like.'

'That question about Strachan . . .'

'About his medical knowledge?'

'Yes. He'd know basic first aid. He could probably start a heart and keep someone breathing, but that's about all.'

'It's his ability to stop them breathing that worries me,' said Sam tartly.

Hammond smiled. 'Look, there's another hangar dance at the base next month and I was just . . .'

'Wondering if I'd like to come? Sounds like bribery to me.'

Hammond was suddenly embarrassed. 'No, look, not at all, it was just we had such a good time . . .'

Sam let him off the hook. 'I'll have to see if Tom's working or not. Let me have the date and I'll let you know.'

'And if he is? Working, I mean.'

A loud rap on the door saved Sam from having to answer. Jean appeared, carrying a pile of files on top of which was Sam's diary. She seemed surprised to see

Hammond still there. 'Oh, sorry, I thought you'd all gone. I'll come back later.'

Sam stopped her. 'No, it's all right, Jean. Major Hammond was just leaving.'

Hammond took the not-so-delicate hint and stood up. 'Well, I must be on my way. See you again *soon*, I expect, Doctor.'

Sam tilted her head slightly to one side. 'Maybe.'

He smiled at her. She was playing games with him but he didn't mind. He pulled his Air Force cap into place and, giving Jean a polite nod, went out. Sam couldn't help thinking that perhaps Tom Adams was right. Perhaps she was a sucker for a pretty face.

It was mid-afternoon before Hammond got back to Leeminghall. The front entrance of the base was surrounded by an army of press and television reporters, who crowded round his car, peering eagerly in to see if he was important or worth talking to. Fortunately, no one recognised him, or had any idea who he was, so he managed to get through without too many problems. He parked outside the officers' mess, and walked quickly across the baseball field to his office.

The moment he opened his office door he felt an unusual atmosphere and realised that all was not right. The feeling was so strong that he didn't even bother taking off his cap. He glanced across at his assistant, Sergeant Jenny Groves, who stood up immediately.

'Well?' he asked.

Groves had worked for him for just over a year and he knew by now that he could smell trouble. She started her explanation nervously with an excuse. 'I tried to get you on your mobile, sir, but it was switched off.'

Hammond had turned his phone off during the PM so as not to disturb the proceedings and had forgotten to switch it back on.

'Get on with it, Jenny.'

She breathed in deeply and looked straight ahead, concerned at his reaction and unwilling to look him in the eye. 'Colonel Cully's compliments, sir, and he would like to see you in his office.'

'When?'

'As soon as you got back, sir. Er, now.'

Hammond sighed, smiled reassuringly at her and went out. It took him only five minutes to cross the base to Cully's office. As he passed the numerous airmen and airwomen who swarmed all over the base at this time of the day, and returned the numerous salutes they threw up, he could feel their tension. He could see the trouble in their eyes and on their faces as they searched his face for information about the previous night's events. Like most uniformed service personnel, they were proud of their units and when one of their number went bad they felt that it reflected on the rest of them.

He remembered the rape of the Japanese girl only a few years before. It wasn't just the perpetrator the local people would blame, but the entire US Air Force. It seemed unfair but he could understand it. For the past fifty years the relationship between the locals and the base had been good. They'd brought with them economic prosperity for the surrounding area and even married into the local population. Now that relationship was under threat and everyone was worried. Cully would know that better than most. Until he assumed command of the base, he'd been part of an official inspectorate which travelled through both America and Europe examining Air Force bases and reporting on their efficiency.

When he arrived at Cully's office, he was ushered in immediately by a very nervous lieutenant.

'Major Hammond, sir.' The lieutenant went straight out again, closing the door quickly behind him.

Cully was standing with his back to the door, looking out over the base through one of his office windows. Hammond stood to attention and saluted. Although Cully couldn't see him, he knew he'd be listening for it.

Without moving a muscle, Cully said, 'Seen the papers?' His previous almost hysterical tone had gone, replaced by an intense and forced calm.

Hammond was aware that Cully could explode at any moment so he knew he had to be careful. 'I haven't had the chance yet, sir.'

Without turning Cully pointed to the top of his desk, where several tabloid newspapers lay unopened. They didn't need to be opened: the front pages were enough. Hammond picked a couple up and read the headlines: 'GIRL SLASHED TO DEATH ON AMERICAN BASE', 'AMERICAN RIPPER LOOSE IN CAMBRIDGE'. The rest were in a similar vein. Where the press had got all its information from, and so quickly, he couldn't guess, but however they'd done it it was yet another problem that Cully would expect him to deal with. Farmer was going to be pissed off when she read them, too.

Cully said, 'Apparently the papers back home are full of it too. Bad news travels fast. I've imposed a curfew on the camp. No one enters or leaves without a good reason.'

Hammond knew nothing of this order and it helped explain the troubled looks he'd received. 'It'll blow over,' he said. 'It always does.'

'Maybe,' said Cully tensely, 'but not before it's destroyed me, Bob.'

Hammond realised it was hopeless. Cully was on the brink and nothing he could say right now was going to bring him back.

'Do you know how long it takes, Bob?'

'Sir?'

'To get where I am, do you know how long it takes?'

'No, sir.'

'Twenty years. Twenty years. Twenty years of working hard, making all the right moves, knowing who to talk to and when . . .'

'Being an arsehole.' Although Hammond had no more than whispered it under his breath, Cully had turned and was facing him when he said it.

'Sorry, Major, what did you say?'

'It must have been very hard, sir.'

'It was very hard. Christ, I even married the general's daughter.'

Hammond didn't like the way Cully referred to his wife as if she were some appendage to his career, another pip on his shoulder, another stripe on his arm. Hammond knew Sarah Cully, a bright, attractive woman who charmed everyone she met. For the life of him he couldn't work out why she'd ended up with Cully. But they'd been married for over fifteen years so he must have something going for him. Besides, after one divorce and two failed long-term relationships what did *he* know?

'Do you know what I wanted, Bob? Do you know what I wanted?' Cully had an annoying way of repeating everything he said, as if he wanted to emphasise his importance or beat you to death with the point he was trying to make.

'No, sir.' But he was sure Cully was going to tell him.

'I wanted to go all the way, right to the top, to the White House. Christ, I'll be lucky if I get to the shit-house now.' Cully pointed angrily at his desk. 'See that desk, Bob, see it? That's where my arse stops the buck. Even the fucking ambassador's coming tomorrow, all because some stupid little bitch got herself murdered on my base.' He was starting to become hysterical again.

Hammond thought, I'll pass on your sympathies to her family, Colonel, sir. It was the first he'd heard about the ambassador, though, and he knew he'd have to move fast. As head of the base's police, he was in charge of all security matters, including the visits of all dignitaries.

'What time's the ambassador due, sir.'

'God knows. Talk to my aide – he's got all the details.' Cully had calmed down again. He sat down in his wide-backed chair and looked up pathetically at Hammond. If Hammond hadn't despised him so much he might have felt sorry for him, but he didn't.

'We've got to get this mess cleared up, Bob, for both our sakes.'

Hammond recognised the veiled threat, but it didn't bother him. He'd been threatened by experts, and Cully was far from that. He'd sort things out – he always did – but not for Cully. Cully had already asked too much of him, compromised him, made him question his own best judgement.

'I'm sure it will be, sir.'

'Have they picked up Strachan yet?'

'No, sir, not yet, but the British police are sure they'll get him. He's got nowhere to go, and they're very good.'

'You think so? Christ, they don't even carry guns.'

There was a knock at the door and Cully's aide entered. 'Sir, the two men from the embassy are here to see you. You said to let you know as soon as they arrived.'

Cully eyed Hammond, who remained impassive. 'Show them in.'

His aide disappeared back into the main office, making way for two blue-suited diplomats.

Thanks to Trevor Stuart taking her afternoon list, and with Jean's help, Sam managed to get through the mountain of paperwork remarkably quickly and arrive home early for once. She'd already made plans for these unexpected hours off and intended to catch up with the gardening. As she turned into her drive, the security light flickered on. She didn't need it just then, but was glad it was working again. Must have been a loose wire, she thought. She really would have to get a handyman. Picking up her bag from the driver's seat, she made her way across the gravel path to the back of the cottage. The conservatory door was already open and a muddy pair of wellington boots stood outside it.

As soon as she went into the kitchen she recognised the aroma of Irish stew. She hadn't smelt it for years. The table was already laid, with a bunch of wild flowers and a large bottle of red wine breathing at its centre.

Liam came in. 'Nice to have you home,' he said, and kissed her on the cheek.

'This is all very nice. How much is it going to cost me?'

'A few nights' bed and board, that's all. I think you're getting a bargain.'

Sam smiled at him and, while he checked on the contents of the pot, pulled off her coat and went through to the hallway to hang it up.

She called to him, 'How did you know what time I'd be home?'

'I rang your office, talked to . . . Jean, is it? What a lovely woman. She told me. Seemed very interested to know who I was and where I was staying.'

Sam winced. She went back into the kitchen. 'Yes, well, she would. What did you tell her?'

'The truth, of course.'

'Which, your truth or the real truth?'

'That we were lovers determined to take up where we left off many years ago.'

Sam glared at him.

'On the other hand, I may have just said I was here for a job interview and would be returning to Ireland in a few days.'

Sam smiled. She could never be sure with Liam. Whichever it was, it would be around the hospital by now, spread by the old 'now don't mention this to anyone else' school of gossip.

'Well, that's me branded a scarlet woman.'

'Good, then you've got nothing to lose. Sleep with me.' He smiled mischievously at her.

She ignored the invitation. 'Did anybody ring?' She was hoping that Tom had made contact.

'Not that I know of, but I was outside most of the time.'

The answerphone wasn't bleeping, so she knew no one had rung while he was outside.

Sam walked across to the stove, where the Irish stew was bubbling happily away. She put her nose carefully down to it. 'Smells great. How long will it be?'

'Why, have you got an appointment?'

'No, but I was hoping to get a bit done in the garden.'

Liam looked out of the window. 'Oh, you mean that bit of preparing that needed doing at the back there?' Sam followed his gaze. 'I've done it. Did it this morning. Put those plants in as well. Take it you wanted them put where you dropped them?'

Sam was taken aback and wasn't sure whether to be grateful or annoyed. She was glad it was done, but had rather been looking forward to doing it herself. When she was gardening was the only time she really relaxed and could think things through. She decided it would be ungracious to be annoyed: he was only trying to please. Besides, she could think of a hundred and one other things that needed doing.

'Thanks. I don't know what to say.'

'Thanks will cover it,' said Liam cheerfully. 'I fixed the security light too, so you can thank me twice.'

She was taken aback again. It seemed to be her evening for that. 'Really? You fixed it?'

'I'm a wizard with the screwdriver and the spoon. Now, if you sit down I'll dish up.'

Sam went over to the table and began to pour the wine, while Liam ladled out helpings of stew.

An hour later they were both slightly drunk, comfortably bloated and relaxing in the sitting-room, finishing off the last of the brandy. Sam was stroking Shaw, her cat. Liam was stroking Sam's bare feet, which rested on his lap.

'Have your mother and sister forgiven me yet?' he asked.

'Wyn has, and Mummy's too ill to remember or care.'

'I heard she wasn't well. No better, then?'

'Worse. There is no getting better.'

'I'm sorry.'

'You aren't. Not really.' Sam changed the subject before the conversation became too intense. 'So, tell me, why are you here? It's not just to see me, I know.'

'Well, almost, but not quite.'

91

'So?'

Liam had always had a way of dancing around even the simplest of questions. 'I'm applying for an arts fellowship at St Michael's.'

'To do what?' she demanded, amazed.

He seemed surprised at her question. 'Poetry, of course.'

She knew that he'd always read and written poetry, but had no idea it had become so serious. 'I'm impressed. I thought it was just a hobby.'

'So it was, but when I stopped the travelling I decided I had to make a living if I wasn't to starve, so I made up my mind to teach poetry.'

'Do you think you'll get it?'

'The fellowship? Shouldn't think so for a minute, which of course means I can at least go in there with no nerves and tell them exactly what I think.'

'That should go down well.'

'If they want me, they can have me, Irish warts an' all.'

Sam smiled at his self-confidence. There was something innocent about it.

'I seem to remember,' he said, 'you always had your nose stuck in one of Shaw's books.'

She quoted, 'Woman's dearest delight is to wound man's self-conceit.'

Liam grinned and matched her quotation: 'The only way for a woman to provide for herself decently is for her to be good to some man who can afford to be good to her.'

'I'd be wasting my time with you, then.'

'Right now, maybe, but one day you'll be begging to have me back.'

She laughed but refused to take his bait.

He tried again. 'I do not know whether women ever love. I rather doubt it. They pity men.'

Sam was more relaxed than she had been for months. She was enjoying Liam's company, as she had before when they were teenagers together and were both experiencing the first taste of love. Like Romeo and Juliet they played out their roles to the bitter end. It all seemed very silly now but then, oh, the intensity. Nothing had ever been quite like it since.

'What about something you've written,' she suggested.

'Are you sure? You might not like it, and me pride couldn't take that.'

'I'll like it, I promise.'

He wasn't convinced. 'Try a bit of Yeats first.

I will arise and go now, and go to Innisfree,
And a small cabin build there, of clay and wattles
   made.
Nine bean-rows will I have there, a hive for the
   honey-bee,
And live alone in the bee-loud glade.'

Sam had forgotten over the years how beautiful Liam's voice was. Like a cascade of warm water, it washed over and through her. She leant deeper into the settee and put her head back on the cushions listening, absorbing every word.

'And I shall have some peace there, for peace comes
    dropping slow,
Dropping from the veils of the morning to where
    the cricket sings;
There midnight's all a glimmer, and noon a purple
    glow,
And evening full of the linnet's wings.

I will arise and go now, for always night and day
I hear lake water lapping with low sounds by
    the shore;
While I stand on the roadway, or on the pavements
    grey,
I hear it in the deep heart's core.'

Sam didn't hear the last few lines for sleep had finally
taken her tired mind and given it rest.

Shaw's wet nose, rubbing against Sam's face, woke
her. She opened her eyes with a start, and at first couldn't
think where she was. It took her a few moments to pull
herself together. She was still lying on the settee where
she'd drifted off to sleep the evening before, the only
difference being the blanket which was now wrapped
awkwardly round her. She lay there for a moment
gathering her thoughts and stroking Shaw, who had
settled on her stomach and was enjoying the attention.

She didn't feel too bright and breezy this morning.
Never again, she resolved, well, not till next time, at
least. She'd never been very good with drink. Those
three glasses of brandy after all the wine with dinner
were quite a bit more than she usally drank. She glanced

across at the old school clock that hung beside the fireplace. Nine-thirty. It didn't register for a moment then, realising her list began at ten, she threw back the blanket and, sending Shaw sprawling across the room, raced up the stairs two at a time to shower.

In fact, having missed the early-morning rush hour, Sam arrived at the hospital earlier than she'd expected, though not early enough to begin her list on time. Liam had still been asleep when she left. His interview wasn't until two so she'd set her alarm for eleven and put it by the bed. Liam had always been a nocturnal animal, sleeping all day and playing all night. It was nice to know, she thought, that some things didn't change. She'd just had time to write him a good-luck note, which she left on the kitchen table. Despite his bravado she guessed that he would be nervous, so the note seemed appropriate:

That secret of Heroism, never to let your life be shaped by fear of its end.
  Lots of love, Sam. XX.

Fred had everything ready and was prepping the first body, which lay on one of the mortuary's half-dozen stainless-steel tables.

Pulling on her surgical gown and boots, she asked, 'Any difficult ones, Fred?'

'Not really. Two heart attacks, one suspected stroke, and a couple of malignancies.'

'Couldn't make me a quick coffee, could you? My mouth feels like the inside of a chauffeur's glove.'

'The sins of the flesh shall find you out. Repent, O sinner, repent your evil ways less the Lord . . .' His voice disappeared with him into his room.

These PMs shouldn't take long, Sam reckoned. She wasn't looking to break any records but she did want to finish early so that she could get herself up to the science lab and see Marcia. With a bit of luck they should know what the object was she'd found on Mary West's body. As she cut into the first body she thought how lucky she was. There had been a week of particularly hot weather and that normally had them dropping like flies. Too hot or too cold, and down they went. For some reason this year the rush hadn't started yet, but she had every confidence that it would. She started dictating her notes.

Hammond had sent a car to the hospital early to pick up Sam's report, in the hope that she'd completed it. He needn't have worried. When the driver arrived, it was all bound and ready for him to collect.

Hammond read it quickly, making notes about the more 'interesting' aspects. He picked up the green form that had been lying in his in-tray for the past two days, and began to fill it out.

Any murders committed on American soil, wherever that soil might be, had to be reported to the FBI academy at Quantico for inclusion in their Violent Criminal Apprehension Program, normally referred to as Vi-Cap. The idea was to have an international network of information regarding certain types of crime, such as murder, rape and terrorism, in which the culprit might be American or in which the victims were American citizens or the incident occurred on American territory. The activities of the German international serial killer Jack Unterweger, who murdered several women in a number of different countries, including the USA, had demonstrated the importance of this type of international approach to serious crime.

It took him just over an hour to fill out the form and write a covering report outlining the aspects of the case which he felt were important but which were not covered on the form. When he'd finished, he walked across to the office fax machine and fed it through. Technology never stopped amazing him. Although he'd used the fax hundreds of times, he was still impressed by the fact that a report he'd written could within minutes be in the hands of an FBI agent, being acted upon.

Once the report had cleared through, he checked his watch. The ambassador would be arriving in a few hours, and he'd better be ready. Slipping his cap on to his head and pulling the jacket of his dress uniform smartly down, he decided to have one last look round the base, just in case.

Elizabeth Kirkland had worked at the FBI academy at Quantico for almost two years. Her husband had been posted there as an instructor, and when the job as receptionist had come up she'd taken it. With both boys now at college, she'd found she had a lot of time on her hands and the job helped fill it. The extra money was welcome, too. It was used as their 'Holiday Kitty' and had paid for a whole month in Europe the year before. The job's only drawback was the shifts. They were normally only early mornings and late afternoons and she could cope with that – at least it gave her part of the day to catch up with things. Occasionally, however, a night shift was called for and during those weeks she seemed to be permanently tired. The night shift consisted mainly of taking phone messages and filing faxes ready for delivery the following morning. It was quite easy and, with no one else to talk to, quite boring. Still, she told herself, it was an opportunity to catch up with her reading.

The fax machine by her side hummed into life. She turned away from her book and watched as the paper spilled out of the machine. As soon as it stopped she pulled the sheets away and glanced at the cover-sheet. It was addressed to the Behavioral Science Unit, Quantico, and was from the US Air Force base at Leeminghall, Cambridge, England.

She remembered Cambridge from their trip. They'd had a choice, Cambridge or Oxford, but remembering the film *Chariots of Fire* had decided to see where it had all happened. They hadn't regretted it. It was a wonderful place, so ancient, one of the great seats of learning.

She began to read the fax now, more interested in it than in her book. Strictly speaking, you weren't supposed to, so of course everybody did. This one concerned the gruesome death of an English girl on the base. She remembered reading something about it in the papers the day before, but the article hadn't included any of these details. Protecting the family, she supposed.

She wondered what the English would think of the case. An American boy killing an English girl was bad enough, but the way he'd done it ... Christ, he must have gone mad. Shaking her head in disbelief, she dropped the fax into the appropriate file and returned to her book.

Early that afternoon, Sam parked in front of the forensic science lab at Scrivingdon. As she stepped out of the car, the sound of the surrounding bird life was almost deafening. Scrivingdon was situated in the centre of an ancient woodland, having been built before the environmental lobby became so vocal. The block was surrounded by a high metal fence topped by razor-wire. There was only one way in or out and that was guarded by two uniformed security guards. Scrivingdon was not only the centre for forensic analysts for the eastern district, but also covered all firearm enquiries outside London. As a result it had a massive arsenal of weapons secreted in a giant safe under the laboratories.

Sam made her way to the reception area and signed in. After passing through various and increasingly ingenious hi-tech security checks, she finally arrived at Marcia Evans's lab.

Marcia was expecting her. 'Morning, Sam. Coffee's ready.' She handed her a piping hot mug and the two of them went over to one of the worktops, where Marcia was working on the clothes and the debris taken from Mary West's body.

'Anything interesting?' asked Sam.

Marcia picked up a clipboard and scanned it. 'A few

99

interesting bits. The print Knight found on the body was smudged, and if he's going to get any joy from the ones he found in the shed he's got a lot of elimination prints to take. Most of the footprints came from the Air Force policemen who found the body, although there are several others that have yet to be explained – probably voyeurs'. And the blood they found at the back of the hanger: it didn't belong to Mary West.'

Sam stared at her in surprise.

'Wrong type. Interestingly, it's the same type as Strachan's.'

'How do you know that?'

'Called the base. They were very helpful. Trouble is it's a very common type: O. The West girl was AB.'

Sam put in, 'So there's still a chance it's not his?'

Marcia nodded. 'A slim chance. We'll have to wait for the DNA results to be sure.'

Sam didn't understand what Strachan's blood was doing there. Perhaps Mary West had injured him during the struggle. If so, he must have been quite badly hurt – there was too much blood for it to have been a minor injury – and if he was that badly hurt she didn't think he'd be running anywhere except perhaps to the nearest hospital. But if that's what he'd done, why was it that, as Farmer had pointed out, there was no trail of blood? Why was it in just the one area? Why? why? why? Sam's head began to spin with the questions, but Marcia interrupted her thoughts.

'Come and look at this.'

Beckoning Sam to the other side of the lab, Marcia

checked the focus of a microscope on one of the worktops, then gestured to Sam to take a look. Sam set her eye firmly to the eyepiece. Beneath the powerful magnification a different world seemed to open up before her. She saw a strange object, triangular except that the lines between its corners were convex, not straight. The surface reminded her of lemon peel, lined, coarse and bobbled. At each of the triangle's points the object seemed to open up like the edge of some gigantic volcano, only in miniature. Sam knew by its appearance and structure that what she was looking at was pollen; she'd seen enough of it in her time, both professionally and through her enthusiasm for gardening. She also knew that pollen fibres had solved more that one case over the years and hoped this might be the break they were looking for.

She looked up. 'It's pollen, but what kind I've no idea.'

Marcia took her place at the microscope. 'That's a shame because neither have we. It's not a home-grown one, that's for sure.'

'People do keep non-indigenous plants in greenhouses, conservatories, garden centres, even in their sitting-rooms.'

'It's possible. More likely to have been anemophilous, though. Wind-blown.'

'Had she been abroad recently?'

Marcia shook her head. 'Don't know yet. The police are checking.'

'What about Strachan?'

'They're looking into that too. They're sending his

clothes across this afternoon to see what we can find on them. If we can match the pollen, and with the DNA evidence, it should be an open-and-shut case.'

'Who's helping to identify the pollen?'

'We're going to send some samples down to Kew to see what they can come up with.'

'What about trying Professor Osbourne?'

'I thought he'd retired.'

'He has, but you know what they say—'

'Old botanists never die,' Marcia cut in. 'They just germinate.'

'He still does the odd lecture. You'll find him across at the Botanical Gardens most days.'

'Most of the samples have already gone to Kew, but if you think it will help I've still got a couple you could show him.'

Marcia walked across to a small boxed set of glass slides and began to search through them while Sam nosed round the lab.

'Anything on the butterfly wing I found on the body?' asked Sam.

Marcia found what she was looking for. She pulled one of the slides from the box and handed it to Sam. 'I'd like it back when you've finished.'

Sam nodded and put the slide carefully into her handbag. She looked back up at Marcia and asked again, 'The butterfly wing, anything on it?'

Marcia returned to the box of slides and removed another. 'I heard you the first time. Give me a chance.'

She set the slide under the microscope and, putting her eye to the eyepiece again, adjusted the focus. 'Another mystery. But it's not a butterfly wing, that much I can tell you.'

She stood back and Sam took her place at the microscope. What she saw dazzled her for a moment. It was like looking at a fraction of a summer sky. The colour was a clear, bright turquoise, which radiated outwards despite the object's translucence. Oval in shape and criss-crossed with fine white veins like a spider's web, it took on all the exotic characteristics of a bird of paradise or some other wondrous creature from a far-off place. It was a strikingly beautiful object viewed under the microscope, and seemed an odd thing to find on the cold greyness of a dead body.

'And it you don't know what this is either?'

Marcia shook her head. 'Not having a good week, am I? But no, I haven't got a clue about this one either.'

'So what are you doing about it?'

'I've had it photographed and sent copies all over the place in the hope someone will recognise it, but how long that's going to take is anyone's guess.'

'Let's just hope our killer holds back until we find out what it is.'

'I did mange to identify something, though.'

Marcia picked up a photograph from one of the tables and showed it to Sam. It was a large blow-up of several thin strands of fibre.

'Where are they from?'

Marcia picked up a large plastic bag and held it up. 'Found them in here. It had been thrown in a corner of the shed. Three of the strands, we're pretty sure, came from an American Air Force uniform—'

'He wore the bag over his uniform while he committed the murders?' interrupted Sam. She was sceptical, but Marcia had a plausible answer.

'No. I think he probably put his clothes inside before he committed the murder in order to keep the blood off them. We discovered a couple of other strands as well, but we're not quite sure yet where they came from. But we'll get there.'

Sam examined the plastic bag, turning her mind back to the time she'd spent inside the shed. 'Was there some kind of bloodstained sheet of paper amongst the exhibits?'

Marcia scanned down the list of exhibits. 'Only the scrap you found attached to that nail.'

Sam nodded and put her eye back to the microscope for one last look at the unusual object she had found on Mary West's body. The absence of the paper surprised her and she realised that there were still many mysteries yet to solve.

Detective Sergeant Chalky White approached Detective Inspector Adams and pushed another pile of completed worksheets towards him. Adams looked at them and sighed, 'Is this it?'

White smiled. 'For now.'

'How far have we got?'

'Door-to-door and the searches are finished in the immediate area. Just beginning to expand the search now.'

'Any leads?'

White shook his head. 'Not a peep, sir. He's lying low somewhere.'

'What about the press, the TV and radio?'

'Locals and nationals have covered it, sir. It's a bit soon for *Crime Watch*.'

Adams grumbled, 'Probably shacked up with some tart who can see no wrong in him. Thanks, Chalky.'

He wasn't sure whether he was more annoyed at the lack of progress in catching Strachan or at Sam's attitude towards him. He wasn't sure what he had to do, or what he was doing wrong. Sexually they were certainly compatible – well, she'd never complained, quite the opposite in fact. When they went out or were alone together, they enjoyed each other's company. Perhaps she only ever thought in the short term; a user. Her career seemed to be everything. Didn't she realise that there was more to life than bodies and mortuaries? What about love, family, memories? All those things seemed to have passed her by. She'd be sorry one day, he thought, when she was old and retired and people had stopped caring.

He forced his attention back to the statements. He wasn't sure what he would spot, that others hadn't. They had computers to 'spot' things these days, to pick up inconsistencies, cross-reference alibis and weed out the rubbish. He wondered sometimes whether there'd still be a place for the old foot-sloggers in a few years' time or whether they'd be replaced by robocop machines, armoured and infallible.

He didn't really understand why an incident room had been established when they had their suspect and the weight of evidence against him was massive. Still, he supposed the law had to be seen to be done. He looked through yet more statements describing Strachan. Most said he was 'a great guy', who would never get involved in something like this, though one or two inevitably said the writer had always suspected there was something weird about him.

Adams had met a few killers in his time and Strachan certainly didn't seem to fit any of the stereotypes. He wasn't a loner. In fact, he seemed to be one of the most popular airmen on the base. He had plenty of girlfriends and was considered by his senior officers to be well-balanced and to have a good future ahead of him.

The two most interesting statements, however, came from former girlfriends. They didn't actually accuse Strachan of rape, but they made it clear he wasn't a man to take no for an answer and could be quite forceful and aggressive. Still, Adams considered there was a big difference between that and murder, especially a murder committed with the savagery of the West killing. It was a special kind of mind that had been responsible for that one.

His concentration was suddenly broken by a hand being laid gently on his shoulder. He turned his head slightly and found himself looking up at Detective Constable Liz Fenwick. She had been with the squad for just over six months and was a welcome addition.

In her late twenties, she was tall and slender with a thick crop of long, mousy hair. She also had legs that seemed to go on for ever and she wasn't frightened to show them off, despite Farmer's continual cutting remarks about her 'tarty' dress sense. She'd got guts, too, and soon sorted out the loud-mouths within the unit – without making enemies, which was a difficult balance to strike. Liz was also a good copper. Not only had she been involved in a number of major arrests, but she'd felt a few collars of her own.

She smiled down at him. 'All work and no play, sir? Fancy a liquid lunch?'

As she spoke, Adams noticed the other DCs sit up and take notice. Liz was popular, but surrounded by continual rumours and gossip, most of which was rubbish and more to do with their own sexual fantasies and inadequacies than anything to do with Liz. He stared them down, but he could almost see their ears twitching as they strained to hear what was said.

He wasn't in the mood for their lads' games, so he decided to make it easy for them and raised his voice. 'Yes, I'd like to have lunch with you, Liz. The Eagle, is it?'

She was taken aback for a moment, then, sensing the growing tension in the room, joined in the game. 'No, I know somewhere far more out of the way and intimate, sir.'

They smiled at each other briefly, then Adams slipped on his jacket and they made their way out of the incident room.

It had gone eleven by the time Edward Doyle arrived at work. Solheim and the rest of the team were already there, as fresh and crisp as mannequins in some downtown shop window. Solheim looked up and gave him a brief wave. He looked for a hint of sarcasm in the gesture, but there was none.

He'd been at Sally's Bar the night before, and had stayed late, chewing the fat and putting the world to rights. He'd promised himself an early night but then he did every night, and still ended up going to bed late. His bed, like his apartment – and for that matter his life – was cold and empty and there seemed little point in wallowing in his own solitude. At least the bar kept him in the company of other people. Once, he used to work late regularly, absorbed in his work and determined to make his mark. When it didn't happen he lost interest and did what he had to do and no more. Others, like the sharp attractive Solheims of this world, were moving in and above him. People he'd trained were already senior to him. He was dead wood, on his last case and going nowhere.

Pulling the messages, letters and faxes from his basket, he began to go through them slowly. He had discovered that by leaning back in his chair and changing the focus of his eyes, he could give the impression of reading his messages while in reality watching Solheim.

She was as smart as ever, dressed in some designer black skirt and white blouse. The blouse was sheer, and against the light of the window you could see through it comfortably. The white lace bra beneath did little to hide the fullness of her ample breasts or the dark shades of her nipples. Her skirt had ridden up, as it always did when she sat down, exposing her thighs and the tops of her tights. He wasn't sure whether she did it on purpose or whether it was just a result of the current fashion for shorter skirts.

Still, he wasn't complaining. He'd been having fantasies about her almost from the moment they'd met. At first these just involved having sex with her, in his car, in the men's restroom, at his flat. But recently they'd become more violent and involved kidnap and rape. He wasn't sure whether they were a product of his own insecurities, the average man's average fantasy, or whether he'd been doing the job too long and was slowly becoming what he'd spent his life fighting.

Solheim suddenly looked across at him and Doyle realised he'd been reading the short message in front of him for far too long. He put it down and picked up the next message, staring back at Solheim long enough to display his lack of interest in her expectant look.

The message consisted of a faxed Vi-Cap form, from an Air Force major called Hammond at some place called Leeminghall in England. Vi-Cap had been established at Quantico in 1985 and had quickly grown into a truly international information system. Its primary objective was to reveal early signs of serial-killing patterns, with a view to acting quickly against perpetrators and bringing about early arrests. Doyle considered ruefully the time before the system was running. What a difference it would have made in the David Berowitz murders in New York and the Wayne Williams killings in Atlanta, when it took the police over a year even to admit that they had a serial killer on their hands.

Doyle read the fax wearily, waiting for the right moment to re-focus his eyes on Solheim's body. When he reached the section that outlined the killer's modus operandi, he suddenly sat bolt upright. He read the section again, then again.

Solheim noticed the change in him and called across, 'Everything all right?'

He waved the fax at her. 'Come here and read this.'

As he handed it to her, he picked up the receiver and punched in a number. 'Hi, Edward Doyle here at the BSU. I need two tickets to England on the earliest possible flight . . . Nothing before tomorrow . . . That'll have to be fine then . . . Thank you.'

He put the phone down and looked up at Solheim, who was staring at the fax.

'What do you think?' he asked.

She put the fax down. 'I think our man's gone global.'

CHAPTER FOUR

It was late morning when Adams woke. He blinked his eyes hard and rubbed the sleep from their corners as he tried to focus on his surroundings and collect his thoughts. Staring up at the ceiling, he tried to recall the previous evening's events. The ceiling was unfamiliar, Artexed, not painted plaster as it should have been.

It wasn't until her slender, soft body stirred beside him that he remembered where he was and, more importantly, who he was with. He turned his head slowly towards her, trying to control the hangover which had allowed a demon with a hammer to enter his head and pound mercilessly upon his skull each time he moved. He'd woken up next to a few strangers in his life, and, as he was sometimes too drunk to remember what they looked like until the following morning, had experienced some nasty shocks.

Liz Fenwick was lying on her back, one arm by her side while the other rested above her head. The thin duvet which covered them both had fallen away from the top half of her body exposing her small, ripe breasts and firm stomach. Her hair lay in a disorganised mess across her face and pillow.

Adams pulled himself up on to one elbow and looked down at her. She was certainly beautiful, and young, very young. She was all that men of his age were supposed to dream of, especially when they reached their dangerous middle years. He fell back on to his pillow wondering what he had got himself into. He, like the majority of the squad, had fancied Liz since she'd arrived, but, unlike the majority of the squad, hidden his interest behind a mask of aloof politeness. He began to wonder if anyone would find out what had happened. If they did, it was sure to get back to Farmer and then one of them would almost certainly be off the squad, and he wasn't entirely sure which one it would be.

His hangover was worsening and an ominous churning of his stomach forced him to make a move. Carefully, he sat up and swung his legs out of bed. The movement disturbed Liz, who reached across the bed, her hand searching for the warmth of his body before tucking itself back under her pillow when she realised he'd gone. Adams had never intended this to happen; somehow it simply had. A combination of drink, desire and, he had to admit, revenge.

Since he'd been with Sam he'd never strayed, even when opportunities had presented themselves, which had been often. They were a couple and his future, he thought, was with her. They came from different worlds but he had always consoled himself that opposites frequently did attract and stranger relationships had worked and worked well. Recently, though, he'd begun to wonder about the foundation of their relationship, how deep the feelings were and whether there was any real commitment on Sam's part. That was why he had begun to press her for a deeper commitment, testing the strength of her feelings for him. Eventually, he knew, this would bring about a crisis and resolve the uncertainty.

Recalling the previous evening's events, he felt a bit ashamed. He'd hurt Liz when they made love. It was as if all his anger and frustration had been concentrated in his penis and he was using it as a weapon to beat out his own anger. Even when they had been locked passionately together in bed, he knew Liz's cries hadn't just been the results of her sexual peaks. He'd hurt her and, which alarmed him more, had enjoyed doing so.

When the storm had passed she hadn't been angry with him: he'd have felt better if she had been. She'd rolled across his body, run her hands gently down his chest, and asked, 'What was all that about, then?' There was no malice in her voice, just understanding. 'Things not going so well with Doctor Ryan?'

Her insight disturbed him and he didn't know what to say, so he lay silent while she kissed and stroked him. Finally, he said, 'I'm really sorry.'

'What for, the rough stuff?'

'If I hurt you.'

'I enjoyed it.'

He wasn't sure if she'd meant it or whether she'd just wanted him to feel better. Whatever the reason, it helped. He realised from that moment that Liz would probably make him happier than Sam ever could. He and Sam were too different, too far apart, and searching for different things. Liz came from the same side of the street and her needs and desires would be the same as his. He began to examine his motivation in fighting to keep Sam. Surely life was too short.

He dragged himself into the bathroom, turned on the shower and adjusted the temperature to suit. Stepping in, he let the water run over his face and body. He'd never before been so unsure about his life and what he wanted from it. He had to pull himself together. Was he just being pathetic or were his worries justified and reasonable? Only time would tell, he thought.

The shower door opened, and Liz joined him under the warm cascade. Pulling herself up on his shoulders she kissed his wet lips, her tongue darting around the outside of his mouth while she wrapped one of her legs round his waist.

'Let's try again, shall we? This time with feeling.'

He pushed her gently against the tiled wall and wrapped her other leg around his waist. This time he wasn't angry. This time he just wanted her.

Tuesday was, in essence, Sam's day off. It was the only day she got free from working in the mortuary and, barring court appearances and call-outs, she generally used it to catch up with her reports and letters and to study any forthcoming court cases.

Appearing in court was an important part of any pathologist's job and presenting the evidence correctly was vital. She had seen many cases fail because of the way inexperienced or incompetent scientific witnesses presented their findings in court. Scientists and pathologist who had spent hours studying a case, so that the evidence was both accurate and strong, could see it destroyed by adversarial cross-examination from a clever barrister, seeking to put doubt into the mind of an untrained lay jury. The trick for the pathologist was to make the evidence easy enough to understand but at the same time not so easy that it lost its scientific validity.

The introduction of pathologists for hire was a worrying trend as well. Most pathologists brought in by the defence gave a fair account of what they had discovered, perhaps with a slightly different interpretation. However, more recently there seemed to be a trend towards pathologists giving the evidence the defence thought appropriate, with a view to destroying the expert opinion given by the Home Office pathologist. It was a worrying situation, and one that could ultimately bring into doubt pathologists' forensic evidence.

Someone banged hard on Sam's office door. At first, given the urgency and loudness of the knock, she felt sure it must be a policeman. She shouted, 'Come in.'

The smiling face of Trevor Stuart appeared from behind the door. 'Morning, Sam.'

Sam wondered what this politeness meant. Trevor usually just barged in as if he was expecting to find her 'up to something' in her office. 'Not like you to knock,' she said drily.

He looked rapidly round the room, and seemed to relax when he found no one there but Sam. 'Ah, told off by the Demon Queen last time. Still recovering. She wasn't outside at her desk so I thought she might be in here waiting to pounce.'

'The Demon Queen' was his nickname for Jean.

They had crossed swords on many occasions, and despite Trevor's seniority he always seemed to come off second best.

Sam laughed. 'You're quite safe, she's taken the day off.'

Relief showed in his face and his confidence returned as he strode across the room and helped himself to a chair. Sam liked Trevor, in spite of herself and in spite of Jean's misgivings about his morals. At forty-something, he was tall and slim with handsome, chiselled features and a crop of jet-black hair (she was never quite sure whether the colour was natural or out of a bottle). Although he was 'happily' married for the second time, he was a bit of a ladies' man, and with no little success. How his wife ever put up with this Sam wasn't sure but they'd stayed together and seemed happy enough.

Sam waited until he'd sat down and made himself comfortable before she spoke. 'Thanks for taking my list the other day.'

'Pleasure. You've taken mine often enough. How are you getting on with the murder at the air-base? Quite a nasty one, I understand.'

'I've done my bit. It's up to the police now.'

Trevor gave an incredulous laugh and peered closely at her.

She frowned. 'What are you doing?'

'Looking for the spots that have changed.'

She had to acknowledge that he had a point. 'Well, I suppose there are a few interesting aspects to the case.'

'Which of course you feel honour bound to follow up.'

'Something like that.'

'Well, what have you got?'

She eyed him for a minute, wondering if it was a good idea to tell anyone just how much the case interested her and that her interest extended well outside the mortuary. Finally, she pulled open an office drawer and lifted out a large, official-looking file. From it she took four large photographs, which she handed to Trevor.

'What do you make of those, oh master?'

He looked at them. Each showed in close-up the weal Sam had found on Mary West's neck.

Trevor paused over the last photograph. 'I like the "master" bit. Any chance of keeping that part going?'

'Depends what you tell me.'

Encouraged, he pulled a small eyeglass from his pocket and began to study the mark intently. Despite his rakish reputation, Trevor Stuart was a first-class pathologist with a quick eye and even quicker brain. If that hadn't been the case, she doubted that the hospital would have tolerated him for so long.

'It's a burn mark, probably made by some sort of electric shock.'

'I'm impressed, but how did you come to that conclusion?'

'Remember the boy who was killed pulling his kite off the high-powered cables last month?'

Sam nodded.

'There were similar marks all over him.'

'But this is only one mark.'

'Agreed, but it's still a burn mark. Are you sure it's

connected to the murder? Might have happened before – accident at home or something like that.'

'Farmer's supposed to be checking that for me now. But it's in such an odd place.'

'That's what happens with accidents, or they wouldn't be accidents. Let me know the outcome. Might be a short paper in it, you never know.'

Sam picked up the photographs from the desk and looked through them one more time, puzzled by what he'd said.

Trevor stood up. 'Look, going back to the bit about lists, I was wondering if you'd take mine.'

Sam eased back in her chair. 'Why?'

'I'm organising a talk by some civil rights workers at the Union Society. People Against Torture, or something like that.'

'You, getting involved in politics? You'll be voting Labour next.'

'Already do, dear girl, already do. So I can take it that's a yes?'

'Yes.'

'Brilliant. I suppose I should jump across the desk and kiss you, but with my luck that would be the cue for the Demon Queen to enter and lobotomise me, holiday or no holiday.'

'If she didn't, I would.'

Trevor put on a pained expression and went out. Sam returned to the photographs.

It was the end of a long and anxious day for Hammond. The ambassador, the Honourable Henry Strong, had stayed longer than expected. Hammond wasn't normally impressed by politicians, believing that when they weren't kissing babies they were stealing their sweets. Strong, however, seemed to have a streak of genuine compassion. When they'd first arrived at the Wests' home, high tension and hostility had emanated from her parents and other family members who had gathered to have their say about Mary's murder.

Strong had made everyone – his own advisers, even General Brown, who had stayed on for a few days before returning to the States to retire – wait outside while he went into the house alone. The meeting was meant to last thirty minutes, but two and a half hours later he was still inside. At one point an aide became so concerned about the ambassador's welfare that he plucked up the courage to defy his boss's direct order and marched up to the front door and knocked, only to be sent away with a flea in his ear by Strong himself. Half an hour after that the ambassador finally emerged. He hugged each member of the family in turn and gave Mrs West a kiss. As he went back to his car, Hammond could have sworn he saw tears in the old man's eyes.

After Strong had finished at the West house he insisted on seeing and speaking with the two men who'd found Mary's body. Hammond had hoped that Strachan would be in custody by now, but despite the British police's best efforts he was still at large and keeping the story on the front pages of most of the papers. With luck, the ambassador's visit might at least take the edge off some of the more stinging editorials, especially those in the tabloids.

The ambassador next made a general inspection of the base, even stopping off to hit a few balls with some astonished airmen who were enjoying a day out with their families, finally sharing their picnic and drinking several bottles of root beer. Both Brown and Cully, who had arranged a sumptuous affair for him at the officers' mess, pretended to join in, but it was clear that their hearts weren't in it and they were less interested in the game than in getting their photographs in the American papers.

After the game the ambassador insisted they went off to collect another crate of root beer and soft drinks from the camp's base exchange to replace the ones they had drunk. If you didn't know Cully you might not have noticed the blind rage behind the false smile, but Hammond did and felt a certain amused contentment about it.

At last, and to everyone's relief, the ambassador left, in company with General Brown and Colonel Cully, to attend a dinner and choral concert at King's College. As the motorcade sped out of the gates, Hammond pushed his hat to the back of his head and sighed noisily. With Cully gone he could perhaps enjoy a quiet evening in front of the TV watching the New York Yankees thrash the Miami Dolphins on their way to the Superbowl. But then, he thought that every year and was normally disappointed. He turned to leave and came face to face with his assistant, Jenny Groves.

She threw up a smart salute and handed him a note. 'This came for you this morning, sir. First chance I've had to give it to you, with the ambassador being here and everything. Sorry.'

The note was from the FBI's Behavioral Science Unit at Quantico. It said, 'Agents Edward Doyle and Catherine Solheim due to arrive at Gatwick airport at 20.50 local time. Can transport be arranged to Leeminghall air-base? Wish to interview Major Hammond and any other person connected with the Mary West murder.'

Hammond looked at his watch. It was just before four. He decided to collect them himself and find out what was going on before Cully stuck his nose in.

He said to Jenny, 'Arrange two rooms at the officers' mess for our guests.'

'How long will they be staying, sir?'

'No idea, better make it open-ended. If there's a problem, try and get them into a hotel in Cambridge.'

She nodded, saluted smartly and, turning, made her way across the base towards the officers' mess. Hammond looked down at the note. Something was wrong, something was very wrong. FBI agents with this sort of pedigree would not normally turn out for a local murder, no matter how horrible. Something serious was happening and he wanted to know what. He headed quickly towards his car.

Sam had arranged to meet Professor Clive Osbourne in his rooms at the back of the city's Botanical Gardens. Although Osbourne had been a Fellow at the university for as long as anyone could remember, he had always chosen to live out, having fallen out with his old college over some long-forgotten academic point in the mid-1930s. Despite this, he was still as much a part of the college as the ancient stonework of which it was built. Dressed in flamboyant clothes that were as old in style as they were in years, he could quite easily, by the unwary and uninitiated, be mistaken for one of the many elegant-looking tramps who strolled the narrow streets, dressed in ancient garb and looking for all the world like eccentric dons from a different age making some philosophical protest against the coming of the modern regimes.

According to the ancient and honourable guild of college porters, the source of all the university's knowledge and gossip, Osbourne was well into his seventies, but he was still an imposing figure. Tall and straight, his thin ungainly body was perched precariously on top of slightly bowed legs. His face, too, was long and thin, which emphasised his long, pointed nose, on which he balanced a set of gold-rimmed half-moon spectacles, which he had a habit of peering over whenever he spoke. He was a stickler for procedure and wouldn't interfere with his day's routine for anyone, including Sam whom he had known and liked – as much as he could like anyone – for years.

Sam had decided to avoid the car-polluted streets and make her way to his rooms through the gardens. They were beautiful and relaxing, a place you could wander through for hours enjoying all the pleasures the wide diversity of plants and flowers had to offer. Although the route was longer, it was far more pleasant and interesting. As she strolled through the lines of plants and shrubs, she'd stop occasionally to smell one or make a note of another's name. She hadn't visited the gardens for some time and was regretting it. If anything could confirm her sense of smell was functioning properly, and hadn't yet been destroyed by the numerous chemical aromas in the mortuary, this aromatic place could.

Eventually, tearing herself away from the gardens, she crossed the road to Osbourne's rooms. He was waiting for her and answered the door before she had time to knock. Sam looked up at him, surprised.

'I was watching you from the window,' he explained. 'Thought you might come through the gardens. I take it you still have your six senses?' He tapped the side of his nose.

'Yes, thank you.'

'Good. I think I've found what you were after. Follow me.'

He marched ahead of her along the corridor, his lanky legs taking huge strides. As he disappeared into his study, Sam closed the front door and began to follow expectantly.

Osbourne pulled a book from the top of his old, creaking bookcase and dropped it with a thud on a large oak table at the centre of the room. He opened it and began to flick through the pages with his thumb.

'Found it in here. Quite an old book but still the best one ever written on the subject.'

Sam joined him by the table. 'Who wrote it?'

He blinked down at her, as if bemused by the question. 'I did, of course.'

He was utterly serious and Sam had to fight the desire to grin broadly.

He ignored her while he searched for the page he wanted. 'Here it is. Interesting, very interesting.'

She tried to move things along a little by adding a note of urgency to her voice. 'Something unusual?'

It didn't work. She hadn't really thought it would and realised she would just have to be patient and wait for him to get to the point in his own sweet time.

'Not unusual. Rare, but not unusual.' He considered his words and seemed to change his mind. 'But then again perhaps it is, perhaps it is – for Cambridge, that is. Let me demonstrate.'

He pointed to a double-page spread. 'I think this is what you were looking for.'

On one side of the page was a large map of North America, with the names of some of the southern states shown in bold type. On the opposite page were drawings and photographs of a plant with long oval leaves and small round fruit pods. By the side of these were several detailed photographs of the plant's pollen grains: they were identical to those Sam had seen earlier beneath the lens of Marcia's microscope. The plant was identified as '*Myrica indora*, odourless bayberry from the wax-myrtle family.'

Sam looked intently at the pictures.

'Sorry the photographs are in black and white,' said Osbourne. 'If they were in colour you'd notice that the plant has yellow, granular, dotted leaves with an indehiscent, waxy coating.'

Even in an informal place like his own study, he sounded as if he were lecturing to a group of first-year students. Sam gritted her teeth and tried not to be irritated.

'It flowers between February and July, depending on which state it's growing in.'

'I take it it isn't indigenous to this country, then?'

'You take it right. Southern states of North America, mostly. You'll find it in shrub-tree bogs, non-alluvial acid swamps, pine flatwoods, hillside bogs, cypress ponds, that sort of place.'

He ran his finger across the map. 'The best chance of finding it is across these states, Georgia, Alabama, southern Mississippi, some close to the Florida pan-handle.'

'And you're sure it's not grown over here?'

'Pretty sure. It would be difficult, very difficult, need an expert, and I'm sure by now either I or Janet Blackwood at Kew would have been contacted if someone had decided to try and propagate it.'

Sam asked, 'You think the murderer's American, then?'

'Almost certainly. It would make sense, you see. Has he been home recently?'

She shook her head. She began to feel a bit awkward, as if she'd turned up with only half the information and was wasting his time. She hated to appear unprofessional. 'Don't know,' she said. 'Sorry. I'll see what I can find out.'

He looked at her long and hard over his spectacles. 'Remember, every contact leaves a trace.'

Sam knew Edmond Locard's phrase well and it annoyed her to hear Osbourne using it as if she were some rank amateur in the presence of a great forensic master. Locard had worked under the great Alexandre Lacassagne at Lyon University until 1910, when he'd left to establish the influential police laboratory. There he expanded Lacassagne's methods and began to apply forensic medicine to cover more and more fields of science. As a result, he was associated with many celebrated criminal cases. It was after reading Locard's book *Trait de criminalistique* – even though it was now out of date – and absorbing his passion for forensic science that Sam had decided to become a forensic pathologist.

She looked at the map again. 'It's such a wide area. Is there nothing within the pollen that could perhaps narrow it down a little?'

'Not really. It is what it is. Unless you have something else? Then perhaps we could cross-match and narrow it down a little.' He paused for a moment, his mind clearly working fast. 'Or perhaps even a lot.'

Sam dipped into her bag and produced one of the photographs of the turquoise object she had discovered on Mary West's body. 'I found this on the body. I've never seen anything like it before. What do you think?'

Osbourne scanned it intently, lifting the glasses from his nose to get a better view. 'Looks like you've found a set of fairy's wings. Where's the rest of her?'

Sam smiled. 'I wish I knew.'

He studied it for a few more moments. 'Sorry, can't help. The only thing I can say for certain is that it's not part of any plant. Probably animal, but then possibly not.'

He shrugged and handed the picture back to Sam. She

took one last look at it before slipping back into her bag, wondering who on earth to try next.

The traffic around Gatwick airport was as bad as ever and Hammond found himself transferring from queue to queue. He'd set out in what he thought was plenty of time and expected to reach the airport comfortably, perhaps even to have time for a coffee. He had, however, forgotten to allow for the normal clutter of roadworks, accidents, and British lorries which, for some unknown reason, shed their loads all over the road with alarming frequency.

It was early evening and he was over an hour late by the time he finally stowed his car in one of the large impersonal multi-storey car parks and hurried through to the international arrivals lounge. As he hadn't a clue what the two FBI agents looked like, and didn't want to stand like some company chauffeur holding out in front of him a card bearing the appropriate names, he'd remained in uniform and hoped that there weren't too many other US Air Force majors doing the same thing.

He glanced up at the information board, praying that the plane had been delayed. They often were, so he still had a chance of saving some face. But he was out of luck: the plane hadn't arrived on time, it had been a little early – which was unusual, to say the least. It clearly wasn't going to be his day. The passengers must have disembarked some time before, and either his guests were waiting for him somewhere inside the airport or else they'd already left and were on their way to Cambridge. He surveyed the people sitting and standing around the lounge, hoping two of them might wave or walk up to him, or show some sign that they were the people he'd come to collect. No such luck. He felt himself grinding his teeth, which had become a habit when he was anxious or upset. Given recent events, he was surprised he had any teeth left at all.

He was considering putting out a message on the PA system before making his way back to base when he was tapped firmly on his left shoulder.

'Major Hammond?'

He knew immediately it was them. The voice was slow and laid-back with a giveaway Southern twang. Hammond turned and found himself facing a giant of a man, at least six feet three and almost as broad, it seemed, as he was tall.

The man held out a huge hand. 'Edward Doyle, FBI. I take it you're Major Hammond?'

Hammond shook the proffered hand. Even for a large man, Doyle's handshake was surprisingly firm, as if he were already trying to make a point and establish who was in charge.

Hammond pulled his hand free. 'Yes. The uniform gives me away every time, doesn't it?' He tried a smile, but it wasn't returned. He knew Doyle was playing games – after all he was a psychologist and mind-games were his business. As there was little Hammond could do about it, he decided to let it pass and play his own games later.

'Sorry I'm late. Traffic around here is as bad as in LA.'

Doyle's expression remained bland. He was clearly

uninterested in excuses. He introduced his partner. 'This is Agent Catherine Solheim. She'll be working with us on the case.' He said it as if he resented her presence.

Hammond hadn't noticed her at first, because she had been shielded by Doyle's large frame but as soon as she emerged from behind her partner's bulk he was impressed. It was a long flight from the States and most people emerged from the plane tired and more than a little jaded. Not this girl, though. She looked as cool and unruffled as if she had just stepped out of her apartment on her way to work. She was beautiful, too, tall and sophisticated, with everything from her clothes to her make-up and hair in the right place and used to maximum effect.

Hammond reached over and shook her hand. 'Major Hammond. Pleased to make your acquaintance.'

She smiled warmly at him. 'Good to meet you too. You look great in your uniform.'

Her confidence and fresh outwardness were in such contrast to Doyle's glumness that Hammond was taken by surprise. He looked at her more closely. Her face was fresh and unlined and her eyes the bluest he could ever remember seeing. Lost in them, he held on to her hand for a moment or two longer than was normal and she was forced to pull it away firmly but gently. Hammond realised what he had done and stood back, embarrassed.

He recovered quickly. 'I've arranged for you both to have rooms at the officers' mess on the base while you're staying with us. It's pretty good accommodation, better than most hotels. I think you'll be comfortable there. Any luggage?'

Doyle said, 'It's on the trolley. I'll get it. Where's your car?'

'Just across the road. It's only a few minutes.'

Doyle nodded and moved off to collect the luggage. Hammond noticed as he went that he did not so much walk as lumber.

Solheim said apologetically, 'He's a man of few words.'

'But lots of attitude.'

Solheim raised her eyebrows expressively. They both turned and watched as Doyle made his way slowly back towards them.

As Sam pulled into her drive she saw Tom's car parked by the front door, although there was no sign of him. She was glad that Liam was in Cambridge and hadn't been there to meet Tom when he arrived. She didn't think his sense of humour would have suited Tom's mood and it would probably have led to more confrontation, which she didn't need.

She parked beside Tom's Vauxhall and stepped out of her car. As she passed the Vauxhall she instinctively felt the bonnet. It was still warm: he hadn't been here long. Time to kiss and make up, she thought. Picking up Shaw, who was as usual hanging around the front door waiting to be fed, she went inside. Tom had had a key to the cottage for some time, so she assumed he'd be lounging around inside somewhere and she called out, 'Tom! Tom, are you here? Where are you?'

There was no reply. She went down the hallway to the kitchen, and looked out of the window. She saw him sitting on a log at the bottom of the garden, gazing over the fields towards the woods beyond.

She walked down the slate path towards him. 'Long time no see. Where have you been?' She sat next to him on the log and kissed him on the cheek.

He smiled down at her. 'Remember this log? It was the first place I ever kissed you.'

'Almost kissed me. As I remember it, you got a call from Farmer and left me frustrated, cold and alone in this big dark garden.'

'You're right, I remember. I knew you were big enough to look after yourself.'

'The first time you kissed me was when you came to collect me from the hospital.'

Tom nodded. 'Great memory, great kisser.'

Sam followed his gaze across the fields towards the woods. She'd known him long enough to realise he was only making small-talk and that there was something far more serious on his mind. She decided to force the issue. 'So, what's been the problem?'

He shrugged as if he were reluctant to talk about it.

She tried a guess. 'Liam's only a friend, you know, a person from my past who returns to haunt me every now and then. There's nothing between us.'

He picked up a small stone and threw it hard at the wooden fence which marked the boundary of Sam's garden. 'It's not him, not directly anyway, although he probably made me wake up to the reality of the situation.'

Sam stared at him but he wouldn't meet her eyes. She felt a surge of unease, almost panic. She knew exactly what he meant, but wasn't ready to admit it just yet.

'And what reality is that?' she asked.

He turned to face her. 'Us. We're not going anywhere and we aren't likely to, are we?'

'I'm happy the way it is.'

His voice became firmer. 'Well, I'm not. I want more. You might think that's selfish of me, but it's the way I feel.'

Sam found herself asking questions to which she already knew the answers. 'What do you mean by "more"?'

He turned his entire body to face her as if he wanted to emphasise what he was about to say. 'You, all the time, not just at weekends and the odd evening. I want to come home to you, or be there when you come home. To wake up with you, go to sleep with you, eat with you . . .'

She smiled at him. 'The number of call-outs I'm getting, are you sure that's a good idea?'

There was no answering smile. 'It's not a joke.'

'Sorry, I didn't mean to be flippant.'

'Yes you did. It's the way you cope with relationships. Keep everything cool, at arm's length. Nothing too serious, no involvement, nothing that might jeopardise your precious career and lifestyle.'

There was a difficult silence. For once, Sam didn't know what to say. She didn't want to lose him. She was happy with him, comfortable. Eventually, she heard herself say, as if her subconscious was controlling her mouth, 'You can move in if you want, stay all the time, live with me.'

It was a concession she'd never thought she'd make and she was aware that even now she was not offering full commitment. Tom looked at her deeply for a moment and Sam thought he was about to kiss her before whisking her off her feet, making love to her and then starting to discuss plans for the future. She was wrong.

'It's gone beyond that. I shouldn't have to have this argument with you. You should want me without this.'

'I do want you or I wouldn't—'

'Then marry me, have my children and become part of a family, our family. Because that's what I want.'

Sam swallowed hard. Her mind was racing, trying to sort out what to do, what to say, to find a way out, a compromise.

Tom looked at her as if he were reading her mind. 'It's all right. You can stop panicking.'

His instant assessment of her dilemma took her by surprise. 'I'm not panicking.'

'Yes you are. I can see it in your eyes. Even if you said yes now you'd regret it later, and then things might be very hard. We're different people. You need different things and we've taken it as far as we can.'

'I'm sorry. It's my fault.'

'It's no one's fault. It's just the people we are.'

Sam was struggling to understand. 'Is there someone else?'

'No,' he lied, 'there's no one else. It's been very good. I won't forget.'

Sam nodded, too upset to speak. Half of her wanted to throw her arms round his neck and agree to everything he wanted, while the other half knew that what he'd said was right. If she'd taken the time to give any serious thought to their relationship recently, as Tom had, she would have come to the same conclusion as he had, but she'd been busy and her work, as always, had been interesting and absorbing. Their relationship had become just comfortable enough to need no further analysis and so she had given it none. The mild irritations which had developed between them recently had not intruded on her emotions sufficiently to disturb her concentration at work and so she had ignored the warning signs.

Tom stood up and looked down at her. 'See you around.'

Sam only nodded, determined to keep her emotions in check. She refused to look up or watch him walk away and instead kept her eyes firmly fixed on the distant woods through the haze of her tears.

As Tom rounded the corner of the cottage, he passed Liam walking in the other direction. He nodded but didn't speak, almost afraid of what he might say.

Liam tried to start up a conversation. 'Is Sam in the . . . ?'

Tom ignored him, walked on, jumped into his car and drove away. Liam went round into the garden. Looking down the path he saw Sam at the bottom of the garden, her head in her hands. He made his way towards her and, sitting down on the log, put his arm round her shoulders. He thought he could make a pretty good guess at what had happened.

'Now has the big bogey man upset you, then?'

Sam shook her head. 'It's me that's upset the big bogey

man. What the hell am I doing with my life, Liam? Just what the hell am I doing?'

She buried her face in his shoulder, and he held her more tightly. He'd been there a few times himself, and he knew there was nothing he could say or do. She'd just have to let it all out and come to terms with it in her own sweet time.

Frank Strachan watched as his wife rolled up the sleeve of her summer dress, exposing the white fleshy arm hidden beneath. She still seemed to be in a state of shock, unable to take in the magnitude of the information the two FBI agents had just outlined to them about their son.

They'd been married for almost thirty years and he'd never seen his wife like this before. Her face was white, bland and listless, as if she was going along with life without actually living it. He knew he would have to be strong for both of them. The FBI agent at his side firmly but gently pushed the needle into his arm and the syringe began to slowly fill with blood. It didn't hurt and it was over in a moment. The puncture mark was wiped with antiseptic and a plaster stuck securely over the top. When it was finished, Frank stood up and joined his wife on the settee, holding her hand and stroking it gently.

The day had started well enough. He'd finally got around to repairing the fence at the front of the house while Helen had baked cakes and savouries in the kitchen in readiness for Sunday, when the family were going to spend the day with them. They had three sons and two daughters. Ray, the youngest, was the only one away, but he was due back the following year, and he kept in regular touch with them by phone and letter. The rest of the family lived close by and visited regularly, bringing with them the all-important grandchildren. Frank and Helen's most earnest hope was that they were going to be around long enough to see them grow, and maybe even become great-grandparents.

The two FBI men arrived about lunchtime, together with Ed Chiasson, the local sheriff, a good man and one the family had known for years. He introduced them and they all went into the house together. When the FBI men told them about the murder and their son's suspected role in it, Helen had gone a deathly white and almost fainted.

It was good that Chiasson was there. He might be the sheriff but he was also a friendly and familiar face, and they needed one of those right now. He'd had already sent word to Abraham, their eldest son, who lived about fifteen miles away. Abraham was already on his way over.

It wasn't just the awfulness of what the FBI agents told them that was upsetting them, but a strong feeling of guilt. They were the ones who had brought Ray up, therefore they must be the ones who'd made the mistakes that had led to his becoming a killer. Frank could hardly bring himself to think about it. It had taken a while for the full horror of what they were being told to sink in, but when it did it was more than they could bear.

Helen had gone quiet, unconscious with her eyes wide open. Frank found himself asking the same questions over and over as his mind simply rejected what he had just been told. Even though they said Ray was only a suspect in the killing, it was clear from their tone that he was the only suspect, and they were as certain as they could be that he had in fact committed the murder.

Of all the people in the world, Ray seemed like the last person to commit a murder but then, Frank thought, if murderers were easy to spot there wouldn't be any. He was trying hard to keep his emotions under control and be rational, but it wasn't easy. Ray had been a little wild in his youth but nothing serious. He'd never been in trouble with the police and, as far as they knew, never taken drugs. Most of his energy had been taken up with sports and he'd played both football and baseball for his college, something the entire family had been proud of. It was Sheriff Chiasson who had helped Ray get into the Air Force. They'd had a party and Ed had come along with his wife. It had been a great day.

Now this. They'd searched his room, even taken away some old school exercise books. Then they'd asked dozens of questions, not just about the murder in England but about others that had taken place in the States. Did he keep a diary? What was his home life like? Did he have a normal sex life? They wanted the names and addresses of old girlfriends. They even had the nerve to ask them whether Ray had been abused or beaten when he was a child. What kind of people did they think they were?

Ed was reassuring, but Frank was becoming increasingly angry. Finally, the FBI agents had asked for blood samples so they could do some kind of DNA match, prove once and for all that Ray was guilty. Frank wasn't going to do it at first, not help to see his son locked up. But Ed pointed out that it might prove Ray's innocence as well, and persuaded them to co-operate. Frank began to think about the murdered girl and – to his own surprise and shock – to feel angry that she had been foolish and careless enough to be murdered and cause this trouble for his son.

CHAPTER FIVE

Sam was trying hard to be well-organised. She'd made a long list of essentials and ticked them off as she packed them away ready for the picnic.

A small plastic cold-box sat on the kitchen table full to the brim of tall, colourful cans of a foreign lager to which Liam seemed addicted. Sam's green and gold Harrods bag was propped up against the box, twisted and misshapen by the flasks of tea and coffee which had been shoved haphazardly into it. Lastly, there was the ageing, elegant wicker picnic basket, in which the plates and cutlery nestled neatly between the sandwiches, salads and strawberries. Sam ticked off the final few items and then she was ready.

She didn't feel like going, but the picnic had been planned for weeks and she'd be letting the whole family down if she didn't turn up. What she really wanted to do was immerse herself in the solitude and serenity of the garden. She needed a little time to get over her unhappiness, to clarify her thoughts and feelings so that she could move ahead with the changes in her life.

The real difficulty was that Tom was right: the relationship might have dragged on for a little while but not for long. She was confused and annoyed with herself for allowing foolish and unfounded emotions to take over like this. She was selfish where her work was concerned. It was important to her and, yes, everything else did come second.

Was that so wrong? Couldn't she have both a career and a social life? Men had managed it for years, so why couldn't a woman? Or were the sexes different, with different needs and desires? It wasn't that she didn't like the idea of a committed relationship, but she wasn't ready for one yet. There was still so much to achieve. Relationships required time and energy. They could become all-consuming and emotionally demanding and she hadn't the time just now. Then again, perhaps she just hadn't met the right person yet.

These and a hundred other thoughts raced through her mind over and over again as she analysed herself, Tom and society's structure in general. She'd tried a little retail therapy and bought herself a new summer dress but it hadn't helped. She'd instinctively wanted to show it to Tom, and then was angry with herself for wanting that. Even her precious garden was being neglected and she'd never let that happen before. It was pathetic. She was behaving like a teenage girl who'd just lost her first boyfriend and had decided to make high drama of the whole thing.

She really must pull herself together. She knew these feelings would pass, but at the moment . . . Even seeing the log at the top of the garden upset her, so she'd decided to have it removed and replaced by a wooden bench. The men were coming today to take it away, and she was glad she wouldn't be around to watch it go.

Her thoughts were interrupted by Liam rushing into the kitchen, his hair still wet from the shower. 'Come on, are you ready? We're really late.'

And that, thought Sam, from a man who had been out of bed for all of thirty minutes. Liam grabbed the cold-box and picnic basket and made his way to the front door, almost treading on Shaw, and cursing all cats on his way out. Sam collected the rest of the bags and followed.

It was a beautiful day, at least. The air was fresh and fragrant with summer, the sun was out and there wasn't a cloud in the sky. As she threw the bags into the back of the car and opened the sunroof, her spirits began to lift and she thought she might enjoy herself after all.

After parking the car in New Court, Sam and Liam made their way back through the court and out towards Trinity Bridge. Just before they reached the bridge they turned left down a small dirt track which ran parallel to the Cam and took them to the wooden punting sheds at the back of Trinity College.

The rest of the family were already there. Ricky was sitting on the bank with his latest girlfriend, Tracy, throwing stones far out into the water and watching as the ripples spread outwards in ever-expanding circles. Sam's mother was sitting on a worn-out plastic chair, sheltering from the sun in the shade of a willow tree whose branches hung low around her and dipped into the water. She'd been dressed in her best summer clothes and was wearing a wide-brimmed straw hat. The last time Sam had seen her wearing it was at Wyn's wedding and that was some years ago. It had looked awful then and it had not improved with age. Still, it served a useful function.

Wyn, on the other hand, looked wonderful. Sam hadn't seen her for a few weeks. She knew her sister was on a diet but the weight loss was dramatic and she'd also had her hair lightened and cut short. She too was wearing what looked like a new summer dress, long and flimsy, with a pattern of flowers in pastel shades.

Sam kissed her warmly. 'You look fantastic.'

She stood back admiringly while Wyn did a twirl. 'Size twelve – and I didn't have to force it on.'

Sam smiled at her pleasure. 'You'll be borrowing my clothes again soon.'

'Borrowing your clothes? It was you who used to borrow mine as I remember it. Where's Tom? I thought he was coming?'

For a moment Sam was at a loss, searching for some not-too-lame excuse, reluctant to tell Wyn what had happened. She wasn't ready for explanations, not just yet anyway.

She was saved by Liam, who suddenly appeared around the corner of the boating shed and said admiringly, 'A size twelve? You look more like a ten to me.'

Wyn said, 'There's a voice from the past, twice as big and still full of—'

He silenced her with a quick kiss. 'Charm?'

She smiled, said, 'Something like that,' and kissed him back.

As she did Liam picked her up and whirled her round.

'It's good to see you again, Wyn Ryan. Good God, look, I can still get me arms round you.'

Wyn roared with laughter. It was the first time Sam had heard her sister laugh like that for many years. She was glad they were getting on; she hadn't been sure they would. Liam had been her first boyfriend, but he was a Protestant while she was a Catholic, so almost inevitably the relationship was hated by both families. Liam's mother had actually gone to the expense of hiring a private detective to follow them. When he tracked them down he'd rung Liam's parents and they had turned up, together with Sam's mother.

Liam was sent off to boarding-school in England. Keeping in touch had been very difficult, though with the help of friends they'd smuggled through an occasional card or letter. It wasn't until many years later, when Sam was at university and they were both free of their families' influence, that they managed to see each other again.

They'd considered re-kindling the relationship, but the passion had gone. Time had changed them both and they'd become different people, the innocence of youth replaced by the reality of their emerging adulthood. They both realised it could never be the same again and because they were now 'mature adults' they decided to stay friends.

Consequently, Sam didn't hear from him again for more than a year, after which he popped up from time to time, to catch up with her life and tell her about his, before disappearing again until the next time, whenever that happened to be. Occasionally, she would receive a postcard from a far-off place and wonder what he was doing, but it was only ever a passing thought, in the middle of doing something more urgent.

Sam walked across to the willow and, taking her mother's hand, crouched down beside her. She sat passively, looking along the bank at a swarm of gnats dancing across the water, their movement capturing her attention for a moment.

'Hello, Mummy. You're looking very summery.'

For a moment her mother's head turned and she looked down at her younger daughter, but there was no spark of recognition in her eyes, just emptiness.

Ricky came over and sat down beside Sam. 'She gets worse every day,' he said quietly. 'Mum won't be able to cope on her own for much longer. She doesn't even know who I am any more.'

Sam wasn't sure if her nephew's comments were a criticism of her or just concern for his grandmother.

'I remember when she was all right,' he went on. 'She used to moan a lot, but she could be good fun too. I used to play noughts and crosses, and squares with her.'

Sam remembered playing the same games with her mother when she'd been young.

'Now you can't even wipe your own bum, can you, Grandma?' He kissed the old lady's hand and laid it back on her lap.

Sam said sadly, 'It's a tragedy that this should happen, isn't it, Ricky?'

He looked up at his grandmother's vacant face. 'If ever I get like this, Aunty Sam, you will kill me, won't you?

Put me out of my misery, stick something nasty into my arm. You'll know what.'

She could see he was serious and would resent a flippant reply. This was an unusual mood for Ricky, but Sam's Catholic upbringing had instilled a strong belief in the sanctity of life and she couldn't agree to his request, however hypothetical.

'Where there's life there's hope,' she hedged. 'All life is precious.'

'That's bollocks and you know it. Grandma died when she got this. Now it's just a case of when we bury her.'

The punt was pushed firmly against the bank and held in place while the family clambered aboard with all their baggage and sorted out who'd sit where. Ricky sat at the front with Tracy, their feet dangling in the green water. Wyn and her mother sat at the back facing the direction of travel, while Sam shared the front seat with a collection of cold-boxes, picnic baskets and plastic bags. Liam stood at the back of the punt, pole in hand, and pushed them away.

Sam was surprised at Liam's dexterity with the pole. Avoiding the inexperienced punters who zig-zagged up and down the river, shouting excitedly in a dozen different languages, he kept the boat running not only straight but smoothly. They glided past King's College with its imposing chapel, making their way towards Queens' rather rickety wooden bridge. Sam leant back against the cushions and enjoyed the warm sun dancing over her face and the tips of her fingers skimming over

the cool water. She closed her eyes and began to drift
gently away.

Hammond had arrived early at the officers' mess with
the intention of having breakfast with his two guests.
He'd always found it easier to discover what he wanted
over a meal. The informality of the occasion meant that
people often let their guard down and so were easier to
manipulate.

Normally he avoided working weekends, leaving that
dubious honour to the more junior ranks. However,
Cully, who was becoming increasingly paranoid, had
ordered him to stick to the two agents 'like shit to a
blanket'. Cully was terrified of being found wanting and
it was clearly Hammond's job to steer the two detectives
in the right direction and ward off any criticism of both
Cully and the base.

He wasn't too worried about Solheim. She was eager
enough but fresh and inexperienced and was still walking
in her partner's shadow. Doyle, though, was a very
different matter. Although he didn't like the man much,
he'd quickly formed the impression that he was not only
dogged but astute and perceptive. Life wasn't going to
be easy for the next few days, and possibly weeks.

Hammond made his way to Solheim's room. As he
passed the mess he'd spotted Doyle sitting at one of the
tables waiting for them, and so was reassured that he was
occupied. He knocked on Solheim's door and waited. A
few moments later the door was opened wide. Solheim
stood in front of him holding a short white towel in
front of her with one hand, while the other mopped

her dripping hair from her face. There was no attempt at modesty. Hammond's eyes became almost glued to her body. Her long brown legs seemed never to stop, disappearing beneath the thin towel that clung to her slim wet body, the top half of the towel gently lifted by her firm breasts, which pressed enticingly against the towel's edge. Behind her, at the back of the room, was a full-length mirror and in it Hammond could see her naked back and tight, high bottom.

He was speechless. She looked up at him through her hair, which hung in a disorganised mess around her head and clung to her face.

'Major Hammond?' Her words woke him from his trance.

She seemed surprised to see him so he reminded her, 'We were due to have breakfast. But if it's a problem . . . ?'

'I'm sorry, you'll have to forgive me. I'm still a bit jet-lagged, I think. Give me ten minutes and I'll be ready.'

Hammond kept his eyes fixed firmly to her face, careful not to cause her, or for that matter himself, any further embarrassment. 'I'll see you there in a few minutes, then.'

She pushed some strands of hair away from her face and smiled. Even without make-up she was beautiful. 'Fine,' she said. 'See you there.'

Hammond nodded stiffly and, like a little tin soldier, turned and marched down the corridor. He wondered whether she always answered the door like that, or whether it had been done for his benefit.

Solheim watched him go. She liked Hammond. She'd

always liked older men, had a bit of a father fetish, she thought. He was tall, strong and obviously intelligent, and, for a man in his middle years, in remarkably good shape. She pushed the bedroom door closed before dropping her towel to the floor and looking at herself in the mirror. She looked good and knew it. Her looks had always given her the power to manipulate most men, and some women, for that matter, although she'd always been careful about the way she did it. She often used to lie in bed working out how long it would take her to make it to the top, against how long her looks would last. It was a near-run thing but she was sure she would make it.

Fortunately, she'd also been blessed with a good, incisive mind, so when she reached her final goal she was sure that she could remain there for as long as necessary. Her father had called her 'subtly ambitious'. He was right, and as long as no one knew how far her ambition extended she'd make it.

Breakfast was a complete failure. Doyle remained tight-lipped throughout the meal, while Solheim chatted artlessly about her desire to see Cambridge until Hammond took the hint and offered to show her the sights before she returned to Washington. He wasn't sure whether she was flirting with him or not, but whatever her motives it was an occasion he was looking forward to.

When the meal was at last over, Hammond escorted the two agents across to his office.

'Do the local police know you're here?' he asked.

Doyle squeezed his large frame into one of Hammond's office chairs. 'No, not yet. We were kind of hoping to be in and out quickly. No point in causing too much fuss.'

In reality, the last thing Doyle wanted to do was alert the British authorities to the fact that they might have a major serial killer on their hands. He remembered with some trepidation the Ted Bundy case, and how the team investigating him had had their thunder stolen when he was arrested by other officers. One of the things Bundy had taught the law-forcement agencies was that the more a serial killer murdered the more proficient he became, and that, Doyle reckoned, made his quarry about as dangerous as they come.

He badly wanted to catch this man. Serial killing was not a familiar phenomenon to the British police, who hadn't, to his knowledge anyway, experienced anything like the epidemic that had hit America over the last few decades. However, they weren't fools, and one lucky break was all it would take for him to be left scavenging for the scraps. He wasn't about to let that happen.

Bundy, shortly before his execution in 1989, had told Doyle that, contrary to the opinion of many psychologists, serial killers did not subconsciously want to be caught. They were not prone to leaving subtle clues in the hope that the police would catch them and prevent them from killing again. They enjoyed killing. It was what made them tick. Many found the excitement of notoriety and the thrill of outwitting the police an added bonus. Doyle hoped that when 'his killer' made a mistake, he, Doyle, would be the only person around to capitalise on it. This was his case and his collar, and no one was going to take that away from him.

There was one more thing bothering him. He asked Hammond, 'Have any other ... agencies ... been in touch with you about this case?'

Hammond looked directly into his face without hesitating, something he realised might give him away. 'Like who?'

'Not sure. They're all suits to me. Someone from the embassy, perhaps, asking questions about the case?'

Hammond shook his head. 'No, no one. We were a little surprised that the FBI had any interest in a case so far from home, to be honest.'

If he was lying, Doyle couldn't detect it. He relaxed back into his seat.

Hammond handed Doyle Sam's PM report, Strachan's personnel file and all the statements he'd taken from base personnel, but this didn't seem to satisfy him.

'Are these all the witness statements you've got?'

'The local police have got the rest.'

'Have we got copies?

Hammond shook his head again.

'Why not?'

Hammond didn't like Doyle's tone but answered civilly, 'It's a local police matter. We have no jurisdiction.'

'Any chance of seeing them?'

'I could ask, but they'd want to know why.'

'What about the two security guys who found the body?'

'I've got their statements. I can arrange for you to interview them, if you like.'

'Do that, would you?'

Hammond nodded, and without a word of thanks Doyle returned to the files. He flicked through Sam's post mortem report on Mary West first, every now and again stopping to study a section more intently before making notes in a small black notebook and then handing the page to Solheim. She read each page quickly, then dropped it back into the file while she waited for the next. Hammond thought she looked unenthusiastic, as if she felt their involvement was a futile exercise.

Doyle looked up from the file. 'There appear to be no photographs with the PM report.'

'The file was given to me unofficially by Doctor Ryan. She's one of the government pathologists. We have an understanding . . .'

Doyle thought, 'she', eh? He wondered what 'understanding' meant – probably that he was sleeping with her. Doyle didn't like Hammond's type, too smooth by half. In his experience men like that were all show and no substance. The fact that he hadn't managed to get the statements from the British police illustrated that. He didn't like the way he was getting on with Solheim, either. She was here to work, not to go sightseeing with some over-sexed Air Force major. He'd have to have a quiet word with her. If Hammond tried anything in the meantime, there'd be hell to pay.

Doyle continued, 'Any chance of seeing the body?'

'Difficult – without the local police knowing, that is. If you want their co-operation I think you're going to have to tell them why you're here.'

'You say you have an arrangement with this Doctor

Ryan. Couldn't you "arrange" for us to view the body unofficially? I'm sure you'll be able to make it up to her later.'

Doyle's words dripped sarcasm, and Hammond could feel his anger rising. He fought it down.

'I think Doctor Ryan has stuck her neck out far enough,' he said. 'I'd hate to see her get her head cut off. Besides, I don't want my relationship with the local police jeopardised. This isn't the only case on which I've liaised with them and so far they've been fine.'

But Doyle wasn't a man to give up easily. 'Well, see what you can do. I'm sure it will be appreciated in Washington.'

Hammond knew Doyle was bullshitting but was unsure how much political clout he really had.

At last, Doyle closed the file and sat back in his chair. 'I'd like to see the murder scene now if that's not too much trouble.'

Hammond resigned himself. It was going to be another bad day.

The trip along the Backs and then on to Grantchester was one of the pleasantest in England, Sam thought, and Granchester itself was her favourite village in a county well-known for its quaint and beautiful villages. It had been made famous by the poet Rupert Brooke in 'The Old Vicarage, Grantchester'. One of the beautiful young men of his day, he had died, young and celebrated, during the Gallipoli campaign in 1915.

The journey took about an hour. Once everyone was ashore, the rugs were spread out and the food and drink laid on top. Before they had time to finish filling the plates, Ricky and Tracy had grabbed handfuls of sandwiches and crisps and were carrying them down to the river's edge where Ricky had left his fishing rod and line. Sam wasn't sure that it was the fishing season but they seemed happy enough so she decided to leave them to it.

With Ricky and Tracy gone the three of them spent the time reminiscing about their days in Belfast. Between them they remembered a remarkable amount. People, places, embarrassing incidents. Sam laughed until tears rolled down her cheeks. Finally, Wyn got up and decided to give her mother a slow walk along the bank.

As she took the old lady's hand she said to Sam, 'Do you know, I sometimes wonder what's going on in her head. She talks about the old times too, as if she were still there, waiting for Da to come home.'

'Perhaps she is. It's when she was happiest.'

As Wyn walked away with her mother, Sam jumped up and, leaving Liam sipping at a can of lager and looking thoughtfully after Wyn, walked down the shallow grassy slope towards Ricky and Tracy.

'How're you doing?'

Ricky held up a large fish which was still struggling in his warm hands. 'Got a perch. Not a bad size, eh?'

'What are you going to do with it?'

'Put it back when I've finished.'

'Not going to cook it over a camp fire?'

'Not this time, but I expect I'll be doing quite a bit of that soon.'

'Why?'

'I'm . . . we're' – he gestured towards Tracy – 'going away. Didn't Mum tell you?'

'No. Where are you going?'

'Around the world, backpacking. It'll be good.'

Sam thought Ricky still had problems finding her cottage. The idea of him travelling around the globe with only a map and the stars to guide him filled her with alarm, almost with panic.

'You're not old enough, surely?'

'I'm nineteen. You'd left home by then, according to Mum.'

'That was different. I went to university not to some God-forsaken country in the middle of nowhere. What about money?'

'I've been saving. Just about got enough.'

'Just about! You'll need every penny you can get. What if you get into trouble, become ill, lose your way? There are a thousand things that can go wrong.'

'Tracy's dad is in insurance. He's sorting out a policy for us, so we'll be OK.'

Sam wanted to grab him and hug him and tell him he couldn't go, but realised it would be futile. Half of her knew it would do him good while the other half was frightened for him. Ricky dropped the perch back into the river with a splash and Sam saw it swim away and vanish in the green water.

Ricky put his arm around her as if he realised what she was thinking. 'I'll be fine, Aunty Sam, really. I need to do this, just to see if I can. It'll make a man of me. I'll come back a completely different person.'

Sam stroked his hair. 'Just come back.'

With all his faults, he was the closest thing Sam had to a child of her own, and she worried about him almost as if he were.

Hammond escorted his two guests across the air-base to the storage shed where Mary West had been found. It was still taped off and a security guard strolled the perimeter, keeping away any intruders and sightseers. Spotting Hammond, the guard stood to attention and saluted smartly. Hammond returned the salute, before lifting the tape and allowing the small party to duck beneath it. Doyle stood and looked at the shed and then slowly scanned the area around it, taking in the scene and already coming to a few conclusions.

Hammond said, 'It was used as a sort of storage room for sports equipment, stuff that was broken or out of date.'

'Was it kept locked?'

'Should have been, but the lock got broken some time ago and everyone figured, "Who'd want to steal broken sports equipment?" so it was given a pretty low priority.'

Doyle began to lumber towards the shed. Solheim made to follow, but Doyle put a hand up and stopped her. 'Wait here. I expect there's already been far too many people getting their muddy paws all over the scene.'

She obeyed. Experience told her there was no point in arguing. Short of sleeping with Doyle, an idea that disgusted her, she'd done everything she could to make him more co-operative and helpful, but he was a belligerent old bastard whose life revolved around his work. Besides, she knew he saw her more as a rival than as a colleague, and wouldn't hesitate to do the dirty on her if he could. Well, two could play at that game . . .

She watched as he slowly examined the roof and walls, and the ground around the shed. He always brought his own camera with him and took photographs of anything and everything. She wasn't sure what he was photographing or why, and probably never would be. Doyle then examined every aspect of the surrounding area, including the lighting, taking more photographs.

Hammond stepped forward and stood beside her, looking down at her from beneath the peak of his highly polished cap. 'How do you put up with him?'

She smiled. 'It's what they pay me for. And for what he can teach me, which isn't much right now.'

Hammond nodded thoughtfully. 'When would you like your sightseeing trip?'

'It will have to be in the evening when Doyle's finished with me.'

'No problem. When?'

'It will have to be a last-minute thing. Is that OK?'

'Sure. Fancy a spot of dinner after? Be better food than in the mess.'

'Then back to your place for a nightcap and to examine your etchings?'

Hammond was taken aback by her forthrightness. 'I haven't got any etchings.'

'Good, that should save time.' She smiled mischievously at him, and he smiled back before turning back to watch Doyle's progress, a shiver of anticipation running through his body.

The shed was old, probably dating back to the war. Its concrete walls were stained and cracked and its roof looked as if it would fly off during the first good wind. After his preliminary examination Doyle moved inside. He was pleased to see that at least the British police had had the common sense to put stepping-plates down; he just hoped they'd also the sense to use them.

The moment he entered the shed, Doyle knew 'he' had been there. He didn't have to see the evidence writ large across the walls. He could almost smell him, could sense his malignant presence. The shed was empty, every loose item having been taken away for examination. The one small window at the far end was coated with a film of silver fingerprint dust sprinkled on liberally by the fingerprint experts, and every surface was heavily stained and soiled with blood. It smeared the walls and ceiling, and had congealed in cracked pools on the floor.

The position of the dead girl's body had been marked on the floor. He knew from the pathologist's report that Mary West had been found face up. He examined the blood-splatter pattern, trying to form his own conclusions about the way she'd been murdered. Like the rest, she'd been alive when the killer started to use the knife on her, and there was the usual array of splashes, spurts and smears.

He pulled out his small camera from his jacket pocket. He always liked to take his own pictures, not trusting anyone else to do it properly, especially not the British. Although the camera was small, it had a fine lens and the reproduction was always of good quality. He took several photographs of the bloodstains, and made a quick drawing, in his notebook, of the murder scene.

The long wall at the far end of the shed interested him most and he took several shots of the omega symbol. He took several more photographs of the splash patterns, and followed this by taking pictures of every area of the shed, from the floor to the ceiling, to the back of the door and the windows, changing his film at least once. Finally, satisfied that he hadn't missed a thing, he went back out into the sunlight.

Solheim was standing where he'd left her. Hammond was standing close to her, and Doyle didn't like that.

He strode across towards them. 'Is there a list of the people who went into the shed after the body was discovered?'

Hammond began, 'I'm sure there is—'

'But the police have it,' said Doyle rudely.

Hammond could only nod. 'I really think it might be as well to let them know you're here,' he said. 'I'm sure they'll be co-operative, especially when they find out what this is all about.'

Doyle ignored the comment. 'Do we know if they're any closer to finding Strachan?'

'No, but they're doing all they can.'

'Which doesn't seem to be enough, or presumably they would have got him by now.'

'They'll get him.'

'Well let's hope he doesn't gut some other poor innocent bitch before they do.'

Although Doyle wasn't entirely convinced that Strachan was his man, he knew from bitter experience that you could never afford to eliminate anyone from an enquiry, and that more often than not the most obvious suspect was the right one. The one thing he was sure of, especially after reading Ryan's report and inspecting the shed, was that whoever had committed the murder was the same man he was looking for.

'Who would I talk to?' he asked.

'About the murder?'

Doyle nodded.

'Superintendent Farmer's in charge of the case,' said Hammond.

'What's he like?'

'I'm told *she* is very good. Bit uncompromising but efficient.'

'She!' Doyle didn't want to lock horns with another clever woman. They bothered him, had an uncanny knack of seeing right through him, and he didn't like it. His wife had been a clever woman. She'd made his life miserable for twenty years, then left him. That was clever women for you. He'd have to be on his guard.

He told Hammond, 'I guess you'd better set up a meeting. Sometime this week would be fine with me.'

'I'll see what I can do.'

Doyle nodded his thanks. Hammond realised it was the first time the man had been polite since they'd met. Perhaps he was making progress.

'In the shed,' Doyle asked, 'was there anything unusual, different, unexpected?'

'It was a murder, so most of it was unusual, I guess. The upside-down horseshoe?' Hammond was well aware that

Doyle was trying to get something out of him without giving away too much.

'No, I expected that. Anything else? Writing? A note of some sort?'

'No, nothing like that I don't think. The local police would know if there was.'

This time, however, there was hesitation in Hammond's voice, and both Doyle and Solheim noticed it. He was lying and both agents knew it, but for the moment at least they couldn't understand why. Doyle decided to let it go, and see what developed later. He changed the subject.

'Any chance of seeing the two security men who found the body?'

'I sent for them when we left. They should be in my office by now. I'll take you to them.'

'We' – Doyle indicated Solheim – 'would rather like to see them on our own, if that's OK.'

Hammond could feel himself getting nervous. It wasn't like him, it was out of character, and he tried to disguise it. He hoped they hadn't picked up his hesitation. He should have known better.

'Fine. I'll be in Colonel Cully's office when you've finished.' He saluted and walked briskly away.

Solheim and Doyle looked at each other. Something was wrong.

The day had been a glorious one and, much to Sam's delight, enjoyed by everyone. After Wyn returned with their mother, they had finished the last of the coffee and begun to pack up. Wyn called to Ricky and Tracy, who made their way back along the bank towards them, throwing the fishing rod on to the floor of the punt as they came. There were about half a dozen sandwiches left and Sam offered them to Ricky.

'Finish these off or feed them to the ducks.'

'Ducks? With a growing boy like me around? No chance.'

He stuck his hand out and scooped the lot off the plate in one movement. It was as he pulled his hand away that Sam noticed it. It was only there for a second, a flash of light, like a signal from a mirror. She recognised it at once and, as if scared of losing it, dropped the plate she was holding and grabbed Ricky's wrist. The action was so fast and violent that it took Ricky completely by surprise.

'OK, OK,' he protested. 'I'll give them to the ducks. I'm not that hungry.'

'Hold still, Ricky, for God's sake!'

Still holding his wrist securely, she pulled him across to the picnic basket. Ricky was bewildered and looked across at his mother for support.

As surprised by Sam's actions as everybody else, Wyn said, 'Sam, whatever's the matter?'

The entire family was now watching the strange spectacle. As the couple reached the picnic basket, Sam leant down and, taking a clean knife, scraped it across Ricky's hand. Ricky closed his eyes and looked away, expecting his aunt to cut him at any moment.

'Stay perfectly still, Ricky. There's something on your hand.'

Ricky was becoming genuinely alarmed: the look on his aunt's face told him that it wasn't a joke. She drew

NIGEL McCRERY

the knife across his wrist and hand several times before,
at last, releasing him. Apparently satisfied, she examined
the surface of the knife carefully until she found what she
was looking for.

She showed it to Ricky and asked, 'What do you think
that is?'

As she pushed the knife towards his face, Ricky
stepped back as if he was worried that something was
going to jump off the surface of the knife and bite him.
When he mustered the courage to look properly, he could
see nothing.

'There's nothing there.'

Sam moved the knife slightly to one side so that the
light caught the edge of the object. 'The small silvery
particles along the top. Do you know what they are?'

Ricky was surprised to hear his 'very clever' aunt
asking such a stupid question. 'Yes, of course I do.'

'Well,' she said impatiently, 'what are they?'

'Fish scales, probably from that perch I caught. They
stick to your hands sometimes. They're not dangerous,
though' – he thought about it for a moment – 'are they?'

Sam looked down at them again. Fish scales. So
unexceptional, so ordinary. She was almost shocked by
the discovery. It was another piece of the jigsaw.

Monday couldn't come fast enough for Sam. Even her
feelings about the split with Tom were forgotten in the
excitement of the moment. She'd rung Trevor Stuart and,
despite his initial reluctance, had persuaded him to take
her morning list. Leaving her mail unopened on the floor,
she headed for her car.

Traffic in Cambridge, like everywhere else in the country, was terrible, especially on a Monday morning. The worst day of the year was in early October when thousands of expectant students and their even more expectant families arrived for the start of the academic year. Pride and advice were the currency of the day, while all the students wanted to do was get rid of their families as quickly as possible, let their hair down, and get on with the job of being a student. With the town's population almost doubling for the day, the congestion caused havoc, especially to local residents. Most 'townies' – as non-college residents were known by the students – and Fellows alike stayed at home and waited for the carnival to subside. Sam could cope with it once a year, but it seemed as though every working day was becoming like it, with more and more cars vying for less and less space.

This morning it took her about an hour and a half to get to the forensic science labs at Scrivingdon with her prize, now neatly mounted on a glass slide and sealed. She made her way along the corridors to Marcia's laboratory and prayed that she would be there. She had tried to call her over the weekend but had got only the answerphone, and Marcia hadn't returned her call.

Sam's heart sank when she looked through the glass-panelled door and saw that Marcia wasn't there and there was no sign that she'd started working. It soared again when, as she turned to leave, she came face to face with her friend.

'Marcia, you're here.'

'Where else would I be?'

'You never returned my call, so I wondered.'

Marcia was carrying two cups of coffee. She handed one to Sam. 'I was in London with my brother. I didn't get back until late Sunday and I didn't think you'd want me ringing you at midnight. I was going to call you this morning.'

She pushed the lab door open and the two women went in.

'Anyway, what's so urgent that it brings you all this way on a busy Monday morning?'

Triumphantly, Sam produced the slide from her handbag. 'I think I've discovered what the object I found on Mary West's body is.'

Marcia nodded.

'Shall I show you?'

Marcia sipped her coffee casually. 'Sure, if you must.'

Sam was puzzled. Usually Marcia was as enthusiastic about her work as Sam. Today, though, she seemed subdued. Sam slipped the slide under the microscope, focused it, and stood back, allowing Marcia to fix her eyes firmly to the lens. Marcia looked for a couple of seconds, adjusting the focus slightly before sitting up again.

'Fish scales.'

Sam was astonished.

'From the yellow and black lines running through them, I'd say they came from a locally caught perch.' She smiled across at Sam knowingly.

Marcia, Sam thought, was good but this was a bit too much. 'How the hell did you work all that out?'

'Elementary, my dear Doctor Ryan. A little bit of natural genius. Oh, and I went to the fish section at the Natural History Museum on Friday. That's why I was away.'

'I thought you said you went to your brother's.'

'I did, afterwards. Anyway I met a very nice chap there, Nigel Butterworth. Taught me everything a girl should know about fish and their scales in one easy lesson.'

'But how did you know it was a local perch?'

'The local bit was just lucky, but the perch bit was no guess. It just happened to one of the ones Butterworth showed me.'

'Well,' said Sam, a bit deflated, 'what else did Mr Butterworth tell you?'

Marcia fetched a slide from a container on the far side of the lab, and slipped it under the microscope. 'Have a look at this.'

Sam rubbed her eyes briefly before pushing them down on to the lenses. She recognised it at once. It looked like a metallic blue fairy's wing. 'It's the scale I found during the PM.'

'No, it's a sample Butterworth gave me at the Natural History Museum, but it's the same fish. What you found was a scale from a *Lepomis auritus* – a redbreast sunfish to you and me.'

'Never heard of it.'

'I'm not surprised. It's a bit of an odd one. It's not indigenous.' As she spoke Marcia switched back to the perch slide. The two were dramatically different.

'Most British fish have cycloid scales. If you look carefully at your perch slide you'll notice that the scales have unbroken circular lines with a relatively smooth edge. The colour's a bit of a giveaway as well. Notice the thin yellow and black stripes peculiar to perch. Not many indigenous fish have such a brilliant display of blue.' She switched back to the *Lepomis* slide. 'Now have another look at the sunfish scales. They're catenoid. The rings are broken by a string of teeth across one end, and the surface is far more uneven.'

Her eyes still glued to the microscope, Sam asked her first question: 'Where do they come from?'

'Southern states of America, mostly Alabama and Georgia. Find a lot in the brackish waters around swampland. Kids catch them as bait or pan-frying fish. They're a bit small for anything else.'

Sam finally looked up. 'The pollen you found on the clothes, it comes from the *Myrica indora*. That's found only in the southern states too, Georgia, Mississippi and Alabama.'

'I can't believe our killer came all the way from the States without washing his hands at least once.'

'No, but he could have transferred them to something without knowing, and then transferred them back when he used whatever it was again.'

'Every contact leaves a trace?'

Sam nodded vehemently, but Marcia wasn't entirely convinced. 'Unlikely, though.'

'Not as unlikely as you might think. There have been other cases.'

'Sounds like a trip to see the "good ol' boys" might be in order.'

Sam returned to the microscope. 'Maybe. We'll have to see what happens when they pick Strachan up.'

Marcia finished her coffee. '*If* they pick Strachan up.'

CHAPTER SIX

'Good evening and welcome to the Old Combination Room at Waddington College.' Dr Christopher Dudley's voice was firm but gentle, his fluency occasionally marred by his inability to pronounce his Rs. Tall and gaunt, he was the essence of the art critic, from his soft shoes to his bright red spotted bow tie. 'This evening is a bit of a first for both the college and the Art Society. Instead of having one of the great masters interpreted by an established art critic or historian, tonight we have as our speaker a forensic pathologist.'

He turned and bowed slightly to Sam. Sam smiled a bit nervously and fidgeted on her chair. Although used to giving lectures, this was an entirely different affair. These weren't medical students attending a lecture delivered by a more learned, experienced and qualified person. This audience was made up of professional art critics, historians and experts in every field from cave paintings to Picasso, people whose life's work was art. And here was she, a total amateur, an interested bystander, about to pronounce judgement on one of the most famous paintings in the world. Bronzino's *Allegory with Venus and Cupid* had hung in the National Gallery for as long as Sam could remember. She used to sit in front of it studying every line and stroke until she knew the painting as intimately as she knew herself. She could not rationalise why she loved the painting so much, she just did.

Dr Dudley continued, 'As many of you here already know, Doctor Ryan is the Home Office pathologist for the Cambridge region and has been involved in some of our most highly publicised murder cases over the past few years. Tonight, however, she is going to turn her discerning eye upon one of the great works of Renaissance art, the *Allegory with Venus and Cupid* by Bronzino.' A large print of the painting had been pinned to a board just behind the lectern from where he was speaking.

'Doctor Ryan's views on the painting are as controversial as they are interesting, but most of all, however, I think you'll find them refreshing. So without further ado, allow me to introduce your speaker for tonight, Doctor Samantha Ryan.'

He led the audience in their applause as he took his seat and made way for Sam. As Sam stood, however, Doctor Dudley was back on his feet. 'I'm most terribly sorry, just one more thing' – Sam clasped her hands together in front of her and waited – 'drinks have been arranged in the Fellows' Garden after the talk, so if we could all wait to ask our questions until then, I'm sure it would most helpful, not to mention cooler. Thank you.'

He raised a hand in apology to Sam and returned to his seat. Sam took up her position at the lectern, sipping from a glass of water which stood on a small table by her side. She looked round the room. It was full to capacity, with over two hundred people sitting and standing at every vantage point. She wondered what they would make of her. Close to the front she noticed Hammond. Next to him was a very attractive woman in her late twenties and beside her a large, uncomfortable-looking man, probably in his mid-fifties. She didn't know why but she formed the impression that they all belonged together. Two rows back from them was Liam. She was pleased he'd turned up and that there was at least one friendly face she could concentrate on.

She cleared her throat. 'Good evening, and thank you for coming this evening. I'm sure most of you would much rather be sitting by the river sipping Pimm's, so I appreciate your attendance.'

She glanced round the room again. Most of the audience were at least smiling politely.

'Our main source of reference for the painting is Vasari in 1568. He was then the director of Duke Cosimo's artistic project in Florence. Since that time there has been no real disagreement regarding the personification of Venus, Cupid or Time.' She turned to the picture and indicated the three areas she was discussing. 'The painting's competing interpretations depend to a large extent upon the different identities ascribed by the author to the three subsidiary figures.'

Despite his best efforts, Doyle could feel his eyes begin to close. He hadn't completely recovered from the journey yet and he wasn't as fit or as healthy as he once was. Although the room was large, it was packed. She could certainly pull an audience, he thought, but what the hell she was talking about he didn't have a clue. He was hot. It wasn't natural for so many people to be in one room at the same time. They'd opened all the windows but it made little difference. Where was the goddamned air-conditioning? He pulled out his handkerchief and mopped his face and neck. He noticed Solheim glance across at him and hoped he wasn't beginning to smell. He slipped his handkerchief back into his pocket and tried once again to concentrate.

'So Vasari's interpretation of the painting pointed out that love was very contradictory. My contention is that Bronzino was depicting love as dangerous, even lethal.'

Sam was beginning to feel uncomfortably hot. She wished a fan had been provided. She soldiered on. 'Before the Renaissance, the study and practice of medicine was for centuries based upon corruptions of Galenic principles, the teaching of the Arab school of Avicenna and Stoic reliance on astrology, the re-examination of the Classical texts of Hippocrates and Galen, and the new interest in rational methodology.'

It was no good, Doyle thought. If it got any hotter he would have to leave. It would look rude but it would be better than collapsing on the floor in a dead faint. If he'd understood anything that Dr Ryan was saying it might have helped keep his mind off his discomfort, but he didn't, so he only had himself to think about.

By now Sam was in full swing. 'The first crucial test of this new age of medicine was provided by the great pandemic of syphilis which swept across Europe, probably carried by retreating armies, during the sixteenth century. Everything from a punishment from God to a particular alignment of the planets was blamed. However, one of the more enlightened men of the day, Giovanni de Vigo, surgeon to Pope Julius II, eventually recognised that the disease was contracted through copulation with an infected partner. In his *Practica in arte chirugica copiosa*, published in Venice in 1514, he accurately described the progression of the disease: the darkening of the complexion, headaches, stomach cramps, and finally the swellings with hard knobs or knots.'

Although Doyle had begun to understand what she was saying, it was too late. Hauling himself to his feet, he pushed past the people near him and strode quickly out of the room. His head was swimming and for a moment he didn't think he was going to make it. At last, he reached the outside and sat down on steps close to the doorway, taking in great lungfuls of air and steadying himself with his hand. A few moments later Solheim was by his side with her arm round his shoulders. It was the closest she'd ever come to a show of affection.

'You OK, Ed? You look like shit. Want me to call an ambulance or something?'

Doyle waved the offer away. 'No, no, I'm fine. It was just too damned hot in there.'

A grey-suited and bowler-hatted porter approached them. 'Are you all right, sir?'

Doyle nodded and the porter produced a tall glass of cool water. 'I'd just sip at it, if I were you, sir.'

Doyle ignored his advice and swallowed the entire

glass in a few gulps, before handing the glass back without a word of thanks.

Solheim covered for him. 'Thank you. That was very thoughtful.'

The porter said, 'If you need me again I'll be just inside the door,' and went back to his post.

Doyle belched loudly and turned to Solheim. 'You go back inside. I'll be fine now. I'll meet you both here when she's finished.'

'If you're sure?'

'Yeah, I'm sure. See you later.'

Solheim stood up and went back inside, leaving Doyle on the steps to regain his composure and colour.

Sam had watched as the large man sitting two seats down from Hammond staggered and bumped his way out of the room. She wondered for a moment if she should follow and see if he needed help. His face was certainly ashen and she was unsure whether he was having a heart attack or whether it was just the heat. Her mind was made up for her when the woman sitting next to him followed him out. If there was anything seriously wrong, she was sure to come and get help. Her return a few moments later reassured Sam that the problem was just the heat. She continued her lecture.

'The figure on the far right of the picture is depicted in a semi-foetal flexion. His hand is pressed firmly to his head, the mouth is wide open and the neck muscles contracted. The figure is therefore clearly in distress. You will note further that the figure's skin is darkened and

172

that the ocular *scera* are reddened. We can also observe that he has several teeth missing.'

As Solheim resumed her seat, Hammond leant over and muttered in her ear, 'How is he?'

'Fine.'

'Shame. I thought it might be a heart attack.'

'Wishful thinking.'

'What about tomorrow evening?'

'For the trip?'

Hammond nodded.

'Sounds fine,' she whispered. 'Sure you'll be able to manage in the heat?'

'I've walked around hotter places than Cambridge.'

Solheim looked him straight in the eye. 'It wasn't the walking I was thinking about.'

Hammond swallowed hard, but let it go as a firm 'shush' from the people behind re-focused their attention.

'His fingers are remarkable for their periarticular nodal swellings and evidence of sero-sanguineous discharge. There is evidence of hair loss as depicted by the hair we see here and here.' She indicated the figure's left cheek and right shoulder. 'All these stigmata, as we have seen, are associated with syphilis or with its treatment during the sixteenth century. In conclusion, then, it is my belief that Bronzino was telling us not that love could be contradictory, but that it could lead to the scourge of sixteenth-century Europe, syphilis. Thank you.'

Doctor Dudley stood and led the applause, turning and smiling at Sam as he clapped.

'Bravo, bravo!'

As the applause eased, Dudley turned back to face the audience. Hands shot up all over the room as people struggled to be noticed in order to ask the first question. Dr Dudley was firm, however, and waved their hands down.

'First, I would like to express the thanks of the Art Society, and I'm sure of all present, to Doctor Ryan, for one of the finest and most unusual reinterpretations of an old master I have ever heard. It is not often that a small society such as ours is privileged to hear such a refreshingly different lecture.' He bowed to Sam, who smiled at him. 'As I said before, drinks will be available in the Fellows' Garden and any questions you would like to ask can be put to Doctor Ryan then. She has very kindly supplied us with copies of her paper, which the porter will hand out to all those who want one as you are leaving the room. Just to remind you, the next meeting of the society will take place on September the 2nd, when Mr William Melville will be reading us his paper on the emergence of African art within a European context. Many thanks.'

As the room emptied, with the usual loud clattering and scraping of chairs, Dr Dudley turned to Sam. 'Wonderful, quite wonderful. You must be very pleased.'

Sam was embarrassed by the warmth of his praise, but pleased that her talk had gone down so well.

Adams felt slightly sick when he received the order to attend Superintendent Farmer's office. It wasn't that it was unusual, and normally he'd have been fine about it. But he was told she wanted to see DC Fenwick at the same time.

Although he was sure about ending his relationship with Sam, he was less sure about starting another up with Liz. 'On the rebound', they use to call it, and he began to examine his motivations for his relationship with Liz. On the plus side were her age, looks and, he had to admit, enthusiasm. He couldn't remember a time when sex had been so plentiful or so enjoyable. On the negative side was the fact that not only did they have to work together but he was her boss.

Although the way she called him 'sir' in bed was quite nice. Liz had a habit of secretly flirting with him in the office while other members of the team were about. She showed a little too much leg, leant across his desk so that he could look down her cleavage and had even, on occasions, grabbed great handfuls of his backside and squeezed hard. On one occasion she'd actually tried to have sex with him in one of the store cupboards and it was only when they heard voices outside the door that she desisted. Perhaps the age difference was too much. Perhaps he was too old and women of Sam's age were better suited to him. Unfortunately, it looked as if Farmer had found out. She objected strongly to any relationships, other than professional ones, on her teams and had made no secret of her dislike of Liz, but as she was the only woman on the team Farmer was stuck with her, for now anyway.

As if summoned by his thoughts, Liz came into the room. She was dressed in a lightweight skirt and jacket and looked about as smart as he had ever seen her. If someone had to go, perhaps she was trying to make sure it wasn't her. Typical. Bloody women, they'd be the death of him.

They made their way down the corridor together towards Farmer's office.

Liz spoke first. 'Think she knows?'

Adams shrugged. They reached Farmer's office and Adams knocked. Farmer's voice was loud and clear from the other side of the door. 'Come in.'

Adams opened the door for Liz and they both walked in and stood formally. Farmer looked at them for a moment, chewing her pen, before waving them to the two easy chairs on the opposite side of her desk.

'Sit down, sit down, you're making the office look untidy.'

They obeyed immediately and, like pet dogs, sat. Farmer glanced down at her papers again as if refreshing her memory,

'I have been contacted by the FBI academy at Quantico. They are sending two agents, Doyle and Solheim – sounds like something out of an American cop show. Anyway, they're here to help with the Mary West investigation.'

Adams could feel a wave of relief ripple through his entire body. He glanced secretly across at Liz, who also seemed to relax. He wondered, though, how many more occasions like this one he could stand and, despite the sex, whether his peace of mind was more important than their relationship.

Farmer continued, 'I don't know how you two feel about it but it seems rather odd to me that the FBI have, firstly, become involved in what is, in essence, only a local murder, and why they are sending two of their agents from the Behavioral Science Unit at Quantico, which I understand is an élite unit used to dealing with major crime and, dare I say it, investigations into serial murders.'

Adams said, 'So, ma'am, you think the murder of young Mary might be less simple than we thought?'

Farmer nodded. 'Almost certainly, I should think.'

'Did the FBI send us any information other than who we should be expecting to meet?'

'Nothing. That's why you two are here.'

Liz plucked up the courage to speak. She wasn't so much scared of Farmer as nervous of her and the effect she could have on her career prospects.

'When do they arrive, ma'am? Should we pick them up?'

'They're already here. Apparently they arrived a few days ago and are staying at Leeminghall. Also apparently, they felt it necessary to let the Americans know they were here before they let us know. Major Hammond will be your contact at the base.' Farmer's face became deeply earnest. 'I want you to find out what's going on. If we have got a serial killer on our patch I want to know before some other poor girl ends up with her belly ripped open.'

Adams tensed again. 'And if there is?'

'Then the shit will hit the fan big-time and it will all be going the Americans' way. Any sign of Strachan yet?'

'Nothing, ma'am, and we're beginning to run out of ideas.'

'Interpol? Might have reached the Continent.'

'Done, ma'am. We checked all ferry and tunnel passengers as well. Zero.'

Farmer relaxed back in her chair again. 'If and when you get him, I don't want the Yanks near him until I've finished interviewing him.'

'Might be difficult, ma'am,' said Adams reasonably. 'He's an American citizen, after all.'

Farmer leant across her desk and her eyes narrowed. 'He's also an American killer, as far as I'm concerned. If he comes to my county and commits murder, I don't care if he comes from Timbuk-bloody-tu, he's mine. Am I making myself clear?'

Adams and Fenwick nodded. Farmer wasn't a person to argue with, especially in her current mood.

'Well, off you go, then, and I want to be updated regularly.'

Liz and Adams stood and began to leave the room.

'DC Fenwick.' Farmer's voice cut across the room as Adams opened the door. Liz looked back at her superior officer. 'Nice suit. Keep it up. Tom's clearly having a good effect on you.'

Liz hid her embarrassment. 'Thank you, ma'am.'

'But' – Farmer's face was hard and serious – 'I suggest that you keep your sexual activities for the bedroom and not one of my store cupboards. That'll be all.'

Adams felt his heart sink as he pushed Liz through the door.

Doyle had never drunk anything with cucumber and mint in it before. He was a beer man, but this was more like lemonade and, by the look of them, most of the people here were lemonade sort of people. He'd chosen a cool spot under one of the largest trees in the garden. It shielded him from the sun and kept him reasonably cool. Hammond and Solheim stood a few feet away from him, chatting quietly and, judging by the occasional glance shot his way, probably about him.

He looked around the lawns at the numerous people in their cream suits, flowing dresses and pale complexions. He didn't like the British much. He didn't consider himself a racist or anything as politically incorrect as that. To be a racist you had to hate one or two sections of society because of their ethnic origins. Doyle hated everyone, so he guessed that made it OK.

He'd been surprised by Doctor Ryan. He hadn't expected someone so attractive, but had assumed Hammond had simply taken his opportunity with a rather sad and desperate spinster in return for inside information. Doctor Ryan was far from that: small and slim with a very pleasing face and a hint of hidden sexuality. Hammond had just gone up in his estimation. Solheim had a sort of animal attraction for him but Dr Ryan, well, there was a real woman. Not only would she keep your bed warm at night but he'd bet she could fix you up a great supper as well. If she had a failing it was that she was too smart by half. There was no doubt about it, though. Despite her brain, Doyle was impressed.

The three of them had waited until the long line of people waiting to ask her questions had eased before going across to meet her. When they reached her, she was still talking to Dr Dudley and a rather scruffy young man whom she called Liam.

She seemed pleased to see Hammond. 'Bob!' She leant across and kissed him on the cheek – part of the 'understanding', Doyle thought – 'I didn't know you had an interest in the history of art.'

'Only when you're involved.'

'Flatterer.'

Doyle turned to Dr Dudley, who was still standing beside Dr Ryan. They had important and private matters to discuss, and the last thing Doyle wanted was any prying outsiders listening in. Keeping his face straight and hard, Doyle looked directly into Dudley's eyes. No matter which way Dudley looked, Doyle continued to stare at him, watching him become uncomfortable and then embarrassed.

Liam watched Doyle with some contempt. He hated bullies and Doyle was obviously a bully. Putting his arm around Dudley's shoulder, Liam drew him away from the group.

'Now, Doctor Dudley, what do you make of the premiss of Irish art being the foundation of all things magical?' As they went, Liam scowled back at Doyle just to make it clear that he at least wasn't intimidated by him.

With Sam's other guests gone, Hammond turned his attention to his two companions. 'Can I introduce you to Agents Edward Doyle and Catherine Solheim from the Behavioral Science Unit at the FBI headquarters in Quantico.'

Sam shook their hands. 'Really, I'm very impressed.

I don't suppose you're here to listen to my talk on Renaissance art, so I can only assume it has something to do with the Mary West case.'

She looked up at Doyle. He was a giant of a man, with a ruddy face and ill-fitting clothes, who seemed to sweat from every pore in his body.

He replied awkwardly, like a little boy who'd been caught with his pockets full of apples, 'We have an interest in the case, yes.'

'Must be some interest to come thousands of miles for. Is there something I should know?'

Hammond came to Doyle's rescue. 'I think it would be better if we had this conversation away from the crowd.'

Sam nodded and the three of them gathered up their drinks and plates of sandwiches and decamped to the students' lawns. She chose a secluded part of the lawns and made sure there was a tree under which Doyle could perch himself. The weather was glorious, but although it suited Sam it didn't suit everyone, as the filling fridges at the mortuary all too clearly showed.

Sam waited until Doyle had manoeuvred himself into a comfortable position, then said, 'Shall we get to the point?'

Doyle said, 'About ten years ago I was investigating a series of murders that had been committed in various states. At first the authorities failed to link them, but slowly and through the use of Vi-Cap – that's our computer – a pattern emerged that made it clear we were probably looking for the same killer.'

'How many murders do you suspect he is responsible for?'

'Twelve, or thereabouts.'

'"Thereabouts"? Why aren't you sure?'

'Some of the remains weren't found until some time after the victim went missing, so much of the evidence was destroyed by the elements and by animals and insects. We've had to rely on guesswork, but there are possibly three or four more.'

Sam was becoming increasingly interested. 'What pattern did the Vi-Cap pick out?'

'All the victims were murdered, or went missing, close to US Air Force bases. They were all stabbed to death, probably with a serrated knife, and their kidneys were removed.'

'And you think your killer might have popped across the pond?'

'Yes, although I can't be entirely sure until I've seen the body and the scene-of-crime photographs.'

He was lying. He knew it was the same killer but needed a reason to get at the relevant information and documents.

Hammond put in, 'So we were wondering if . . .'

'I would let you see West's body and the photographs?'

Hammond nodded. Doyle and Solheim were silent, content to let him handle Dr Ryan.

'Does Superintendent Farmer know you're here?' she asked.

'Yes,' said Doyle. 'We're due to see her tomorrow.'

'In that case, couldn't it wait until then?'

'Not really. The earlier I can find out what happened, the quicker I can react, and hopefully stop it happening again.'

Doyle found himself in an odd dilemma. Of course he hoped there wouldn't be another killing. He wasn't so hard-boiled that he'd wish that kind of death on anyone. On the other hand, although he felt that they were closing in on their man, their progress was so slow that he wondered whether they could hope to catch him unless there was another killing.

Sam broke into his thoughts. 'What about Strachan?'

Doyle picked at his teeth, removing a scrap of sandwich. 'Well, I never say never, but his profile certainly doesn't seem to fit the person we're looking for.'

'So you don't think it's him?'

'I didn't say that. Profiles, like all methods of crime detection, are fallible. Mistakes have been made before. I wouldn't eliminate him just yet.'

'Where did he come from?'

Doyle remained silent a moment while he finished a sandwich. These had to be the smallest sandwiches he'd ever seen in his life. It was true what they said about the British: they were tight bastards.

'New York, born and bred.'

'Any connections with the Southern states, say Georgia?'

Doyle looked at her enquiringly. 'Not that I'm aware of. Why? You know something we don't?'

Sam shook her head. She wasn't willing to share her discoveries with him just yet. She asked, 'Your other victims, were any of them raped?'

Doyle shook his head.

'Mary West was.'

'I know, I read it in your report. It's out of character but not impossible. Serial killers are no different from ordinary people in that they're all different. Some are smarter than others, that's all.'

'So they're capable of changing their methods.'

'Oh yeah. They don't all want to be caught. They only have to read one of the many books that some of my more distinguished colleagues have written to confound most of us. Change their MO, locations, type of victim. Makes it hard even to link the killings, never mind catch the bastard as well.'

'Perhaps Strachan's one of them, very clever. That's why the police haven't caught him yet.'

'Maybe. From the information I've just received from the Bureau, I understand he's at least capable of rape. I understand you managed to extract some sperm samples from the West girl. When will you get the DNA results?'

Sam shrugged. 'They're a priority. But it still might take a while. They're not the kind of thing you can rush, otherwise you run the risk of contaminating your samples.'

Normally Sam wouldn't have let them within a mile of the mortuary without the appropriate permission. She was no respecter of pointless bureaucracy – a failing which had landed her in trouble before now – and was frequently frustrated with the delays caused by the need to follow protocol, but she was strict about confidentiality and security. This case, though, was different. This time the police and the public needed every bit of help they could get, through official channels or otherwise.

'How likely is he to strike again?' she asked.

'Who knows? The gaps between the killings have been getting shorter. How much shorter they're likely to get is anyone's guess.'

Sam paused. 'It will have to be a visual examination only.'

Doyle nodded his thanks. 'That's all it will take. Then I'll know for sure.'

'When would you like to do it?'

The question cut across his chain of thought but he reacted quickly. 'Now would be as good a time as any. If that's OK by you?' He judged that this was a time to be polite.

'Fine. Sooner the better, really.'

Doyle decided to press his luck a bit. 'And the scene-of-crime photographs, when can I see them?'

'After you've viewed the body, if you like. They're in my office.'

He seemed pleased. 'Fine.'

Sam picked up her things and got ready to leave. Before she moved away, she stared at each of the Americans in turn. 'This is between the three of us,' she said firmly. 'It goes no further.'

Hammond and his two companions nodded.

'Bob, you know the way, don't you?'

He nodded again.

'OK, I'll see you there.'

It was over an hour since DC Fenwick and DI Adams

had arrived at the base and they were still waiting outside Colonel Cully's office. Neither Hammond nor the FBI agents were at the base and no one seemed to know where they were, although Adams suspected Cully or one of his aides knew exactly where they were but wasn't saying.

He began to regret not phoning before he came. He had hoped to catch them cold and off their guard. It usually got results. Against trained FBI agents it might not have worked quite so well but he'd thought it was worth a shot.

They'd been on their way out when they had received the message from the base commander. A large American airman in a smart green uniform with a semi-automatic rifle slung across his shoulder had stopped them and 'requested' that they return to the base commander's office, where he was waiting to see them. It was an offer they couldn't refuse and so they did as they were bid. Cully wasn't there when they arrived and, as it had been at his request that they had returned, Adams was particularly aggrieved. He knew it was one of these stupid seniority games that they were taught at the staff colleges to try and demonstrate who was in charge, but he could have done without it right then.

While Fenwick sat quietly looking out of the window, lost in her thoughts – doubtless concerning Farmer and what she knew or only suspected, and worrying about the effect it was going to have on her career – Adams flicked through a number of American magazines piled on a rather grand-looking coffee table in the centre of the reception room. Cully's secretary had provided both of them with coffee, but Adams had found it almost undrinkable and left it on the side. He was tempted to ask for tea but felt it was rude and far too English.

Finally, the tall, gaunt figure of Colonel Cully strode into the office. Adams and Fenwick stood up as Cully hung his cap on a hook behind the office door before pulling his jacket smartly into place. Finally, satisfied with his appearance, he turned to the two detectives and introduced himself.

'Colonel Cully, base commander.' He shook their hands firmly. 'Sorry I'm late. Last-minute hiccup. These things happen.'

He stood back and waved them into his office. 'Coffee?'

Adams replied quickly, 'No, thanks. We've just had one.'

Cully directed them to chairs and took up position behind the large oak desk at the far end of the room.

Adams waited to see what he wanted; he didn't have to wait long.

'I take it you're here about the West murder? Tragic, quite tragic. We're helping the family all we can, you know. Any sign of Strachan yet?'

Adams thought he sounded about as sincere as a game-show host, but said merely, 'No, nothing. He's gone to ground. He's got to surface sometime, though, sir, and then we'll be waiting.'

'I'm sure you will, I'm sure you will.'

'How long have the FBI agents been here, sir?' asked Fenwick.

Cully leant back in his chair. 'Only a few days. They'd

have been in touch before but I think they were bit jet-lagged. It takes a seasoned campaigner to be able to buck that sort of thing,' he said, puffing out his chest.

'Bit dramatic to bring in two FBI agents for what, in essence, is a local murder, isn't it, sir?'

'Well, Inspector, I think Washington is taking a dim view of it. American airman murders local British girl. Doesn't go down too well, especially after that business in Japan. Probably want it cleaned up as much as you do.'

'Election year in the States, isn't it, sir?'

Cully nodded.

'Time to be tough on crime, eh?'

Cully bridled. 'I'm sure that's got nothing to do with it.'

'Then why have the FBI dispatched two of their top agents from the Behavioral Science Unit? Look, sir, if there's something going on that we don't know about, I think you'll find that we would take a dim view of it.'

'I'm sure there isn't, Inspector, just hands across the ocean, but you'll really have to talk to the two agents about that.'

'We intend to, sir. I was just hoping you might have been able to save us some time.'

Cully felt uncomfortable. This wasn't the reason he'd decided to talk to them. He wanted information out of them, not the other way around.

'When do you expect them to return?' asked Adams.

'Depends on how long the talk lasts, I should think. These things tend to go on, as I'm sure you're aware.'

Fenwick asked, 'What talk, sir? Where?'

The edge in her voice made Cully realise he'd said something wrong. However, he was committed now and couldn't see a way round it. 'The one Doctor Ryan's giving at Waddington College, something about the history of art. Wanted to go myself but my schedule didn't permit.'

Adams remembered Sam telling him about it, and finding her working on the paper at two o'clock one morning. He'd had to pick her up and carry her to bed or she'd have been there all night. It was a good memory and one he wished he could forget.

He forced himself back to the present. 'What time was the talk due to finish, sir?'

'I've no idea, but I'm sure that if you ring the college they'll let you know. I believe there were drinks after. It all sounded very English.'

Adams didn't really need the information; he already had a good idea where Sam would be. He stood up. 'Well, thank you for seeing us, Colonel. I'm sure we'll be seeing a lot more of each other over the next few weeks.'

Cully thought it sounded like a threat and responded, 'I have no jurisdiction at all over the FBI agents' actions. They're very much their own people. I do hope there's not a problem?'

Adams shook his hand without replying and the two detectives left the office.

As they went, Cully picked up the phone. 'Get me the number of Waddington College.'

Sam had phoned Fred from her mobile on her way to

the mortuary and asked him if he minded turning out to help. She couldn't pay him but she did offer to give him double time off, which seemed to do the trick. Fred lived in a small cottage about a mile from the hospital and cycled in each day no matter what the weather. He was an odd fish but Sam liked him.

He was at the mortuary and Mary West's body was already in position by the time Sam and the others arrived. They all changed quickly and entered the mortuary. Doyle went straight across to the body and began his examination. He spoke into a small tape-recorder which he produced from his capacious pocket.

Sam decided to remind him of the rules. 'Visual only, remember?'

Doyle nodded and continued, 'The body is that of a white female, in her late teens or early twenties. She is of average height and weight and well nourished . . .'

Sam waited and watched as he carried out his own brief, but precise, examination. When he reached West's neck he made a point of examining the small burn mark that Sam had noticed during the PM.

'Any idea what caused this?' he asked.

'I was hoping you could tell me.'

He returned to the mark. 'I've seen it before, or something quite like it. It was on some of the other bodies, the ones that hadn't become too decomposed.'

Sam moved across to his side. 'It appears to be a burn but so far we've been unable to determine the cause.'

'Could be, but we need to know for sure.'

Sam was impressed. Despite his size, he moved well and treated the body with a degree of reverence. Every now and again he would stop and fire a question at Sam, waiting until he was satisfied with her reply before starting again. The whole process took about twenty minutes and Sam couldn't think of a thing he'd missed. He turned off his tape-recorder and began to change while Fred packed the body away.

Doyle threw his gloves into the bin and turned to Sam. 'Can I have a look at the scene-of-crime photographs now?'

She nodded and guided the team out of the mortuary and up to her office. As the lift doors closed she asked, 'Well, was it your killer?'

Doyle didn't move. He'd been almost sure before, but now he was positive. 'Oh yes, it was him all right.'

On entering the office, Sam went straight to her shelves, pulled down the appropriate file, opened it and withdrew all the relevant photographs. She handed half of them to Doyle and the other half to Solheim. They took them over to Sam's desk and began to sift through them slowly, swapping them back and forth while Hammond and Sam watched.

After a few minutes Doyle's impatient voice broke the silence. 'Is this all of them?'

'I shouldn't think so. The police have most of them.'

Doyle nodded, clearly disappointed.

'Perhaps if you gave me a clue to what you're looking for I could be more help,' suggested Sam.

Doyle said, 'At every other murder scene a note's been found. It's odd that there wasn't one here.'

'What sort of note?'

'I'm sorry, that's confidential. Nothing personal but it's the one scrap of information I've managed to keep from the press. Helps eliminate the nutters when they come to confess.'

Although Sam was a bit annoyed, after all the unofficial help she had offered Doyle, she could see his point. She decided to tell him what she'd found. 'There was something.'

Doyle looked at her sharply.

'I think a note had been hung on an old nail above Mary West's head. There was a small section of paper still attached to it, as if someone had ripped the note down.'

'How do you know it wasn't an old note?'

'The blood-splatter pattern surrounding the note. It didn't sit right. I'm sure the note was there when she was murdered.'

'Who would have ripped it down?'

Sam had no idea. 'Your killer?'

'Then why put it up in the first place?'

He was right it had been a stupid suggestion.

'Who else went into the shed after the body was found?' he asked.

'The two security policemen.'

'I've interviewed them. If they'd anything to hide I'd have known by now.'

'The SOCOs.'

Doyle didn't understand.

'Scene of Crime Officers.'

'Would they have taken it down?'

Sam shook her head. 'Not without telling someone.'
'Anyone else?'

She shrugged. 'The police will have a full list.'

'Any chance they might have missed someone?'

'Not after they got there. Perhaps before, though. The base security police should have their own list.'

They both turned to Hammond. 'Handed it over to the British,' he said. 'Besides the colonel and me, there were only the two men who found her on the list. Sorry there's not more I can tell you.'

Again, Doyle felt sure Hammond was hiding something. He'd left it before, but time was getting on and he needed to know the truth. He didn't want to confront him here and now, but he'd have to get around to it soon.

Sam changed the subject. 'Were any of your victims found in the area of Atlanta, Georgia?'

She'd asked a similar question before and Doyle was keen to find out why. 'Two, including the last one. Why?'

'We found some pollen grains on the girl's clothing, from a bush which apparently only grows in that area, and a scale from a fish which is also exclusive to the swampland around there.'

Doyle was surprised, pleased and angry all at the same time. He growled at Sam, 'Why the hell haven't you mentioned this before?'

Sam was damned if she was going to be addressed like that in her own office, especially after she'd stuck her neck out for them. 'Because I've only just met you. The British police are aware, so perhaps if you'd got

in touch with them immediately you arrived, instead
of worrying that a bunch of Limeys would steal your
thunder by arresting your serial killer,' she said acidly,
'you might have been known a little earlier.'

Doyle was clearly taken aback, and Hammond and
Solheim couldn't help but smile. Doyle realised he'd
overstepped the mark and, not wanting to alienate
someone who could continue to be helpful, tried to
smooth things over. 'OK, we were out of order, but
it's been a long haul to try and catch this bastard. I'm
due to see your Superintendent Farmer tomorrow.'

'Good, then I'm sure she'll fill you in on all the latest
developments.'

Doyle nodded. For the first time in nine years the
clouds that had surrounded his killer were beginning to
lift. It was just a goddamned shame that it was a woman
who had helped to bring this about. His thoughts were
interrupted by a loud knock on the door and two police
officers entered the office.

Tom Adams looked across at Sam, who appeared
none too pleased to see him. 'Up to your old tricks
again, Sam?'

The smell from the toilets in the sports hall was appalling
and seemed to be getting worse by the day. Finally,
unable to play the inter-camp basketball final because
the changing rooms had become unusable, they sent for
a plumber.

Jim Smith had been a plumber in the local area for
almost forty years and was seriously thinking about
retiring. There was a rumour that with all the spending

cuts the American air-base would be closing and as he, like the rest of the local community, relied on the base's personnel for employment, he thought he might as well get out while the going was good.

He tried to clear the blockage from the gents' toilets but, despite spending several hours and all the ingenuity he could bring to bear, he was no farther forward. There was no choice in the end but to get himself down the drains and see where the problem was. He pulled open the inspection trap and began to climb down. At least the sewer was fairly large.

Stepping off the last rung of the ladder, he shone his torch around until he found the exit pipe from the hall. He crouched down low and aimed the torch along the length of the pipe. After only a few feet the beam picked up a large, dark obstruction. At least he had discovered what was causing the problem. Crawling into the pipe, he grabbed it. It felt like some kind of wet cloth bundled up and then packed tightly inside the tube. Probably someone's idea of a joke, he thought. He gave it a tug and, to his surprise, it gave at once.

The sudden freeing of the obstruction and the force of the sewerage which instantly poured along the pipe sent Jim flying backwards against the far wall, knocking all the breath out of him. He'd realised the moment he'd done it what a stupid thing it was to do. Stuck on all fours, trying to get his breath back and retching from the ageing sewerage he'd taken in the face, he picked up his torch and shone the light back to see whether the blockage had completely gone. As he put his hand forward it fell upon something firm but soft. It could have been one of a hundred things, each more unpleasant than the last.

Wiping the slime from his eyes Jim Smith looked down at his hand which was pressed down firmly over the head's wide-open mouth, while his fingers dangled inside the empty sockets that had once been Strachan's eyes. For the first time in his life, Jim Smith screamed.

CHAPTER SEVEN

Sam had been to some unusual crime scenes but the interior of an underground sewerage system was a first, even for her. She arrived with Tom Adams and the rest of the murder squad, having received the message in her office at the same time as Adams.

The call had come not a moment too soon and had prevented what might have been an ugly scene. Sam couldn't remember ever seeing Adams so angry. He didn't rave or shout, but his face revealed his battle for self-control. She knew she'd have to face him in the end and tell him why she'd broken the rules and let Doyle see West's body, but she wanted to put it off for as long as possible, giving him time to calm down and her a chance to come up with a suitable explanation.

As they drove through the camp's main gate, Sam had a strong feeling of déjà vu. As the last time, Colin Flannery and his team were already there, scurrying about like white ants, tying off tapes, erecting flood-lights and pushing stepping-plates into place. Although it looked chaotic, there was a practised and impressive organisation behind the activity.

Flannery handed her a white boiler suit, a pair of

wellington boots and a disposable hat and face-mask. 'It's pretty evil down there,' he said. 'We don't want you catching anything nasty, do we?'

Sam smiled at him, but groaned inwardly. She hated face-masks: they were hot and uncomfortable. She often wondered how surgeons coped with them, especially during some of the longer and more complicated operations they performed.

The drain shaft was about twelve feet deep, with a large sewerage pipe running along the bottom. A metal ladder had been dropped inside and with Flannery's help Sam climbed slowly down. When she reached the bottom of the shaft, she stepped off on to one of the tight-fitting plastic platforms which Flannery's team had wedged into position around Strachan's body.

The force of the unblocked sewerage had washed the body out of the pipe, and it lay broken and twisted at the bottom of the shaft. Strachan's arms were splayed loosely above his head and his legs had been bent and forced up behind his back as if in some ghastly yoga position. He looked like a macabre rag doll which had been thrown down the shaft by a spoilt child in a fit of uncontrolled temper.

Sam scanned the walls and floor quickly, looking for the omega sign or a note. There was nothing. Opening her bag, she removed her notebook and pencil. There was no point using the tape-recorder: she'd never hear herself properly through the mask. Her nose had already begun to itch irritatingly, like a broken limb inside a cast.

There was very little room to work. Every time she

moved, her body touched the wall or floor smearing her suit with some of the dark black slime which covered everything. It clung to the walls and dripped slowly into the shaft, like treacle falling from a spoon.

Although Strachan had only been missing a week, his body was already badly decomposed. There were also areas which had been gnawed at, eaten by the numerous rats which lived and bred within the sewerage system. Sam could hear them as she worked, squeaking and scratching as they complained to each other, annoyed at the invasion of their privacy. The high-intensity lights positioned within the drainage shaft were keeping the creatures at bay for the moment, but Sam wondered how much longer that would last. Rats were brave, tenacious creatures, which adapted quickly to almost any situation. She remembered stories from police officers and SOCOs about having to beat them off bodies with shovels and truncheons. 'Rats as big as your head,' one SOCO had reported. She shuddered inwardly and hoped she got out before they decided to return to their unfinished feast.

Not only was the body badly decomposed but it was covered in a thick layer of the sludge that clothed the rest of the shaft, and this made the initial examination difficult. Sam was unable to wash clean any of the areas she wished to examine, for fear of destroying or removing trace evidence at the same time. She began to write.

'Drainage system beneath Leeminghall US Air Force base, 10.42 p.m., 30th May 1996. The body is that of a white male believed to be Airman Ray Strachan. The remains are badly decomposed and have been attacked by rodents, probably rats.'

She turned his head carefully from one side to the other, looking for injuries. 'There is' – she took measurements with a six-inch clear ruler – 'a half-inch hole to the left side of the head, possibly a gunshot wound. I will need to make a closer examination to be sure.'

She turned to the next item. 'By the side of the victim's head, with a small section fixed under the head, is a clear plastic bag.' She opened it slightly with her ruler. 'The interior of the bag is heavily bloodstained.'

Although it was only conjecture on her part, she was certain that the bag had been forced over Strachan's head after he was shot. That would explain the lack of blood at, and leading to, the scene. She looked over the rest of the body, but, given the state of the remains, there was little more she could do for the moment. It would have to wait until she did the post mortem.

As she began to pack her equipment away, she saw a sudden darting movement at the far end of one of the long drains. She saw it for only an instant, caught in the half-light that stretched out from the drainage shaft along the pipes before whatever it was disappeared into the enveloping shadows. That was enough: without taking time to shut her bag properly, she jumped on to the ladder's first rung and climbed as fast as she could, grateful for the welcoming hands of two white-suited SOCOs, who pulled her clear of the drain before descending into the disgusting depths themselves.

She pulled off her face-mask and opened her mouth

wide, taking in great gulps of fresh air and letting the night breezes cool her face. Her nose twitched, and only at the last moment did she remember to drag off one of her latex gloves before giving her nose the scratch it had been craving for the past quarter of an hour.

'Bit rough down there, isn't it?'

Sam looked up to see Colin Flannery. 'A *bit*? If you don't lose at least one SOCO to the rats I'll be surprised.'

Flannery laughed. She ripped off her protective suit and kicked her boots across the field, keen to escape the filth and smell which had permeated every fibre. He patiently collected all her kit and dropped it inside a black exhibit bag.

She sighed guiltily. 'Sorry.'

He was understanding. 'At least he wasn't cut open.'

'No, I suppose that's something. How long before you get the body out?'

'We haven't quite finished with the drain yet. Say a couple of hours. It's going to be a tricky one.'

'They always are.'

'True enough. What time do you intend to do the PM?'

Sam looked at her watch. 'It's getting on a bit now and I'm all in. Let's leave it until tomorrow, shall we?'

'Nine o'clock?'

'Make it half past. Give me a chance to catch up with some work – and sleep.'

'Half past it is. What about the plan-of-action meeting?'

'Let's wing this one. See what happens.'

Flannery was not keen on the idea of 'winging' anything. It went against the grain. He decided, however, that this wasn't the time or place to get into an argument about PM procedure and that he'd sort it out in the morning. Turning on his heel, he rejoined his colleagues at the top of the drainage shaft.

Sam headed back to her car, her one thought to get home, plunge her hot, sticky body into a cool shower and wash away the traumas of the day.

Tom Adams's voice cut into her reverie. 'I take it it is Strachan?'

'Yes. Why? Someone else from the base gone missing?'

Adams shook his head. 'Someone's going to get their arse kicked over this. We've already spent most of the force's overtime budget and he was here all the time.'

'Difficult to spot, though, stuffed up the drainage pipe.'

'If the idle sods had got their act together and gone down the shaft, instead of just having a quick look down it, we could have saved ourselves a lot of time and trouble. Now we're back to square one.'

'You don't know they didn't.'

'Don't I?'

There a brief pause, then Tom asked, 'How did he die? Or do you want to wait until you've had time to tell your friends from the FBI first?'

Sam kept walking. 'I've told them nothing I hadn't already told you.'

He wasn't appeased. 'You shouldn't have told them anything without checking with us first. You knew that.'

Sam stopped walking and turned to face him. 'Are you going to tell Farmer?'

'I should. But I won't.' He was well aware of the problems it would cause, not just for Sam but for everyone else too, if Farmer found out what had been going on.

'Thanks.'

'But don't rely on me, Sam. I'm a professional doing a professional job and I always thought you were too.'

'It won't happen again.'

'Where have I heard that one before?'

Sam knew she had no real defence, so changed the subject. 'Where is Farmer, by the way?'

'Away. We've tried to contact her but she's not answering her bleeper and no one seems to know where she is. She was supposed to be seeing your friends the FBI agents tomorrow, but we've had to cancel that. There'll be a row when she finds out about Strachan.'

Sam walked slowly on, and he resumed his questioning. 'So how did he die?'

'Can't be entirely sure. He's in a bit of a mess. We'll have to get him cleaned up a bit, but it looks as though he's been shot in the head.'

'Not cut open?'

'No, nothing like that. Just a good old straight-forward murder. I'll be able to tell you a lot more after the PM.'

He realised there was little point in pursuing the subject: she'd told him all she could for the time being. And they had other things to discuss. 'So,' he said, 'how have you been?'

'Well, I haven't had a mental breakdown yet.'

'I didn't want it to end like this, but it would never have worked. We just want different things out of life, that's all.'

'I know.'

Adams halted in mid-stride as Liz Fenwick ran up behind him. 'Excuse me, To—' she noticed Sam staring at her '—sir, but the Crime Scene Manager would like to talk to you about moving the body.'

'Oh, right. I'll be along straight away.'

Sam gave Liz Fenwick the once-over. She was young, with smooth skin, a taut body and extremely long legs. There was also a familiarity in her voice when she talked to Tom that Sam didn't like.

He turned back to Sam. 'When do you intend to do the PM?' He was all cool professionalism again.

'Nine-thirty tomorrow.'

'Bit late, isn't it?'

'Not really. Flannery and his team are still working on the scene and it will be a while yet before they get the body out. Then it has to be taken to the mortuary and prepared, and, most important of all, it's late and I'm tired.'

Adams acquiesced, not wishing to make an issue of it.

Sam glanced across at him. 'Will you be there this time?'

'I'll have to be, especially if Farmer hasn't turned up.'

'Good. Only you missed the last one, remember?'

Sam turned and walked away before he had a chance to reply. She was angry and upset. It was something about the way the policewoman had spoken to him and his immediate change of attitude towards her. She had no proof, but she sensed that he'd lied when she asked him if he was involved with anyone else at the time of their split. There wasn't anything she could, or would want to, do about it, but the fact that he'd lied to her and the youthfulness of his new girlfriend made her unreasonably angry.

When she reached her car, Hammond was standing beside it. She wasn't in the mood for him or anyone else at the moment. 'Not now, Bob, not now.'

Hammond wasn't put off. 'I just need to talk to you about Strachan. It won't take a minute.'

'Ring me in the morning, or come to the PM.'

'What time?'

'Nine-thirty.' Sam checked herself for a moment. 'But I'd clear it with Inspector Adams first. I think we've upset him enough for one day.'

Sam noticed Doyle and Solheim standing a few yards behind him. She said to Doyle, 'No, there was no note, no omega sign, and he wasn't disembowelled.'

With that she climbed quickly into the car and threw her bag into the back, before pulling out of her parking place and racing down the road to the entrance of the base. As far as she was concerned, if she never saw Leeminghall again it would be too soon.

The now familiar smell of Irish stew bubbling on the hob greeted Sam when she dragged herself back into her cottage. While Liam was around she knew she wouldn't have to rely on her heavily scented garden to remind her that her sense of smell was still intact and working efficiently. She hung her jacket on the wooden stand by the front door and wandered into the kitchen, to find Liam stirring a giant metallic pot with one of her wooden spoons. Although it was good of him to have dinner cooked and ready when she arrived home, she wasn't in a particularly grateful mood.

'Is stew all you can make?'

Liam stopped stirring. 'Now that depends on what you mean.'

He was dancing around the question again. It was as if he enjoyed parodying himself.

'I mean, is stew the only thing you can cook?'

Liam had gauged Sam's mood the second she'd slammed the cottage door, and had decided to try and change it by being flippant. It was a risky strategy.

'Well,' he said, 'yes and no.'

Sam stared at him impatiently.

'You see, there's all sorts of stews and I can make most of them. Although they're all called stew, they're all different. So some would say that, yes, I can only make stew but, no, it's not the only dish I can cook because there are lots of different ones. If you see what I mean?'

Sam crossed to the table and poured herself a large glass of red wine. 'How did you know what time I'd be coming home? It's too late to ring the hospital.'

'I didn't. I made this about six, then when I heard your car in the drive I began to heat it through. It's almost ready.'

Sam turned away and went to the door. 'I'm not hungry.'

She went into the sitting-room and threw herself on

to the settee, almost spilling her wine. Picking up a magazine from a side-table, she began to flick aimlessly through the pages.

Liam watched her go. He'd seen her in this mood before and knew she'd have to be allowed to come round in her own time. He switched off the heat, put a lid on the pot, poured his own glass of wine and followed her into the sitting-room.

He joined her on the settee, making sure he sat far enough away not to invade her privacy but close enough to be able to listen.

'So, besides having to deal with yet another awful murder, what kind of a day have you had?'

Sam looked at him in surprise.

'Before you ask, it was on the news just before you got home.'

She took another swallow of wine. 'They'll be reporting them before they happen soon.'

She threw her magazine on to the floor in anger and frustration and searched for the TV remote control.

Liam spotted it first. 'It's on top of the television.'

Sam grunted. She couldn't be bothered to move, so she just pulled her knees up under her chin and sat staring blankly in front of her.

Liam guessed what the problem was. 'You saw Tom, then?'

She didn't react.

'You had to at some point. You're working on the same case.'

She turned her head towards him. 'Would you say I was still attractive?'

'Very, but then I'm biased.'

'For my age, I mean.'

'For any age.'

'He's got another woman. A girl.'

'Told you that, did he?'

'Didn't have to. I saw her. All legs and hair, with smooth skin.'

'Doesn't sound like Tom's type to me. Sounds like my type, though.'

'Oh, I know, young and pretty, that's everybody's type.'

He decided to play along with her. 'Not so much a woman, more a trophy?'

'Exactly.'

Sam was pleased that Liam understood so well; she hadn't expected him to.

'Are you quite sure about this girl?' he asked.

'Oh yes. You should have seen them together – little secret intimacies.'

'Who is she?'

'A policewoman on Tom's squad. I've seen her before and, boy, does she like to show it off.'

Liam hid a smile at Sam's jealousy. It was so unlike the calm, intelligent professional she had become over the years. When it comes to affairs of the heart, he thought, we all seem to come down to basics and logic goes right out of the window.

'He told me there wasn't anyone else,' Sam went on. 'He lied. That's what makes me so angry. I wonder how long it's been going on for? How long they've been laughing behind my back?'

He found all this highly irritating. 'I wish to Christ you'd stop feeling sorry for yourself. You wanted one thing out of life, and that's fine. Tom wanted something different, and that's fine too. If he is having a relationship with this girl, it's more to do with company and comfort than anything else, and, if you'll take my word for it, as soon as he's got over you he'll get rid of her.'

'Do you think it could have worked?'

'Maybe, if you'd both been different people, but you're not and that's all there is to it. You've got to move on.'

'Move on to what?'

'At the moment, Sam, your work is everything, and until you can find someone willing to share you with your ambition, you're going to have to be very patient.'

Sam pouted. It wasn't what she wanted to hear, even though it was true.

'Besides, this isn't so much about losing Tom as about who you think you lost him to.'

Sam put her hands either side of her face and pulled her skin tightly backwards. 'Do you think a facelift would help?'

'No. You'd end up with one of those permanent smiles on your face. Like those dreadful Hollywood wives.'

He drew an exaggeratedly wide smile across his face, which made Sam laugh. She began to relax and stretched her legs out across his lap. He picked up her foot and stroked it.

'Who was that big ugly bastard in the students' garden?' he asked.

'Edward Doyle. He's an FBI agent helping us out with the murders.'

'You watch yourself with that one. He's a bully and a man who likes his own way and doesn't much care what he has to do to get it.'

Sam was touched by his concern. 'I can handle the Ed Doyles of this world.'

He smiled at her, unconvinced by her bravado.

She began to run the ball of her foot idly up and down his leg. 'We were good together once, weren't we?'

'Once.'

'Think we could be again?'

'Who knows? Maybe. Depends whether I could cope with your ambition or not.'

'Perhaps we could capture the passion again, for old times' sake?'

Liam grinned. 'Now there's the best offer I've had for years.'

Sam waited, her eyes fixed on his face.

'Normally I couldn't think of anyone I'd rather say yes to, but right now I feel I'd be taking advantage.'

'Rejected twice in one week. I'm not sure I can take it.'

'Only twice? Besides I'm not rejecting you.'

'More Irish logic?'

'You don't want me, you just want to get even with Tom. Besides, I'm not into one-night stands.'

'Might not be a one-night stand.'

'I'm afraid it would. I'm leaving tomorrow.'

'*What?*' Sam sat bolt upright in alarm.

'I was going to tell you but you weren't around much and the right moment never seemed to arrive.'

'What about the Cambridge job?'

'Didn't get it. Gave it to some sculptor from Glasgow. Apparently he can drink more than I can.'

'Why didn't you tell me?'

'As I said, it was difficult, and you had enough of your own problems. Thought I might hang around and see it through with you before I bugger off.'

'What are you going to do? Where are you going to go?'

'I've got a job in Sydney.'

'Australia?'

'Well it's not Donegal.'

'Sure it's far enough away?'

'It's all I could get. Besides, the English have been sending Irishmen to Australia for years.'

Liam thought Sam looked suddenly desperate. 'It's only a short-term contract, twelve months to be precise.'

Sam still felt a slight twinge of panic at the thought of losing him. 'Doing what?'

'University post. Teaching English.'

Suddenly, Sam pushed herself across to him and, sitting across his lap, ran her hands through his greying black hair and kissed him passionately on the lips, letting her tongue explore the inside of his mouth for the first time in over twenty years.

After a few moments he pulled away from her. 'I told you,' he said gently, 'I'm not going to take advantage of the situation.'

Sam said nothing, just sat breathing deeply and looking into his eyes, her fingers stroking his face and pulling at his hair.

It was more than he could take. 'Oh, to hell with this, let's play the advantage rule.'

Cupping his hands behind her head, he pulled her back towards him and kissed her deeply. Then he picked her up and carried her up the stairs to bed.

It was still dark when Sam woke. The dawn chorus had only just begun and was filling the air with sweetly piercing song. Normally she enjoyed it, but not today. Today she was just too tired.

She glanced across to see if Liam was still there, but he was gone. A note was held in position by a pale-pink rose. He was on an early-morning flight and had booked a taxi for 4 a.m. She'd told him to wake her but he'd chosen to slip away and leave her sleeping on. Given her current state, he was probably right.

The note was pinned upside down in mock Australian style. She sat up and pulled it carefully from under the rose. Although the rose was beautiful and its scent filled the air, it was, like many wild things, still dangerous and its thorns could quite easily pierce and cut the flesh. Sam wondered if he was using poetic irony to try and tell her something. The note was short.

> I'm no prince to wake you with a kiss,
> But looking at your face, it's one that I'll miss.
> Lots of love, Liam. XX.

She got out of bed, went over to her large mahogany chest of drawers and took out of the bottom drawer an old shoe box. In it she kept all the letters and notes that

Liam had sent her over the years. There weren't many, and they fitted comfortably into the small box. She dropped the note into the box, smiling at the memories its contents brought back and wondering when she'd see him again. Not for years, probably.

She didn't regret sleeping with Liam – in fact she'd enjoyed it. She wondered if that was because it was safe. He was leaving, so there was no chance of it leading to anything more. Perhaps that was what her sex life was all about: occasional passionate meetings with no complications. It certainly fitted into her lifestyle, but what of the future? She was too tired to consider that now. She put the box back in the drawer and wandered into the bathroom to shower.

By the time Sam arrived at the mortuary all the early preparation had been completed. The samples from the body had all been collected and preserved, the X-rays taken and the body washed. Flannery and his team must have been there all night, she thought, and not for the first time. Colin had a way of instilling into his team a loyalty and passion which kept them working long hours in the most inhospitable of places and enjoying every moment.

Tom Adams was changed and waiting outside the mortuary when Sam breezed purposefully past him into the room. To her surprise, Farmer was still missing. As the chief investigating officer, she should have been there. In all the time Sam had conducted PMs, especially of this importance, she had never known Farmer to miss one. She glanced up towards the gallery. Again to her surprise, Doyle, Solheim and Hammond were there. They must have made their peace with Tom, she thought, although how much Doyle had told him about the case was another matter.

Strachan's naked body lay cold and grey along the top of a stainless-steel table, his head raised slightly on a moulded plastic block. At least he now looked like a human being, not the evil apparition that had greeted her when she climbed down the drainage shaft.

She moved quickly through the basic examination, noting his height, weight and any apparent injuries and marks, measuring them as she moved her way along the body. Fred then pulled the body on to its side giving her a clear view of the underside. At first there seemed to be nothing obvious and then, just as Fred was going to drop the body back into position, Sam noticed something.

'There is a small, thin injury to the back of the neck' – Fred handed her a ruler and she measured it – 'measuring two and a half inches.' She handed the ruler back to Fred. 'It matches the one found on Mary West's body almost identically, in everything except the location of the wound.'

She stepped back from the table. 'I'd like plenty of photographs of this, please.'

The SOCO photographer came forward and took several shots. Once he was done, Sam continued. She took scrapings from beneath all the nails and then clipped them short. This was followed by vigorously combing through all the visible hair, both head and pubic. Everything was dropped into exhibit bags and sealed for later analysis. Next, Fred handed her swabs of various lengths. Taking them one at a time, she ran them around and inside Strachan's nose, mouth and anus.

As she pushed a swab deep into Strachan's penis, Adams closed his eyes and looked down at his feet. No matter how many times he saw it done, it still made him wince.

Now to the skull. Sam had already inspected the X-rays and seen that there was some hard object buried inside Strachan's head. When she'd first viewed the body she'd thought the head-wound must have been caused by a bullet, but the object piercing Strachan's brain was too long and thin and was flattened at the end. It was like nothing she'd seen before, and she was eager to discover what it was.

She stood back while Fred first cut and then shaved the area around the wound with a disposable plastic razor. When he'd finished, Sam measured first the diameter of the wound and then its distance from the top of the right ear and from the centre of the head. 'The wound is three-quarters of an inch in diameter,' she dictated, 'four inches from the top of the subject's right ear and six and a half inches from the centre of his head.' These measurements helped establish the wound's position in relation to the rest of the head and made it easier for a lay jury to understand exactly where the injury was situated.

She turned her attention to the entry wound and examined it first by eye, then with her fingers. 'There is some powder tattooing to the scalp, indicating that the shot was fired at close range, probably point-blank.' She would normally have expected more powder marks, but, given the circumstances in which the body was found, they had probably been washed, or even wiped, away.

'The skin around the absorption ring has been stretched. It's smooth and discoloured, brown. There are also some splits and abrasions to the skin around the wound.'

Fred passed her a scalpel. She made two incisions, one behind each ear, before drawing the scalpel across the top of the head and joining the two incisions together. Using only her fingers, she began to reflect the scalp, pulling the skin down to expose the skull beneath. Again she measured and examined the entry wound. This time the pattern was ragged and irregular, with fracture lines, caused by the impact of the projectile, radiating outwards from the injury. The skull itself, however, had stayed in one piece, which was a help. Powerful impact wounds could shatter a skull and then the only thing holding it together was the flesh covering it. When that was removed the skull would fall to pieces in her hand. Fred passed her a cranium saw and she began to saw around the skull cap.

In the gallery, Doyle grimaced. The sound always reminded him of the dentist's drill, and the drill was precisely why he hadn't been to the dentist for over ten years.

The skull cap was removed by Fred and placed on a tray. Sam began her examination of the brain. It was swollen and had been badly disturbed by the projectile's entry, with sections damaged and torn in different directions. Sam could see the tip of the object. It was a few centimetres inside the bloody remnants of the brain. She pushed her fingers into the soft tissue and carefully pulled the object out.

Adams stepped forward, and in the gallery Doyle craned his neck to see, both men as interested as Sam in seeing what it was. Holding it in the flat of her hand, she showed them. It was not, as the two detectives had expected, some kind of specialist bullet, but a two-inch masonry nail.

Back in her office, Sam held the clear plastic exhibit bag up to the light and looked closely at the object it contained. She had dealt with some bizarre and unusual deaths in her time, but never before had she seen anyone who'd had a nail driven through their skull. In view of the circumstances in which Mary West had been found, Sam thought it would have been more appropriate for him to have been found with a stake through his heart.

A knock at the door announced the arrival of Adams, Doyle, Solheim and Hammond. They came into the room two steps behind Jean, who indicated that they should sit in the three armchairs in the centre of the office.

'Tea?' Jean's voice was as efficient as ever.

'I'd prefer coffee, ma'am, if that's not a problem.' Doyle was unusually deferential. Jean had that effect on people. They seemed to be almost afraid of her.

'Not at all. Coffee it is. Is that OK for everyone?'

They all nodded and Jean went out, closing the door firmly behind her.

Sam asked Adams, 'Where's Superintendent Farmer?'

'Otherwise engaged.'

The truth was that he hadn't a clue, but he didn't want to admit that in front of the Americans. The phone call he'd received from the divisional commander revealed that the top brass didn't know where she was, either. He'd decided to give it until the end of the day before he started looking for her. If she was following up some independent lead, she wouldn't thank him for interfering.

'So what can you tell us?' asked Doyle.

'The cause of death was massive brain injury caused when this' – she held up the masonry nail in its exhibit bag – 'was driven into the back of his skull. But how it was done I'm not sure. Obviously a great deal of force was used.'

'Nail-gun?'

Everyone turned to Hammond.

'We've got workmen on the base at the moment. They're doing some repair work to one of the hangars. I noticed they were using nail-guns when I made one of my inspection tours a couple of weeks ago.'

'But there were powder burns to the skin,' objected Sam.

'It operates almost the same way as a gun, so that would be consistent.'

Annoyance clear in his voice, Adams said, 'There weren't any workmen on the list of base personnel you gave me.'

'They're not base personnel. They're outside contractors, local guys. Besides, they'd finished working the day before Mary West was killed.'

'They never reported the theft of a nail-gun?'

'Not that I know of. But then there's a lot of petty theft on the base, so I don't always get to hear.'

'Do you think you could find out?'

Adams's sarcasm reminded Sam of Farmer. She might not be there in person but she certainly was in spirit.

'I'll get it done as soon as we've finished up here,' promised Hammond.

'I'll want the name of the company you employed to do the work as well.'

Hammond nodded.

Sam turned back to Doyle. 'Were any of the other victims killed like this?'

He shook his head. 'No, they were all stabbed. Well, the ones where we could establish a cause of death – some were too far gone. No nails, though, I'm sure of that.'

Adams was sitting on the edge of his seat. 'What other victims?' he demanded furiously. 'Will someone tell me what the bloody hell is going on here?'

Doyle hastened to enlighten him. 'We think that both Mary West's and Strachan's deaths could be linked to a series of deaths that I've been investigating in the States over the past few years.'

So Farmer was right about the FBI's reason for being there, thought Adams. His anger grew. 'And you've only just decided to tell us?'

'We were going to tell your Superintendent Farmer this afternoon, but the meeting was cancelled.'

'But in the meantime you thought it better to talk to your local friendly pathologist before you talked to us?'

'No point bothering you if we were wrong. Didn't

want to make fools of ourselves. Doctor Ryan just helped to point us in the right direction. Now we believe it is the same man, we are more than happy to liaise with the British police.'

'Good of you,' he said acidly, and glared across at Sam.

She ignored him and said, 'There was a mark on both Mary West's and Strachan's bodies, like an electrical burn.'

She pulled a photograph from a file on her desk and handed it to Doyle. It was a colour shot of the mark she'd found on Mary West's neck. 'Seen anything like it before?'

He studied it for a moment, moving it around in his hand to see the injury from different angles. 'I'm not entirely sure but I think I have. I'll have to get my hands on some of the PM photographs to be positive.' He gave a half-laugh. 'Never linked them before.'

Doyle was annoyed at himself. He'd thought he knew everything about this particular killer and the way he operated. He didn't, and it had taken a woman to point that out. It was a hard lesson.

Sam could feel her excitement mounting. 'Can you remember which of the women had the marks?'

'No. It rather depends whether the pathologist noticed it or not. It might have been missed or marked off as an incidental injury.'

Remembering her own initial assumptions about the injuries Sam could understand how that might happen. 'How long before you can get copies of the photographs?'

'I'll fax Quantico this evening. Couple of days.'

Adams interjected, 'So several of these woman did have similar injuries and the FBI never made a connection? Not very impressive.' Adams was still furious at being left in the dark about the case, and was looking to bite back.

Doyle stayed resolutely calm. 'Several of the victims were dead and buried before we became involved. Others weren't discovered until after their bodies were badly decomposed, making it almost impossible to obtain any worthwhile evidence from them. Perhaps if we'd had the luxury – if that's the word in the circumstances – of two murders at the same location over a very short period of time, and all the bodies had been easily recognisable as human beings, then perhaps we wouldn't have missed things either.'

The two men's eyes met in a hostile stare.

Hammond hastily intervened. He asked Sam, 'So what do you think happened?'

Sam glanced at Adams, looking for signs of disapproval before speaking. He seemed to have relaxed a little, so she said, 'Strachan was either raping or having violent sex with Mary West when he was shot in the back of the head with the nail-gun. That would explain the presence of his blood at the back of the hangar. After which our killer forced a plastic bag over his head, stemming the flow of blood to the ground. I found one stuck under Strachan's head. It was probably ripped off when his body was forced through the pipe, which would explain why there was blood at the scene and nothing leading to the sewer pipe.'

'Because it was caught in the bag?' asked Hammond.

Sam nodded.

'Clever.'

She continued, 'He then dragged or carried West to the shed, where he killed her.'

Adams jumped in. 'Who did he move first, Strachan or West?'

Sam shrugged. 'Strachan, I would think.'

'Leaving West alone? Wouldn't she have taken the hint and legged it?'

Doyle could also see the hole in her argument, but was more cautious in his criticism. 'Could the West girl have been immobilised in some way' – Sam thought he made her sound like a car, but let it go – 'giving the killer time to dump Strachan's body before returning to collect the girl? The shaft was only a few yards from the hangar. It couldn't have taken him that long.'

'There were no marks on her wrists and ankles,' Sam said, 'and no indication that she had been beaten unconscious. Could there be more than one person involved? That would certainly answer some of the questions.'

Doyle was adamant. 'No, there is only one person involved in this.'

Adams pressed the point. 'How can you be so sure of that?'

'I'm sure. I've been chasing him for long enough. I know him better than I know myself.'

'Then why haven't you caught him yet?'

Adams knew the question would annoy Doyle. He also knew that the real reason Doyle had kept the enquiry secret until the very last moment was that he was worried that the British police would step in and take all the glory. Adams knew this because, to be honest, he'd have done just the same. Doyle must be feeling like a marathon runner who'd been in the lead for the entire race, only to be beaten at the finishing tape.

Jean came in with the coffee tray as the visitors were getting up to leave. 'Oh, you're all going?'

All three men apologised and Jean took it with good grace, smiling and beginning to back out of the room again. As she did, Trevor Stuart appeared beside her and lifted one of the cups from the tray.

'For me, Jean? Wonderful. And I didn't even have to make an appointment.'

Jean scowled at him, before resuming her backwards retreat from the office.

Sam introduced him. 'This is Doctor Trevor Stuart, my colleague in pathology. This is Agent Edward Doyle, from the FBI's Behavioral Science Unit in Quantico, and his colleague, Agent Catherine Solheim. Inspector Adams you know, and this is Major Robert Hammond, the senior security officer from Leeminghall air base.'

'Bob, long time no see. Still having those wonderful parties, I hear.'

'When we get the chance.'

Clearly taken with her, Stuart turned to Solheim. 'How long do you expect to be staying in Cambridge?'

'Not too sure yet,' she said. 'Depends on the enquiry.'

He nodded understandingly. 'Where are you staying?'

'Leeminghall.'

'Excellent. Have you had a chance to see our wonderful city yet?'

Hammond said firmly, 'That's already taken care of, Doctor Stuart.' He took Solheim's arm and guided her towards the door.

Stuart looked disappointed. 'Really? What a shame. Another time perhaps.'

Hammond shook his head. 'I doubt it.'

As the remainder of the team prepared to leave, Doyle turned to Sam. 'Any chance of seeing the pathology report?'

'You'll have to ask the inspector. I think I've done enough favours for one lifetime.'

Adams stared at her, stony-faced. He wasn't placated by her conformity and was convinced it wouldn't last. He said to Doyle, 'I think you're going to have to wait until after your interview with the superintendent. It will be up to her.'

'Whenever that will be.'

Adams shrugged indifferently and went out. Sam sank, greatly relieved, into her chair.

As soon as everyone had gone, Trevor Stuart put his coffee down and pulled Sam's jacket off its hook on the back of the door. 'Come on, I'm taking you out.'

He lifted her out of her seat and began to slip her jacket around her shoulders.

'Where? I'm busy. I don't have time for this.'

'The abattoir at Morton.' He took her arm and half dragged her towards the door.

'Where? Well, you certainly know how to show a girl a good time.'

He paused and smiled confidently down at her. 'I think I've discovered what caused that mark you found on Mary West's neck. Interested now?'

Sam pulled her jacket on properly and willingly followed him out of the office and down to his car.

As soon as they were clear of the city traffic, Stuart looked shrewdly across at Sam and asked, 'What's going on?'

Sam shrugged and shook her head, trying her best to look as though she didn't know what he meant.

But he knew her too well. 'Oh come on. FBI agents from the States, Hammond sitting in on meetings. Not exactly another day at the office.'

'You know why. They're investigating the murders of Mary West and Ray Strachan at the base. It's officially American soil, so they're taking an interest. That's all.'

'These are local murders, normally dealt with by local plods. Don't make me beg.'

Sam smiled. She'd known Trevor since she'd arrived at Cambridge and, although he was going through a mid-life crisis of mammoth proportions, he was a good friend and colleague and she trusted him.

She gave in gracefully. 'They're linking the deaths to several similar ones in the States.'

'A serial killer?'

'Looks like it.'

'How have they linked them?'

'They're all women, and although there's no particular type the MO is very particular. And recently they've identified a link with American Air Force bases.'

Trevor thought this over. 'Raped?'

'No. Well, not that they know of.'

'West was raped.'

'But not by our killer. We think she was probably raped by Strachan, who was then murdered.'

'Because he got in the way?'

Sam nodded. 'We're still waiting for the DNA evidence but I think it will support my theory.'

'Look, I know you like getting involved in your cases outside the lab, but I think you should leave this one alone. If you're dealing with a serial killer, that's as dangerous as it gets. You're getting in over your head this time, Sam.'

'Don't start worrying. I'm a big girl now. Besides, I've almost finished. There's not much more I can do.'

'Good.'

'Unless they find another body, of course.'

He realised it was hopeless. He'd just have to keep an eye on her for a little while and, if things did get a bit hot, arrange for her to be taken quietly off the case. He still had enough clout with the hospital to do that, and after all it was for her own good. In the meantime, he'd better concentrate on his driving.

Morton was a pretty little village, about twelve miles outside Cambridge, dating back at least four hundred years. In an age of new developments and out-of-town shopping centres it had remained largely untouched, and had consequently been gradually taken over by affluent commuters and those able to afford two homes. The announcement, about five years previously, that an abattoir was to be built there had aroused fierce opposition from the villagers, who collectively wielded a lot of political and monetary power. Eventually a compromise was reached, and the buildings were erected two miles to the east of the village – though even there the development still caused much offence.

When they arrived, Trevor parked in the spot marked Managing Director and jumped out. As he walked towards the main door, a large, overweight man in a smart blue suit came out to meet him. They shook hands, then Trevor brought him across to meet Sam.

'Sam, this is Peter King, the abattoir manager. He's going to help us solve a small problem. Peter, this is Doctor Ryan, the pathologist I was telling you about.'

King held out his hand and Sam shook it. There was nothing firm about his handshake. In fact it was soft and flabby and made Sam uncomfortable.

'Pleased to meet you, ma'am.'

The American accent took her by surprise for a moment. Then she remembered that this and several other similar abattoirs up and down the country had been built by an American company. It was a large multinational, with abattoirs and meat-processing plants all over the US, and was now moving into Europe in a big way.

In one hand King was carrying something wrapped in a white rag. Sam was curious but didn't ask what it was. She guessed that if it was relevant he'd show her in his own sweet time.

He gestured towards the slaughterhouses. 'If you'd like to step this way, I think we should be able to get the demonstration over quite quickly.'

As Sam followed the two men towards the slaughter-houses, a consignment of sheep and pigs arrived. Sam was used to death and no vegetarian – she thoroughly enjoyed meat – but she found the sight of these hapless creatures being shepherded out of the lorries to their slaughter disturbing. She just hoped that they had been treated well beforehand.

The way to the slaughterhouses took them through several of the sheds where animals and meat were in various stages of being processed. Sam didn't like the place. It smelt of death, and the pathetic bleating sounds of the animals as they were lined up before being killed was truly awful.

At the far end of the factory, there was a small holding shed with metal pens of all sizes. They made their way to one of the small pens at the centre of the shed, where a solitary pig was waiting. The pen was so small that the animal could move neither backwards nor forwards but only stand and move its legs from side to side in a desperate effort to get comfortable.

King looked down at it, not with compassion but almost with contentment. It sent a shiver up Sam's spine, and she wondered what he and Trevor had in mind. King unwrapped the object he'd been carrying. It looked like a Y-shaped gun with a black button or trigger on the side; on the inside of each Y section were small metal tips. King handed it to Trevor Stuart, who held it up in front of Sam and pressed the button. There was a sudden flash and a loud crackle as a thin steak of blue and white electricity, like a lightning bolt, spat across the Y-shaped tip of the object from one metal point to the other.

Trevor smiled at Sam's startled face. 'It's a stun gun.'

He passed it to her and she examined it closely, taking care to keep her fingers well away from the trigger.

'Remember that civil rights conference I spoke at?' he said.

She nodded.

'I was shown some photographs of political prisoners after they'd been tortured. Bodies mostly – they certainly don't muck about in some of those countries. Anyway, I noticed that some of the injuries were similar to the ones you'd shown me on the PM photographs of Mary West and also to the ones I'd seen on the young boy who died trying to retrieve his kite. So I asked about them. They were caused by one of these being pressed against the flesh and then discharged.'

'But where the hell would anyone get them from?'

'Us mainly. Apparently we sell quite a lot.'

Sam was flabbergasted.

'Anyway, by controlling the amount of electricity that flows through the machine you can either seriously hurt, especially if the instrument is applied to certain vulnerable parts of the body, or, if necessary, stun somebody, knock them out. They're becoming popular with muggers, apparently. Are you catching my drift?'

She was.

'Let me show you. Peter?'

Peter King placed the device against the back of the pig's neck and pulled the trigger. The result was immediate. The pig's legs buckled and, despite the limited space, it collapsed immediately to the floor. Sam was horrified. The photographs would have been sufficient to convince both her and the police. There really was no need for this. All it did was satisfy Trevor's love of the theatrical. He beckoned her across and they crouched down by the still-twitching animal.

'Have you killed it?' she asked King.

'No, ma'am, just stunned it a little. It'll be OK in a few moments.'

'Then you can slaughter it?'

King shrugged.

'Look, look at this,' said Trevor.

Sam looked where he was pointing. On the back of the pig's neck was a long thin burn mark identical to those she'd found on Mary West and Ray Strachan.

CHAPTER EIGHT

Solheim's tour of Cambridge took the whole of the afternoon and most of the evening. After their meeting with Superintendent Farmer had been cancelled Doyle had decided to go over his notes to reassure himself that there was nothing else he'd missed, so she'd found herself with a free afternoon. Hammond was quick to respond and, armed with a tour guide, they managed to visit all the old colleges and even a couple of the new ones, after which Hammond took her for a short punt along the Backs followed by dinner at a small, intimate restaurant by the side of Magdalene Bridge.

He was the perfect companion, pleasant, attentive and informative. She felt happy and relaxed enough with him to take his arm as they strolled through the streets that afternoon, enjoying the illusion that they had been together for years.

At the end of the evening they went back to Hammond's apartment. As they went in, Solheim automatically reached out to turn on the light, but his hand on her arm stopped her. The room wasn't entirely in darkness. Moonlight shining through the windows gave enough cool blue light to see by, glazing all the surfaces with the silvery mystery of a summer's evening. Hammond turned her to face him and, cupping her chin in one hand, tilted her head up to his and kissed her. She responded at once, returning his kiss with passion and running her hands across the back of his neck. Their caresses became more urgent and intense, and Hammond lifted her and carried her into his bedroom.

Laying her gently on the bed, he whispered in her ear, 'Are you sure about this?'

She smiled and ran her finger across his lips, silencing him. As he caressed her body, her response was immediate. Her mouth opened, her arms stretched above her head and she moaned gently. Hammond felt that if he didn't get his pants off soon he would explode with excitement. She stroked his neck, running her long fingers over the back of his head as she pulled him down towards her.

Once Sam found out about Ricky's proposed adventure she had promptly become involved in the preparations. It was wrong of her, she knew. There had to come a time when he stood on his own two feet, and if anyone had tried to interfere with her plans at the same age she would have resented the hell out of them. But Ricky, she told herself, was different. She had been more mature, knew a little more about the way of the world.

His route had been planned, his passport checked and all his visas acquired. She'd even ended up re-packing his backpack while Wyn stood to one side protesting, 'He's got to learn to do it on his own.'

Sam had ignored her sister and continued with her

demonstration, while Ricky and Tracy watched with a detached air from their seats at the kitchen table. When she'd finished, Ricky stood and walked over to her.

'You know what's going to happen, don't you?' he said.

Sam looked at him, puzzled.

'The first thing I'm going to need will be at the bottom of the bag and I'll have to take everything out to get it.'

She was having none of it. 'The bag has been packed logically, so that shouldn't happen.'

'That's fine if you're dealing with a logical person. But I'm not logical.'

Sam stared at him for a moment in silence, while Tracy tried not to giggle. He was right, of course, and eventually he would have to do it his own way, just as Wyn said, but at least she could give him a good start.

She'd offered to drive them to London, and then suggested that, having travelled that far, she could easily take them as far as Dover. At that point Ricky became alarmed, convinced that his aunt was going to follow them to Katmandu, and said firmly that they would revert to the original plan. Sam had to content herself with ferrying them to Cambridge station.

The roads into Cambridge seemed busier than usual. There was no obvious reason, apart from the sheer volume of traffic, but they were already late and Sam was becoming increasingly anxious. It had taken longer than she'd expected to collect Tracy from her parents' house and for them to say their goodbyes, and now this. It would be ridiculous if the two young people missed the train, the first stage of their trek. The traffic eased a little, and she managed to make up some time, reaching Station Road fairly quickly.

The war memorial at the junction brought a lump to Sam's throat. It was a large bronze of a young man going cheerfully off to war, waving encouragingly to others. It was silly and over-dramatic but for a moment the statue's face looked like Ricky's. She pushed the thought away and drove on to the station. She found a parking spot near the entrance. Everyone spilled out of the car and helped unpack Ricky and Tracy's backpacks and various carrier bags, full of assorted staple foods, which Wyn had insisted they take.

When they reached the platform, the London train was already in, so they hastily bundled everything aboard and made sure that the two travellers had decent seats. Then they climbed back down on to the platform to say their farewells.

Sam waited while Wyn gave Ricky and Tracy a final hug and kiss, then took her nephew in her arms and gave him a warm hug.

'Now listen, you've got my number. Any problems, any at all, and you call me, you understand? You call me.'

Ricky hugged her back. 'Thanks for everything, Aunty Sam. I might not have made it without you.'

'Don't be silly, of course you would.'

She squeezed his hand, forcing a further £50 pounds into it.

'I think you've already done enough for us,' he said. 'There really is no need.'

He tried to hand it back but Sam wouldn't take it. 'It's to pay for all those phone calls you're going to make to your mother and me.'

'You gave me a phone card for that.'

'You might lose it. Who knows?'

The guard blew his whistle, and, after giving everyone one last hug, Ricky and Tracy jumped back on to the train. Seconds later it was moving out of the station, gathering speed rapidly. Sam looked across at her sister and saw tears running down her cheeks. She put her arm around Wyn's shoulders and, as the train disappeared from sight, gave her a hug.

'Don't worry too much about him,' she said gently. 'It's not so much about whether Ricky is ready for the world as whether the world is ready for Ricky.'

Wyn managed a smile. Thousands of young men and women did the same thing every year and they all came home safely. But Wyn, unlike her more adventurous sister, had never experienced the open road and couldn't be easy in her mind about cutting her only son loose.

Sam slipped her arm inside her sister's. 'Come on, let's have a cup of tea. The café here's supposed to be quite good, and if it makes you feel any better you can pay.'

'That makes me feel much better.'

They turned their backs on the empty tracks and retraced their steps along the platform.

As he finished knotting his tie, Hammond looked across the bedroom at Solheim. The sight of her firm body lying under a thin white sheet made him want to undress again and join her. He watched, almost mesmerised, as she arched her back and bit her bottom lip. Hammond had slept with a number of women during his career. Some had been beautiful, some not, but in all his life he could never remember seeing a woman as stunning as Solheim looked at that moment. Just the memory of her young body beneath his hands was enough to make his heart race. He was glad he'd kept in shape. That, combined with good looks and a charm born of a genuine interest in, and love of, female company, had brought him continued success with women, even though he was now in his middle years.

But, however much he wanted her, he wasn't sure he could manage another session. It was going to be a long day and he needed all the strength he had left. General Brown was due to make his last inspection before flying himself back to the States, and Hammond knew that, no matter how good the work was, the general would inevitably find fault – if only in order to justify his existence.

He finished dressing and walked across to Solheim, leant down and kissed her on the mouth. Before he realised what was happening, her arms were around his neck and her lips pressed hard against his. He tried to stand, but found that he was lifting her up with him, her grip strong and unshakeable. He chuckled, and reluctantly disentangled himself from her hold, leaving her kneeling naked and wistful on the edge of the bed.

'I'll see you tonight,' he said.

She lay back, looking at him through half-closed eyes. 'Maybe.'

He waited.

'Or maybe I'll call that nice Doctor Stuart, see what he's doing.'

Hammond was not to be drawn. 'I'll see you tonight. And don't be long – Doyle is bound to start looking for you.'

He went out, closing the door quietly behind him, and made his way across to his office.

Solheim got slowly out of bed and headed for the bathroom to shower. She'd enjoyed the previous day's and night's activities. Hammond was a good lover, taking the lead without being overbearing, and for a man of his age he had impressive staying power. They hadn't slept much so she was tired and hoped that Doyle hadn't arranged too strenuous a day. She wondered whether she ought to meet Hammond that evening and decided that she would; she could catch up on her sleep when she got back to the States.

Drying herself, she wandered into the sitting-room. The room was large and, unlike her own, which was a permanent mess, perfectly tidy. She couldn't help reflect, however, that it looked more like an office than a sitting-room. Everything was spotless. Arranged around the walls were numerous photographs of Hammond in uniform and on a variety of military courses, along with the certificates he had obtained from attending them. Strangely, there were no photos of friends, family or girlfriends. Various bits of memorabilia decorated the tops of his cupboards and shelves: police helmets from England, Germany and France, as well as several from the States. His books consisted mainly of military law, though there were also a number of works of literary criticism, some poetry and several biographies of writers.

She didn't like the room. It was too 'just so': no warmth, no deep-rooted personality. She wasn't sure if this was Hammond's fault or the fault of the military. This was a society which always seemed to be on the move, forcing people to live their lives one step ahead of the next posting. She went back into the bedroom to dress.

After dropping Wyn at home, Sam set off back to the cottage. She'd hoped to see her mother, but it was her afternoon at the day centre and Wyn appreciated the break. Sam had booked the remainder of the day off and was determined to spend most of it in the garden, catching up with all the jobs she had neglected over the past weeks. She felt terribly tired, almost drained, and was ready for a break. She stopped off at the local travel agent on the way home and picked up armfuls of holiday brochures. All she wanted was a quiet beach in a far-away place, a beach towel and a novel to read.

When she got home, she dumped the brochures on the settee along with the crumpled papers and letters. She knew the cottage needed a good clean and tidy but when it was a choice between house and garden the garden won every time. She had advertised for a cleaner but was still waiting for a response. She loved the cottage's remoteness, but that remoteness, when viewed as a prospective place of employment, seemed to put people off.

She changed into her gardening clothes and wellingtons and went outside. As she headed towards the shed, she heard the familiar sound of car wheels on the gravel drive. For a moment she was cross; she hoped it was nothing urgent. She went round to the front of the house where, to her surprise, Harriet Farmer was standing by the front door.

'Superintendent?'

'Doctor Ryan, I hope you don't mind me calling. I need a quick word.'

The moment Farmer had turned towards her, Sam noticed a difference. Her hair was no longer pulled tightly to the back of her head but lay loose across her shoulders, held in place by a black hairband. The formal dark suit and sensible shoes had gone too, and been replaced by an attractive summer dress and sandals. Her face seemed calmer and more relaxed.

Sam was intrigued. 'Coffee?'

Farmer nodded and followed her round to the back of the cottage.

Sam brought the two coffees out to the patio. She found Farmer admiring and smelling a particularly beautiful clump of heliotrope.

Sam put down the cups. 'Beautiful, aren't they?'

'Yes, they are. I've always wanted a big garden.'

'What have you got at the moment?'

'A green and brown postage stamp. Very practical, very lifeless.'

Sam nodded, wondering when Farmer would get to the point.

She did so at once. 'I've resigned – well, retired – on medical grounds.'

Sam was stunned, not just at the thought of Farmer

leaving the police force, which she knew was her life, but at her reason for leaving. Medical grounds? She'd always looked the picture of health.

Farmer was just as frank about this subject. 'I've got cancer, breast cancer.'

'How long have you known?'

'A while. Found the lump a few weeks ago.'

'What's the prognosis?'

'I'll need a mastectomy, possibly followed by radiation treatment. I found it early, so the outlook is optimistic.'

'Is that why you went AWOL?'

Farmer nodded. 'It frightened me more than I realised. When I found out . . . I don't know . . . it was bit like being jet-lagged.'

'If the outlook is good, why are you leaving? You'll find you recover very quickly from the operation. The mental adjustment can be more difficult but you're a strong person. I'm sure you'll get yourself back to normal fairly quickly.'

'No I won't. I'll never be the same again. I've had enough. It's nothing to do with physical disfigurement – I can cope with that. It was the jolt I got when I realised I was mortal and my time on this earth was limited. Funny what the touch of the angel's wing can do to you, isn't it?'

Sam was silent. Farmer wanted to talk and had, for some reason, chosen Sam to talk to. She felt honoured.

'I followed my dad into the force, you know. Seemed to be the right thing to do at the time, women's lib and all that. I think I was swept along on the new radicalism.

You know, women had to have a career, compete with men, be up there with the rest.'

Sam knew only too well.

'But do you know what I really wanted to do?'

Sam shook her head.

'Have a big family, a large garden and a scruffy dog. But I couldn't because that's not what was expected of me. I'd have been looked down on. We spend our lives doing things because it makes other people happy with us. So I fought my way to the top of my particular greasy pole and then wondered why.'

'Harriet, you've done very well. You've nothing to feel ashamed about.'

'I don't feel ashamed, I just feel as if I've lived my life for the benefit of others. For years the "right ons" have looked down on women who chose to be mothers and wives, made them feel like second-class citizens. But what's wrong with wanting that? It's just as important as any career they might have chosen.'

Sam had often felt the same pressures, but let that go for now. 'What are you going to do once the operation's over?'

'Travel.'

'On your own?'

'No, I have a friend, Eric. Would you believe, we go walking together most weekends? He's older than me, a friend of my father's actually, but we get on and share a lot of interests. I could do worse.'

'Marriage?'

'Who knows? Why not, if that's what we feel like

241

doing? Anything but the bloody rut I've been in for the past twenty years.'

'Hello, world.'

Farmer smiled. 'Yes, it feels a bit like that.'

'You're sure you're making the right decisions?' It was a rhetorical question, but Sam felt she should ask.

'I've never been so sure about anything in my life.'

Sam could sense Farmer's conviction and was reassured. She felt a moment's doubt about her own life choices but quickly pushed it to the back of her mind. Everyone lived their life differently and found their happiness in different ways.

'Things do come in threes, don't they?'

Farmer looked at her enquiringly.

'You're the third person I know to leave this week.'

'Who were the other two?'

'An old friend, Liam – he's gone to Australia – Ricky, my nephew, who's decided to trek round the world, and now you.'

'If I bump into either of them, I'll say Hi for you.'

Sam smiled. 'I think I'm going to miss you.'

'Better the devil you know?'

'Something like that. Who's taking over from you?'

'That's yet to be decided. It'll be the night of the long knives. Superintendent Paul Reid will take over for the time being, though.'

'What's he like?'

'Not as clever as he likes to think he is. Career officer, cocky as hell but limited results, and he likes interference less than I did, so be careful.'

242

Sam realised it was friendly advice and nodded her appreciation.

'I was sorry to hear about you and Tom. I think you would have been good for him.'

Sam shrugged. 'One of those things.'

Farmer became earnest again, as if she were about to interview her about a serious crime. 'When I was in charge of a case I tolerated your interference because you were bloody good, and I recognised a similar spirit to my own. But being the best isn't as important as living your life. Don't make the mistakes I've made, Sam. When my name was screwed off my office door that was it. As far as the force which I've given a lifetime to was concerned, I was yesterday's woman, to be forgotten and ridiculed. I've already got too much catching up to do.'

Sam had never seen Farmer like this before and doubted she ever would again. What really disturbed her was that Farmer was expressing thoughts she herself had been avoiding for some time.

Solheim took her time dressing. She wanted to make sure she looked her best and didn't have that 'recently laid' look, which Doyle might spot. As she turned to leave, her glance fell on the bed. It showed unmistakable signs of the night's activities. The blankets were everywhere and the sheets were a crumpled mass in the middle of the bed. Normally she'd have left things as they were, but everything else in Hammond's apartment was so spick and span that she felt obliged to restore some semblance of order here. The least she could do was make the bed.

As she tucked the edges of the bottom sheet under the mattress, her hand touched something hard, the corner of a book. She pulled it out and looked at it. It was Aldous Huxley's *Brave New World*. She knew the book well. Why did Hammond have it in his bedroom, she wondered, and why on earth did he feel he had to keep it hidden under his mattress? Hammond was the sort of man who would have a very good reason for anything he did, so this might well be important.

She flicked quickly though the pages: nothing. She turned the book upside down and flicked through it again. A long strip of white notepaper floated slowly to the ground. It had been concealed about half-way into the book. It must have been a makeshift bookmark of some kind. She picked it up and was about to tuck it back into the book when she saw, drawn in ink at the top of it, Ω. Solheim stared at it in uneasy surprise. It looked like no more than a doodle, but the sight of it was disturbing. She wished she knew which page or passage of the book the paper had been marking. Was this grounds for suspicion? Should she investigate further, in case there was something else? She put the book down on top of the bedside cupboard and thought hard.

When Hammond reached his office, his assistant, Sergeant Groves, was already there. She stood up and saluted as he came in.

'Any messages, Jenny?' He hung his cap on the hook behind the door and checked that his uniform was immaculate.

'No, sir. There's a bit of mail but it's all routine. Couple of signatures should cover it.'

She had laid the relevant papers out on his desk, ready for him to sign. He went over to the desk, feeling in his picket for his pen. To his surprise, it wasn't there. He checked the top of his desk, but it wasn't there either.

'Jenny, have you seen my pen?'

'No, sir, not this morning.'

Hammond thought back to the day before, and remembered leaving it on top of his bedside cupboard after finishing a long report on the murders of West and Strachan.

'You can borrow mine, sir,' offered Groves.

Hammond appreciated the offer but was particular about his pen. It had been left to him by his father, and the only thing he'd inherited that he actually liked.

'No thanks, Jenny. I know where it is; it's in my room. I'll go and get it. It'll only take a few minutes.'

He put his cap on, adjusted it until he was satisfied it was at the right angle, then made his way out of the office and back across the base towards his rooms.

Solheim made a slow, methodical search of Hammond's rooms, careful to put everything back in place. The last thing she wanted was to raise Hammond's suspicions, especially if she was wrong. She carried out the search the Bureau way. The Bureau had its own way of doing everything from suspect searches to full surveillance. Some agents she knew didn't follow the code, but she did. Although the search pattern was slow, it was methodical and usually successful. The ideas and methods had been learnt and improved over the years, and she certainly didn't think she was any better than the instructors who had used the help and advice of hundreds of highly experienced agents.

But she'd found nothing so far, apart from a report on Hammond's desk outlining the British police's actions to date. It was written in the strictest diplomatic language, praising the police effort but concluding that, despite their efforts, they still hadn't managed to arrest anyone or to identify a strong suspect. She'd seen reports like it at the Bureau, and was pleased that they weren't the only ones to use the police as an excuse for failure.

Having drawn a blank in the sitting-room, she tried the bathroom. She searched the cabinet over the wash-basin, taking each item out in turn and examining it before returning it to its original position. Nothing.

That left only the bedroom. It was sparsely furnished, but what was there she examined. Apart from a few papers, the bedside cupboard was empty. She examined the bedside lamp, checking the underside of its base and running her fingers along the inside of the shade. Again nothing. Finally, removing the rather elegant pen which was lying on top of the cupboard, she unscrewed it, checking for anything that might be concealed inside. It was empty. She screwed it back together and replaced it on top of the cupboard beside the copy of *Brave New World*.

Was there anywhere, anywhere at all, she hadn't searched? Not that she could think of. Suddenly, she heard the door open and Hammond enter the apartment.

Slipping the bookmark back between the pages, she hastily slid the book back beneath the mattress and smoothed the sheets before going through to the sitting-room.

Hammond looked surprised to see her. 'Still here?'

'Only just. Making sure I don't have the "well screwed" look about me before I see Doyle.'

Hammond smiled, flattered. He took her in his arms around her and attempted to kiss her but she pulled away.

'It took me ages to get my make-up right. You'll have to wait until this evening if you want to smudge me.'

Hammond's smile broadened. 'Something to look forward to, then.'

Solheim decided that now was a good time to try and get what she wanted, while he was relaxed and his defences were down. It was an old ploy but it there was no reason why it shouldn't work. She needed to know how much significance there was in finding the book.

She moved across to his bookshelf and ran her fingers across the spines of the books. 'What do you do when you're on your own?'

'I'm seldom on my own.'

'Oh, I see, you have them queuing at the door, do you?'

'I wish. No, I'm just too busy.'

'You must have some time off. What do you do then, when you're alone in your room?'

'I try to avoid my room. It's a very lonely place. Well, most of the time.'

Solheim was becoming impatient. 'Don't you get time to watch some TV, read? You have some books.'

He laughed. 'Can't stand British TV, except perhaps Agatha Christie and Morse. I prefer music.'

'But you read sometimes as well?'

'Reports mostly. I keep pretty much up-to-date with regulations, too.'

She decided she'd have to press the point. 'Books. Which books do you like to read?'

'Why is it so important?'

'I don't know. They say you can judge a person's character from the books they read.'

Hammond joined her by the bookshelf. 'I don't have much time unless I'm on vacation. Then I like to find something that stimulates my mind – I can't read trash. What does that tell you about me?'

'Not much more than I already knew.'

Solheim's heart sank. She hadn't a clue how to get any more information out of him without giving herself away. So she left it while she considered other strategies.

Hammond glanced across at the clock on the wall. It was 10.20. 'Christ, doesn't time fly when you're enjoying yourself?'

He started to search the room.

'What are you looking for?'

Hammond replied without looking up, 'My pen. I know I had it yesterday morning but now . . .'

'It's on top of your bedside cupboard. I saw it there when I was dressing.'

'Thanks.' He went into his bedroom and saw at once

that the bed had been made. He was pleased that she'd taken the time to do that, but also concerned.

He picked up his pen and went back into the sitting-room. 'Thanks for making the bed but the cleaners would have done it.'

'I helped mess it up, so it was the least I could do. Well, I guess I'd better find out what Doyle's up to. See you this evening.' She walked across to Hammond and kissed him on the cheek. 'Your place or mine?'

'Mine. I'll get a bottle of something nice in.'

'You don't have to get me drunk but it helps. Bye.'

As soon as the door had closed behind her, Hammond ran back into his bedroom and felt around under the mattress. To his relief, he found the book where he had left it. For a moment he'd doubted the reason for Solheim's sexual enthusiasm and his ego was already taking a beating. He relaxed again and flicked through the pages to his bookmark. It was in the wrong place, twenty pages on from where he'd left it. He sat down on the bed and punched the covers hard. He'd made a big mistake.

Tom Adams was reading Sam's report on the marks the stun gun had made on the pig's neck. It was certainly another line of investigation and with a bit of luck might produce a few more names.

Not that he didn't have enough of them already. After Strachan's body was found, the enquiry doubled in size. The press were on their backs too, screaming for a solution and making vague hints of incompetence. The chief constable had poured the last of his already stretched resources into the enquiry, and even this might not be enough. Three more days and there would be no more overtime money left and the team would have to work for time off later – though when they would be able to take that time off was anyone's guess.

For now, it was a matter of number-crunching and getting through as much work as possible to convince the press that, on paper at least, the force was doing all it could. It had been decided to interview and take statements from everyone who had been on the camp on the night of the murder and during the previous day, and to feed all their stories into the computer in the hope that a few of the stories wouldn't cross-match and a suspect would emerge. It was a long shot but it was all they had.

He'd also asked Doyle to supply him with a list of the Air Force bases in the States near which the bodies of the other women had been found. The idea was to cross-reference all the personnel on those bases with the people stationed at Leeminghall and hope that a common name popped up. Doyle assured him that the FBI had already done this and drawn a complete blank, but Adams wanted to do it himself, and Doyle had agreed. The door-to-door enquiries had begun again as well, this time with a brand-new set of questions. They too would have to be cross-referenced to see if anything emerged. This was the humdrum and frankly balls-achingly boring aspect of detection work which never got on to the television screen.

As Adams stared across at the duty board, trying to remember when his next day off was due, the door to the main office flew open. Everyone in the incident room looked up. Superintendent Paul Reid stood framed in the doorway for a moment, eyeing each of them in turn as if trying to sum up their potential threat, before striding confidently across the room and into Farmer's former office. He was followed by a smart, well-dressed woman in her early thirties.

Adams knew Reid of old and, like the rest of Cambridgeshire CID, thought he was an arsehole of the first order. The general consensus was that his promotions had been more to do with the masonic lodge he belonged to than with his ability as a police officer. The woman was a stranger, but Adams guessed she was Detective Inspector Sarah Holmes, who had arrived in Cambridge shortly after Reid. They had apparently worked together for years and the word was that she was his mistress, although Reid was careful and there was no proof, just a lot of rumours and innuendoes.

Farmer's desk had already been cleared and her name removed from the office door. It was almost as if, overnight, Superintendent Harriet Farmer had ceased to exist. Her premature retirement had come as a shock to all of them. Tom had thought he was close to her but she hadn't said a word. It had been left to the divisional superintendent to tell them, and he hadn't even had the courtesy to tell them in person, but simply sent a round a brief memo: 'Superintendent Harriet Farmer has taken early retirement from the force. She will be replaced by Superintendent Reid from Monday.'

Adams had tried phoning her but got only her answerphone. He'd left messages but she hadn't called back. Visiting her home had proved equally fruitless. Either she wasn't in or she wasn't answering the door. What the hell was all this about? In his frustration, he pressed his pencil so hard on the paper he was doodling on that the lead broke.

The sound caught the attention of Sergeant Chalky White, who looked across at him. 'Do you know what's going on, sir?'

Adams shook his head. 'I haven't got a bloody clue.'

Reid called from his office, 'Tom, can I have a word, please?'

As Adams went across to Reid's office, White looked at him sidelong. He knew what it was about. Reid wanted his own assistant, and it wasn't going to be Adams.

Ross said, 'Tom, let me introduce you to Detective Inspector Sarah Holmes. She'll be joining the team as from today.'

The two inspectors shook hands. Adams thought she was a hard-faced woman with all the charm of a snake about to strike. She and Reid suited each other.

Reid waved Tom to a seat. He wasn't subtle in his approach. 'Tom, as you are aware, I'm taking over the West enquiry as from today and as the new broom I'm afraid I'm going to have to sweep clean.'

Adams asked, 'So I'm out?'

'Right. Nothing personal, but I want my own people around me and you were very much Farmer's man. It's not a reflection on you or your competence, just the way things have worked out.'

'So what happens now?'

'I've arranged for you to work on South Division. You'll be taking over from old Sid Reid. His thirty's up and he's decided to run his own security business, God help us all. I think you'll fit in well. It's a tough division but worthy of a man of your calibre.'

The words of his probationary tutor came to Adams's mind. 'If you can survive South Division, you can survive anything. It's where they put all the flotsam and jetsam of the police force, people who have upset the system, embarrassed their boss, or just arrested the wrong person at the wrong time. If the world had a bum, this is where it would be.'

Adams knew Sid Reid too. Sid had jumped just before he was finally pushed. He was so bent that not even the pictures on his wall hung straight, but then it was that sort of division. Adams knew he'd have to make the best of it and get out when he could. Reid had always disliked Farmer and anyone associated with her, so he, Adams, was bound to be top of the shit-list.

Reid continued, 'So, if you'll bring DI Holmes up to speed – and considering the amount of progress Superintendent Farmer has made in this enquiry that shouldn't take you long – I think we need detain you no longer.'

He looked at Adams expectantly. Adams took the hint and without another word returned to the incident room. He was angrier than he could ever remember being before but refused to show it. He could at least deprive Reid of that little satisfaction.

Plonking himself down on his seat he gave Sergeant White the thumbs-down sign.

'South, sir?'

Adams nodded.

'You won't be the only one, sir.'

As he spoke, Reid called again. 'Sergeant White, got a minute?'

This time it was Tom's turn. 'See you next week?'

White nodded and made his way across the office like a French aristocrat going to the guillotine.

Sam was in the garden when the phone rang. She was in two minds about whether to answer it. But it might be important, not just Jean reminding her about yet another court case or lecture that she had to attend. With a sigh, she went indoors, kicking off her boots and throwing her gardening gloves on to the kitchen table.

'Doctor Ryan.' She always answered the phone formally in case it was work. Not this time. It was Wyn, and she was crying. 'Sam, come quick, come quick!'

Instantly alarmed, Sam said, 'What is it? Whatever's wrong? Is it Ricky?'

The reply was short and almost hysterical. 'It's Mum. She's dying, Sam, she's dying.'

Sam fought to stay calm. 'Where are you, Wyn?'

'The Park, I'm at the Park. Come quickly, please. Before it's too late.'

'Where at the Park?'

'Casualty.'

'Stay there. I'll be as quick as I can.'

Sam put the phone down, slipped into her shoes and grabbed her car keys – which she found immediately for once. She was tempted to ring Casualty and find out what the hell was going on but she resisted the temptation. She ought to get there fast, rather than wait around for them to find the right doctor. She ran out to the car.

The traffic and the lights were kind to her and she arrived at the hospital quickly. She parked in one of the doctors' spots and hurried into Casualty. There was no sign of Wyn, so she asked at reception and was directed to her mother's cubicle.

The second she pushed open the doors of the ward, she heard Wyn's sobbing and knew she was too late. She walked across to the cubicle and pulled back the curtain. Wyn was leaning across her mother body, crying bitterly, while a nurse tried to comfort her.

She raised her tear-stained face as Sam entered. 'You're too late. She's gone, she's gone.'

Sam glanced at the nurse for confirmation, and the nurse nodded. Sam looked down at her mother: her face was calmer than it had been for years and she looked truly at peace. Sam took Wyn's hand and held it firmly, while with her other hand stroking her mother's thinning white hair. To her puzzlement and distress, Sam found she lacked the ability, or even the desire, to cry.

CHAPTER NINE

W yn was crying again. Sam stood with her arm
around her sister's shoulders as their mother's
coffin slowly disappeared from sight behind a set of
faded yellow velvet curtains and the priest said a final
few words. Almost immediately they were guided out of
the chapel and through a back door, bursting suddenly
into bright light and cool, fresh air.

It was a little like being tipped off the end of a conveyor
belt. As Sam had arrived for her mother's funeral the
previous one was just concluding, and now, as they left
the chapel, yet another was waiting to begin.

The funeral had been a simple affair with few mourners.
Most of her mother's friends and close family were dead,
as infirm as she had been, or still living in Ireland. Wyn
had put a notice in the Belfast *Herald*, *Post* and *Tele-
graph*, which had brought many letters and telegrams of
condolence. The sisters were touched to find that some
were from people they hadn't heard from for years but
who had remembered them and taken the time to extend
their sympathy.

They'd decided not to tell Ricky. He'd been close to his
grandmother and would regret missing her funeral, but

the disruption and cost of dragging him back from his trip might have resulted in the collapse of the whole project. He'd have a chance to make his farewells when he got back. Wyn and Sam had agreed to return their mother's ashes to Belfast, to be laid alongside their father's. That was what she had always wanted and it seemed only right that the couple should rest together in their homeland. For Ricky's sake, they'd wait until he returned and could make the sad little pilgrimage with them.

Wyn dried her eyes and began to read the cards on the wreaths and bouquets sent for their mother. Sam watched dark smoke emerging from the tall chimney at the back of the crematorium, and tried not to think of what it meant.

She was glad when Tom Adams's voice broke through her thoughts. 'I'm really sorry, Sam.'

He put his arms around her and hugged her tightly. Despite what had happened, it still seemed the natural thing to do, and she was glad he was there. She couldn't help wondering, though, how he'd managed to get time off work to come.

The whole of East Anglia seemed alive with police, as the enquiry expanded to take in every part of the region. Although the story now made only the inside pages of the national papers, it was still front-page news locally, and she knew the police were under a lot of pressure to make an early arrest. Yet, for all their efforts, they seemed no nearer to a solution than they had the night of Mary West's murder. Tom must be working all hours of the day and night.

As if he'd read her mind, he released her. He took her

hand and looked down at her. 'I've got to go. If you need me, you know where I am.'

'Incident room?'

He didn't think it was the right place or time to tell her he'd been thrown off the enquiry, so said, 'Try me at home. It's the same number.'

Sam nodded. He kissed her on the cheek and made his way back to his car.

As he walked away Wyn joined her. 'I think you made a mistake there.'

Watching his car disappear down the drive, Sam felt the pain of lost life, love and opportunities.

When Sam got back from the funeral, she was annoyed to find Catherine Solheim waiting, her huge Jeep Cherokee parked exactly where Sam usually parked, right outside the front door. Sam sighed. She'd hoped for a few hours on her own to reflect, remember and try and work out why, since her mother died, she hadn't shed any tears. She was giving herself a mental battering and the continual self-analysis made her mother's death even harder to bear.

As Sam stepped out of her car, Solheim came over. 'You look very smart,' she said, taking in Sam's classic-cut, short-sleeved black dress.' Special occasion?'

'My mother's funeral. I suppose that is quite special.'

Solheim reddened with embarrassment. Her instinct was to get back into her car and return to the base, but Sam was the only person she was able to trust and it was important that she talk to her, even at such a difficult time.

'I'm sorry. I didn't know. No offence intended.'

Sam looked at Solheim stony-faced and without a hint that her apology had been accepted, before making her way across to the front door. Solheim followed and persisted.

'I can see this really isn't a good time, but I have to talk to somebody, and to be honest you're the only one I can think of right now.'

'Is it significant that Doyle isn't with you?'

Solheim nodded. Resignedly, Sam opened the door. She still wasn't in a forgiving mood but was now interested enough to want to hear what Solheim had to say.

As she ushered Solheim inside, she said, 'I hope this won't take long.'

'It won't.'

While Sam went upstairs to change, Solheim made herself comfortable in the sitting-room. The place was everything she expected from an old English cottage, old, low, oak beams, a large open brick fireplace and small windows and doors. The only thing that seemed out of place was the clutter. Papers and books littered the floor and every armrest and table top seemed to hold a half-finished cup of tea or coffee. Sam might be meticulous in the mortuary, thought Solheim, but her domestic life left a little to be desired.

A large tabby cat appeared from nowhere, jumped up on to her lap and began to settle himself comfortably. She was about to push him off, in a vain attempt to protect her dark business suit from his claws and loose hairs, when Sam reappeared.

'His name's Shaw, after George Bernard.'

Solheim nodded and made a show of stroking him, but Sam could see her heart wasn't in it, so she scooped him off Solheim's lap.

'He's a lovely cat but hairy. He'll ruin your suit if you're not careful. I'll take him out.'

She carried him through to the kitchen and let him out into the back garden. When she got back to the sitting-room, Solheim was standing up, brushing her skirt and jacket vigorously but ineffectually.

Sam handed her a clothes brush. 'Every contact leaves a trace. Try this. It usually gets the job done.'

After several sweeps with the brush, Solheim sat down again. Sam poured herself a large brandy. She raised her glass questioningly, but Solheim shook her head. Sam took a good, reviving swallow, and sank on to the sofa opposite her guest. She pulled her knees up under her chin.

'This had better be good,' she said.

Solheim dipped into her handbag and took out a small piece of paper, which she unfolded and passed to Sam.

'I was wondering if you'd ever seen anything like this before.'

Sam took the note and read it. The first part was in Latin: 'Si monumentum requiris, circumspice.' She knew it meant 'If you would seek his monument, look around you.' She read on: 'I ate civilisation. It poisoned me; I was defiled. And then I ate my own wickedness.' The note was signed 'John Savage'.

She said, 'John Savage is a character from Huxley's book *Brave New World*, and I think both the quotes are from there as well – although the original of the first one's over the north door of St Paul's Cathedral.'

Solheim nodded.

'But why are you showing me?'

'Different passages from the same book have been found at all the other murder scenes, and they have all been signed "John Savage". Well, until the last one that is.'

'Doyle's big secret?'

Solheim nodded again. 'You see I think it was there but had been ripped down before the authorities could find it.'

More pieces of the puzzle were falling into place. Sam said slowly, 'You mean the scrap of paper I found attached to the nail?'

'Yes. As you pointed out, we know from the blood-splatter patterns that something was there before West was murdered, but had gone by the time you and the police arrived.'

'So what's your point?'

'Well, as our killer wouldn't have torn it down, it only leaves me one conclusion: that the note was ripped down by someone trying to mask the identity of our murderer.'

'But who would do that?'

'It could only be one of four people. Either the two security policemen who found the body, and as far as we can tell they had nothing to gain from moving anything, or—'

'Hammond or Cully.' Sam beat her to the punch.

'Right. After the body was found, the continuity of evidence in the shed was recorded. No one that we know of, except Hammond and Cully, went into the shed.'

'What about before the body was "officially" discovered?'

'If the two security guys are right – and I see no reason to doubt their statements – they chased the killer from the shed. After which one of them was at the shed at all times.'

'As you say, *if* they are correct and the person they chased was the killer,' warned Sam.

'Who else could it have been?'

'The person who took the note.'

'What about the bag he was carrying? The one we think her organs were in?'

'We don't know that for sure. There might have been anything inside it.'

'The only footprints found inside the shed belonged to the two security guards, Colonel Cully and Hammond.'

'What about our killer?'

'Nothing. He must have been very careful.'

'Which must,' said Sam thoughtfully, 'have been difficult in a blood-drenched shed in the middle of the night.'

'Exactly.'

'You obviously have a theory. Want to share it?'

'Hammond. I think Hammond removed it.'

Sam was stunned into silence, but recovered quickly. 'Why Hammond and not Cully?'

'Because I think Cully's probably our killer and Hammond's covering for him.'

'Why not the other way round?'

'Cully covering for Hammond? Cully's not the type. He'd sell his old lady for a promotion.'

Very scientific, Sam thought.

Solheim continued, 'Besides, Cully's profile's closer.

Paranoid, few friends, and there is a rumour that he indulges in rather unorthodox sexual practices.'

Sam wondered fleetingly what they were.

'He also spent many years travelling around different Air Force bases in the States on inspection tours. Sort of a military drifter, ideal for committing a murder and then moving on before the authorities have a chance to discover who you are.'

'A sort of Henry Lee Lucas with medals.'

Solheim gave a half-laugh. 'Good way of putting it.'

'How sure are you about this?'

'As sure as I can be for now. I've sent a few messages back to Quantico to see if we can match Cully's base inspections with the dates of any of the murders, but it will take a little while.'

'And in the meantime?'

'I'll just keep an eye on the bastard until I'm ready to move.'

'You say "I". Do I take it that Doyle isn't part of your plan?'

'I was certainly never part of his.'

Despite all the circumstantial evidence Sam still wasn't convinced. 'Well, for what it's worth, I think you're wrong about Hammond. He's too much the policeman to do something like this. I don't know about Cully. Apparently he's not well liked or respected, but I only have that on Hammond's say-so. I think he's a crass, sexist bore and I'd string him up just for that, but it doesn't mean he kills people for kicks.'

'We'll see. But for now he's my best suspect and I'm sticking with him.'

Sam shrugged.

'There's something else perhaps you ought to know as well. I found a copy of *Brave New World* in Hammond's room. It was hidden under his mattress.'

Sam didn't enquire what she was doing in Hammond's bedroom in the first place, merely said, 'Bedtime reading?'

Solheim smiled sarcastically.

'Who else knew about the notes?'

'Besides Doyle and myself, a few local sheriffs and police officers whose people discovered the bodies. Certainly not an Air Force major stationed in England.'

Sam thought back over all that she'd heard. She had to admit it that Solheim had made a pretty strong case.

But Solheim hadn't finished. 'Is there any forensic evidence that might help link Cully to the murder?'

'You're better going to the police for that kind of information, I don't have it.'

'But you could get it?'

'No.'

'You did it for Doyle and Hammond.'

'I had some control over what I showed them. I have no control over the British Forensic Science Service.'

'But you have friends within the various departments who might be helpful.'

'I wouldn't consider involving other people in unofficial intrigues.'

Sam was not being entirely honest. In fact, she hadn't hesitated to request access to information from Marcia and number of other scientists in the past, but that had been for her own use and she would never jeopardise the careers of others by passing such information to a third party.

'So you won't help?' asked Solheim.

'Can't. I'm sorry. Look, I'm sure if you spoke to Tom Adams, he'd be as helpful as he could.'

Solheim shook her head. 'And take the chance of Doyle finding out? No thanks. Thought we might be able to sort this out woman to woman.'

'Well, woman to woman, there are rules and regulations, and if you break them you stand a very good chance of some clever bloody lawyer dismissing your evidence and throwing out your case because you didn't act within the rules. You should know that better than most, having worked within the American system.'

Sam had had enough. Solheim's attempt to invoke some pseudo-sisterhood in order to enlist her help was not only clumsy but annoying. Still raw from the shock of her mother's death, she craved genuine friendship and affection. Solheim's show of blatant ambition raised her hackles more than it would normally have done. She stood, making it clear it was time for her visitor to leave.

Solheim took the hint. At the door she turned and said, 'I hope I can rely on you. I'd hate this information to go any further.'

'Woman to woman, you mean?'

Solheim realised that she'd set Sam's back up, and would just have to hope she'd would be discreet.

Tom Adams looked down at his empty desk and the cardboard box on the chair next to it. He'd been surprised that all his stuff had fitted into such a small box. He wasn't sorry to be going. The enquiry was in a complete mess. Reid had removed all the experienced officers and replaced them with yes-men who couldn't detect a cold on a winter's day. Not there was much left for Reid's new team to do. Pen-pushing, mostly, and basic enquiries; they'd done the rest.

You always knew when an enquiry was getting nowhere because the senior investigating officer, in this case Reid, would suddenly decide that anyone with a criminal conviction within the past ten years for an offence similar to the one in question had to be seen, interviewed and if necessary taped. It rarely made a difference to the enquiry, but at least the force could say that they had left no obvious stone unturned and it made the interview rate look bloody impressive on paper. The truth was, in all the years Adams had been on the squad not a single lead or arrest had ever been made using these methods. It cost a fortune, but it saved the chief constable's blushes and kept the press at bay so that was all right.

He glanced towards Reid's office. Reid was at his desk, talking on the phone while Inspector Holmes hovered over him, waiting for Adams to go so that she could swoop down on his desk and take it over. Chalky White, who had sat opposite him for the past year and who been as near a good friend as a sergeant could be to an inspector, was gone. White had already rung and told him that South Division was as bad as ever. His replacement was a sour-faced sergeant from Central Division, called Winterbottom, who spoke in grunts and was clearly not keen to be seen on friendly terms with Adams, especially when the boss was looking.

Adams sighed inwardly. He and Chalky had had a joint leaving party at the Maypole in Cambridge. It was the friendliest pub in town, and the one with the best ale – squad piss-ups normally started there. Everyone had got very drunk and had a high old time swapping tales about past arrests and unpopular senior officers. At closing time, they fell out of the pub into the nearest curry house. It had been well-attended do. Reid, Holmes and, of course, Winterbottom, hadn't shown up, but they weren't greatly missed.

But neither had Farmer, and Adams was genuinely sorry about that. He still hadn't managed to talk to her. It was as if she wanted to cut herself off from every-thing and everybody. From the serious rumour squad he'd learnt that she had cancer and – which was much more surprising – that she had a boyfriend, with whom, after she had finished her treatment, she was going on holiday. Adams had always flattered himself that he knew Farmer well and that he was closer to her than anyone else in the force was, which, considering her rather frosty personality, was something he was proud of. But she had been living a secret life that neither he nor, as far as he knew, the rest of the force was aware of. He began to wonder just how much he knew about anyone.

Adams had spent the past week with Inspector Holmes. If he hadn't liked her when they met, he hated her now. He'd gone over the entire case with her: statements, inter-views, names and personalities. No matter what he said or did, she continually found fault and was about as officious as they come. She was obviously keen to make her mark and didn't care who she trod on to make it.

With Reid's help, Adams was sure she would make it too. If she was having an affair with Reid – and that, after all, was only a rumour – Adams reckoned they deserved each other.

She was also unnecessarily aggressive in her approach to both her colleagues and suspects. He knew, probably better than most, how difficult it was for a woman in the force, probably more difficult than for a member of the ethnic community. But there was no point being aggressive unless you had to be, and if problems arose there were now more channels than ever before for filing grievances. No, he decided, she was just an unpleasant, rather loud woman with more chips on her shoulder than McDonald's. After Holmes, he reckoned South Division would seem like paradise.

His last act before he finally vacated his desk was to ring Sam. Despite the abrupt end of their relationship, she was one of the few people he still trusted and right now he needed to see her. She wasn't at work and the cottage phone was answered, as always, by her infernal machine. He left a brief message saying where she was most likely to find him and a selection of new phone numbers.

He became aware of someone standing beside him. It was Liz Fenwick.

'Sorry, Tom,' she said, so quietly that no one could have overheard.

'Thanks. One of those things. At least you're staying.'

'For now. I can't see Inspector Holmes and me getting on too well.'

'You survived Farmer.'

'Pussy cat in comparison. Are we still on for the weekend?'

Adams glanced across at Reid's office to see Holmes staring at them inquisitively. 'Be careful,' he warned. 'We're being watched.'

'Good. Perhaps they'll send me to South Division as well. I hear they've got a very big lost property office.'

He smiled. 'Behave yourself. Well, until Friday night, anyway.'

She returned his smile and went back to her desk. At least, he thought, she'd reminded him that he had one good thing to look forward to.

He stuffed the last couple of items into his box and turned to the rest of the team. 'See you on South Division, people.'

Some, the old hands, waved and shouted good-luck wishes. Others, the new ones, Reid's lot, refused to acknowledge him and kept their heads down as if nothing was happening. As he went out, Holmes walked across the room and, after casting a predatory eye over the rest of the room, made the desk, and the prestige that went with it, hers.

Sam waited a couple of days before going over to her sister's house. She'd rung each morning and evening to see how Wyn was coping, and her forlorn loneliness was plain. She was finding her three-bedroomed house echoingly empty, too big for just one person. Sam worried at the thought of her sister brooding there alone. Although they had never been very close, Wyn was still her sister and

Sam felt a responsibility towards her. Yes, she thought, it was high time she went to see her.

They had a cup of tea in the kitchen, Wyn reminiscing as always about Ireland and the good times they'd spent with their parents. Sam listened quietly, seeing how much brighter and calmer Wyn was for the chance to talk. She waited until her sister's flow of talk began to dry up, then said, 'I'd like you to come and live with me.'

Wyn was startled. 'At the cottage you mean? I thought you enjoyed your privacy.'

'I do, but there's a big difference between privacy and loneliness.'

'And what if you want to bring a boyfriend back for the night?'

Sam shrugged. 'You'll have to sleep in the shed.'

Wyn laughed. 'If my memory of your lovemaking is anything to go by, I'll still hear you out there.'

Sam felt her face begin to colour. Her sister had never brought this up before and Sam, for one of the few time in her life, was speechless.

'If I do move in with you you'll have to buy a gag.'

Sam buried her face in her hands and laughed. 'Wyn, what are you suggesting? Anyway, with the way things have gone recently, I doubt there will be any men around, and if there are I promise I'll be discreet. Now, what do you say?'

Wyn liked the idea. The last couple of weeks had made her realise just how much her mother's need for constant attention had shielded her from loneliness. She was determined, though, not to be a burden on Sam.

She said firmly, 'I'll want to pay rent.'

'There's no need.'

'Yes there is,' Wyn insisted. 'I don't want your or anyone else's charity, thank you.'

'Look, as you know, I'm a little on the scruffy side and not very practical around the house—'

'Tell me about it!'

'Yes, well, don't rub it in. What I thought was that you could perhaps take over that side of things for me instead of paying rent.'

'Be your skivvy, you mean?' asked Wyn angrily.

'No, I *don't* mean that. I'm out at work all day, so I don't get a chance to get around to most things domestic. I could bring someone in to do it but I'm not sure I'd trust them.' Sam paused for a moment to emphasise her final point. 'You're about the only person I would trust or who I think could put up with me. What I'm trying to say is, I probably need you more than you need me.'

Wyn's anger subsided. But she still had one serious reservation. 'You're a bit isolated out there in the middle of nowhere.'

'I'll get you a car.'

'What about when Ricky comes back?'

'He can move in too if he wants, although I expect he'll be ready to launch out on his own by then.'

'And what if it doesn't work?'

'Then I'll help you get a smaller house or a flat, but we can give it a try until then.'

Wyn thought it over for a moment. 'OK, it's a deal. When can I move in?'

Sam gave her sister a warm hug. 'As soon as you like. I'm sure we'll have a great time.'

'We'll see. Let's just try living together without killing each other first.'

Sam smiled and hoped for the best.

When Sam got home, she found on her answering machine a message from Tom, inviting her for a drink at the Crown in Snersburgh. She guessed that he wanted to tell her what had happened. She would at least be a friendly shoulder to cry on. If she went, she thought, should she try to look her very best? Or should she not bother? She'd seen his new girlfriend and couldn't hope to compete with her youth. Still, she'd have a bloody good try! That short green dress always looked good – and she wouldn't wear too much under it. There was just time to wash her hair and to do her make-up properly for once. She ran up the stairs two at time.

She found Tom sitting at one of the Crown's corner tables. He seemed nervous, constantly checking the room as if he were looking for someone. He'd even parked his car at the far side of the village and walked. She got a couple of drinks from the bar and went to join him.

'Thanks.'

'Expecting trouble?' she enquired.

'You never know.'

She waited for him to explain, but instead he abruptly changed the subject. 'You look great, but then you always did.'

She raised her glass to him. 'Not bad for an old 'un.'

He knew exactly what she meant, but refused to take the bait. 'Not bad for a young 'un.'

'Now, to what do I owe this honour? From the way

your nerves are reacting, you're clearly doing something you shouldn't be.'

Tom smiled her. 'You were a bad influence on me.'

'So what is it?'

He leant across the table and handed her a large blue file. 'That's all the information on the Mary West and Strachan case to date. I've left out all the irrelevant stuff.'

Sam was puzzled. 'So what are you giving it to me for?'

He took a good swallow of his drink, and said, 'I'm off the squad. I was going to tell you at your mum's funeral but it didn't seem appropriate.'

'I already knew.'

'How?'

'Force bongo drums.' Nothing was ever a secret for very long within the force.

'New broom, sweeping clean. I'm seen as Farmer's man so I was out.'

'That's bloody ridiculous! What about all your knowledge?'

'Passed on to the new inspector.'

Sam shook her head in disgust. The weight of the file in her hand reminded her that he hadn't answered her question. 'Look, I am sorry about what's happened, and I don't want to appear unsympathetic, but I'm still not sure why you're giving this file to me?'

He leant back in his seat and took another mouthful of ale, swilling it around his mouth and savouring its taste for a moment before swallowing. It was a habit Sam hated.

'Do you remember John Rochester?' he asked.

'The old chief constable? Of course I do. He was a good man.'

'Yes, he was. He's commander of the staff college at Cromwell Park now. He could be very helpful to us.'

'Us?'

'You.'

'I thought the college was just a training establishment.'

'It covers a bit more than that. Anyway, he's formed a new squad to track serial killers.'

Sam put her drink down and began to listen more intently.

'The police have thought for some time now that hundreds of serial crimes, especially murders, are going undetected each year. You know that thousands of people are reported missing each year. Many are found, or we have a good idea where they are or why they went missing, but hundreds more simply disappear without trace. Nothing. Like the women they found at Cromwell Road. None of them were reported as crimes. They were just marked off as missing from home, when in reality they were buried around Fred West's house and in various parts of the country. Anyway, the idea behind the squad is to bring the very best brains into one place – you know, computer experts, forensic scientists, lawyers, psychologists, detectives – and turn them into a squad of people specifically trained to hunt these killers down.'

'And detect crimes that have never been reported. Novel idea.'

He nodded. 'Something like that. The Home Office is funding the project and the team are available to any force that wants to use them.'

'Sounds like the beginning of the British FBI to me.'

'It is, just disguised slightly for now. It's all very political.'

'So why haven't you used them on this enquiry?'

'We were about to when Farmer left. I mentioned it to Reid, but he didn't want to know, arrogant git. Hoping to take all the credit for any arrest and move himself one step closer to becoming chief constable.'

'So you want me to go trolling down to Hampshire with this file and see if I can get Rochester interested?'

Another nod.

'And what, when he sees me with a confidential file I have no right to have in my possession, do I do if he decides to ring Reid?'

'He won't.'

'It's easy to speak with confidence if you're not taking the risks, I've found.'

'He hates Reid. Did all he could to get him off the job when he was the chief.'

Sam raised her eyebrows at him and he looked away, annoyed. But he brightened up when she picked the file up and dropped it into her briefcase.

'You'll do it, then?'

'I'll see. I'll read it tonight and if I think it's worth the risk maybe I'll give Rochester a call. But no promises.'

Tom smiled broadly. 'Knew I could rely on you.'

'I said "maybe".' She rattled her empty glass on the table top. 'Nasty sight that.'

He took the hint and made his way back to the bar, leaving Sam to ponder what he'd just asked her to do.

*　　*　　*

An hour later, Sam was back at the hospital and on her way up to her office. As she approached the door, Jean came rushing up to her.

'Doctor Ryan, thank goodness I've caught you,' said Jean in an urgent whisper. She was breathless with tension and concern. 'There's a Superintendent Reid and Inspector Holmes in your office. I tried to put them off but they said it was urgent.'

She had to meet them some time and now seemed as good a time as any. At least it was on home ground. 'OK, Jean.'

As she was about to go in, she stopped herself, pulled the blue file Adams had given her from her briefcase and gave it to Jean. 'Hang on to this would you, Jean? Lock it in one of your drawers. I don't want anyone seeing it.'

Jean took the file. 'What have you been up to now?'

Sam said, trying hard to sound indignant, 'Jean, I'm sure I don't know what you mean,' and swept into her office.

Reid and Holmes stood up as she went in. She'd decided that her best form of defence was attack, so before either of them could speak she said, 'I understand that my secretary has already told you I'm busy. I don't normally see people without an appointment but as you're here I'll make a brief exception so you'd better be quick.'

Ross had got his speech all prepared but was totally wrong-footed by this attitude. Pulling himself together, he said, 'My name is Superintendent Reid and this is Inspector Holmes.'

Holmes nodded in Sam's general direction. She had a notebook in her hand and was writing down everything Reid said.

'We've just taken over the Mary West and Strachan murder enquiry,' Reid went on, 'and thought we'd better come and introduce ourselves.'

Sam was still acting prickly. 'I know all that. Is that it? As I said, I'm very busy.'

Reid had come for a particular purpose, however, and was determined to have his say before he left. 'I understand, Doctor Ryan, that you have a reputation for taking your pathological investigations outside the four walls of this hospital and into my domain.'

Sam said nothing, but she could feel her anger rising.

'Although occasionally, I understand, your help has been appreciated' – *occasionally?* thought Sam – 'I'm here to tell you officially that you are no longer to interfere with this or any other enquiry I am dealing with, except in your official capacity as one of the county's forensic pathologists. Any additional information you might come across during the course of your work is to be forwarded to either me or Inspector Holmes here for our attention. I do hope I'm making myself clear, Doctor Ryan?'

Sam folded her arms. 'Perfectly. Is that all?'

'For now.'

'Good, then would you mind leaving? I have an important post mortem list to prepare.'

Holmes wrote furiously for a few seconds. Then she got up and followed Reid to the door.

'Please close the door on your way out.'

When they were gone, Sam leant back in her seat with a sigh of relief.

Jean came in. 'Are you all right? They didn't look very happy.'

'Good.'

'I think you should be careful there. He looks a nasty piece of work.'

A voice the doorway said, 'He is, Jean. A very nasty piece of work.' Trevor Stuart strode into the room and took his normal seat opposite Sam. 'So you've met the new team, then, Tweedledee and Tweedledum.'

'More like Heckle and bloody Jeckle.'

Stuart laughed. 'Yes, well, they came to see me first.'

'Why?'

'They wanted me to take over the case.'

'*What?*'

'Decided they needed a more mature view of the forensic evidence.'

'And what did you say?'

'That they had the best help that money could buy, and I wasn't interested.'

'The bastards! Well, that's going to get them both a complaint.'

'For what? They're well within their rights.'

'After all the additional information they've got out of me I—'

'Sam, you know that you, or for that matter I, have no right whatsoever to interfere with any police enquiry over and above our professional role in the case. You've been lucky so far. Let it go, leave it with them. Then, when they fall on their faces, they can't drag anyone else down with them.'

Sam wasn't sure which annoyed her most, Reid questioning her professionalism or the underhand way he'd tried to get her thrown off the case.

'The pompous ass,' she snorted.

'Let it go. Just do what you have to do and forget it.'

But she had no intention of letting it go. If she hadn't been sure about seeing Rochester before, Reid had just made her mind up for her.

Sam stopped briefly by the security gate that led into Cromwell Park while the security guard checked her pass and established who it was she had come to see. Cromwell Park was the National Police Staff College, which all police officers wanting to reach a senior position within their respective forces had to attend. But it was like no other police training college she had ever visited. There were no whitewashed walls and neat parade grounds here. The beautiful eighteenth-century house was surrounded by acres of unspoilt park, and was approached down a long drive which led across an ancient bridge spanning a stream, then rose slightly towards the great house.

The security guard completed his checks, handed back her pass and raised the barrier. Sam parked on the gravel forecourt in front of the house, dutifully locked her car, and climbed the stone steps to the entrance hall. There she checked in at reception and was issued with a visitor's badge. Another guard escorted her down a long corridor and up a winding staircase to the commander's office.

She had known John Rochester since his time as chief

constable in Norwich. He was a born leader and career police officer, determined to make his mark on the force before he retired. Before moving to Norwich, he had served with the Met in London and been in charge of, or attached to, just about every department in existence, gathering a wealth of experience as he went. He was also the possessor of a hatful of commendations and awards, several for bravery.

Carol Wing, his secretary, met Sam at the door. 'Doctor Ryan?' They shook hands. 'Mr Rochester's expecting you. Go right in.'

'Thank you.'

Carol Wing led her through an outer office, where she and Rochester's staff officer worked, to the inner sanctum. John Rochester was sitting behind his desk, speaking into the phone. He looked up and smiled broadly. Waving Sam to a chair, he gestured to his secretary to make some tea and she went out. At last he finished his call and came across, saying, 'Sam, it's good to see you again.'

She stood up and they exchanged chaste kisses.

'It's good to see you too. This is a bit different to your office in Norwich.'

'Just a bit. Nice, though.'

Rochester wasn't a man for idle gossip and, besides, he had a shrewd idea that the visit wasn't just social. 'So what can I do for you? Still sticking your nose in where it's not wanted?'

Sam knew him quite as well as he knew her, so she came straight to the point. 'There've been a couple of murders in Cambridge over the last few weeks—'

'I thought that might be it.'

'And I was hoping your new squad might be able to help.'

'Maybe. The problem is we have to be invited into an enquiry. We can't just turn up uninvited on their doorstep.'

'Can't I invite you in?'

'Nice idea, but it has to be the senior investigating officer.'

'No chance there, from what I understand.'

'I know you've had your ups and downs with Farmer, but she's a good police officer and would put the enquiry above everything else.'

'Farmer's gone. Superintendent Cross has taken her place.'

Rochester was astonished. 'But I never heard a thing.'

'Most people didn't until it was all over. It was all a bit unexpected, I think.'

It was Rochester who, as the area's chief constable, had first spotted Harriet Farmer's potential as both a detective and a future commander. He'd watched her career carefully and been instrumental in her rise through the ranks. He, like many others, felt hurt that she hadn't seen fit to let him know her plans or even seek his help if there was a problem.

'Do we know why?' he asked.

'Cancer.'

'Christ, that's bad.'

'Well, at least they think they've discovered it soon enough, so it shouldn't be life-threatening. But the treatment's going to be a trauma.'

'I'll give her a call.'

'I shouldn't. I think she wants a bit of space. I'm sure she'll be in touch when she feels up to it.'

There was a pause while Rochester digested this. Then he moved on. 'Well, while you're here, we might as well have a quick, unofficial look at your case. What can you tell me?'

'These are all the relevant case notes.' Sam took from her briefcase the blue file Tom had given her and passed it to Rochester. Doing so was taking a chance, but she'd decided to risk it.

Rochester leafed rapidly through the pages. 'Same old Sam. I take it Adams gave you these.'

Sam couldn't hide her consternation at his immediately identifying the source of the file.

'Don't look so surprised, I might not have found out about Harriet yet but I do keep in touch with my old patch. Can't Adams persuade Reid to come to us for help?'

'He's been moved off the enquiry.'

Rochester gave a humourless laugh. 'Night of the long knives, eh? Well that was always Reid's way. Where's he gone?'

'South Division.'

'Poor Tom. Let's hope he survives.'

Sam said, 'That was the other thing I wanted to talk to you about.'

'Whether I could bring Tom Adams here on attachment?'

'Yes.'

'He's a good man and we do still have a few vacancies to fill. Are you sure he'd want to come?'

'I'm sure.'

'OK, I'll see what I can do. I can't promise. It'll be up to his new chief, but as I know him well I shouldn't think there'll be a problem.'

'Thanks.'

Rochester put the file down on top of his desk.

'There's something else,' she said.

He leant back in his chair expectantly. She rummaged in her bag and took out a slip of paper. 'Catherine Solheim, one of the FBI agents who are over here to investigate the case, gave me this.'

Rochester inspected it.

'They're lines from Aldous Huxley's *Brave New World*. They've been found at the scene of every murder except West's. We suspect that the note was there but was removed before we got there.'

'Why come to you? Why not go to the police?'

'I think she's after a gold star from her boss. Wants to make the arrest herself.'

'OK. So who do you think moved the note?'

'Well, Solheim thinks it was the head of the base's security police, Major Hammond, covering for his boss, the base commander, Colonel Cully.'

'And what do you think?'

'I think she's wrong. Hammond is a policeman through and through. I don't see him getting involved in this sort of intrigue – and what possible motive could he have?'

'Is he a policeman first or a soldier first?'

Sam wasn't sure what he meant. 'Sorry?'

'Where do you think his real loyalties lie, with the military or with justice?'

Sam hadn't a ready answer. She would have liked to have said justice, but realised that in truth she didn't know Hammond that well.

Seeing her uncertainty, Rochester changed the subject. 'Come on, I'll show you the nerve centre of this little operation. You never know, we might learn something. I'll introduce you to some of the team as well.'

He led her through the hall and out of a side door, down through the park to a set of modern buildings close to the lake. They pushed through a set of swing doors and went down a long staircase.

'How many on the team?' asked Sam.

'About twenty so far, but we're still recruiting. It's quite hard. We want only the best and the forces, not surprisingly, are reluctant to part with their best people.'

'Sort of thinking man's nick?'

Rochester was nettled by this description of his pet project, and replied curtly, 'Something like that.'

At last they reached the control room. It was a large open-plan room full of the usual paraphernalia associated with a squad room – briefing boards, computers, televisions – and there were side offices and the all-important small kitchen. Most of the desks were still unoccupied, and the room had a slightly deserted feel to it. But those who were there were hard at work.

Rochester led Sam across to a young man who was working at a computer terminal.

'James, let me introduce you to Doctor Samantha Ryan. She's the forensic pathologist for Cambridge. Dr Ryan, this is DC James Morgan.'

The young detective stood up and shook hands shyly.

'It's Sam.' It was unusual for a police officer to be shy and she found it rather charming.

Rochester went on, 'Doctor Ryan's dealing with the Cambridge serial case. Managed to pick anything up?'

Sam looked at him in surprise, and he explained, 'When I heard you were coming I didn't think it was for my company. As I said before, I guessed what it might be all about and got James here to do some preliminary work on the case before you arrived. It's nice to be one step ahead of you for once.'

Sam smiled.

'James is working on our new computer system, funnily enough called Catchem, which stands for Centralised Analytical Team Collating Homicide Expertise and Management. It's similar to the FBI's Vi-Cap computer, only better. It's already linked into the European network, Interpol, so hopefully we can track serial criminals no matter where they might decide to roam around Europe.'

'Are you linked into the FBI system yet?'

'No, not yet. There are a few hurdles to cross before we get to that one, but we will.'

'So what makes it better?'

'It's more analytical. It's capable of pointing out patterns and analysing them – a sort of mechanical psychologist. James has been feeding in what information we've been able to glean on your murders. Any joy?'

Morgan shook his head. 'Nothing I'm afraid, sir. Not enough data.'

'Well, sorry about that,' Rochester said, 'but it's early days. Your file should help.'

Sam's eyes were gleaming. 'Ask your computer how

many women have been murdered or gone missing close to American Air Force bases in the UK over, say, the last five years.'

Morgan looked up at Rochester, who nodded his approval.

'How close to the bases do you want me to go?' Morgan asked.

Sam thought for a moment. 'A mile. Try a mile.'

'Any particular type of woman? Age, build, colour of hair?'

'Not really, but you could try between sixteen and fifty.'

'That's pretty wide but I'll try.'

Morgan began to enter instructions on the computer key-pad. His fingers were fast and it only took a moment. The screen became blank apart from the flickering cursor, as the computer began to analyse the information. Suddenly it came to life and information began scrolling down the screen. There were eight entries in all, each with name, date of birth, the time, location and date of disappearance, and the name of the investigating officer. Rochester bent close to the screen, frowning. It looked as though something was bothering him.

'Is that unusual?' she asked.

Still peering at the screen, he said, 'Maybe.' He told Morgan, 'Try ten years.'

Again Morgan's fingers flew, and again the cursor flickered as they awaited the answer. This time four new names appeared on the screen, together with all the relevant information. All the women had been reported missing.

Rochester gave another order. 'What about men in the same area?'

Again the instructions were fed in and a few minutes later the information came back. There were only two.

'Print the screens off for me, James, and order up all the files on the missing girls. Get them faxed across. Bill!' A detective at the far side of the room looked up. 'Have you got a couple of men free?'

The man looked around the room before his gaze fixed on two detectives sitting at a desk close to where Rochester and Sam were standing. 'Dan, Harry, are you free for a couple of hours?'

Their despairing look clearly showed they weren't.

'Good, then can you liaise with the commander?'

They nodded reluctantly.

Rochester was unsympathetic. 'There's a file on my desk. Can you get it copied – I'll probably need about six copies. Then have a word with James and make sure the "missing from home" files from the computer printout are sent straight down to us from the relevant forces.'

'What if they want to know why we want them?'

'Stonewall them until we've had a chance to check a few things out. Any problems, tell them it's a Home Office enquiry and if they want to answer to them they're more than welcome. That should keep any inquisitive noses out.'

He crossed to Morgan, who handed him a copy of the printout while his colleague made his way quickly out of the room to collect the file.

Sam was as impatient as ever. 'Perhaps you could tell me what's happening?'

'We might have expected to find one or two missing girls within a certain distance of a particular point but not twelve. It might be just one of those coincidences –

I shouldn't think they're all victims – but it's odd never-theless.'

'You mean you think our killer might have been at it for years?'

'We won't know that until we start getting a bit more information in, but it's got to be checked out, and quickly.'

'What happens now?'

'If I'm right, we seek Home Office approval to investi-gate the cases and start pulling the team together.'

'You should talk to the two FBI agents. They're staying at Leeminghall American Air Force base. It's all in the report.'

'Right, well, can I suggest we retire to my office and go through the report page by page together. And we'd better see what we can do about having Tom Adams across here as soon as possible as well.'

Sam nodded, well pleased.

'Come on,' he said. 'You've got a lot of explaining to do.' And he led her out of the building and back to his office.

After they'd finished going through the file, they went back to the control room, where a briefing was held. As hour after hour passed, the squad's activity became more and more frantic, with phone calls being made, faxes sent and received, and detectives scurrying in all directions. Despite her interest in what was happening, Sam felt separate from it, like a student watching one of her PMs through a glass screen. If there was going to be a role for her to play in the enquiry, this wasn't the time.

It was late by the time Rochester called it a day. He tried to persuade Sam to stay the night but, as she had no change of clothes or make-up with her, she decided she'd rather make the long trip home.

It was the early hours of the morning when she arrived. She was both physically and mentally exhausted, and only just had the strength to drag herself up the stairs, pull off her clothes, take the phone off the hook and fall into bed. She was asleep in an instant.

A loud noise jolted her awake. She sat up, her heart thumping. What could the noise be? Was it a window banging? Or had she dreamt it? Then it came again. Some one was hammering on the front door.

She turned on her bedside light and looked at her clock: 4.15 a.m. It was highly unusual for someone to call at this time of night without phoning first and she was nervous. Slipping into her dressing-gown, she ran downstairs and turned on the outside light, then ran back up to her bedroom and looked out of the window.

She saw the car first – a Cherokee Jeep – then heard a familiar Southern American drawl: 'Doctor Ryan? Doctor Ryan!'

At the instant she recognised the voice, Doyle and Solheim came into view. Sam said wearily, 'What the hell do you want? Do you have any idea what time it is? Why didn't you ring first?'

Doyle said, 'I'm sorry, but your phone was permanently engaged.'

Sam remembered that she'd taken it off the hook. 'So what's so urgent that it drags you out here at four o'clock in the morning to disturb other people's sleep?'

'Commander Rochester wants us at Cromwell Park immediately. There's been some kind of development.'

CHAPTER TEN

The journey to Hampshire was hair-raising, with Doyle's driving leaving much to be desired. Sam wondered at times if he'd forgotten he was in England and had reverted to driving on the right. Fortunately, apart from the occasional milk-float and a smattering of early-morning shift workers, there was little on the road to threaten them.

By the time they arrived at Cromwell Park, it was full daylight. The early-morning freshness blowing through the trees in the park lightened Sam's mood and chased away the lethargy that had hung over her during the journey. She felt hungry and realised that she hadn't eaten for over twenty-four hours. She wasn't sure what the food was like at the Park but hoped she would at least be offered breakfast.

They were cleared quickly through the gate by an agitated security officer, who looked cold and tired. Sam directed Doyle to the gravelled car park in front of the house. Emerging from the car, she stretched until she felt she might snap in the middle, in an effort to ease her stiffness after the long journey.

A uniformed police officer came down the front steps

to greet them. 'You didn't waste much time.' He shook hands with Sam. 'Chief Inspector Terry Lambert. I'm Mr Rochester's staff officer.'

'Doctor Ryan, Samantha Ryan.'

'Glad to meet you at last. I think we must have missed each other last time you were here. You've caused quite a stir.'

Sam gestured to her companions. 'These are Agents Catherine Solheim and Edward Doyle from the FBI's Behavioral Science Unit at Quantico.'

'It's good to have you here,' said Lambert. 'I understand you've agreed to help us with the enquiry?'

Doyle wasn't having that. 'On the contrary, I thought it was you who'd agreed to help me.'

Unwilling to get involved in an argument, Lambert merely smiled. Doyle took Lambert's smile for a sign of weakness, and was pleased that the British police were going to be so easy to 'deal' with.

'Well, if you'd like to follow me,' said Lambert, 'Mr Rochester is expecting you.'

Instead of going up the steps to Rochester's office, as Sam had expected, he took them round the side of the house, towards a set of modern buildings at the back, where Sam knew the incident room had been established.

Rochester was standing at the far side of the room talking a detective who was inputting information into a computer. Lambert led them across to him. 'Sir, Doctor Ryan and party.'

Rochester looked up and smiled at Sam. 'Sam, thanks for coming at such short notice.'

Doyle, annoyed at being relegated to a mere member of Sam's party, said, 'Agent Ed Doyle from Quantico. I'd just like to say thank you for agreeing to help us with this enquiry.'

The implications of his words weren't lost on Rochester. 'Anything we can do to help our American colleagues. I passed that message on to your Mr Bartoc only yesterday.'

Doyle stiffened. Bartoc was head of the FBI unit at Quantico, a ruthless man who wanted political office and stamped hard on anyone who made his tenure at the Bureau look anything but perfect. Of all the people Doyle had ever dealt with it, Bartoc was the one he most feared.

Rochester followed up on his verbal victory. 'He's already assured me of your – the FBI's – fullest co-operation. He's sending us all the appropriate files on the US murders so we can update our computer.'

Doyle had been outflanked, and he knew it. He said, with as good a grace as he could manage, 'Good. I'm sure they'll be of great help.'

'Did you bring the files I requested?'

Doyle had not. He hadn't forgotten, but had deliberately left them behind. He wasn't sure precisely what was going on, or how much of a threat this new agency might be to his personal success in this investigation, and until he could establish that he'd decided to co-operate as little as possible.

'No. I'm sorry. It has all been a bit of a rush. I forgot them.'

Rochester's sceptical look made it clear he was aware

of the lie. 'Well, no matter. Luckily Mr Bartoc's having them faxed across to my office. They should arrive very soon.'

Having dealt effectively with Doyle, Rochester turned to Solheim. 'From Mr Bartoc's description, you must be Catherine Solheim.' They shook hands. 'He speaks very well of you, a future star of the department I'm informed.'

Sam looked at Doyle out of the corner of her eye. Although he had himself well in hand, she could see his anger rising. It seemed that Rochester intended to keep the two agents apart – not that that was going to be difficult, given their already strained relationship.

Rochester turned back to the computer screen. 'Well, I suppose I'd better tell you why I've dragged you all down here at such short notice.'

They looked at him expectantly.

'Although it hasn't been properly established yet, we think that the murders committed in Cambridge may be linked not only to the ones the FBI are investigating in America but to a number of missing women both here and in Europe.'

Doyle asked, 'How many women are we talking about?'

'There are possible links with the disappearance of at least eight women over a ten-year period in Britain, but we're still looking.'

'What are the links?'

'We've established that they all disappeared within a one-mile radius of an American air-base and, to date anyway, not one of them has been found, only listed as missing from home.'

Doyle nodded. 'That could be a pattern.'

'Are such patterns out of the ordinary?' asked Sam.

'Yes,' said Rochester. 'We've looked at other patterns, such as the number of males who went missing in the same area over the same period and done an analysis of general statistics for missing people. We've established a significant anomaly associated with the air-bases, which merits further investigation, although it's still too early to be absolutely sure.'

Doyle was poised to ask another question, but Solheim got hers in first. 'Are you sure about your information?'

'Catchem is still quite new but its system works well. But there's a bit more to it than just the US and British angle. DC Morgan decided – for reasons best known to himself, but we're grateful for his initiative – to link into the Interpol computer in France. He fed in the same search information as we used for our computer. Over the areas of Europe with which Interpol have connections, they've established that during the past ten years, over fifteen women have been reported missing within a one-mile radius of US air-bases. We're making a note of the missing women's names. The body of one further woman was discovered in a wooded area about half a mile from an American base in Germany about a year ago. She'd been stabbed to death and both her kidneys removed. The murderer was never arrested.'

The Special Operations team had been out since first light. Bill Smethurst and his partner, Andy Clough, like the rest of the unit thought it was a complete waste of time and taxpayers' money. They hated last-minute jobs, which played havoc with their social lives and put their marriages and relationships under extra strain.

Susan Dench had been missing for over three years. Smethurst remembered looking for her when she disappeared. It had been a pretty low-key affair. She'd gone missing two or three times before and had turned up after three or four days, having spent her time with some unknown male. So in Dench's case it was a matter of going through the motions. After all she was just another sad statistic in a world full of sad statistics.

The fact that this time she failed to return home was no great cause for concern: it was bound to happen. There had been several alleged sightings of her in London, so they were pretty sure that, like a northern moth, she had flitted her way towards the bright lights of Soho. The only people still convinced something awful had happened to her were her parents – and what did they know? They'd campaigned for a while and aroused some local media interest, but the fuss died down along with the investigation.

Why they were looking for her again, after all this time, Smethurst had no idea, unless the bosses knew something the unit didn't. The bosses seldom did tell them anything interesting, working on a need-to-know basis, and in most cases it was considered that they didn't need to know. It must be important though, he thought, because they'd called out every unit they'd got, even calling people in from their rest days and holiday to help with the search, and that was going to cost them a packet in overtime.

Surprisingly, in view of the size and nature of the search, there was no media coverage and no civilians were involved. Normally, the police were grateful for all the help they could get, and more than enough volunteers usually turned out for something like this. This time, however, it was police only.

They'd started from different points around the perimeter fence at the US air-base, forming a giant blue circle, then fanned outwards, stopping and searching any likely places. They'd even got police frogmen searching the local lakes and ponds, which seemed a bit of a waste of time after so long: they'd be lucky to find her teeth. But at least it made it look as if they were taking things seriously. From time to time the whistle went and the line halted, as something was found and examined before being bagged and taken away for analysis. Then the line moved on again.

Smethurst's section finally reached Alexander's Place, an area of rough woodland covering about a hundred acres. Thick and unkempt, the undergrowth was difficult to get through. Smethurst dug his stick into a tangle of thornbushes, weeds and grass and prodded around in the hope that he'd strike something interesting. He did. He recognised the sound at once: corrugated iron – he'd moved enough of it in his time.

He called across to Clough, 'Over here!'

His partner stopped what he was doing and came over. Smethurst hit the object again for Clough's benefit.

Clough wasn't impressed. 'A piece of corrugated iron.

Well done, PC Smethurst. You'll probably get a medal for this. Well, in you go and get it. Might have a confession written on the back.'

Smethurst ignored the sarcasm and forced his way through the thorns into the undergrowth. Stamping down hard, he heard the corrugated iron crack and then shift beneath his feet. As Andy Clough watched, his partner first shouted, then screamed, then disappeared in a cloud of dirt and foliage.

Rochester left Doyle and Solheim going over the information from Interpol while he took Sam out of the control room and up to his office. To her surprise, sitting at the large round table at the centre of the room was Tom Adams. Next to him was an elderly man she didn't know. Both men stood up as she came in.

Rochester said, 'Sam, I think you and Tom Adams know each other. And this is Professor Boyd Charlton from the other place.'

Sam took 'the other place' to be Oxford, Rochester having been not only a former chief constable of the area but also educated at Trinity College, Cambridge, and proud of it.

He went on, 'Boyd holds the chair for ancient studies and has a particular interest in ancient writings and codes.'

They all sat down round the table.

'So what's that got to do with the case?' Sam asked.

'The writings at the scenes of the murders,' said Rochester. 'I faxed Boyd some copies and he thinks he's come up with the answer.'

Professor Charlton was more cautious. 'Well, I haven't come up with the answer yet, but I do think there's a strong possibility that I might get somewhere with it.'

Sam still couldn't see how ancient writings were relevant. 'What have you got so far?'

Charlton asked Rochester, 'Did you manage to get some more of the sheets?'

Rochester picked up from his desk a file of faxes, which he handed to Charlton. The professor slipped on a pair of half-rimmed spectacles and buried his nose in the file. He took his time over it, while the rest of the party waited patiently. Sam caught Tom's eye several times. There was a lot she wanted to say and even more she wanted to ask, but this wasn't the right time or place: she'd just have to wait.

At last, Charlton put the papers down. 'Well, there's nothing obvious. A bit of time might draw something out.'

Rochester said, 'Well, we'll leave it with you, professor. How long before you can give us anything concrete?'

'Shouldn't take too long. If it's there I'll find it.'

Rochester pushed the small brass bell on the side of his desk. 'I've arranged for a taxi for you. It should be here by now.' He shook hands with the professor, and saw him to the door. 'The very best of luck, professor, and don't forget to keep me informed.'

As he came back to the table, he said, 'Sam, I want you on secondment to the squad until this matter is cleared up.'

Sam felt that things were moving out of her control,

and wasn't at all sure that she like the feeling. 'I'm not sure that's a particularly practical idea, and, besides, I'm not sure either the university or the hospital would tolerate it.'

Rochester smoothly cut the ground from under her feet. 'I've cleared it with them both. Trevor Stuart has offered to take on the bulk of your work' – *now* Trevor chooses to be helpful, Sam thought – 'and anything he can't cope with Jean tells me she can take care of for him. Impressive lady, your Jean. The hospital and university authorities are on-side as well. So what do you say?'

She capitulated. 'As long as I don't have to share a room with Charlton.'

Rochester smiled. 'You ask a lot but it's a deal.' He turned to Adams. 'Tom, as I'm sure you and Sam have a lot to talk over, can I trust you to take her back to the control room while I arrange for her to have an office and room?' Adams nodded. 'By the way, Sam, I don't know if you already know but we have our own lab and mortuary here. If you want to go and have a look at them, feel free.'

Rochester stood up abruptly, always a sign that a meeting was over and it was time his visitors left. Adams and Sam made their way across to the door. As they reached it, Rochester called across to her, 'Your friend Hammond has gone, by the way.'

'Gone? Gone where?'

'Recalled to the States this morning, travelled on an American Air Force cargo plane, of all things. Obviously keen to go.'

'Do we know where he is now?'

'Funny thing, no one seems to know. State Department, Pentagon, Washington, they're all keeping quiet.'

'What about Cully?'

'Oh, he's still there. I've still got a bit of checking to do, but I don't think he's our man. Killers don't tend to be so anxious about their careers.'

'Do you think Hammond is—?'

'Our killer?' Rochester shrugged. 'I don't know. They're playing some sort of game. I just wish I knew what it was. These are deeper waters than we thought.'

As Sam turned back to the door, Rochester warned her, 'Don't get too comfortable, Sam. I've got a feeling you're going to be very busy very soon.'

When Bill Smethurst recovered, he found himself lying on his back at the bottom of an eight-foot-deep pit. Above him he could see the treetops and above them blue sky with clouds scudding across it.

Andy Clough's face came into view. 'Bill! Bill, you all right?'

Smethurst felt his arms and legs. All present and correct. The fall hadn't hurt, just surprised and winded him. 'I'm all right, Andy. Just me dignity that's taken a bit of a knock.'

He sat up and looked round. The pit was square with sheer sides, and was clearly man-made. In one wall there was what looked like the opening to a tunnel. Its entrance was about five feet hight and made of concrete, and the tunnel seemed to slope down deeper into the ground. By the side of the entrance was a metal switch which he took to be a light switch. He stood up and brushed himself down, then went over and clicked the switch up and down a few times. Nothing happened. If it was a light switch, it was broken. He called, 'Andy, get a dragon light down here, would you?'

Clough nodded. He said, 'Hang on,' and disappeared from sight.

A few moments later he was back and passing down to Smethurst a giant orange light. Smethurst turned it on and shone its broad beam into the tunnel. The way looked clear. Bending down, he went inside and began to make his way cautiously along. The tunnel stank of age and damp. Green slime oozed through the ceiling and long dark patches stained the bottom of the grey concrete walls. Mud and slime had seeped in over the years and formed a slippery carpet across the floor. More than once he almost lost his footing.

The beam of his light flickered around the walls of the tunnel as if it had a life of its own. He looked down at his hand: it was shaking. He grew cold and his legs began to weaken. He was more than frightened. For the first time in his police career he felt real terror – of what, he didn't know.

All his instincts told him to get out, to get back to the safety of the sunlight. But at the end of the tunnel, about fifty yards away, he could see the entrance to some kind of chamber, and he knew he had to check it out. With a supreme effort of will, he forced himself on, down to end of the tunnel.

He flashed the light round the chamber, not daring to move from the doorway. The light came to rest on a large table in the centre of the room. He held the beam there for a few seconds, trying hard not to believe what he saw. Then his nerve broke and he fled headlong back along the tunnel, plunging the horror into merciful darkness again.

Tom Adams and Sam went down the stone steps towards the car park, but Tom, instead of turning towards the operations room, took Sam's arm and led her to the opposite side of the building, from where they could look out over the formal gardens and the park. 'How's the family coping?' he asked sympathetically.

'Fine, thank you.'

There was a pause, then he said, 'I understand I owe you one.'

'Not really.'

'If it hadn't been for you I'd have been fighting a rearguard action against the press on South Division.'

'You were the best man for the job. You've been on the enquiry from the beginning. You understand what's been going on and I'm sure you'll help the squad towards a successful conclusion. I just pointed him in the right direction, that's all.'

'Why did you do it? After what happened I'd have thought . . . well . . . you know . . .'

'I'd hate you for ever and try and stitch you up first chance I got?'

'Something like that. Should have known you better, shouldn't I?'

'Yes, you should. If you did, perhaps we'd still be together.'

Tom took her by the arms. 'We still could be.'

She pulled away. 'No, we couldn't. I might not have liked what you said to me in the garden, but it was true none the less.'

He let her go, realising it was a lost cause. He wondered whether she'd contrived his transfer to this job just to get him away from Liz, in the hope that it would break them up. A woman scorned, he thought. But Sam wasn't like any other woman he'd ever met, and he didn't think she'd stoop to such petty intrigue.

He changed the subject as they walked on. 'Do you think Rochester's right?'

'About the extent of the serial killings? Yes.'

'He's only got circumstantial evidence.'

'I wouldn't have called the murders of West and Strachan circumstantial evidence, would you?'

'I'm talking about linking them together. You know, America, Britain, Europe. It all seems a bit unlikely.'

'Unterweger did it.'

'He was a one-off.'

'All serial killers are one-offs.'

Tom thought for a moment. 'There's enough circumstantial evidence to sink a boat and, given time, I think more substantial evidence will turn up.'

'Like what?'

'Charlton's codes, fibre evidence. Don't forget the fish scale and seeds you found on West. And the reports from the FBI might help.'

'Maybe your boys in blue will turn something up.'

'The woodentops? You never know – they've been lucky before – but don't hold your breath.'

They heard Chief Inspector Lambert calling urgently, 'Doctor Ryan, Inspector Adams, you're wanted, straight away. They've discovered something.'

The journey through Wiltshire and into Kent was exhilarating. To reach a murder scene, Sam usually had to find her way through some inhospitable landscape to an unmarked spot on a map. This time, however, there were police cars and motorcycles, all with their sirens screaming, and she, Dr Samantha Ryan, sat beside Commander Rochester in the back of one of the unmarked cars like a member of royalty or a senior member of the government. The difference was that people were usually pleased to see members of the royal family and Sam was not at all sure what her reception at the murder scene was going to be like.

Despite their protests, Doyle and Solheim had been left behind. No police force liked outsiders interfering in a crime on their patch. A new squad – no matter how specialist – from outside the area taking over the investigation would be hard enough for the local force to swallow. Representatives from a foreign force, especially the FBI, might have caused not just friction but open warfare. Rochester knew this was a unique opportunity to convince the Home Office of the need for his squad, and he wasn't about to let a couple of FBI agents spoil that.

Nor was it just the police reaction which worried Sam. The forensic pathologist for the area, Dr John Alexander, was hardly likely to welcome Sam's interference in his work. They had worked together in London some years before, and she knew him to be a good man and a first-rate pathologist. Unfortunately, he was also pompous and a bit of an individualist, who didn't suffer fools – or people who interfered with his work – at all, let alone gladly. Sam hoped fervently that she wouldn't have to deal with him, that one of the county's other pathologists had been called out, but she had an nasty feeling that it would probably be John.

The sight of a silver fighter plane flying low overhead warned her that they were close to their destination. A few minutes later they reached the police cordon, which was under siege from the media with all their equipment and the inevitable buzz of speculation. The journalists were well aware that something out of the ordinary was happening and would stop at almost nothing to find out what. The fact that they were already present indicated that their inside informants had been at work. The sight of the motorcade brought an immediate response: every camera, light and microphone was turned on the cars. Sam was taken aback by it all and, to Rochester's amusement, shielded her face like a Hollywood starlet caught with someone else's husband.

The cars moved slowly past the army of news-hounds, through the police cordon to the murder scene. At last they stopped and Rochester and Sam emerged into the warm afternoon air. He was immediately greeted by a uniformed police superintendent and they began an earnest conversation. Sam look round at the landscape of fields and woodland. It was remarkably unspoilt for an area with one of the highest populations in the country. She wondered if it was the existence of the base which had allowed it to remain in this virgin state and whether it would stay unspoilt once the base had gone.

The police activity around the scene wasn't as frantic as normal. It was as if they were all waiting for something to happen. Sam suddenly realised that indeed they were, and that what they were waiting for was her.

Rochester said, 'Doctor Ryan, over here.' When she joined him, he said, 'Allow me to introduce you to Superintendent Clarkson. He's to be our liaison officer while we're here.'

There was not the glimmer of a smile on Clarkson's face as they shook hands. His face was serious, even bleak, and he had a voice to match. He said to Rochester, 'If you'd like to follow me, sir, I'll take you to the scene.'

As they moved off, Sam asked, 'Is there anything you can tell me before I begin to examine the body?'

'Bodies.'

'There's more than one?'

'At least two, maybe more. They're in one of the old defence pits. There are dozens of pits scattered around the woods and countryside. They were built as the first line of defence in case the Russians invaded during the Cold War. Mostly used by kids as dens now, and by courting couples. The policeman who found it got himself in a bit of a state. Afraid of the dark, I think.'

Sam recalled her own loss of nerve at the scene of Mary West's murder and felt a rush of sympathy for the unknown PC. 'Have the other pits been searched?'

'We're doing that now. Problem is that after all these years, the base aren't sure where they all are. Their location was a big secret until a few years ago, and by then they weren't considered important enough to survey properly.'

'Well, someone certainly seems to know where they are.'

Clarkson wasn't happy about Sam's line of questioning and kept looking across at Rochester for support. But he got none.

'We think one body is that of Susan Dench, a twenty-two-year-old local girl. She went missing from home a few years ago. Bit of a bad lot apparently, slept around, few convictions for theft. She'd gone missing before, usually off shagging with some local thug.'

Sam was angered by the way he spoke of Dench, as if she didn't matter, as if being young and irresponsible was a hanging offence. 'So you just wrote her off?'

Clarkson was taken aback. 'We didn't exactly write her off. We did what we could under the circumstances.'

'And what was that?'

'Door-to-door, friends and family, notices to other forces.'

'Yet three years later you managed to find her within twenty-four hours when a bit of pressure was applied. Doesn't that suggest something to you?'

Clarkson bristled. 'This search was Home Office-funded. We don't have the cash to go looking for every half-baked youngster who decides to run away from home for the bright lights of some God-forsaken town.'

Sam knew he was probably right. It made her wonder

just how many more missing people weren't found because of lack of funds. It was a depressing thought.

Almost equally depressing was the fact that, when they reached the defence pit, the first person she saw was John Alexander, who was standing beside the pit looking down into it.

She decided to get the worst over quickly and went across to him. 'John.'

He glanced up at her and then back into the pit. 'Sam. We have become important these days. They wouldn't even allow me inside until you arrived.'

'Sorry. For what it's worth, it was nothing to do with me. The decisions are being made at a very high level.'

'So I understand from Clarkson. So how did you get involved in all this?'

'Wrong place, wrong time.'

Before he could say any more, a short, stocky man carrying the regulation white boiler suit came up to her and introduced himself.

'John Haze. I'm the Crime Scene Manager on this one. Welcome. You'll be needing one of these.'

Sam thanked him and began to pull the overalls on.

Haze went on, 'I'd like to come down with you, if that's all right?'

Sam was glad that he had the courtesy to ask; perhaps there wasn't going to be as much friction as she'd feared. She smiled up at him and nodded. 'Has anyone else been down the pit yet?'

'The big-footed plod who fell down it. And we've had to get some lighting down there. It's pretty unpleasant – no wonder that copper had a funny turn. Other than that, I've kept everybody out. I was ordered to, actually. Is there something special about this one?'

Sam smiled again but didn't answer, merely picking up her bag and slinging it over her shoulder.

'Don't tell me,' he said resignedly. 'Need-to-know basis and I don't need to know.'

He gripped the top of the ladder firmly, steadying it for Sam as she climbed down into the pit. It was a lonely, unpleasant spot, probably ideal for their killer. The tunnel in front of her was now well-lit and she could see down it into the chamber beyond. It reminded her of an Egyptian burial chamber with passages and secret chambers. She'd heard stories about buildings retaining the essence of dramatic and horrific events, which gave such places a frightening atmosphere. This, she thought, was one of those places. She felt a definite reluctance to walk down the tunnel and face what was at the end of it, and was glad she didn't have to do so on her own.

As soon as Haze and Alexander had joined her in the pit, she began to make her way along the tunnel, moving with caution on the slippery concrete. As she got closer to the chamber, she thought heard an unearthly scream in the distance. Startled, she looked round at the others. They gave no sign of having heard anything. It must have been just her imagination.

Nevertheless, it was a relief, when she reached the chamber, to find it empty of apparitions. It was large, about twelve feet high and thirty feet square. Decaying maps of the area were still pinned up around the room. But what stopped her in her tracks was a giant symbol on one wall. It was badly faded, but she recognised it at once: Ω.

In the middle of the room was a large table, lying across which were the skeletal remains of a human being. The skull faced Sam, leaning slightly to one side, its jaw hanging open in a wide, ghastly smile. The floor was strewn with bones, probably the result of animal activity. There was a neat pile of clothing at the foot of one wall, and, at the far end of the room, another skull. She couldn't tell how many people these bones had constituted, but of one thing she was absolutely certain: this was one of his killing chambers.

She became aware that the others had joined her in the doorway. Their silence was as appalled as her own.

Sam straightened her shoulders resolutely and asked Alexander, 'Do you want to have first go?'

Matching her tact, he said, 'No, no, it's your shout. You go ahead. I'll just watch from the background.'

And wait for me to get it wrong, Sam thought wryly. She pulled her tape-recorder from her bag and began to dictate. 'Alexander's Place woods, East Stratton. The scene is a chamber at the end of a tunnel extending from a large pit dug into the earth. It is believed to be part of an outer defence network built to protect the base during the so-called Cold War. It hasn't, however, been used for many years. It is about twelve feet high and approximately' – she looked around the room again – 'thirty feet square. Maps of the area are pinned to the walls, and on one wall is the omega symbol seen at the Mary West murder scene. There is a pile of clothing by one wall. There is a table at the centre of the room, on top of which are the unclothed skeletal remains of a human torso. Both arms have been secured above the skeleton's head with a pair of handcuffs before being tied to one of the table legs by a rope. The right leg has also been secured to one of the table legs, while the left leg is missing.' She paused, went across to the table and looked the skeleton up and down, before taking a closer look at the skull. 'A red rag of some description has been pushed deep into the skull's mouth and fixed there by a piece of cord.' From her bag she took a pair of tweezers with which she carefully removed the dried-out rag. She held it up it in front of her and studied it.

Alexander stepped forward, trying to see more clearly. 'What do you think it is?' he asked.

'It looks like a pair of pants but, given the state they're in, I couldn't be entirely sure. Probably the deceased's.'

Alexander nodded and stepped back again. Haze passed Sam a small exhibit bag and she dropped the object into it.

She resumed her examination of the skull, starting with the nose. 'The sciatic notch is comparatively wide. The supra-orbital ridge and nuchal crest, on the other hand, are relatively small.'

'What about the pelvis?' demanded Alexander.

'The pelvis,' she said, refusing to be put out by the interruption, 'is wide and low. On preliminary examination the skeleton would appear to be that of a female, a little over five feet in height and in her late teens or early twenties. She has been dead for several years.'

That was about all she could reasonably establish for now. The rest would have to wait for the PM.

Haze was standing quietly next to Alexander, waiting for her to finish. She told him, 'You can remove the body when you're ready.'

'I'd like to have the area thoroughly searched and photographed before we move anything, Doctor, if that's OK.'

Sam went to the second skull and crouched down by it.

Haze joined her. 'Alas, poor Yorick,' he said.

Normally Sam would have considered such a comment to be in the poorest possible taste, but just now she was grateful to him for lightening the grim atmosphere. She examined the skull. She was sure it was female but, again, that was all she could say until the PM.

She stood up and turned to Alexander. 'Is the hospital ready to do the PM?'

'It's all been prepared. Do you want me to assist?'

'If you don't mind.'

'I promise I won't get in the way,' he said sarcastically.

Sam appreciated that Alexander's nose had been put more than a little out of joint, but there was nothing she could do about it and she was irritated by his sarcasm.

'Good.'

The remark clearly annoyed him and Sam hoped it would shut him up for a while. She began to examine the walls, carefully checking each map.

Haze watched with interest. 'I think you'll be lucky to discover any trace elements after all this time, Doctor.'

'I'm not looking for trace elements. That's your job.'

'What then?'

Sam said nothing, and continued her minute search of the walls. Although the omega sign was clear enough, there was no sign of the all-important writing so she turned her attention to the pile of clothing. She crouched down and examined it. There was a green floral-patterned dress, a pair of light-brown tights and a small white handbag. No shoes. She checked the floor around the pile, but they weren't there. Opening the handbag carefully, she examined the contents. They were pretty much what she had expected: make-up, a purse containing a few pounds, the usual clutter found in any woman's bag. And there was also an envelope printed with the name and address of the Social Services. The postmark was just legible: 1992. The envelope was addressed to Miss S. Dench.

After reporting her findings to Rochester, Sam decided to wait for the remains to be removed before making her way to the hospital. There were several friendly faces here and she wasn't sure what her reception would be at the local mortuary, especially since Alexander had gone on ahead.

A makeshift canteen had been set up. She collected a plastic cup of coffee, and sipped gratefully. It was vile, but nowhere near as vile as the air in the pit, which she could still taste at the back of her throat. There was a low wall nearby, and she perched on it, turning over in her mind what she'd seen.

Tom Adams came over to join her. 'Not much to tell yet, I hear.'

'You hear right. We'll have to hope the SOCOs pick

up something relevant. If not we'll just have to go by the circumstances and informed guesses. It's how you solve half your cases, isn't it?'

He let the crack pass. 'If they're victims of the same killer, the balloon's going to go up.'

'I thought it already had.'

'It'll be good for Rochester's new squad, especially if he can get a result. There are one or two politicians not in agreement with the concept who've tried to put their oar in. This should convince them of its merits.'

Sam smiled grimly. 'Hell of a way to convince anyone, isn't it?'

Adams shrugged.

'Tom, there's a small favour I'd like.'

He looked at her suspiciously.

'The samples that are collected from the scene: I'd like them sent to Cambridge. Get Marcia to have a look at them. She already knows the case and is more likely to be able to spot the unusual.'

'Or we could bring Marcia down here, make her part of the team for a while.'

'Whatever, but I would like her to have a look at things.'

Adams nodded. 'I'll see what I can do.'

Haze suddenly appeared from within the wood and waved frantically to Sam. She jumped down from her perch and jogged towards him, followed by Adams. Haze was already half-way back to the pit by the time she caught up with him.

'What is it?'

'I think it's what you were looking for earlier. You remember, need-to-know basis.'

The pit was cluttered with the black body-bags and large polythene sheets that would be used to remove the girl's remains. They picked their way through them and Haze led the way briskly down the tunnel. When he reached the room, he went over to the table and stood waiting beside it. Sam and Tom hurried to join him.

He said triumphantly, 'I take it this is what you were looking for?'

They looked down at the table's surface, which had been brushed clean and wiped. Carved into the wood were the words

FRY, LECHERY, FRY.
JOHN SAVAGE.

Sam recognised the words immediately. They were spoken in *Brave New World* by John Savage as he recalled what Thersites said as Thersites, Troilus and Ulysses watched the seduction scene between Diomedes and Cressida. It was when Savage finally decided that Lenina – if not all women – was a strumpet. Sam looked at the pathetic remains scattered around the room. Some other words from the book seemed suddenly very relevant: 'Pain was a fascinating horror.'

CHAPTER ELEVEN

O nce the chamber had been cleared, Sam made her way to the local mortuary with the rest of the team. The remains of the bodies had been collected in large plastic bags. Haze was certain they had found almost all there was to find, though the search for very small items, such as slivers of bone, was still going on.

Sam had just finished changing into her PM clothes, when there was a knock on the door.

'Come in.'

A young, smiling face looked round the door. 'Afternoon. Doctor Ryan?'

'Guilty.'

The smile broadened. 'Robert Young.'

The name rang a bell in Sam's memory, but she couldn't place him.

'I'm the anthropologist.'

'Oh, I'm sorry. I'd no idea they'd called one in. I'm not the local pathologist, I'm afraid, so some messages have yet to come through to me.'

'So I understand. Your Mr Rochester seems to have ruffled a few feathers.'

Sam smiled at him. 'He's good at that.'

As she spoke, recognition dawned. Of course, *that* Robert Young. He'd made his name working on the Romanovs' remains when they were discovered in eastern Russia. It was largely thanks to him that the Tsar's family had been identified and the causes of their deaths established. Without his work, the work done later by Gill and Ivanov at Aldermaston would not have been possible.

He was a tall, gangling creature, with the sort of scruffiness that comes from lack of interest in appearances. Sam guessed that his work absorbed him almost entirely, leaving little room for thoughts about trivia like clothes. She looked forward to working with him.

Young said, 'I've been asked to arrange what we have into some semblance of order. I take it you don't mind my interference?'

'As long as you don't mind me hovering around in the background and watching an expert at work.'

Young gave a half-laugh, clearly flattered. 'Well, I should say it would be a privilege. Shall we dance?'

Sam nodded, and together they made their way into the mortuary.

Although it was larger than the mortuary at the Park Hospital, it wasn't as modern and looked like a product of the late 1930s. Five of the white-porcelain-topped tables were lit by overhead lights, and on each was a large plastic bin-bag, containing some of the remains found inside the chamber and sketch-maps showing precisely where each bone had been found. Later the photographs would arrive, but for now Young seemed content with his sketches.

He called across to Haze and asked what was in which bag.

'Bags one and two have the remains we found on the table, and the ones we found on or near the table. Four and five contain the second skull and the fragments we found close to it. The final bag contains all the other bits that we couldn't identify immediately. They might come from a third body or they might be lots of bits from the other two.' He shrugged, 'Who knows?'

'Have the bones been labelled?' asked Young.

Haze said that, yes, each bone had been labelled with an exhibit label and number, and its position marked on the sketch-plan as it was collected.

'Shall we get on, then?'

The SOCO photographer came over. Young opened the first bag. As each bone was removed and laid on the table, photographs were taken. Sam watched and waited, as the bags were slowly emptied,

The public gallery was well filled. She saw not only Rochester and Adams but two uniformed officers whom she didn't know but who were obviously senior, plus two dark-suited officials. They were all watching the proceedings intently. Also there, of course, was Alexander, not so much watching proceedings as watching Sam's every move, criticism written plainly on his face.

Young recovered the skulls and set them on their respective tables. They were then X-rayed, so that the oral structure could be examined for identification. Human dentition tends to outlast all other body tissue after death, and dental work and restorations such as false teeth are particularly resistant to chemical and physical degeneration. The almost infinite number of permutations of aspects of dentition means that any given configuration is, for all practical purposes, unique, as fingerprints are.

Putting the skeletons together was like doing a giant 3D jigsaw. Young completed the first body quite quickly. It was the one from the bunker table-top and its position had largely protected it from hungry animals. Except that the left leg was missing, the remains were largely intact.

The second skeleton took longer. Apart from the skull, only about half of it had been found. The left leg was largely intact, but the right leg, part of the right hip and most of both arms were missing. The one consolation was that the remains at least resembled a human being. The third body did not. What was left of it covered barely a third of the table. It was merely a collection of dirt and brown bones placed in an approximation of their supposed positions: no skull, only part of one leg, part of one arm, fragments of the rib-cage, a twelve-inch section of the spinal column and some small pieces of bone which not even Young could identify.

Set aside on another table were further fragments of bone which he had discarded. Sam picked one of them up.

'What are these?' she asked.

'Animal bones,' said Young. 'Couple of foxes, I think. Probably died last winter. They're the most likely suspects for the scattering of the bones.'

Sam nodded and put the bone down again.

'Well that's about it,' he said. 'I've run out of pieces.'

Sam looked round the tables and their pathetic burden. The women must have endured terror upon terror – and then to end like this . . . The thought sent a chill of horror through her.

She forced herself back to the matter in hand. 'So what can you tell us?'

'Two white females, one black female. All in their late teens or early twenties. With a bit of luck, we shouldn't have too much trouble identifying the first two.'

'We already have some ID for the one we found on the table.'

'Good, good. The third one, unfortunately, I think you might have trouble with. As you can see there's not a lot to go on.'

Sam looked at the few bones which were all they'd found of the third girl, and had to agree. 'What about a DNA profile?'

'As long as the bones haven't been too heavily contaminated. But even then you're going to want a match and I can't see the authorities willing to match the DNA to the parents of every young girl who's gone missing over the past few years. Not very cost-effective.'

Again, she had to agree.

'They were all stabbed if that's any help,' he said. 'Look at the sharp-edged marks on the side of the rib-cage. They're consistent with a sharp instrument being forced upwards through the body and scratching across the rib-cage as it went. All three skeletons have similar injuries.'

Sam looked closely at them and then at other marks

along the rib-cage and across several of the other bones. 'What are these?'

Young inspected them briefly. 'Animal bites. Rats, foxes and badgers, I should think. I'll need a little more time to be sure.'

'How long do you think they've been dead?'

'Years rather than months, and I think they were probably killed around the same time. If you can establish when the first two girls went missing, it might help you narrow down when the third girl did. It's a bit thin, I know, but I assume anything helps.'

Sam nodded.

'Well, I'll leave you to finish up. Good working with you, and I'm sure we'll see each other soon.'

Sam shook his hand. 'You did all the hard work. There's only the finishing off to do. Thanks a lot.'

'Pleasure. I'll get my report in the post to you tomorrow.'

With that, Young swept out of the room, leaving Sam to examine what was left of the three young lives.

The meeting with Rochester after the PM was a short one. Sam could tell him little that he didn't already know, and what there was she would submit in her report. He told her that the two uniformed officers she'd seen in the gallery were the chief constable and assistant chief constable for the district. The two suits were civil servants from the Home Office, presumably there to be convinced of the need to establish Rochester's new squad and fix his place in police history.

She asked him to prepare a list of possible forensic

pathologists. With almost every force in the country now taking a renewed interest in its missing-from-home files, the likelihood of further bodies being discovered was that much greater and Sam knew she couldn't cope with it on her own. Rochester seemed to have accepted that it would be far easier if the local pathologist for a particular area conducted the initial PM and the report was forwarded to Sam for her inspection. They knew enough about their killer by now to recognise his modus operandi without too much trouble. It might also stop pathologists like Alexander from taking offence at the invasion of their domains by outsiders.

She was desperately tired. She hadn't had a good night's sleep for ages, and the frantic activities of the last twenty-four hours had left her feeling drained both emotionally and physically. She wasn't like Rochester, who seemed to go on for ever and still look fresh and alert in the morning. She felt grubby and was hungry. All she wanted was a long soak in a hot bath full to the top with the smelliest bubble bath she could find, with a plate of sandwiches by her side. Rochester arranged for her to be taken home in a police car, and she dreamt about that bath all the way home. He'd tried to persuade her to say at the college until the investigation was over, but she wanted home and Shaw and all her familiar things around her.

When they reached the cottage, she was startled to see that every light in the place seemed to be on. She was about to ask her police driver to wait while she went in and checked that all was well, when she remembered that Wyn had moved in. What's more, Sam had promised to help her but in all the excitement had completely forgotten.

She leant against the door for a moment, summoning up the courage to face her sister. Finally, sliding her key in the lock she turned it and pushed the door open. From the moment she went in, she noticed a difference. She felt like one of the seven dwarfs coming back to their clean and tidied cottage. In the sitting-room the changes were even more obvious. There were no newspapers on the floor, the grate had been cleaned out and the fire lit, and even her desk had been tidied. I'll never find a thing now, Sam thought. She ran a finger along the mantelpiece: it was clean.

She heard the kitchen door open and her sister call, 'Is that you, Sam?'

'You'd better hope so,' she called back, and headed for the kitchen.

Wyn had just brought in a basket of vegetables from the garden. She took one look at Sam and said, 'You look tired. Where the hell have you been?'

Sam sank wearily into a chair. 'Kent. Sorry I wasn't here to help you move in.'

'That's OK. The removal men were very good. I've arranged for them to send you the bill.'

'Thanks a lot.'

'Pleasure.'

Sam looked around the kitchen. It was as clean and tidy as she could ever remember it being.

Wyn dropped the vegetables into the sink. 'I don't know how anyone can live in these conditions.'

'Thanks a lot.'

'My pleasure. You been dealing with those bodies they found at the American air-base?'

Sam nodded.

'No wonder you look tired. It's been the main news all day.'

'Has it? Well, I'm not surprised.'

'How many bodies were there?'

'Three.'

'Well, there you go. Shouldn't believe everything you hear on the news. They said between six and twelve.'

Typical, Sam thought. Anything to try and make something more dramatic just so they could sell a few more papers.

'Looks like you could do with a bath and an early night,' said Wyn.

'You sound just like Mum.'

'Good. You used to do as she told you – well, most of the time.'

Sam dragged herself out of her chair and headed for the stairs. From half-way up, she called, 'Couldn't make me a plate of sandwiches, could you?'

Wyn put her head out of the kitchen door. 'I think you'll need something more substantial than that. Go and have your bath and it'll be ready when you come back down.'

Sam smiled her thanks, and trudged on up the stairs.

After Sam had eaten, they dumped the dishes in the sink and went through to the sitting-room.

'So what's the problem?' asked Wyn. 'I thought you loved a juicy murder.'

'Is it that obvious?'

Wyn nodded.

'I know it sounds stupid, but I feel a strong sense of evil about them.'

'I'd have thought there was an evil about all murders.'

'There is, but I've never sensed its presence so strongly before. You can almost touch it.'

'Shut up. You're giving me the willies.'

'Sorry.'

'If you're so unhappy, why don't you tell them you don't want to work on it any more?'

Sam sighed. 'If only it was that easy! I'm not happy but I do want to see it through to the end if I can.'

'I'm damn sure I wouldn't if I was as frightened as you are.'

'Yes you would. You're as nosy as I am, really.'

Wyn smiled affectionately at her sister. 'Well, if you don't get some sleep you won't be working on anything. Your eyes look as if they're on fire.'

Sam blinked. 'They are a bit sore. I'll hit the sack.' She hauled herself to her feet and plodded upstairs. From the top, she said, 'It's really good to have you here and thanks for everything. We are going to have a really good time.' Her final words tailed off into a huge yawn.

'Tell me that in six months' time,' Wyn said under her breath as she went into the kitchen to wash up.

Sam's bedroom curtains were flung open. She grunted crossly and pulled her duvet over her head to try and escape the bright light which streamed into the room.

But Wyn, after opening the windows wide, ruthlessly pulled the covers off her.

Sam scrabbled for the bedclothes. 'I'm not Ricky,' she complained. 'I'm a grown woman who is more than capable of knowing when she wants to get up.'

'Really. Well there are two policemen downstairs who want to see you.'

Sam felt she'd seen enough of Rochester and Adams for one lifetime, but if they'd come all this way it must be urgent, so she forced herself out of bed. Standing on her bedside cabinet was a cup of tea. She picked it up and took a mouthful. It was stone cold.

Wyn was unsympathetic. 'It was hot when I brought it up to you half an hour ago.'

'What time is it?'

'Half-past eleven.'

'*What?*'

Sam looked disbelievingly at her clock.

'I'll put the kettle on. I shouldn't keep your guests waiting too long if I were you. They don't seem the patient type to me.'

Sam fell backwards on to the bed, trying to summon the energy to move.

When she went downstairs, Wyn handed her a large mug of steaming coffee before disappearing back into the kitchen. To her surprise, she found not Rochester and Adams but Reid and Holmes waiting for her.

She looked at Reid and raised her mug. 'Like one?'

'No, thanks. Your cleaner's already made us one.'

There was a shout from the kitchen: 'Sister, actually. I just look like the cleaner.'

Reid was clearly torn between a wish to apologise and a reluctance to shout back. Enjoying his discomfiture, Sam sat down in her favourite position in the corner of the settee, where she was at once joined by Shaw.

'So,' she said, 'to what do I owe this unexpected visit?'

'The murders in Kent. I understand they might be linked with the two we had at Leeminghall and I was wondering what you could tell us.'

Sam stroked Shaw. 'I'm not sure I'm in a position to do that.'

'You're the Home Office pathologist dealing with the case, and I'm the senior investigating officer. Why shouldn't you be in a position to tell me what's going on?'

'Because at this point in time I am no longer working for you but for Commander Rochester at Cromwell Park and via him directly for the Home Office.'

'This is a local murder that needs solving and quickly. No matter where you might be attached at the moment, you still have a duty to keep me and my team informed of progress in this case. The other thing which you ought to remember is that at some point you will have to return to this force.'

Sam could feel her hackles rising. 'Are you threatening me?'

'Not at all. Just making you aware of your situation.'

'My situation is very clear. If you want any further information on this case, I suggest you speak to Commander Rochester or Inspector Adams. If they authorise me to pass information or reports on to you, I will. Otherwise you're going to have to take up any complaints you may have about the way the enquiry's being run with the Home Office and see how far it gets you.'

Reid became conciliatory. 'Look, we're all professionals, and we've all got our jobs to do. All I want is some idea of what's going on, in the hope that it might help the enquiry at this end.'

Sam refused to budge. 'As I said, make any requests you have to Commander Rochester. I'm sure he will be as helpful as he can be.'

There was a pause while Reid took in what she'd said. They were both well aware of how Rochester felt about Reid, and that there was no chance whatever of Reid getting anything from Rochester.

Before he could try again, the doorbell rang. Sam pushed Shaw off her lap and went to answer it but Wyn was there first. 'It's all right, ma'am, I'll get it.' She tugged her forelock as she spoke.

Sam smiled at her sister's sarcasm but neither Reid nor Holmes flinched. Wyn came into the sitting room with Tom Adams at her heels, and said unnecessarily, 'It's Tom.'

He looked as surprised to see Reid and Holmes as Sam had been. Reid stood up and held out his hand. 'Tom.'

Despite his deep-rooted dislike for Reid, Adams thought it best to be diplomatic and shake hands. 'Superintendent,' he said curtly.

One of Adams's own private rules was that he never called anyone he didn't respect 'sir'. But he was careful not to fall foul of service discipline, and so addressed such people by their rank, for which he couldn't be criticised.

'Can I ask what you're doing here, Superintendent?'

Reid was clearly annoyed at the question. 'I was going to say the same as you, but from what I understand, your relationship with Doctor Ryan isn't entirely professional.'

Adams decided that remark didn't deserve an answer. 'Again, Superintendent, I must ask you what you're doing here.'

'Investigating the murders, Inspector.' His lip curled with contempt at the word 'Inspector'.

'As you are well aware, all enquiries regarding this particular series of killings must be made through Commander Rochester,' said Adams evenly.

'Look here,' said Reid with sudden anger, 'you remember who I am. I'm your boss. I'm the one whose boots you lick when I tell you to lick them. You don't tell me where to go and who to talk to. I tell you.'

Adams was unruffled. 'You don't tell me what to do any more and never will again.'

For a moment Sam thought Reid was going to explode. She intervened quickly. 'Inspector Adams might not be able to tell you where to go and who to talk to, but while you're in my house, I can. So if you wouldn't mind leaving . . .'

Reid glared at Adams, who met his eye without blinking, then returned to Sam. 'I'll be seeing you again.'

'Very likely.'

Adams said coolly, 'I'll be making a full report of

this incident to Commander Rochester and the Home Office.'

'You can do what you bloody well like.'

He nodded to Holmes, who stood and followed him out of the room.

Wyn opened the front door for them. 'Don't come back soon.' She slammed the door behind them and joined Adams and Sam in the sitting-room.

'Did you tell him anything?' he asked Sam.

'Of course not.'

'Sorry. Just being in the same room as that bastard gets my back up.'

'Really? I never would have noticed. You were impressively cool.'

Wyn asked Adams, 'Fancy a coffee?'

'No, thanks. Don't think I'll have time. We have to get back to see the boss.'

As Wyn headed back to the kitchen to make sandwiches for lunch, Sam asked crossly, 'Have we? Well, I've got a few of my own plans before we do that.'

Adams looked impatiently at her and then at his watch. 'Like what?'

'I've got an appointment with Marcia Evans at the lab.'

'Well, if we get a move on you can still see Marcia and we shouldn't be too late back at the Park.'

Sam considered for a moment. 'OK.' At the door a thought struck her, and she turned back to him. 'Have they identified the three girls yet?'

'Two of them. One was Susan Dench and the other was a girl called Elizabeth Carr from Ealing in London.'

'That's not close to any air-bases, is it?'

'She was on her way to see friends in Suffolk, hitching. So she could have been taken from anywhere *en route*. Disappeared about three weeks after the Dench girl.'

'What about the third girl?'

Adams shrugged. 'Cast of thousands. If she wasn't local and could have come from as far away as London, then you're dealing with a lot of missing girls.'

Sam knew it was the sad truth. It could be a long, long time before they found out who she was – if they ever did. She sighed, and said, 'I'll be five minutes.'

Adams looked at her sceptically, then called, 'I will have time for that coffee after all, Wyn.'

Sam scowled at him and disappeared up the stairs.

Sam spent the journey to Scrivingdon scoffing the mountain of bacon sandwiches Wyn had made – since getting home the evening before, she seemed to have been permanently hungry. Selfishly, she hadn't offered Adams so much as a bite, but her stomach still felt empty.

When they reached Marcia's lab they found her in her usual position, glued to a microscope. She ignored their arrival. Adams cleared his throat, but she didn't move.

'I know you're there,' she said. 'I'm not deaf. But if I don't finish this now it will be hanging around for days.'

Only when she had finished and made a few quick notes on her pad did she turn to face them.

'Morning, Sam. I was hoping you'd turn up at lunchtime so you could buy me some. I think you owe me that.' She nodded to a big pile of plastic evidence bags.

'Sorry about the extra work, but I couldn't think of anyone else I trusted to handle it.'

Marcia smiled sardonically. 'Make new friends. Do you know what? I think I'm going to die a virgin.'

Sam let her jaw drop in mock amazement and Marcia gave her an appreciative grin.

'Anyway, I've got what you wanted over here.'

She led them to the far side of the lab. Hanging on hooks were two apparently identical jackets.

She picked one up. 'This is the jacket Strachan was wearing when his body was discovered stuffed down the drain shaft.

Sam winced. 'Don't remind me.'

'It's the standard-issue jacket for privates and NCOs in the US Air Force.' She hung it up again and took down the second one. 'This, on the other hand, is a US Air Force *officer's* jacket. Similar in appearance but not the same. This one came from the quartermaster's store at Leeminghall.'

She put it down on a nearby workbench, and went over to one of her many microscopes. She checked the focus, then invited Sam to have a look. Sam bent over the instrument. She saw a dark, twisted fibre.

'The fibre you're looking at there,' said Marcia, 'came from Strachan's jacket and is typical man-made fibre. Now, using both spectrometry and thin-layer chromatography, we can analyse the dyes used in the fibre. The ones we found in the plastic bag in the shed where Mary West's body was discovered are different from the samples we took from Strachan's jacket.'

'We know that, because I think it's reasonable to assume that Strachan didn't kill Mary West.'

'Agreed, but I'm only using it as a comparison.'

Sam waited expectantly.

'The kind of dyes we found on the fibres inside the plastic bag are military, but are more commonly found on officers' jackets, not the rank and file's.'

Adams asked, 'So you're saying our murderer is an Air Force officer?'

'No. What I'm saying is that the threads found in the plastic bag came from an American Air Force officer's jacket.'

Adams glanced across at Sam. 'No wonder Hammond disappeared so quickly.'

'Bit premature, isn't it?' she said. 'I'm sure there's more than one officer at Leeminghall.'

'But only one who's on the run.'

'Sorry, I thought he'd been recalled to the States. I didn't realise he was on the run.'

Adams looked pointedly sceptical.

'There is a difference,' she said. She still couldn't believe that Hammond was capable of any kind of murder, let alone these vicious, sick serial killings. She asked Marcia, 'What about the coloured thread you found?'

Marcia shrugged. 'Still not quite sure where that came from.'

As Sam turned away from the microscope, her attention was caught by the officer's jacket lying on the workbench. She stared at it. There was something odd about it, but she couldn't think what. She tried to visualise the jacket being worn by one of the men, picturing it in her mind's eye as clearly as possible. Of course! That was it! There were no medals on either of the jackets, and the American armed forces prided themselves on the number of medals they issued. She couldn't understand why she hadn't noticed it before.

'Medals,' she said. 'Where are the medals?' She hurried across the lab, took up the two uniform jackets and pointed out where medal ribbons were normally displayed. 'See? No medals. That's where your unidentified thread's come from. It's from a medal ribbon.'

'Did Hammond have any medals?' asked Adams.

'A chestful – but then so do most officers with his length of service.'

'I suppose it will all depend on what kind of medal the ribbon came from,' said Marcia.

Adams looked at her questioningly.

'Some medals are common and most officers will have them. Others are rarer, so we might be able to narrow the field down a little.'

'How long before you know which medal ribbon it came from?' he asked.

'As soon as I can get a list of American medals and their comparison colours. It shouldn't take too long. I'll get working on it straight away.'

'Good. I'll see what I can do about tracing Hammond.'

Sam glared at him as he strode out of the lab.

The drive from Cambridgeshire to Cromwell Park was

a long one and undertaken in almost complete silence. As they reached the main gates, Adams stopped the car and turned to Sam.

'Why are you so convinced he's innocent?'

Sam stared straight ahead. 'Why are you so convinced he's guilty? I thought it was the basis of British law that a person was innocent until proved guilty.'

'I think we've got enough evidence already.'

'As I pointed out before, it's all circumstantial.'

'Oh come off it, Sam. If it had been any one else but Hammond, you'd be agreeing with me.'

Sam rounded on him, flushed with anger. 'That was a bloody ridiculous thing to say. I don't think he's guilty because I don't think there's enough evidence against him. Your problem, Tom, is your policeman's vision. Under pressure you've decided he's guilty, so any evidence that helps you establish his guilt, no matter how half-baked, you accept. Any evidence that might prove the contrary you ignore. And while you're all giving yourselves a big pat on the back, the killer is still out there and likely to strike again!'

She turned sharply away and folded her arms. He knew it was pointless continuing the argument, so restarted the car and drove in silence up the drive to the house.

When they went into Rochester's office, Doyle and Solheim were already waiting. Rochester came over to greet Sam. For a moment she thought he was going to give her a kiss, but his hand came out smartly and she took it.

'I understand congratulations are in order,' he said.

Sam glared across at Adams, who taken a seat at the far side of the room,

'Well, I think it's a little premature for that,' she said.

'Perhaps, but the fibres, and with a bit of luck that medal ribbon, should make the case against Hammond that much stronger.'

He offered Sam a seat and returned to his own. 'I'm afraid our friend Professor Charlton was rather less successful than yourself. He could make nothing of the notes. So it would appear our man is just a nutter.'

Doyle shook his head firmly. 'He's no nutter. He knows exactly what he's doing and enjoys doing it.' Though Doyle hated the killer, he also had a strange respect for him. If the killer hadn't been clever, they would have tracked him down long ago.

Rochester went on, 'I think the other thing you ought to know is that Agent Solheim here has been doing some background work on Hammond's locations during the period of several of the murders, and they just about seem to fit.'

Sam looked at Solheim. 'Just about?'

Solheim was less confident than Rochester. 'I've still got some work to do, but the ones we have checked put him in about the right location around the right time.'

'"About"? "Around"? What exactly does that mean?' demanded Sam. 'On the base, close to the base, same county, state, what? At least one of the girls we found in Kent didn't even come from the area.'

Doyle said, 'Within a close enough distance to reach

337

the location and commit the murders, but far enough away not to bring suspicion down on himself.'

'I see. So the facts no longer fit the crime but the crimes do fit the facts.'

'We're pretty sure about him,' said Solheim.

Sam turned on her. 'You were "pretty sure" about Colonel Cully as well.'

Rochester and Adams were surprised by this, since the good colonel had been dismissed from the enquiry some time before, but Solheim knew exactly what she was getting at and her resentment was clear.

Sam wasn't put off. 'I just think we're all jumping to conclusions. All of this is pure speculation, based on nothing but assumption.

'Then why did he run?' asked Adams reasonably.

'As I've already said, are we sure he did? I thought he'd been summoned back to the States.'

Rochester shook his head. 'That's what we were told, but apparently it was a story that Hammond put out himself. The Air Force are denying knowledge of any such order.'

The revelation took the wind right out of Sam's sails. She sat back, deflated.

Rochester went on, 'We also think we've tracked the major down to the Georgia area, probably just outside Atlanta, which' – he looked meaningfully at Sam – 'I understand fits in very nicely with some of the fibre evidence that was found both at the scene and on the body.'

'Yes,' she admitted, 'the seeds and the fish scale. How did you manage to track him down?'

Rochester gestured to Doyle and Solheim. 'With the help of our friends in the FBI. They're flying out to Atlanta to try and find him tomorrow morning.'

'Good luck,' Sam said. 'I'd appreciate being told if you do manage to arrest him.'

Doyle looked quizzically at Rochester, who said, 'I don't think there'll be any need for you to be told. We were hoping you'd go with them.'

She gaped at him.

Tom Adams was clearly as surprised as she was. 'Do you think that's a good idea, sir?'

'Yes I do, otherwise I wouldn't have suggested it.'

'In that case, sir, shouldn't one of us go too?'

'No. This is an American show now. I'm sure Doctor Ryan will represent us very well. However, I expect it depends what Doctor Ryan's thoughts are on the matter.'

The last thing she wanted to do was muscle in on an FBI investigation. There must be *some* way of getting out of it. 'What good would I be?' she asked. 'I'm sure the FBI have their own people who are more than capable of providing anything I could bring to the investigation.'

'Apart from Agents Doyle and Solheim here, you're closer to this enquiry than anyone else. I' – he gave Doyle an ironic glance – '*we* feel that your knowledge of the case, combined with the FBI's, would bring this case to an early resolution.'

He was lying, of course. Doyle didn't want even his fellow agent Solheim there, let alone a busybody from the British police – and a woman to boot. This was a ploy of Rochester's, to make sure one of his own people stayed close to the investigation, and she wasn't going to be allowed to refuse.

She asked Doyle, 'Will I receive the full co-operation of the FBI?'

Rochester answered before Doyle could. 'Mr Bartoc has assured me that everything will be done to make sure you remain an important part of the team.'

Bartoc's name had its usual effect on Doyle: he nodded with a show of enthusiasm, but clearly resented having to do so.

Sam wondered whether there was any help to be had from Tom. She was sure he didn't want her to go – not on her own, at least. But no, she couldn't ask any more of him. The look Rochester had given him when he spoke showed clearly that any further protest from him would go down badly – the names of South Division and Reid had hung in the air. Tom must be left out of it. She suddenly felt very alone.

CHAPTER TWELVE

The flight arrived in Washington during the early afternoon. A car met them at the airport and whisked them into central Washington. Doyle and Solheim dropped Sam at her hotel to unpack and freshen up, while they pressed on to Quantico to update and brief Bartoc and the rest of their team.

Sam was much impressed by the hotel: its five stars were well deserved. Her room was luxurious, large, air-conditioned, with fresh flowers and a basket of fruit on a side-table. The views over Washington were wonderful and she spent a little time picking out some of the more famous landmarks.

But what she wanted most was a bath, and her bathroom had a Jacuzzi. She'd never tried one before and was keen to see what it was like – she'd save the power-shower for another time. She slid gratefully into the hot water and turned on the Jacuzzi. The bubbles tingled on her skin and pummelled her tired muscles into relaxation. She couldn't help giggling. She felt like a teenager preparing for her first date. Despite the grim reason for her visit, she thought she might actually enjoy herself if this was anything to go by. She leant her head on the end of the bath and began to daydream. Her reverie was interrupted by the shrill of the telephone – there was, naturally, an extension in the bathroom.

'Dr Ryan.'

The caller was Solheim. 'Look, I realise you're probably a little tired but I was wondering whether you'd like to have dinner with me tonight. My treat.'

Sam thought about it for a moment. She wasn't keen: another session of Solheim trying to enlist her support against Doyle was hardly an attractive proposition. 'I'd love to normally but I'm—'

'Look, I know what you're thinking,' Solheim cut in, 'but I'm not trying to play you off against Doyle. I just thought it might be good for both of us to have an evening off. Ever seen Washington by night?'

'I haven't had a chance to see it by day yet.'

'It's better by night. You don't see all the dirty marks.'

Despite her reservations, Sam found herself saying yes.

'Good. Well, that's a date, then. I'll pick you up at eight. We'll go somewhere smart, so it's the little black dress if you've got one.'

Sam put the phone down, slightly disappointed and annoyed with herself for not having the courage to say no. Any chance she had of relaxing was now gone. She pulled herself out of the bath, wrapped herself in a towel and slumped into a chair, too lethargic to dry herself. Washington might be more interesting at night, she thought, but she'd still have preferred to see it in the day.

Fortunately, she did have a little black dress with her. She slipped it on and made up her face, trying to summon up some enthusiasm for the evening. As she was putting on her shoes, reception rang to tell her Solheim had arrived. Sam made her way down to the foyer. As usual, Solheim looked stunning. Her clothes were never over the top; there was just something about the way she wore them. As she stood waiting, several people, including the receptionist, were openly admiring her. Sam felt small, insignificant and dowdy. Why on earth had she said yes?

After a short drive they arrived at a small restaurant near the commercial district. Solheim was obviously a regular and was welcomed warmly. They were led to a secluded table at the back of the restaurant and handed the menu. It was in French. Sam read it with interest. Whether it was excitement or stress she wasn't sure, but her appetite seemed to have returned with a vengeance.

Solheim looked across at her. 'If you need any help?'

Sam peeked round the side of the menu, feeling slightly insulted. 'No, it's OK. I did pass my GCE French.'

'Excuse me?'

'It doesn't matter. Just an old exam.'

They ordered, and Solheim chose the wine. After the first glass, Sam began to relax.

Inevitably, Solheim chose to talk about the case. 'You still don't think Hammond's guilty, do you?'

Sam shook her head. 'No. I know some of the evidence points in that direction but I'm still not convinced. Just a gut reaction, I suppose.'

'Pity you can't use gut reactions in court. For what it's worth, I don't think he's our man either.'

Sam hadn't expected this. 'You seemed sure enough in Rochester's office.'

Solheim shrugged. 'That was for Doyle's sake. He wanted a bit of solidarity.'

'So why are you so sure? Gut reaction?'

'Sort of, but not quite the same type. I slept with him.'

Sam wasn't sure whether she was more surprised by the fact that Solheim had slept with Hammond or by her frankness in revealing the fact.

Calmly, Solheim went on, 'He was a gentle lover. Considerate, no fantasies, or force. My pleasure was more important than his. I like that kind of thing in a man.'

'Sounds like you enjoyed yourself.'

'Oh I did. Did you sleep with him?'

Taken aback, Sam shook her head. 'No.'

Solheim smiled at her. 'He was certainly interested. I thought perhaps that's why you were so support-ive.'

Sam shook her head again. 'If I had slept with him and discovered later that he was our killer, I'd have given him up.'

'Embarrassing.'

'Maybe, but I would still have done it.'

The first course arrived and was ceremonially placed in front of them.

When the waiter had gone, Solheim said, 'Who do you think did it, then?'

'No idea. But whatever the answer is, I think we'll find it here, not in England.'

Solheim nodded. 'I think so too.'

There was a pause while they ate, then Solheim asked, 'Have you had any problems with the investigation?'

'No. Well, nothing out of the ordinary. Why?'

'After about body six we suddenly started getting a couple of unwelcome visitors. They used to turn up at the scene and we had to forward all statements and interviews to them. Doyle was really pissed about it.'

'I'm not surprised. Who were they?'

'We were never told. Everything was funnelled through Bartoc on a need-to-know basis.'

'And you didn't need to know.'

Solheim nodded.

'We have a similar system in Britain. Who do you *think* they were?'

'CIA, Air Force intelligence, State Department – might even have been a different department of the Bureau. Who knows? They're so busy fighting among themselves for supremacy that it might even have been all of them.'

Sam was pleased to learn that kind of stupidity went on on both sides of the Atlantic.

With due ceremony, their empty plates were removed and the entrée brought in. Sam took a mouthful. It was delicious.

Solheim looked across at her. 'Food's great, isn't it?'

Sam nodded her approval.

'Now, tell me about you and that Inspector Adams. I know you slept with him. I thought he was really cute.'

Dinner over, Solheim summoned a cab and they set out to see the sights. Solheim's interpretation of the word 'sights' was a broad one: they visited not only the city's floodlit monuments but also one of the loudest, hottest discos Sam had ever been to. At first she refused all offers of drinks and invitations to dance, but then, aware she was being ungracious, she began to accept and, to her surprise, found herself having fun. Most of the men she danced with were younger than she was but they didn't seem to mind, and nor, after helping Solheim polish off three bottles of wine at dinner, did she.

When she returned, exhausted, to the hotel in the early hours of the morning, there were three messages waiting for her, two from Rochester and one from Tom, asking her to ring him back at his Cromwell Park office. She went up to her room and showered quickly before crawling into bed. Wearily, she reached for the bedside phone.

Tom answered at once: 'Inspector Adams.'

'That was very formal.'

'I'm a very formal man.'

'Since when? I half expected your new friend to answer.'

Adams refused to be drawn. 'I've got no new friends.'

Sam was too tired to pursue that particular line of conversation. 'So what do you want? It's late and I'm tired.'

'Where have you been?'

'Seeing the sights with Solheim.'

'Girls' talk, eh?'

'We were talking about you, actually.'

'Me? What's so interesting about me?'

'She wanted to know what you were like in bed.'

Sam's unaccustomed frankness took him aback. 'What! Have you been drinking?'

'Only a lot. I think I deserve it and you still haven't told me what you want.'

'I was just making sure you'd arrived safely and everything was OK.'

'I'm fine. Quantico tomorrow. If anything develops I'll let you know. There was one thing . . .'

'What?'

'Has anyone tried to interfere with the case?'

'Like who?'

'I was hoping you could tell me that. It's just something that Solheim said.'

'Not that I know of. I'll check with Rochester, if you like.'

Sam wasn't keen on that idea. Given the kind of games that Rochester liked to play, it wouldn't have surprised her to find out he was involved in some way. 'No, there's no need. I just wondered.'

'OK. Well, I'd better let you get some sleep.'

'Yes, you'd better.'

'What did you say, by the way?'

'About what?'

'My performance in bed.'

'How could I say you were a lousy lover after only ten seconds?' The last thing Sam heard as she put down the phone was Adams' gasp of astonishment and hurt pride.

* * *

Marcia had decided to work late in order to plough her way through the thick book. *Orders, Decorations and Awards to the United States Armed Forces* wasn't her idea of a good late-night read but she realised she'd have to get it done sooner or later. She was beginning to wish she'd applied to the American embassy for help. She hadn't, because she'd thought it would be quicker to do it herself, but now she was having doubts. She'd already covered foreign decorations, long-service and good-conduct medals and campaign medals, and was moving on to gallantry awards. She was getting bored, and was glad to be interrupted by a knock at the lab door.

Michael Spender put his head round the door. 'I think we're the last two left,' he said. 'Fancy a drink?'

He was a new addition to the lab, a graduate who was clearly going places. But despite being dedicated to his work, he was interesting – and attractive, too. Marcia looked down at the book. It was the last chapter and would wait until the following morning. In the meantime, she'd investigate the possibilities that a quiet drink with young Spender offered.

Marking her page, she closed the book and slipped off her lab coat. 'Your round?'

'Absolutely. As long as it's a Coke.'

Marcia swept past him. 'With a large rum inside.'

Michael Spender smiled and followed her.

The next morning a car arrived to collect Sam at ten o'clock. She was feeling slightly the worse for wear and she skipped breakfast, her appetite having completely gone. Quantico was further outside Washington than she'd realised, and the journey took almost an hour.

Quantico was an impressive sight. It reminded Sam of one of the new universities which were springing up in Britain. She was met at the car park by Solheim, who, annoyingly, looked as fresh as ever. Sam checked in at reception, and they were escorted up to Bartoc's office.

'Enjoy yourself last night?' asked Solheim.

'Very much, but I think I overdid it a little.'

'Doesn't hurt to overdo it sometimes.'

The lift reached their floor, and Sam followed Solheim down a plushly carpeted corridor. Bartoc's office was large and impressive, and a far cry from the standard design. Modern paintings hung on the walls, and pieces of modern sculpture were displayed so as best to catch the light. The only photograph was one of Bartoc's family, which stood on his desk. There was not a single police photo or memento to be seen. Bartoc himself was in his late forties, tall, sun-tanned and handsome. Grey hairs flecked the edges of what was otherwise still jet-black hair. He wore a dark-green modern suit, which Sam thought was probably an Armani, and had a ready smile.

He strode across the room to her. 'Doctor Ryan. I've heard so much about you that I feel I know you already.'

Sam held out her hand. 'Ditto.'

When he came close, Sam realised that the sun-tan was probably false and that he had had at least one face-lift. She began to wonder how much more about him was false.

Doyle was already there. He stood up and shook hands with Sam. Bartoc directed Sam to a seat, before resuming his own.

'I understand from Ed here that the Bureau's managed to locate Hammond.'

'With some help from the local Sheriff's Department,' said Doyle.

'Good. Been traced to Georgia, I understand. It's a big state. What do you reckon are your chances of finding him?'

Sam was ready for the question. 'That depends whether we can trace the seeds we found on Mary West's body.'

'Bit of a tall order, isn't it?'

'Not really. They're rare and grow only in certain areas of the swampland. If we can match the seeds' DNA, we should even be able to say which particular tree they came from.'

'Impressive. But how long's all that going to take?'

Doyle said, 'I've booked us all on a flight this afternoon, sir. I figured the sooner we begin the better.'

'Bit soon isn't it, Ed? I was hoping to show Doctor Ryan round our capital city before you disappeared.'

'I've seen it. Agent Solheim took me round last night. It's a remarkable place.'

Doyle scowled at Solheim, who looked away. Sam realised she'd put her foot in it again.

'That's a pity,' said Bartoc. 'Well, perhaps next time. I'm sure there'll be places you missed.' He dismissed the subject. 'OK, what do you want me to do?'

'If you could arrange some help from the local law-enforcement officers, that would be a help,' said Doyle.

Bartoc nodded.

Sam said, 'There's a forensic scientist down there called Samuel Clarke. He's a bit of an expert on local flora and fauna. I think he might be worth a visit as well.'

'Not a problem. Do you think you'll find Hammond?'

Solheim looked sceptical. Doyle was less so. 'We'll find him. There ain't a state big enough to hide him.'

Bartoc smiled at him. 'Always the optimist, Ed.' He glanced down at his watch. 'Well I've got to go – meeting on Capitol Hill.'

Right on cue, the door opened and Bartoc's secretary entered. There must be a secret button he presses when it's time for people to leave, thought Sam.

They all stood up and Bartoc shook hands with Sam again. 'Well, it was good to meet you, even if it was for only for a short time. Don't forget our rain-check, will you?'

'Indeed I won't,' said Sam. 'Something to look forward to.'

He nodded and the small party was ushered out of the room.

As soon as the door had closed behind them, Bartoc picked up his phone. 'Get me Colonel Terrington at the Pentagon, please.' He put the phone down and leant back in his chair, frowning in concern.

Sam, Solheim and Doyle made their way down to Doyle's office.

'So what happens next?' asked Sam.

Doyle looked down at her. 'We're on the 4 p.m. flight to Atlanta. I've arranged for a car to take you back to your hotel and then on to the airport. We'll meet you there. The sooner we get this thing finished the better.'

He opened a drawer, took out an automatic pistol and checked the magazine. 'It's been a long hot road but we're nearing its end.' He snapped the magazine back into the butt of the pistol and slipped the gun into a leather holster which lay on his desk. Sam wondered what he'd do if he spotted Hammond, and was suddenly concerned that Doyle's sense of justice might be located in the barrel of his gun.

Marcia arrived at work late the following day. The evening with the 'new boy' had gone on longer than she'd anticipated. Nothing had happened – well, almost nothing. They'd just sat in his flat, chatting.

The odd thing was that she hadn't been bored. Normally, talking about work and ambition rapidly turned Marcia off a man, but Michael was different. He didn't instantly make a move on her, either, and that was unusual too. It wasn't until she was about to leave that he kissed her – and what a kiss! It was all she could do to resist the temptation to push him back inside his flat and ravish him on the hall carpet. But she hadn't and was glad she hadn't.

They'd arranged to go out with each other the following weekend, but she wasn't sure she could wait that long to see him again. She'd hadn't felt like this about a man for a long time. She sighed deeply and wished Sam was around to talk it through with. Sam was never around when she really needed her, thought Marcia.

She looked across at the heavy book that sat waiting on one of the work-surfaces. She slipped off her jacket, donned her white coat and picked the book up. She opened it at the last chapter, which dealt with gallantry medals, and turned to the first description and picture. She read the picture caption and then the description of the medal ribbon. With mounting excitement, she read them again. The colours in the book matched, not just closely but exactly, those of the silk threads found inside the plastic bag. She picked up the lab phone and dialled.

Sam didn't get to see much of Atlanta. They were met at Hartsfield airport by a car sent by the Sheriff's Department and driven quickly out of the city. She had no time to do more than form a vague impression of great wealth and great poverty existing side by side. No wonder, she thought, that the crime rate was so high.

After about an hour they were out into open country and pulling through the gates of the Johnson County forensic science laboratory. The labs weren't big but were apparently the busiest in the state. They were expected and, after booking in, were directed along several corridors to Samuel Clarke's lab. The labs reminded Sam of the ones at Scrivingdon and she felt suddenly at home.

Clarke was waiting for them. 'Doctor Ryan, I presume.'

Sam smiled at him. 'Call me Sam.'

'In that case you can call me Sam too.'

'Well, Sam Too, I expect you know Doyle and Solheim from Quantico?'

He shook hands with both of them. 'Your Mr Bartoc told me you were coming. Asked me – well, ordered me, actually – to help. I think I know what you're after, so I've taken the liberty of preparing one or two maps for you to have a look at.'

He walked across to a large table in the centre of the lab where a giant map had been unrolled and held down by glass jars full of different coloured liquids.

He said to Sam, 'I understand you found some samples of *Myrica indora* seeds on the body of one of your victims.'

Sam nodded. 'Can you extract the DNA from them?'

'Sure can, but not overnight.'

'So if I collect a variety of seeds from these bushes, you'll be able to match the DNA until I get the right one?'

He nodded. 'Hell of a job.'

'I thought they were rare.'

'If you're talking the United States, they are. If you're talking around here, they're not.'

Sam felt a twinge of disappointment. 'There was also a fish scale, if it helps.'

Clarke nodded again. 'The pan fish, that helps a lot.'

'Pan fish?'

'Sorry, local name for them. Kids tend to cook them up in small pans. They're no more than a mouthful, though. Used for bait, mostly.'

'They're too beautiful eat,' Sam protested.

'They are lovely things, aren't they?'

Doyle was growing impatient. 'So where do you think is the best place to look?'

'Sorry. Well, to get the combination of the two there are only three areas in the whole country, and fortunately they're all here.'

He pointed to an area of the map. 'The first, and least likely I think, is probably Stamp Creek. There's not too many bayberry bushes there and even fewer pan fish.'

Sam nodded.

'I'm not saying you won't have to search it, I just think it should be last on your list. The second and third areas I'd try are Blue and Soma Creeks.'

'Soma Creek?' Sam put in. 'Why's it called that?'

'It's always been called that as far as I'm aware,' he said. 'But then I've only been here a few years. Why do you ask?'

'Soma was a hypothetical drug used in *Brave New World*. It was a sedative and euphoric, used to control the masses – sort of chemical persuasion.'

'Any links between the book and the other two creeks?' Doyle asked.

Sam shook her head. 'No, I don't think so. Looks like those notes helped after all.'

Doyle looked at her sceptically. 'We don't know that yet, but I guess Soma's a good place to start.'

Everyone nodded their agreement.

'Difficult terrain,' said Clarke. 'Hard to collect samples. Plenty of them, though.'

Doyle's mind was running on other lines. 'Many people live there?'

Clarke shook his head. 'Nobody that I know of. They're inhospitable places. Fishing's poor and the water's difficult to navigate. Insects are bad, too.'

'Could a person hide out there?'

'If he were insane.'

Doyle nodded. Sam looked across at him. Clearly, he was hoping to find more than just bushes.

'I'd take a guide with you there,' suggested Clarke. 'Dangerous place. Deep water, submerged vines, quicksands. There's a few people gone in and never come out. Expect they'll find them when they drain the place for a golf course.'

'Is that's what's planned?'

'I've no idea, but I'm sure they'll get around to it some day. They seem to have destroyed most everything else. Try the sheriff. If he can't guide you, I'm sure he'll find someone who can. Might cost you a few dollars, but it'll be worth it.'

Sam thanked him warmly. 'We'll be back with the samples as soon as we can.'

'Fine. I'll have everything ready when you do. The faster you can get me the seeds, the faster I can do the work. Perhaps we'll have time to talk about the finer points of seeds and pollen grains too.'

'I'll hold you to that.' She shook his hand and followed Doyle and Solheim out of the door.

It took Marcia a few hours to get hold of a sample of the medal ribbon. After fruitlessly trying the American embassy and several US Air Forces bases, she finally located a Congressional Medal of Honor in a small military antiques shop near Magdalene Bridge. Negotiations with the owner – who swore it was probably the only one in England, which meant it was naturally expensive – were protracted, but eventually they reached agreement and she arranged for a taxi to pick it up. It was in the lab about half an hour later. A comparison between the ribbon and the fibres found inside the plastic bag showed them to be the same. Once again, Marcia picked up the phone and dialled.

Tom Adams was going through his suspect files again when his phone rang. 'Inspector Adams.' The voice at the other end was high and excited, speaking so fast he had difficulty making out the words. 'Marcia, calm down and tell me slowly what you want to say.'

He picked up a pen, ready to make notes. 'Congressional Medal of Honor? I've heard of it. It's the American version of the Victoria Cross, isn't it? . . . I see . . . OK, Marcia. Well done. Keep in touch.'

Tom put the phone down slowly. Yes, he thought, *yes*! This was it, the crucial breakthrough. What he needed now was just a little more information. He picked up the phone again, rang the American embassy and asked to be put through to the information library.

'Hello. My name is Detective Inspector Tom Adams of the Cambridgeshire police, and I'm working in conjunction with your FBI . . . Yes that's right . . . I was wondering if you had an up-to-date list of serving officers who've been awarded the Congressional Medal of Honor . . . Yes I'll wait.'

He sat back in his chair and crossed his fingers. A few

moments later the librarian was back on the phone. Tom picked up his pen. 'Yes I'm ready.'

The librarian began to read out the names. The first three meant nothing, but the fourth he recognised at once. 'Christ, are you sure? Can you read that name again?'

There was no doubt.

He slammed down the phone and ran across the room towards Rochester's office.

Soma Creek was only about half an hour away from Clarke's laboratory. They stopped *en route* to pick up Sheriff Mark Conack, who, having learnt a little about the case, was keen to be involved.

As the day progressed the heat became more and more oppressive. Sam was glad the car was air-conditioned and dreaded the moment when she would have to get out and begin the search.

The moment came only too quickly. Pulling into a small dirt car park beside the creek, where two small wooden boats awaited them, they emerged into the humid heat of one of Georgia's finest swamps.

Doyle looked across at Solheim. 'If you go with the sheriff here, I'll take Doctor Ryan.'

She shook her head. 'No, you take the sheriff. I'll go with Doctor Ryan.'

They glared at each other. This was insubordination and they both knew it. There was no time to argue the point now, Doyle thought, but he'd certainly put a report in later. Perhaps it was the excuse he'd been looking for to get rid of her.

'OK,' he said. 'You take Doctor Ryan.'

The sheriff said dryly, 'Well, if you've finished fighting over me, can I suggest that the ladies take the east and we take the west? That's not meant as an insult to your abilities, ladies, only that the west side of the swamp is considered to be more dangerous than the east, and I know them a little better than you.'

Solheim could see the sense in what he said, and agreed.

The sheriff continued, 'Ever driven a boat before?'

Sam shook her head but Solheim nodded. 'I know how to handle one.'

'That's good. Keep your speed right down and take your time. That way you won't miss anything, and if you hit something you shouldn't do too much damage.' He climbed down into one of the boats and prepared to cast off.

Doyle cut in, 'Are you armed?'

Solheim pulled back her jacket to reveal a Smith & Wesson .38 revolver.

'Good. I hope you know how to use it?' Doyle knew she did but couldn't resist taking a sideswipe at her. 'And if you do find anything other than bushes, get back here and report in. Is that clear?

Solheim nodded.

Sam looked across at Doyle. 'Are you sure you know what you're looking for?'

'Hammond?'

Exasperated, she said nothing.

'I know what the bushes look like,' he said. 'I'll get you samples.'

'Remember, as many different bushes as you can find. Clarke said there weren't too many around here, so it shouldn't take long.'

Bored, Doyle turned away and climbed into the boat beside the sheriff.

Sam reminded him, 'And don't forget to mark which bush it was, and make a note of its location.'

Doyle waved. The sheriff started the outboard motor and they began to move away from the bank.

Solheim caught Sam's eye. 'Right, let's get to it.'

They stepped into the boat and, with Solheim at the helm, headed slowly for the interior of the swamp.

As they moved out of earshot, the radio in the sheriff's car crackled into life. 'This is Control. We have an urgent message for Doctor Ryan or Agent Doyle. Come back.'

Control would continue calling for some time, but wouldn't receive an answer until it was too late.

The small boat chugged into the swamp. Almost at once, the trees closed over their heads, blocking out the light and, what was worse, locking in the humidity. Vapour rose off the water and shrouded the trees and bushes in mist, creating bizarre, eerie shapes. Sweat dripped from their noses and ears as if they'd been locked in the nearest Turkish bath. Their clothes were already sticking to them, and Sam found her breathing was becoming laboured. Completing their discomfort was something Sam hadn't expected: the noise. It was deafening, as thousands of insects and a few animals vied to be heard.

They had decided to cover as much of the swamp as possible by boat, and to leave as little as possible to do on foot. Their first stop was a small island whose banks were thickly covered in bushes and trees. Solheim was patient and even helpful as Sam took sample after sample from the bayberry bushes, dropping each sample into a plastic bag and marking the bush with a small white tag. After noting down the number and location of each bush sampled, they moved on, deeper into the swamp.

The sun dropped low in the sky and the light began to fade. Doyle gestured to Sheriff Conack to turn the boat round and head for home. He'd collected some samples but had been more interested in searching for signs of life hidden within the swamp than in collecting seeds. He'd found nothing. Clarke was right: it was a hostile environment. Doyle wasn't keen to stay there after dark.

The return trip seemed remarkably quick, and Doyle was soon lumbering up the bank and heading towards his car. Sheriff Conack secured the boat and made his way across to join him. As he did his radio crackled into life again: 'Control to Sheriff Conack. Over.'

Conack picked up the handset. 'Sheriff Conack. Go ahead, Billy.'

As the message came through, Doyle's eyes widened.

Solheim looked up through the thick tree cover. It was almost dusk. She peered through the gloom at Sam, who was labelling yet another bush.

'Think we'd better head back,' Solheim said. 'It'll be dark in an hour.'

Sam finished her labelling and looked back along the creek. 'Yes, OK, we can finish off tomorrow. I think I've got enough for Clarke to be going on with.'

As Solheim began to turn the boat, Sam spotted something half hidden behind a clump of trees. She waved to Solheim to stop, and pointed out her discovery. A wooden shack stood isolated on a small overgrown island. Trees and bushes grew thickly around and over it, providing almost perfect camouflage. At the front there was a small landing-stage, from which several steps led up to the door. The two women watched for a moment but saw no movement or sign of occupancy. Whoever owned it was either out or keeping very still.

Solheim whispered, 'I thought Clarke said there were no buildings out here.'

'He did.'

Solheim reached inside her jacket and drew out her gun. She checked the magazine, then clicked it back into place.

Sam looked at her doubtfully. 'I thought Doyle said to report back to the car park if we found anything.'

'And that's just what we're going to do once I've checked this place out.'

Before Sam could stop her, Solheim was out of the boat and wading chest-deep through the water, holding her gun above her head and keeping her eyes firmly fixed on the shack. To Sam's relief she reached the other side without mishap and pulled herself up on to the landing-stage. She turned and gave Sam a quick wave before climbing the steps to the shack. Sam waited, hardly daring to breathe.

There was a momentary sound like frost cracking on a high-voltage cable, clearly audible over the insect calls. Sam instinctively looked up, but there wasn't an overhead cable in sight. In fact, when she thought about it, there probably wasn't one within miles. She checked her watch. It was only a few minutes since Solheim had entered the shack.

Sam was torn by indecision. Should she go back to the car park, as Doyle had wanted, or swim across the short stretch of water to see if Solheim was OK? Probably she should go back and get help, but what if . . . ? She couldn't bring herself to abandon Solheim. She slid over the side of the boat, careful not to make even the smallest splash, and began to swim. The water was strangely warm and thick and foul-smelling, and it felt like swimming through soup. Sam kept her mouth closed tight and breathed deeply through her nose.

After what seemed an age, she reached the shack and, with difficulty, hauled herself out on to the landing-stage. She lay there for a moment, getting her breath back and trying to convince herself that she had probably just got very wet for no reason, before climbing to her feet and heading for the steps. Though she trod as lightly as she could, each step creaked loudly. Anyone inside was bound to hear her.

Sam edged her way to a window and peered inside. The cabin consisted of one large room. At the far end was an unmade bed, beside which were a locker and a tall wooden wardrobe. Behind the bed were several shelves containing large glass jars. There was something in the jars, but she couldn't make out what. At the centre of the room was a large table. On it Solheim lay spreadeagled. She was fully dressed, and her legs and arms hung over the sides of the table. There was no sign of movement.

Sam wondered if she'd be able to find Solheim's gun. Not that it would do her any good as she'd never fired one and would barely know which end to point. Still, Hammond wouldn't know that. Hammond: clearly her subconscious had decided who the killer was, even if her conscious mind hadn't. She inched round to the door, and slipped inside, keeping an eye out for possible escape routes. She moved across to Solheim and lifted her wrist. There was a pulse, though it was weak. Sam checked her for head injuries, but could see nothing.

She shook her, and whispered in her ear, 'Catherine. Catherine, wake up. We've got to get out. Please, Catherine, wake up.'

As she did, she noticed a vivid red weal across the side of Solheim's neck. It was almost identical to the one she had found on West, and explained the noise she had heard earlier. She shook Solheim again, this time with renewed urgency. There was no response. Sam wondered what on earth she should do next. She couldn't leave Solheim, because that would mean certain death if Hammond returned. She wasn't strong enough to carry her, and staying would put them both in danger. Perhaps, she thought, a warning shot might at least bring Doyle and the sheriff running.

As she searched for Solheim's gun, the wardrobe door creaked and began to sag open. Sam cast around desperately for something to defend herself with, but there was nothing. The door opened wider, wider ... Sam watched in terror, waiting for the hidden occupant to reveal himself, but nobody emerged. Slowly, her heart in her mouth, she approached the wardrobe.

It was empty of assailants. Covering its floor and piled half-way up the sides were dozens of pairs of shoes. Different colours, sizes and styles, but all women's shoes.

Feeling slightly less afraid, Sam turned her attention to the glass jars on the shelves behind the bed. She studied them closely. Each of them contained two kidneys. Across the floor were several jars which, to Sam's horror, were empty but still damp. How many unfortunate women the shoes and the jars represented, Sam wasn't sure. But it was a lot.

As she contemplated her next move, she heard a creaking. This time it wasn't the wardrobe but the steps outside. She recognised the sounds from when she'd climbed them earlier. She moved quickly and quietly to the window.

Hammond was coming up the steps. In one hand, he held something that was concealed under a white cloth, in the other, a pistol. Sam didn't like the idea of leaving Solheim, but she could think of no alternative. Running to the far window, she flung herself through it. As she fell she caught a glimpse of Hammond running into the room, pointing his gun directly at her.

She landed heavily, but the ground was soft and, apart from having some of the wind knocked out of her, she felt fine. At least it was firm ground, not water: she wasn't the world's greatest swimmer. There was no time to think. Pulling herself to her feet, she began to run.

She heard Hammond shouting after her, 'Stop! Sam, stop!'

Sam had no idea in which direction she was running and didn't care. All she wanted to do was put as much distance between herself and Hammond as she possibly could. She hadn't gone far when she became aware that Hammond was chasing her. He was still shouting her name, and each shout seemed nearer than the last.

What with jet-lag and too little sleep the night before, she was tiring fast. She stumbled once, twice, and finally fell, exhausted, to the ground. Half crawling, she dragged herself under a bayberry bush – she thought fleetingly how ironic that was. Once in position, she lay perfectly still. Hammond was crashing his way towards her but stopped suddenly, his muddy boots only yards from her face. She closed her eyes, held her breath and waited for him to spot her.

She heard his footsteps moving off. She opened her mouth and took in deep, silent breaths. When she was sure he had gone, she crawled out of her hiding-place and began to run back towards the shack. Her plan was pretty basic: drag Solheim into the water, pull her across to the boat and escape. She just hoped her strength would last and that she could remember how to start the boat's engine.

A numbing pain shot down her arm, and she heard a man's voice: 'Fry, lechery, fry.'

Her body quivered as the electric current passed

through it, then she collapsed. To her surprise she didn't lose consciousness, but just rolled across the ground, holding her arm and screaming. As she rolled, she managed to look up.

She saw not Bob Hammond but General Arthur Wilmot Brown.

He smiled down at her. 'Don't often miss, young lady. Usually like to stun my prey before I butcher it, but it looks like you've been unlucky. Guess that's the way it goes.'

In his right hand he still held the stun gun, while in his left was a large hunting knife with a serrated edge. He knelt down on Sam's body, his knee pressing hard into her chest, holding her in position as he began to lower his knife.

Sam screamed and started to plead for her life. 'Don't kill me! Please don't kill me!'

It was something she'd thought she'd never do, something she'd thought of as a weakness in others. But now, with her own life threatened, she realised that she, like anyone else, would do or say anything to buy time, to stay alive.

A shot boomed out and something ripped into a small tree beside Brown's head. In an instant he had leapt off her and was running through the trees towards the shack. Sam felt herself being lifted off the ground.

It was Hammond. 'You OK?' he asked anxiously.

She wasn't; she felt faint; but she managed a shaky nod. 'It's just my arm. It feels like a horse has kicked it.'

Hammond laid her carefully down and stood back.

She looked up at him. 'Could someone tell me what the hell is going on?'

'Yeah, I guess you are owed an explanation . . .'

The sound of a man screaming for help rang through the swamp.

Hammond gripped his gun tighter. 'Stay here.'

With that he disappeared in the same direction as Brown had done a few minutes earlier. Sam looked around. It was almost dark, and the bushes and trees looked eerie and menacing in the gloom. Sam decided that no way would she 'stay here'. She got unsteadily to her feet and made her way after Hammond as quickly as she could.

She fought her way through bushes and scrubby under-growth for a few hundred yards, then suddenly emerged into a clearing. Hammond was standing motionless watching Brown, who was waist-deep in a stretch of muddy quicksand and sinking fast.

Brown shouted, 'Get me the fuck out of here! Do you hear me, Major? That's an order! Get me out!' His face was twisted and distorted and his eyes seemed to have sunk deep into their sockets. 'Do you hear me, Major? Get me out, get me out!'

Hammond did nothing, only watched as Brown sank deeper.

'For Christ's sake, Major, don't let me die like this. Do something!'

Whatever he had done, Sam couldn't simply stand by and watch him drown. She begged Hammond, 'Help him. Pull him out.'

Hammond said nothing.

The general struggled fiercely but without hope. 'You bastard, Hammond! Don't think I'll forget this. I'll kill you, your family, your friends, even your bitches.'

He pointed at Sam, who with her good arm was trying to break a large branch off a tree, so she could throw it to him. At last it came free. The mud was up to Brown's chest now and his screams were becoming more hysterical. Hammond didn't stop Sam dragging the branch across to Brown, but he didn't help her either.

As she neared Brown, he began to stretch out for the branch. 'Here, you bitch, give it here.' His voice had become a high-pitched shriek. As she pushed the branch towards him, two men in combat jackets emerged from the bushes behind Hammond.

They looked across at Sam. 'Take it off her, Major,' said one.

Hammond reacted at once. Lifting Sam off her feet, he pulled the branch away from Brown's outstretched hand. Brown clawed at it desperately, snatching leaves from the topmost branches.

His screams redoubled. 'No! no! Shoot me, for the love of God, shoot me! Don't let me die like this!'

One of the men nodded to Hammond, who threw the branch away and set Sam down on her feet. He pulled his .45 pistol from its holster and took careful aim. But before he could pull the trigger, he felt the cold steel of a gun-barrel pressed against his head.

'Put the gun down on the floor. And don't try anything stupid or I'll blow your fucking head off.'

Hammond recognised Doyle's voice at once, and knew he meant it. He bent and laid the pistol on the ground. One of the men in the combat jackets moved his hand an inch towards his gun.

Doyle instantly covered him. 'I wouldn't do that if I were you.'

Doyle smiled at him before turning his attention to Brown. The general was fighting to keep his mouth and nose clear, spitting out coarse brown mud and choking for breath. Doyle made sure he caught Brown's eye. He wanted to be the last thing the bastard saw before he died – and he was dammed if that death was going to be easy.

Brown went silent for a moment, eyeing Doyle like a giant cat waiting to pounce on his prey. Doyle had beaten him and even now, at the moment of his death, he raged over his defeat. He made one last desperate attempt to heave himself clear of the quicksand, but he was held fast. With a final scream of rage, he disappeared beneath the mud, which bubbled for a moment and was still again, as if nothing had ever happened.

One of the men in combat jackets looked across at Doyle. 'I'll have your badge for that.'

Doyle was unworried. 'I don't think so.'

He picked Sam up and carried her up to the shack.

They sat in the shack and waited for the forensic science team to arrive – which was going to take some time. It wasn't the best place to wait but it was the only shelter they could find and, with Solheim hurt and Sam exhausted, they were going to need help to get back out of the swamp. The sheriff and one of the unknown men in the combat jackets had set out for the cars about half an hour previously to radio for help.

Solheim had been laid on the bed. She had regained consciousness but she was still in deep shock. Sam had done what she could, which wasn't a lot. Solheim would just have to recover in her own time. Sam sat on the edge of the bed, holding her hand and watching her.

Doyle strode across the room to join them. 'How is she?'

'She's fine, or she will be.'

'She's a stupid bitch! I told her to get back and report. She's too busy trying to impress to know what's good for her.'

Sam's anger overcame her exhaustion. 'And perhaps if you'd included her in the investigation a little more, she wouldn't have had to keep "trying to impress".'

Doyle ran his tongue along the front of his teeth and considered what Sam had said. She was right, but he wasn't sure that he could change, even after this. Too set in his ways, he guessed.

'Are you going to report what happened?' Sam asked.

'I'll have to.'

Sam looked away in disgust.

'But shall we say,' he went on, 'I'll bend the truth a little so we can share the accolades.'

Hammond called across from the table, where he was sitting with the other stranger, 'How is she?'

'What would you care?' said Sam hotly. 'You and your friends nearly got us all killed.'

The stranger intervened. 'No, in fact that's not quite true. We actually kept you alive.'

'Well, perhaps if you told us what the hell's been going on,' said Doyle sourly, 'we might be more likely to believe you.'

The man looked at Hammond and nodded. 'Remember, whatever's said in this cabin today must remain secret. Your lives will depend on it.'

Doyle eyed him. 'Is that a threat?'

'No, Mr Doyle, that is most definitely a promise.' The man paused to let his words sink in, then continued, 'Some years back, in Vietnam, the American government were experimenting with several new chemicals which they hoped would help end the war.'

Doyle interrupted, 'You mean like Agent Orange?'

'Similar. In this case it was a substance called ZO23. Instead of attacking the body, like most conventional agents, this one invaded the mind and induced fear, paranoia. The idea was to spray this on Charlie in the hope that they'd stop shooting at us and turn their weapons on themselves.'

'That explains a lot,' said Sam. 'Did it work?'

'It was never used against the Vietcong. An experiment was conducted with a small group of volunteers.'

Doyle smiled sarcastically. 'I thought the first rule of soldiers was never to volunteer for anything.'

'I'm sure it is. However, they were promised a ticket home and that seemed to do the trick.'

Sam interrupted again. 'How many people are we talking about?'

'Twenty. They were taken to a testing-ground about forty miles from Saigon and, under battle conditions, sprayed. They were then brought back to Saigon for close observation.'

Doyle was almost ahead of him. 'So what happened?'

'What we expected. Fear, paranoia, extreme fits of violence, a loss of their sense of reality.'

Sam was horrified but fascinated. 'How long did this state last?'

'About a week, ten days, or so we thought. Once they had been released and sent back to the States, several of them began to have further reactions.'

'The outcome of which was . . . ?'

'One killed his family, another killed several neighbours and a police officer. One even walked into work one day and killed everyone in the printing works after inviting them to a party.'

'They all reacted like that?'

'Not all, about half. But we couldn't take the chance so we interned all of them. One actually got out and created mayhem for a couple of days, but he's back under control now.'

'And those who didn't have a reaction?' asked Sam.

The man looked at her. 'It would only have taken one more incident and some clever journalist to spot the link and we were all going to be in trouble.'

'But what did the relatives of these men do?'

'Nothing. We told them they were dead, were generous with compensation, and the problem just went away.'

Doyle walked across to the table and sat down opposite the man. 'Until Brown turned up?'

He nodded. 'Until Brown turned up.'

'But how did he become involved?'

'He'd crashed his jet just outside the area and was wandering through the area when we sprayed. We didn't even know he was there.'

'So when did you know?'

'For certain, after the young girl was murdered in England.'

'You were right about the note, Sam,' Hammond put in. 'It was me that removed it. Had to.'

'Why?'

'Recognised the handwriting. The old bastard had sent me a note thanking me for the hangar dance I'd laid on for him.'

'The one we went to?'

He nodded. 'The writing was the same.'

Sam wasn't satisfied. 'And you had no idea it was him until then?'

Hammond shook his head.

'Then why didn't you arrest him when you knew?'

Before he could answer, the stranger said, 'Because we told him not to.'

'And who the hell are you?' she demanded.

'That doesn't matter. But we couldn't have one of our top generals arrested for murder.'

Doyle laughed. 'Look bad at the Pentagon?'

'Something like that.'

Doyle continued, 'So how long have you known it was him?'

'Not long.'

'Before the English girl was murdered?'

The stranger nodded. 'We thought we could control him until we got him back to the States.'

Sam could hardly believe her ears. 'Then what?'

'We'd arranged for him to stay at, shall we call it a secure retirement home, but he gave us the slip.'

'Not very good are you?'

He shrugged. 'It happens. That's when we recalled Major Hammond. A, to stop him having to ask awkward questions and, B, to help us catch the son of a bitch before it all came out.'

Sam shook her head in disbelief. 'Well, it's sure as hell all going to come out now.'

The man said, 'I don't think so. This place is about to be stripped and then destroyed. Wilmot Brown will have died in a tragic accident and taken his rightful place as an American war hero in Arlington.'

Sam said defiantly, 'The British police and Rochester might have something to say about that.'

'Your Home Office and Commander Rochester have been informed. They have agreed to assist us.'

Doyle went over and checked on Solheim again. 'You mean keep their mouths shut.'

The man was silent.

'But what about the PM, the investigation?' said Sam.

'It all ends here.'

'And the families of the women he murdered?'

The man shrugged. 'Casualties of war.'

Doyle came back to the table. 'And what if we decide to go public?'

'You wouldn't be allowed. And if I thought you might, you wouldn't leave this cabin.'

'Casualties of war?'

The man nodded. Doyle knew there was nothing further he could do, but at least he'd stopped the killing.

Sam stood up and stared rudely at the man. 'How many more did you miss?'

He looked uncertain.

'You missed Brown. How many others?'

The man shrugged.

'So right now there could be several other Arthur Wilmot Browns killing at random and with no one knowing what the hell is going on. I suppose all their victims will just be "casualties of war". Well if you remember, Mr whatever your bloody name is, it was people who stopped the Vietnam war, not gases and agents, and they deserve better than you.'

The man smiled, unabashed. 'I'm sure they do but I'm all they've got. Scary, isn't it?'

It was a cold, grey November day in Cambridgeshire when they were at last able to bury the unknown girl found in the pit. The police had tried for months to identify her, but with no success. Dozens of people had made the journey to the mortuary in the hope of finding that she was their missing daughter, sister or wife. They didn't have to come – most details could be given over the phone – but to them it was a pilgrimage, a journey of hope; for all of them, though, it ended in disappointment.

The police, and even families of other missing people, had turned out in force to say goodbye, almost as if she were some kind of 'unknown warrior' whom they could all think of as their missing relative. Sam stood beside Tom Adams, holding his hand, as they lowered the small coffin into the ground. The final words of the service spoken, each person in turn threw a handful of soil on top of the coffin before moving away, most of them deeply moved by the occasion and by their own memories.

Sam had paid for the grave, as she had paid for the headstone. She didn't have to; it just seemed appropriate. She felt she'd let the girl down, and she wanted to make amends in some way. Aware of her sombre mood, Tom Adams put his arm round her waist and gently drew her away from the graveside. As they walked away, Sam thought of the inscription she'd chosen for the headstone.

UNKNOWN

A slumber did my spirit seal;
I had no human fears:
She seemed a thing that could not feel
The touch of earthly years.

No motion has she now, no force;
She neither hears nor sees;
Rolled round in earth's diurnal course,
With rocks and stones and trees.

Sam hoped Wordsworth's lines might make people stop and, for a moment, remember and reflect on this unknown girl's short life.